ANDI JAXON

Hidden Scars by Andi Jaxon
www.andijaxon.com
authorandijaxon@gmail.com

Photographer: Michelle Lancaster
Models: Lochie and Andy
Cover Design: Y'all That Graphic
Editors: Anette King and Encompass Press LLC

DEDICATION

To all siblings everywhere, who fight and bicker and tease each other but at the end of the day, still love each other.

TRIGGER WARNING

Hidden scars is an MM enemies to lovers, hockey romance, with a jealous fuck buddy, plenty of heat, and situations that may be upsetting for some readers.

Trigger warnings can be found on my website at https://www.andijaxon.com/trigger-warnings

PROLOGUE

preston

The plastic sheeting under me crinkles as I breathe, refusing to let my body do any more than lay there and take it. The sharp inhale of breath and the clenching of my jaw is the only indication he gets that he's bothering me.

The scalpel pierces the skin of my abdomen while I lie on our dining room table and stare at the intricate pattern on the ceiling's whitewashed copper tiles. I know there's exactly fifty-two squares up there. I've laid on this fucking table more times than I can count. Probably more times than I've sat here to eat since this is the formal dining room. We don't normally eat in here. No, this room is only used when Father is trying to impress someone.

Blood trickles down my side and onto the plastic. The burn as he slices through my skin in that controlled, smooth motion has my body dampening with sweat and starting to tremble. I close my eyes to focus on my breathing, slowing my heart rate, and convincing my muscles to relax.

"Why are we here, Charles?" My father's matter of fact voice interrupts my breathing, just like he knew it would.

Because you're a sadistic fuck who gets off on cutting up your kid for some perceived mistake that somehow brings shame to our name?

The cutting motion stops, though the scalpel is still in my skin, and Father looks at me. I don't need to look at him to know it. I hesitated too long so now we have to drag this out. What I wouldn't give for a hit of fentanyl or morphine right now, but since I'm drug tested regularly and have no reason for them, I can't have them. The privilege of pain meds was taken away years ago. I had to have been thirteen or so the last time he gave me any. But I'm not shackled to the table, so that's something, I guess.

Who knew being the son of a world-renowned plastic surgeon came with being his guinea pig? Lucky fucking me. Why couldn't he just hit me like a normal abusive father? Oh, that's right, because he can't risk damaging his hands. My corrections are all about him, after all.

"Charles!" Father barks my name and I force myself to refocus on his question. *What did I do this time?* Nothing. I'm being forced to move to fucking Colorado instead of attending Boston University to play hockey. Could I have told him to fuck off? Sure, but then my naïve little sister becomes the new victim. She's too sweet, so this would destroy her. That innocent girl is the only bright spot in my life. She must be protected. So here I am, on his fucking table once again, adding to the scars that already litter my body. This is the last time I'll lie on this table in this room. Next time I'll have the distraction of a new ceiling to study, and unfamiliar sounds. Though, the last few years I've seen more of the inside of the Danbury condo than this one in Boston. I didn't stray far from town when I played for the

Hat Tricks in Connecticut, so Father leased a place for me to be called back to when I needed correction.

"As a reminder of what will happen if I step out of line." My voice is flat, devoid of all emotion. He continues with his cut, it feels about three inches long, between my ribs and hip bone. The scalpel is gone and my body sags in relief. I know I'm not done. He's going to stitch it up, but for a second the air in my lungs flutters and my eyes threaten to roll back as I get lightheaded.

I will not panic. I will not panic. I will not panic.

My body tries to take over, to allow instinct to kick in and protect me, but I can't let it go. I can't get out of my head. Not yet. That comes later. Much, much later.

The sting of the suture needle makes me hiss, and the following slide of the thread through my skin has my body tensing back up. All my muscles tighten as I feel the sutures being placed. It's the worst part. The tug on my skin and the feel of the thread pulling through my flesh turns my stomach.

Bile inches up my throat and saliva pools in my mouth. I gag at the next stitch, my stomach clenching and arching my back just a little.

"Charles. Control." My father doesn't look up, just snaps the words at me. He has always expected perfection from me. Maybe because I'm his spitting image? I get confused for him often, despite being a hockey player and obviously much bigger than him. Do I need a face tattoo for people to stop comparing me to him? He's twenty years older than me, but you'd never guess it. He looks to be much closer to my age. Like a brother.

I manage to get through the rest of the stitches without throwing up and he cleans up the blood, puts a bandage over the wound, and I'm allowed to roll off the table. My shirt is folded neatly on the seat of a chair. Without pulling the chair out, I grab the shirt and slide it on, feeling better with my scars covered. We must appear perfect. Always. Hide the dirty truths behind smiles.

Dad cleans up his supplies while I deal with sanitizing the plastic sheet, folding it, and putting it away. Our ritual after the deed is done. It's happened so many times over the years I don't think about it anymore, my body just does it.

Once the dining room is put back to rights, Father walks me to the door and pulls me into a hug like he always does.

"Thank you," the words tumble from my lips without thought because that is what is expected of me. It's what I've been trained to do.

"If you would behave, I wouldn't have to hurt you, Charles. I just want what is best for you. You will be an NHL star if you keep your focus. I do this for you." His words would sound warm and even encouraging to an outside observer, but to me, they're contriving. He's trying to show everyone what a great dad he is while justifying the abuse. He's making me better, right?

The worst part? I don't know how to make it stop. Over the years, a few have tried to help but they've either been intimidated into silence or disappeared. Gone. And I think the first person who tried to help me was my mother.

It wasn't long after Lily went to kindergarten that our house was broken into, leaving us motherless. I came home from school to find the police and a medical examiner at our house. This house.

Now I'm leaving what few memories I have of her. Leaving the Division One school I picked to play college hockey at to scramble to get another offer from a school in Denver because that's what is closest to him. I could take my pick of schools. I'm one of the best defensive players in junior hockey history, soon to be college history, yet I'm expected to pick up and switch my plans at the drop of a hat.

Make miracles happen while dancing with the devil.

CHAPTER 1

jeremy

The cold air inside the ice rink cools my sweat-slicked skin during practice. The smell of the blood, sweat, and tears that have been spilled in this rink give it history and I am never unaware of it.

After spending most of my life playing hockey, the last two years in the best league in the US, I love that I'm here in Denver, playing for Darby University. It's a Top-Tier Division One school and I am honored to be here. Add in that I get to play with my best friends from Muskegon and this is going to be an amazing year.

We've been practicing for weeks now, getting back in shape for the season. Since we have a new coach this year, we don't really know what to expect from him, but he's kicking our asses so far. Classes start on Monday and we're all falling into our workout and practice routines.

The team is pulling off our practice gear in the locker room after a hard practice when Coach gets our attention.

"Alright, boys, a few things." His gruff voice has the

room falling quiet. "Carpenter, congratulations son. You're captain this year."

The room breaks out in claps and whoops. I cup my hands around my mouth and cheer for him with a big smile on my face. The senior is smiling as he heads toward Coach to grab the jersey, and he holds it up with the embroidered C on it. I don't know him well, but he seems like a good dude.

"Thanks, Coach," he says before turning to face the room. "We're gonna have a bomb-ass season. Work hard and kick ass." The room erupts again, and he heads back toward his spot in front of his cubby, clapping each teammate he passes on the back and ruffling their sweaty hair.

"Next," Coach yells and everyone shuts up. "A few of you still need to get your physicals done with medical. Get on it. Lastly, we have a new transfer coming this weekend. We are very lucky to have Charles Preston Carmichael joining our team. His father has made a gracious donation to our school and to our team. You will make him feel welcome."

The room goes silent, with everyone side-eyeing each other.

Charles Preston Carmichael.

My head goes blank. Empty.

There's no way.

He's expected to be the first defensive draft pick this year. On the ice, he's brutal, focused, angry, and calculating. I faced him before and came back broken and bruised. In all honesty, he's fucking terrifying. I'm not entirely sure how he hasn't caught assault charges for some of the shit he pulls on the ice. Why the hell would he transfer here? Our team is good, but he signed with Boston. What the hell happened?

Our D men are going to be pissed.

"But why?" the words are out of my mouth before I can

think better of it. In the quiet of the space, my question echoes loud enough for Coach to hear it. The angry, intimidating former NHL player meets my gaze. Shit. He's going to murder me.

"He's your new roommate, Albrooke."

Fuck. Me.

Coach leaves the room, and we finish getting undressed and into the showers. We're all sweaty and disgusting.

"That sucks for you, man." Brendon Oiler, my best friend since we were eighteen and playing in the juniors league together, claps me on the shoulder. I'm glad he was able to come here with me after we aged out last season. Since you can only play in the juniors league until you're twenty, we all had to come up with another plan so we all decided on college. Paul Johnson played in Muskegon with us on the Lumberjacks until last year when he turned twenty and talked up this school a lot. He basically talked Brendon and me into applying here. It's weird to be in classes with freshmen when you're twenty-one but it's pretty common for hockey players.

"Fuck you," I grumble, pulling off my base layer and grabbing a towel, the sound of his laughter following me into the showers.

I thought I got lucky and wouldn't have to room with anyone this season. God damn it. I can only imagine how much fun he is to live with. He's probably a major asshole. Cocky and full of himself.

I'm soaping myself up, ignoring the fact that there's hot, naked, muscular, wet jocks around me, and focusing on hockey stats while staring at the wall. Despite the fact that I've been playing hockey since I was eight and showering in locker rooms since I was eleven, I am very aware of how long my gaze stays on anyone in here. I spend most of my time with my back to the room, just so no one gets jumpy if I get hard. Most of the team doesn't know I'm gay. I'm not really hiding it but I'm not announcing it either. They'll figure it out. Why did I have to fall in love with a sport that has men with the sexiest asses? It's just unfair.

Shit. What if Carmichael is a giant homophobe? Cold anxiety slithers up my spine at the thought.

"It's Friday night...party?" Brendon asks as he grabs the shower next to me, wagging his eyebrows at me. He turned twenty-one last month and no longer needs to hide his drinking.

"Getting drunk does sound pretty good right now." I eye him with a smirk. Over the years, we've fucked around a bit. Brendon is bisexual and during the season there isn't much time for dating, so we end up fucking when we need to take the edge off. As far as I know, only Paul knows, since he was around when we first started doing it. "Where are we going?"

"Rocky's." Brendon ducks his head under the water to rinse off. Rocky's is the bar right off campus that the team likes. It's convenient since we can walk back to the dorms instead of worrying about rides.

I rinse off and grab my towel, scrubbing my skin to rid myself of the water. "I gotta grab my shit from my room. Meet me there in ten?"

He turns to lift his eyebrows at me with a knowing grin on his lips and I walk away before I start to chub up. We both know what this means.

Fifteen minutes later, Brendon is pushing me onto my tiny twin size mattress. My shirt is somewhere on the floor, and his hands are on my skin, pulling me closer to him. His lips leave mine as he pulls at my sweats and boxers. I growl when my dick smacks against my stomach. It's been so fucking long, this is gonna be quick.

"Oh fuck." The words are forced from my throat as my

dick disappears into Brendon's mouth. He lays between my thighs, with his hand wrapped around the base of my cock and his head bobbing over the tip.

I dig my fingers into the long red hair on top of his head, encouraging him to move faster. We've been fucking around on and off for two years now. He fucking knows how to do this but he's taking his sweet ass time and I'm not in the damn mood.

His head pops off my dick and he grins at me. "When is your roommate supposed to get here?"

"I don't know, and I don't care. Hurry the fuck up." He chuckles at my impatience but gets back to work with increased vigor. My hips buck off the bed on instinct and electricity hums through my veins. God damn, I'm going to come.

I open my mouth to warn him of my impending orgasm as the door to my room opens.

In a matter of seconds, Brendon is off the bed, my dick is back in my pants, and we're both standing. I don't need to look at him to know his face is bright red, all the way to the tips of his ears. My breathing is ragged as adrenaline and fear tightens my muscles for the incoming attack. I know guilt is written all over me, but I can't seem to look up for more than a few seconds.

The guy standing in my doorway is staring at me. Hard. Unblinking. I can feel it like a physical weight on my shoulders and Brendon won't look at me. In fact, he's looking anywhere but at me or the newcomer.

Shit.

"See ya later, man." Just like that, Brendon is gone, pushing past my new roommate. At least, that's who I'm assuming it is, and leaving me alone to deal with the fallout. Did he see anything? Does he know Brendon was sucking my dick? I think he does but I don't really want to meet his gaze either.

"Charming." The single word spoken in that flat, almost bored tone has my spine straightening.

I will not be made to feel less-than because of my sexuality.

Lifting my gaze off the floor, I make eye contact with the stony face of my new roommate. His spine is straight as a board, jaw set like he's grinding his teeth, with no emotion or thoughts showing through the mask he wears. Great.

"Uh, hey, I'm Jeremy Albrooke." I lift my hand to shake his, but he doesn't take his eyes off mine. It's uncomfortable and awkward. "Okay then." I let my hand drop and cross my arms over my chest.

Carmichael looks so much like his father, it's kinda creepy. He's like a clone. Doctor Andrew Carmichael is basically a celebrity. Everyone knows him. His face is on the side of buses and on TV. He does work on celebrities and professional athletes. The man is charming, always smiling, and comes across as a really nice guy. This dude does not.

"So, uh, this is about it." I shrug, waving my hand around the room. Two twin beds and nightstands, dressers, desks, tiny closets, and a bathroom. There's a mini fridge between the nightstands with a microwave on top of it.

He looks around the room quickly and slides his bag onto the unmade bed. The dude is a beast on the ice when he's in all his gear and pissed off. I've been slammed into the boards by him more than once over the last few years, healed up my fair share of bruises, but this doesn't seem like the same guy.

He hasn't said anything else and everything about him is stiff and tense. I don't understand what I'm seeing here. Who is this guy?

CHAPTER 2

preston

My jaw aches with how hard I'm clenching my teeth together. It's giving me a headache. I'm fucking exhausted and the adrenaline crash is riding me hard.

After being picked up by my father's driver, I was delivered to his new fucking penthouse to have my stitches removed and another new fucking cut added to my body. How dare I be tired from traveling after packing up my dorm room, right?

I haven't had a chance to crash, but it's coming. A few more hours of putting on a fake fucking face before I can disappear into the shower and fall apart.

My shoulders are tense as I lift my suitcase to the bed to unpack it. I force myself to not let out the hiss of pain as my new stitches pull at the movement. The throb at the back of my head is taking over and I can barely think around it.

I don't want to be here, moving into this tiny fucking dorm room that I have to share. Since I was enrolled past the deadline, it was too late to *persuade* the school to give me my own room. Father is not happy about it, but he made this fucking choice. I could have stayed in God damn Boston, stayed close to my sister, who's in boarding school because God knows he's not going to raise his own child. But no. I'm here in fucking Colorado.

"Are you waiting for something?" I snap at the guy I just interrupted getting a BJ. I'm sure this is exactly what he wants to be doing right now. Pretty sure the other dude is also on the team. That should make for some *fun* situations later. I wonder how long it'll take for the boyfriend to give me the "don't touch" speech.

"I guess not." Jeremy stands up a little straighter, his shoulders squaring, and some confidence slides over his face. He's cute when he's got some backbone. Too bad I don't have time for distractions.

"Why aren't you running drills or working out? The season starts soon." I fall back into my asshole ways so fucking easily. Keep him at arm's length so he doesn't land on Father's radar. I work out all the damn time. My body is conditioned much like those who play in the pros since that is what my father wants from me.

It was incredibly frustrating playing for the juniors in a Tier Two division for the NAHL when Tier One teams with USHL have been scouting me since I was seventeen, but I wasn't allowed to leave New England. Can't stray too far from dear ol' dad.

He wants to show off his perfect son, marry off his perfect daughter to the highest bidder, and become invincible. Show his drunk of a father how much better he is because he has money and prestige. Lily is a very innocent seventeen-year-old that has not yet felt the wrath of Doctor Andrew Carmichael. I've done everything in my power to keep it that way.

I just have to make it until her birthday next summer. Then I can tell my father to fuck off and never look back. I don't need him.

I unzip my suitcase to give myself something to do. Even that slight movement pulls on the damn stitches. My body is riddled with scars, from my shoulders to my knees, from my father's scalpel over the years. He's managed to keep most of them from crossing, blaming them on medical procedures anytime he was questioned. He's a highly respected surgeon. Why would he be lying?

Lifting stacks of clothes out of the suitcase, I get them placed neatly in the drawers at the end of the tiny bed I'll be sleeping on for my freshman year.

"We have a workout schedule set by the coach. I follow that so I don't burn myself out or risk injury." His tone is sharper than it was a minute ago. Lookie there, a bit more back bone. My dick almost takes notice.

"If you want to get picked up in the draft, you need to step up your game. You had an unremarkable year last year. You have to do better." My words cut through the space between us with my back to him. I don't plan them. They fall out of my mouth. They are almost word for word what my father told me this morning.

"Uh, no. I want to coach."

Silence falls and it is heavy.

Since my suitcase is empty, I zip it back up and slide it under my bed then turn to face him.

"If you don't want to play, why are you wasting everyone's time and the school's resources? Someone who wants to play could have your spot on the team and be seen by the scouts." Once again, my father's words fall from my lips. I've said it before to my teammates in the past.

He almost flinches but manages to meet my gaze and

hold it. Why do I want to break that strength? Maybe I am my father's son after all.

Jeremy has no response. It's better that way.

I take a step toward him, crowding him against his bed.

"Let me be very clear. I am not here to make friends. I'm here to play hockey to the best of my abilities and I will not let your lack of work ethic drag me down. Get a good night's rest because tomorrow you are all in for a rude fucking awakening."

"You realize that I was playing on a Tier One team, right? You weren't. I think that speaks enough about my work ethic." he snaps back. *Hmm. I do love the fight.*

"I wasn't on a Tier One team by choice. I turned down recruiters three years in a row." I hold his gaze, as confusion crosses his face.

"Why the hell would you turn it down? That's the dumbest thing I've ever heard!" His arms spread out wide as he talks.

"That's none of your business, is it?"

He stares at me for a minute, confused and disbelieving, before a phone buzzes and I watch Jeremy look at his phone on the nightstand next to his bed. Jesus, this room is fucking small. Pretty sure my childhood closet was bigger than this.

I take a step back and force my hands into my pockets. Something about him has my fingers itching to touch, but I can't.

Taking in the shaggy dark blond hair on his head and the perfectly unscarred expanse of his chest, my skin tingles, imagining him against me despite how much my head revolts at the thought of being touched. The muscles of his abdomen flex as he pulls his t-shirt over his head and my mouth waters. He's hot, there's no other way to put it. With his boy-next-door vibe, he appears friendly, but I'm willing to bet he's not so nice on the ice. I vaguely remember playing against him and I can't wait to get to know how he plays so I can pick him apart.

Albrooke slides his phone into the pocket of his sweatpants and runs a hand through his hair. "I guess this means you don't want to meet the team for a beer?" His eyes rake down my body, the muscles in his jaw jumping as he tenses.

"No."

He slides his feet into some worn blue slip-ons, probably Vans, and disappears, closing our door behind him.

Finally, I'm able to breathe. My hands shake, my stomach turns, and my knees give out, dropping me onto my unmade bed. I lean my elbows on my knees and hold my head in my hands while the breath in my lungs stutters in and out of my ribcage. In the blink of an eye, I'm hyperventilating, my eyes fluttering shut as the morning's activities slam into me.

The pull of the stitches being removed from my flesh, the burn of the scalpel as it sliced the skin on my left pec open. My stomach turns and I rush to the bathroom to empty its contents into the toilet. My knees hit the floor hard enough to bruise, but I barely notice the pain. Sweat beads on my forehead as stomach acid burns my throat and nose.

I haven't had a chance to crash until now. The adrenaline high of this morning is finally wearing off, leaving me weak and tired.

"Have you already forgotten your manners? Watch your fucking mouth."

The memory of my father's barely contained rage when I told him I could take the stitches out myself and to leave me alone sends a shiver up my spine. I fucking hate him. Nine months and he can't touch Lily anymore. She'll be an adult, graduated from high school, and finally able to touch the inheritance our mother left her. He won't be able to touch her, which means he'll lose his hold over me.

Dragging my ass off the floor, I don't bother turning the light on before I strip my clothes off and turn the hot water on. I don't want to see the fucking scars anyway.

I didn't put any shower stuff in here, so I grope at the walls and find whatever Jeremy fucking Albrooke has. If he notices, I don't give a shit.

I'm careful to keep the bandage on my chest dry, but I know I'll have to change it and send a picture to dear ol' dad later. Gotta make sure it's not getting infected and that I'm taking care of it properly.

The heat of the water doesn't do much to relax my muscles, but I stand under it until it turns cold anyway. It's peaceful here, in the dark, alone.

Alone is safe.

Turning the water off, I realize I don't have a towel or a change of clothes. God damn it.

I feel along the wall until I find the door and the towel hanging on a hook. Looks like I'm using the roommate's towel too. The rest of my shit should be delivered tomorrow, though I'm not sure how I'm going to explain this if he asks. It's fucking weird to use someone's towel that you don't know.

Quickly, I dry off and grab my clothes from the floor. I don't want to put dirty clothes on, but I can't let anyone see the scars either. They'll ask questions, and if they push it, they will disappear. They always do.

Cracking the bathroom door open, I peer around the room and see it's still empty. I lock the door and hurry to my dresser to grab clothes. Being covered feels better.

I'm fucking exhausted and I have to be up at four AM for a run. How late is this dumbass going to be? Will I be able to sleep or will nightmares wake me up in two hours?

I check my phone and find a message from my father wanting a fucking picture. I find the pack of first aid supplies he shoved at me this morning and head into the bathroom, closing and locking the door behind me. This time I turn the light on and pull my left arm out of my t-shirt, so I don't have to hold it while I deal with the bandage.

Carefully, I remove the gauze that's taped to my skin and clean the wound. I'm patting it dry with a piece of gauze when the door to my dorm is opened and someone tries the bathroom knob. My head swings to the side when whoever is on the other side bangs on the door.

"Hurry up dude! I gotta piss!" Sounds like Albrooke.

"Fuck off," I growl, quickly taking a picture and covering the wound.

"Unless you're taking a shit or jacking off, open the door!" He bangs on the door again.

I slip my arm back through the sleeve and gather my supplies back into the brown paper bag.

Ripping open the door, I stand in the way so he can't push past me.

"What the fuck is your problem?" he yells, cheeks flushed from alcohol.

"You. If I'm in here, I'm not letting you in. I don't care if you're about to shit your pants. Find another bathroom." My empty hand lands in the middle of Jeremy's chest and I push him back out of my way.

He must really need to piss since he doesn't have a come-back and just hurries into the bathroom with the damn door still open. I lift my lip at his lack of privacy and shove the brown bag into the dresser before turning to my bed.

Shit.

I don't have sheets or a pillow. Great.

Digging through my shit, I find a hoodie, fold it into a

pillow, then lie down, back pressed against the wall, and close my eyes.

Should I be working out tomorrow? No. Am I going to do it anyway? Yes. I don't have a reason for the damn stitches so I can't tell the coach I'm ineligible for medical reasons.

CHAPTER 3

jeremy

I hate him.

It's official.

Sweat is dripping down my face and down my back. Every muscle in my body is tired and sore, yet he looks like he's taken a leisurely stroll. I swear he's smirking at me.

"Scrimmage!" Coach yells and the team groans.

We've been running drills for an hour.

"Let's go boys!" Coach blows the whistle, and we break into our normal scrimmage teams, third line versus the second line, so now I have to fight Carmichael to get to the goal.

Brendon, Paul, and I make up the third line forwards. Paul was on the second line when we got here, but after summer camp, Coach moved him to the third line with me and Brendon since we gelled well. Carmichael, however, is on the second line, because of course he is. Show off.

Everyone gets set and I face off against my teammate for the puck. I'm quicker, so I fling it to Brendon, my right winger, and we set off down the ice. With a burst of speed, I'm down the ice and looking to find the puck in Johnson's possession. My left winger sees me and shoots it toward me. The puck has barely made contact with my stick when a brick wall rams into my side, knocking me into the boards, and the puck goes flying back down the ice.

"What the fuck!" I turn on Carmichael but hurry to get back in the game.

"Gotta watch that blind spot, Albrooke," he yells at my back.

I'm fuming. Anger heats my blood more than the physical exertion. One of our D men slams the puck away from the goal and I snag it, quickly turning and racing back up the ice.

"Sloppy footwork, Albrooke," Carmichael calls with a shake of his head as he zeroes in on me, reading my next move as soon as I've thought of it. I shoot for the net, and he blocks it, sending it back over the center line with an insane amount of power.

"My dead grandma is faster than you."

Coach is yelling directions at us from the sidelines, but I don't hear it. The only thing in my head is Preston fucking Carmichael. I'm making stupid mistakes because I'm frustrated and tired. Mistakes he has no problem calling out as soon as I do them.

I'm going to hit him.

I'm not the only one he's doing it to. Everyone on the team is getting the same treatment, but I appear to be getting the brunt force of it. He's not even upset. No, it's all very casual. I think that's worse.

The coach blows his whistle, and we leave the ice. We're trudging down the chute to the locker room, exhausted and limping, most of us sporting new bruises from being slammed by Carmichael.

"Your new roommate is a dick," Brendon says as we get to the locker room and push the doors open.

"No shit. I may suffocate him in his sleep. Fucker was up at four AM."

He was passed out cold by the time I was done pissing and since he didn't have any bed shit, I tossed a blanket over him, trying to be a nice guy, but after today, he can fuck off. I hope he freezes.

"With the season starting soon, practices will be more intense. You all need to work on your endurance. Perfecting little things like footwork and being aware of your surroundings. Longer practices and more workouts in the gym. Carmichael is the only one here that looks ready to play."

I look around the room but don't see mister perfect.

"Hit the showers. Increased gym hours start tomorrow morning. Make sure you're asleep on time. And keep your damn grades up!" Coach leaves the locker room and we finish stripping out of our gear and underlayers.

"This year is going to kill me." Brendon groans as he steps under the shower.

I quickly scan the showers, but Preston isn't in here. What the hell?

Fuck it, I don't care. I'm starving and exhausted.

"Who's up for pizza?" Paul Johnson, my left winger, asks.

"Sounds good to me," I chime in. "But I can't be out late, I gotta finish my homework."

"Yeah, I'll meet you there," Brendon adds in. A few of the other guys agree to head down to the pizza shop as we finish up in the showers and start getting dressed.

"Hey, meet me in my room and walk down together?" I ask Brendon. I need to get off and we were interrupted last time.

"I uh, got something I gotta do first. I'll see you there." He slaps me on the shoulder and leaves before I've got my shoes on. Fuck.

I want to change into jeans anyway, so I head back to the dorms and am surprised when Preston isn't there already. Where the fuck did he go?

Grabbing a pair of jeans out of the dresser, I kick my shoes off and slide my sweats off. Laying back on the bed, I push my boxer briefs down and wrap a hand around my dick. With just a few pumps of my hand, I'm hard. My stomach muscles tighten and despite being tired and sore, the only thing I can focus on is how much I want to come.

And Preston Carmichael.

The dark gray eyes that pierce me when he looks at me. The carefully cut and styled black hair and muscled build I know is under his clothes.

I hate that he's hot. That I want to feel him against me.

My dick leaks precum at the image of him holding me down, losing some of that control he holds so tight to while he fucks me.

My cock throbs and my balls draw up tight against me as my hand pumps furiously.

The image in my head morphs to his hands on my skin. Is he as aggressive in bed as he is on the ice? Would he leave marks on my skin with his teeth?

My orgasm races through me, spilling onto my stomach, and leaving me gasping for breath. Damn it. I should have taken my shirt off.

I lay back on my bed, spent and trying to catch my breath. Footsteps outside the door have me pulling my underwear back up. As I slide out of my cum stained t-shirt, the door opens. Awesome.

I freeze for a second, not sure what Preston's reaction to finding me cleaning up will be. It's obvious what I just did and my cheeks heat with embarrassment. It definitely smells like jizz in here and I'm sure my cheeks are flushed.

He doesn't know you were thinking about him, dumbass. Relax.

I get the shirt balled up as Preston stands in the doorway, holding it open while staring at me. He's freshly showered in clean clothes, the look on his face blank, like he's not really in there.

"Uh, some of the guys are going out for pizza. You can join if you want." I sit up and pull my jeans on, slip my feet into my shoes, and stand to grab a clean shirt. Preston closes the door and eyes me as he walks past to his bed.

"I don't eat that shit. It makes you fat and slow." He looks me over like what he's saying is written on my body. "Clearly." He just drops the words like facts, as casual as if he was talking about the weather.

"Wow. Okay then." I shove my head through the shirt and leave the room. Slamming the door behind me harder than I needed to. What the actual fuck is that dude's problem?

I ignore the looks from the girls that get into the elevator a floor below mine. They whisper back and forth, one of them glancing back at me as I lean against the wall. They're cute, but I'm not interested. Girls don't do it for me.

"You're Jeremy Albrooke, right?" The blonde turns to me.

"Yup." I lean my head back against the wall, trying to tell her I don't want to talk without having to be rude.

"Is it true Charles Preston Carmichael is playing hockey here this year?"

Don't roll your eyes. Don't roll your eyes. Don't roll your eyes.

"Yup."

He's also an asshole that appears to get some kind of sick joy from picking on others. Real stand-up dude.

The brunette with her swoons and it's all I can do not to tell them not to bother, I doubt he'll give them the time of day.

"He's so hot," the girl says, hands waving at her face.

The elevator digs and opens on the bottom floor and I'm grateful for the escape.

"Do you know what room he's in?" the blonde asks, and over my shoulder I say "no," since I'm not giving them my dorm number. Absolutely not.

By the time I make it to the pizza place off campus, the guys have ordered and are taking up half the booths. I slide in next to Brendon and Paul and grab a slice of pepperoni, shoving it in my face.

"Jesus, who pissed in your Cheerios?" Paul looks at me over his cup of soda.

"What?" I snap at him. Okay, take a deep breath and chill out.

I close my eyes and force my shoulders and jaw to relax. I didn't realize how tense I was.

"Who pissed you off?" Brendon asks this time.

"Did you know pizza makes you fat and slow? Carmichael was nice enough to point it out and tell me if I ate better, maybe I would play better. Pompous fuck." I dip a piece of crust into some ranch before shoving it in my mouth and chewing. *Take that, fuck head.*

"Damn, dude is seriously a hard ass. That practice was brutal." Paul shakes his head and grabs another slice of pizza.

"Pretty sure my spleen is bruised from being slammed into the boards," Brendon adds, rubbing at his back.

The guys around us grumble about him too, complaining about bumps and bruises.

"He's going to make us better," Carpenter pipes up, talking to everyone. The captain taking some control over the situation. "He could have gone anywhere, but he came here. We need to learn everything we can from him and work hard to keep up." He looks around the group. "We have the best D man in junior league history on our team. We need to take advantage of that and be a team he can be proud of. Take what he says and learn. He's obviously not afraid to bruise egos, or bodies for that matter. If he says you've got sloppy footwork, concentrate on your damn footwork." Carpenter looks from me to Paul. "If he says you're slow, start doing more speed drills." He takes a deep breath. "None of us are above improvement."

CHAPTER 4

jeremy

By Friday, everyone is beat.

Muscles I didn't know I had are tired. We have two weeks to pull our shit together before our exhibition game against the University of Nevada, Las Vegas, and with the extra practices and workouts Coach added this week, homework has been a bitch to keep up on. Of course, our first game is an away game, so we'll be in a hotel. Hopefully, someone else will be stuck with mister fucking perfect Carmichael.

He's so weird. I've never seen him shower or change in the locker room, he just shows up changed and showers at the dorm. I don't get it. The man is quick to tell us all how much we suck, yet no one calls him on it. It's like what he says is law.

An hour before practice, I'm sitting in the locker room waiting for Brendon. We've tried to hook up a few times but our roommates keep interrupting. Today, we're trying this. Maybe getting off right before practice will help me keep a calmer head and Carmichael won't get to me as much. It's worth a shot, right?

The door squeaks open and Brendon walks into view.

A smile lifts my lips and he grins at me. About fucking time.

When he gets to me, I stand and we head for the showers. It gives us an extra few seconds in case someone comes in early.

Brendon backs me into a corner, kissing and sucking on my neck. My dick is hard when he runs a hand over my pants.

"Someone's eager," he snickers into my skin.

"Yeah, I am. Hurry up before we get caught." My stomach drops at the idea of someone walking in, the awkwardness and possible hostility from a few guys on the team. Most don't know Brendon is bi, but the few that do keep the secret for him.

He grips my ass and pulls me against him, taking my lips in a hard kiss and grinding against me.

Is Preston an aggressive kisser?

God damn it. Focus.

I slide my hands under Brendon's shirt, dragging my fingers over his skin and sliding into his pants.

He groans against me, pulling his lips from mine.

"You want to fuck?" Brendon lifts a lube packet.

"Yeah," I'm breathing faster and spin around, pushing my pants and boxer briefs down, then putting my palms on the wall next to the shower entrance.

My dick isn't as hard as it normally is at the idea of getting laid but I'm trying really hard not to think about it.

Brendon's slicked finger slides against my hole and pushes inside. He takes a few minutes to work me open, one finger becoming two, pushing in and out.

"You ready?" he asks, his mouth next to my ear. Asking

permission is not what I want. I want him to hold me down and take what he wants, but he's too nice for it.

The head of his cock pushes against me and I push back hard enough to surprise him. Taking all of him in one thrust.

"Fuck, dude." He grips my hips and drops his forehead to my shoulder, thrusting slowly at first.

"Just fuck me, I don't need slow," I grit out, dropping my forearm to the tiled wall and wrapping a hand around my dick. Brendon's ragged breath fans across my neck while I jerk myself too hard. Fuck.

I close my eyes and Preston appears in my head. Fucking A. *Stop it.* I don't even know if he's into guys. If he's straight, I really, *really* need to stop thinking about him.

Plus, he's an asshole.

The squeak of the locker door opening has me pausing but Brendon doesn't seem to notice. Soft footsteps pad across the cement floor while my heart pounds in my chest. We're about to get caught. Fuck. I lean slightly so I can see who walks in.

My damn roommate appears around the corner at the same time Brendon grunts. Preston stops moving and takes a step back, peering around the corner until he finds me. I don't know if he can see who's with me, but he lifts an eyebrow and watches me watching him. My cheeks flush and cold fear floods my stomach. Jerking back, I stand back up straight so I can't see him.

Why is my dick getting harder?

My breathing is ragged and it has nothing to do with Brendon pumping into my ass.

Footsteps are quiet and movement from the corner of my eye has me focusing on Preston leaning against a bank of lockers. In the six-inch gap between the wall and the lockers, I see him. He centers himself in the space so I can see him from head to toe, but only a strip of him. His hand slides down his abdomen and into his base layer compression leggings. My gaze focuses hard on the show he's putting on.

Pulling his dick out of his pants, he strokes himself, already hard as fuck. My tongue drags across my lower lip at the drop of precum glistening on his tip.

My cock throbs and arousal hums through my veins as I watch him jacking off to me getting fucked. Jesus, what is happening?

I'm not questioning it. Wrapping my hand around my dick once again, I pump fast. My eyes locked on Preston's like he's told me not to look away. He's holding me there, demanding my attention without a word. His neck flushes. The blush of lust climbing up his jaw onto his cheeks. He bites his lower lip while his hips thrust into his hand.

Oh, fuck, I'm going to come. The electricity shoots through me, my balls tingling and drawing up into me. Cum splatters on the wall in front of me with a groan from my chest. Holy fuck. My knees want to give out. I don't think I've ever come that hard before.

Preston comes, dripping on the floor of the locker room and not giving a shit about the mess. Brendon grunts behind me, filling the condom and almost collapsing against me.

"Damn, that was good."

Unease kills the post orgasm high, but I give him a "yeah," while he cleans up and I pull my pants up.

He leaves the shower area before I do but stops short at Preston standing there with his arms over his chest.

"Oh, uh. Hey, man." Brendon crosses his arms over his chest too. From calm and relaxed to tense and unsure in an instant. The uncertainty hangs in the air around us like a damn weight. We don't know how Preston will react to this but I have a feeling it's not too bad since he obviously enjoyed it. Though Brendon doesn't know that.

Preston just raises an eyebrow at us but says nothing. Dude is weird.

"Come on, let's get ready for practice," I push Brendon toward his locker. From the corner of my eye, I watch the smirk twist Preston's face but I keep moving. I'm not starting a fight right now. I'm pulling my shirt over my head when my phone rings in my pocket. Digging it out, my older sister Stacy's picture is on the screen.

"Hey, what's up? How's my favorite girl doing?" Her scoff at my reference to her daughter makes me chuckle.

"You would ask about Ella first. Ass." The little girl in question babbles in the background, trying so hard to speak. "She's teething so it's a real joy around here."

"Aww poor baby. She needs her favorite uncle and some chocolate ice cream." I slide my jeans and boxer briefs off, and grab my compression shorts.

"Better not let Keith hear you say that. He'll fight you for favorite uncle." Our little brother plays football and thinks he's a badass, especially when his twin backs him up since he also plays. They're both smaller than me, and even together, I can take them.

"Keith isn't even Jordan's favorite, and they're twins." I hold the phone against my shoulder while I sit on the bench and shove my feet through the tight fabric of the compression shorts and stand to pull them up. "I'm getting ready for practice. Did you need something, or can I call you later?"

"Oh, shit, sorry. I just wanted to know if you were coming home for Mom's birthday?"

Fuck.

"Uh, let me look at the schedule but I doubt it. I think we have away games that weekend." Guilt eats at me. This will be the first year I don't see her for her birthday. It's during the season but when I lived in Muskegon, where the team I played for was located, I was able to see her. The best I'll probably be able to do this year is video chat with her.

"Okay, let me know. If we can surprise her, I would like to. If you've got a game close to here, I'll surprise her with tickets to the game."

Guys start filing into the locker room, loud and rowdy.

"Okay, I'll let you know. Tell Ella her favorite uncle says he loves her."

She laughs and ends the call.

"Your sister single yet?" Paul asks, a shit-eating grin splitting his face when I glare at him.

"Fuck off. Even if she was, she wouldn't date your lame ass." I finish getting my gear on and we file out onto the ice.

CHAPTER 5

preston

How are these guys one of the best teams? Sloppy passes and missed goals that should have been easy. Refs are going to hammer them with penalties.

It's going to be a long season if they don't get their shit together and start gelling out here.

Oiler shoots a pass to Albrooke, who races up the center toward the blue line but misses. I snag it and fling the puck toward the opposite side of the ice. The movement makes me grimace as it pulls on the incision. Albrooke growls as he changes direction and keeps moving.

"My blind uncle moves faster than you, Albrooke. And he has no feet."

The goalie behind me grumbles something but I'm not paying attention to his mouth. I don't give a shit what he thinks. These damn pads are rubbing on my new stitches and it's irritating the fuck out of me. The sweat dripping down my skin burns.

Oiler trips over his own fucking skates and falls on his ass, missing the pass Johnson sends him.

"Jesus fucking Christ, my sister skates better than you do, and she's never worn a pair."

"What the fuck is your problem?" Albrooke shoves me but I barely budge.

"Maybe if you focused less on getting laid, and more on the game," my eyes flick to Oiler, images of Jeremy's flushed face while he was getting fucked flashes through my head for a second before coming back to my pissed off roommate, "you'd play better. Get your priorities straight."

"Fuck you!" He shoves me again, getting in my face this time. The strange coloring of his eyes is bright in the lights of the rink. One eye is half blue and half brown while the other is blue with brown spots. It's haunting. "You don't know shit about me!"

"I know you aren't committed to this game or this team. None of you are, or I'd see a lot more of you all in the fucking gym and out here on the ice running drills. You're all doing the bare minimum. Take some initiative. Have some pride in yourself." I shove him out of my space. "Want me to stop ragging on you? Prove me wrong. I dare you."

All this whiny baby bullshit has gotten on my last fucking nerve. I'm done with it. Suck it up and do better or shut your fucking mouth.

Coach blows the whistle to call the end of practice and everyone trudges to the locker room.

I'm the last one off the ice on purpose. I slide my gear off into my cubby but leave my base layer on. I'll shower later in our dorm or in the gym locker room where I can have privacy.

The guys strip down and head into the showers, half of them angry at being called out, the other half hanging their heads as my words hit hard. Hopefully they'll take what I said to heart and start proving me wrong. I want them to.

"Too good to shower with the team?" one of the guys on the first line says on his way past me.

"I'm not done working." I throw back. He stops for a second, looking confused. "I have three miles to run then free weights." Poor kid's eyes widen before he shakes his head and follows along into the showers.

Coach comes along and slaps me on the shoulder. "Good hustle."

"Thanks, Coach."

I slip on my sneakers, grab my gym bag, and head out of the locker room, not caring that the base layer fits like a second skin and leaves nothing to the imagination. I'm in extremely good shape and am not embarrassed by my body at all. The scars are kept a secret because it's easier. It's safer for everyone around me. And it means people don't touch me. I hate being touched.

In one of the stalls in the gym locker room, I change into running shorts and a t-shirt. It's more comfortable than the long sleeves and leggings.

Popping my earbuds in, I find a treadmill and start up my playlist. The loud beat of the NF and Citizen Soldier pounding in my ears matches the tempo of my pulse. There's no one else in here. It's just me and the slap of my feet on the belt. The thoughts that constantly plague me running rampant.

No one can know why I work as hard as I do. Hide the scars and the truth.

"You would be nothing without me. I'm making you better."

"Your sister isn't strong enough to withstand the correction, but I will break her if that's what it takes to keep you in line."

My stomach turns violently and I'm forced to pull the emergency stop rope on the machine. Bent over with my hands on my knees, I breathe through the nausea. Lily has to be protected.

For the first time in a year, I dip out of my workout early. Guilt tries to drag me back.

If you don't keep it up, you're a failure. Father will know and you'll be called back to the house for correction.

I run for the toilet and throw up the water I've been chugging for the last few hours during practice. My knees slamming into the cold tiles surrounding the toilet sends pain shooting up my legs but I can't focus on it. The only thing that matters is making sure I don't throw up on the floor. We must not leave evidence of our shortcomings. The world must believe we are perfect at all times.

No emotional breakdowns, no scandals.

My stomach clenches painfully as the contents are forced from my body. My t-shirt sticks to my back with sweat from my run, the sensation too tight on my body, like I'm suffocating. While I hang on to the toilet for dear life, I have to wonder what it's like to have someone care enough to check on you. What's it like for someone to bring a wet rag or a glass of water or just sit with you when you feel like shit? I haven't had anyone care since my mom died. I was a child. The abuse was getting worse, but I hid it from her too. I had to be strong for Lily and for Mom.

Once my stomach is empty, I sit back against the door of the stall with my knees pulled up and my arms resting on them, my head back against the cool metal. I wipe my face and mouth with the bottom of my shirt and hate the weakness.

Closing my eyes, I allow myself to have this moment. Just this once. To breathe.

When I stand up, I flush the toilet and head to the sink

to rinse out my mouth. I should go finish my run and lift some weights before dinner. I need a shower and don't want to risk taking one at the dorms since Jeremy God damn Albrooke doesn't have any sense of privacy. As much as I don't want to think about him getting off, stroking his dick as I watched him, it flitters through my head anyway.

Fuck it, tonight I'm not finishing the workout. I'm taking a shower and going back to the room to pass out.

I dig out my change of clothes, shower stuff, and a towel from my gym bag and find a shower stall with a curtain. Most of the showers are communal but to the sides there are a few that give you some privacy.

I pull the curtain shut and make sure it doesn't gap open before pulling my clothes off and turning the water on. It's cold as fuck but I don't really have any other option. No one needs to see the damage to my skin. I don't want to field questions about it or see the pity in people's eyes.

The water doesn't get hot enough for my liking, but maybe that's my punishment for not finishing my workout. The tepid water washes down my skin, setting off goosebumps and making my muscles even more tense. The most recent wound stings as the water mixes with sweat.

I hate my skin. The scars that mar my body. Proof of my fuck-ups and the twisted mind of my father. There's never a time I can just pull my shirt off. I'm always aware of the way my shirts fit, preferring to tuck them in most of the time to keep my body covered.

I scrub my body clean and dry off more aggressively than necessary, but I'm fucking irritated. At myself. At my life. At the circumstances of my existence.

As I make my way out of the gym after getting dressed, I pull my phone from my bag and send my sister a message.

Hey brat, how's school?

LILY

Boring. I hate this place.

I know but it's your last year. Did you really want to transfer to a new school your senior year?

LILY

You moved.

Not because I wanted to.

I don't have a comeback for her so I don't respond. Trust me, I didn't want to transfer this year. My last team was good, worked hard, and won the Frozen Four last season.

LILY

I looked up your school, Darby University's hockey team seems pretty good but why did you leave Boston? Didn't they give you a contract first?

I grit my teeth as I push my way through the people standing outside the dorms.

"Hey, you're the new hockey player, right?" a feminine voice calls from behind me a second before a hand lands on my arm. Quickly, I spin around and shrug her off. It makes my skin crawl to be touched.

"Yeah, I guess." I huff at her, completely uninterested. The petite girl with blue hair and black eyeliner drags her eyes over my body and bites her lip. It's almost enough to make me smile. Sorry, chick, I'm not interested.

"I like hockey players." Her tone is seductive but does nothing for me.

"Do they like you?" The words are out of my mouth before my brain has a chance to filter them. The sultry bedroom eyes turn angry and offended. Not really what I meant, but it works. I'm betting she won't be stopping me to talk again.

"What the hell kind of question is that?" She pops a hand on her hip, glaring at me.

"I don't have time for this. You like hockey players, jocks, whatever. Good for you." I turn away from her and enter the dorm building, opting for the stairs to the third floor instead of the elevator since I didn't finish my workout.

The door to my dorm room opens, and Jeremy steps out with Paul and Brendon. They freeze when they see me.

In jeans and hoodies, they look like they're going out somewhere.

"Lay off the carbs tonight." I step past them and enter the room, closing the door, but not before one of them mutters "pompous jackass" under their breath.

I drop my gym bag on the floor and lay down. I'll deal with my dirty clothes later. Right now, all I want is sleep. Curling up on my side, I press my back against the wall and close my eyes, as images of Jeremy Albrooke coming are running on repeat in my mind's eye.

CHAPTER 6

jeremy

It's been a week since Preston watched me get fucked in the showers. Since he jacked off watching me come. Neither of us has said a word about it. He barely spends any time in our dorm room from what I can tell, always waking up at the ungodly hour of four AM to get a workout in before practice. At some point he comes back to nap, I think, then he's gone again for more training. Honestly, he spends more time in the stadium than he does in here. I've never seen anything like it. He's a damn machine.

Even though he blows off the puck bunnies, they still scream his name when they see him. The only person I've noticed him looking at for longer than a second is me, but the only things he says to me are that I'm slow, sloppy, and easy to read on the ice. I don't understand him.

I eventually told Brendon that Preston saw us, but not that he watched and enjoyed the show, so we haven't hooked up since.

Hey, Carmichael should be at the rink for another hour. Wanna hang out before class?

The three dots pop up in the chat I have with Brendon.

OILER

Dude, you sure he's not coming back any time soon? Paul won't fuck off today, I've tried to get him out of here but he's not catching on.

Yeah he's never back this early. We've got an hour easy.

OILER

Done. Be right there.

My skin is itching to be bruised, grabbed, forced. Fucking Brendon won't be aggressive enough so I'm going to have to do it myself. Laying sideways on the bed, I drop my head over the edge of the bed and cross my legs to keep them out of the way.

A knock on the door sounds as it opens and Brendon grins at the position.

"Blowies it is," he chuckles, locking the door behind him and pulling on his clothes to free his dick. He pumps it a few times and eyes the door. I don't give him time to question anything, just grab his thighs and open my mouth. That distracts him enough to lean on the bed.

I suck on him a few times, taking him as deep as he can go before pulling back.

"Shit, did I hurt you?" He tries to take a step back but I keep a hold of him.

"Lean on me not the bed." I want to feel the pressure of being held down. I need it. My dick is barely at half-mast because I'm bored. "Fuck my mouth."

He's average in size, maybe a bit thicker, so he's not going to hurt me. I've been sucking dick for years and my deep throat game is on point. I could handle him in my sleep.

His thrusts are shallow, one hand on the middle of my chest but not really putting any pressure on me. I want to fucking scream. After two years of this, how has he not learned I'm not fragile? Fucking hurt me dude. Take what you want and don't hold back.

I'm not getting off this way and now I'm frustrated.

I reach one hand to play with his balls, gently tugging them, rolling them in my palm. He groans and drops his head back. The key in the lock at the door has me freezing but Brendon doesn't seem to notice.

Fuck. Why am I getting hard now?

Why the hell do I want to get caught *again* by my roommate? What the fuck is wrong with me?

"For Christ's sake, give it a rest." Preston's annoyed voice spurs Brendon into action, turning his back to the door and putting his quickly deflating dick away while mine is now paying attention.

Seriously? What the actual fuck is wrong with me?

With a sigh, I sit up and turn so my feet hit the ground. I hate how I react to this ruthless fucker. I can't ever tell if he's making digs at me because of my sexuality or just because he thinks he's better than me. I guess it doesn't really matter because he's a dick either way.

"What the fuck is your problem, dude?" Brendon goes toe to toe with Preston and honestly, he's about to get taken down a few pegs. He's a good guy, but Preston doesn't care about anything but winning so he's going to hurt Brendon's pride. I stand up in case Brendon loses his mind and swings at Preston. He's my friend so I can't let him get his ass kicked.

"Stop fucking in communal spaces if you don't want an audience or to be interrupted." Preston looks down at Brendon, using every inch of that six-foot-five frame and impressive shoulder width to intimidate. Brendon isn't short but he's a few inches shorter than Preston and definitely not as wide. "You should be running speed drills or working on pass accuracy instead of getting laid."

I roll my eyes at Preston's answer. He needs a fucking life.

Brendon looks at me, "You coming?"

Preston has a smug smile, muttering, "If you can't tell, you shouldn't be doing it," while I shake my head and drop my shoulders. This isn't working anymore. Sleeping with Brendon is not mutually beneficial and hasn't been in a long time.

Both of them are staring at me, digging holes into my body with the heat. One out of sexual frustration and one I'm not sure of but I'm intrigued by it just the same.

"Whatever, man." Brendon pushes past Preston and slams the door behind him.

I shove Preston, taking him by surprise and forcing him to take a step back. His body tenses like I've never seen before, so far past pissed off it's scary.

"Don't fucking touch me!" His voice is so low I almost don't hear it. It has goose bumps breaking out along my skin. My hands immediately go up in a sign of surrender.

Preston's hands grip my shirt tight in his fists, shoving me against my dresser, the knobs of the drawers digging into my back.

"What the fuck are you doing?" I demand, a little more aroused than I'm comfortable with admitting. I'm a strange mix of scared and turned the fuck on. *Why is my dick hard?*

"Shut the fuck up." He growls at me. Blood is pounding

through my veins with every instinct I have on alert and ready to react. My body tight but wanting to melt into him.

Using his forearm across my chest, he leans into me hard enough to hurt while his other hand shoves into my pants and grabs my dick. I'm hard as steel and shocked into silence for a second when he strokes me.

"What the hell are you doing?" I barely manage to get the words out without groaning.

"I said, shut the fuck up," Preston bites out. God damn, my knees are weak I'm so fucking turned on. I'm not going to last.

Reaching for him, I grab on to the loose fabric of his hoodie. His strokes are hard, punishing, almost painful. For just a second he stops, spits in his hand, then goes right back to it. My eyes roll back, and I let the dresser and Preston's arm hold me up. Erotic flutters of lust tickle my stomach. I've never felt anything like this. Every thought in my head is quiet and I'm free to feel.

Preston adjusts his hold on me, his arm now vertical on my breastbone and his hand around my throat. My orgasm hits so hard I'm taken off guard by it. A loud, drawn-out moan escapes my throat and there's not a damn thing I can do about it. I explode between us, my cum dripping down his hand, and onto both of our shirts.

My hands fall to my sides, limp and useless, while my head falls to his shoulder as my brain tries to reconnect to the world.

"Jesus...fuck," I mutter, lifting my head from his shoulder to look up at him. He's got about three inches on me and he uses every centimeter to his advantage.

"Don't touch me." With those words, he shoves me and steps back. "Get your head in the game."

My legs don't want to hold me up so I stay leaned

against the dresser, the knobs on the drawers digging into my back painfully as he walks away. That's probably going to bruise, but that's future Jeremy's problem. *Current Jeremy is riding the orgasm high of his life.*

CHAPTER 7

preston

Y*ou're a fucking idiot.*

My hands are shaking as I tear out of the dorms and all but run to the gym. Today was supposed to be a recovery day but I can't stay in that room right now and I don't have any more classes today. I let my control slip and that can't happen. I have to be in control of myself or it all falls apart.

My heart is beating so loudly in my ears that I can't hear the conversation around me or the music pumping through the sound system of the gym. There are people around, working out, but I don't see them. Not really.

Run. Find a treadmill and run it out.

The treadmills are mostly unused so I grab one in the corner and set myself a hard pace. My legs are tired from yesterday but I'll survive.

I was just on the ice doing drills but I still make sure my muscles are warmed up before going at it full steam.

You're an embarrassment. Your mother is lucky she doesn't

have to witness your lack of control. She would be ashamed of you.

My gut tightens as the words run through my head while my feet pound on the treadmill belt.

You can't save Lily, you can't even save yourself.

Worthless.

Useless.

I push myself harder, trying so fucking hard to make the voice in my head shut up.

Jeremy won't trust you now. He's going to change roommates and everyone on the team will know what a shit show you really are.

But he liked it.

Jeremy *liked* when I touched him. The strange blue-brown of his eyes are burned into my memory. I'll never forget them. I can still feel his dick in my hand, pulsing through his orgasm, and his warm cum on my skin. It took everything in me not to lick it off.

You're a freak for enjoying it. He didn't want you to touch him but you did it anyway.

Monster.

No one will ever want you. No one will love you.

The picture of Jeremy getting face fucked by Brendon flitters through my head. Jealousy at the easy way they touch rears its ugly head. My jaw tightens and my hands clench. I hate how Brendon touches Jeremy.

I hate it even more that I want to be the one touching him.

God damn it. Get your shit together.

My muscles burn and my lungs scream for a break but I focus on the pain, finally quieting my thoughts. Like a weight has been lifted from me, for a few minutes, my head is quiet.

The only thing in my brain is the pounding of my feet and how my body feels.

Everyone thinks I workout like a man possessed because I'm dedicated to hockey but it's because it quiets my thoughts. It works out the sexual frustration of having no life. The only relief I get is in here, forcing my body to do more than it wants.

Or when you had Jeremy pushed up against the dresser...

Fuck off, brain. I don't have time for distractions.

I run until my body starts to break down. Until my knees threaten to give out. Slowing the pace to a jog, I can barely keep my ass on the machine. My entire body is beyond exhausted. My feet stumble on the belt so badly I have to grip the side rails to keep from face planting.

I turn toward the showers on autopilot but I don't have anything with me and I'm not sure I could stand up long enough to not drown in there.

Fuck it.

I force myself out of the gym and toward the dorm. The elevator almost drops me on my ass but I catch myself on the hand rails against the wall. A few people give me weird looks but no one asks if I'm okay. To be fair, if I wasn't, not many people could carry me.

I finally make it to my floor and stumble my way down the hallway to my door.

Please don't be locked. Please don't be locked.

I have literally nothing with me. If that door is locked I'm sleeping in the hallway because there's no way I'm going to be able to stay awake for long.

As I reach for the doorknob, it opens and I almost sag in relief. Doesn't matter that Jeremy is standing there looking awkward and unsure of what to do. Doesn't matter that I want to curl up with him against me. I brush past him, my arm grazing his bare chest and I hiss at the contact, jerking away from him.

I'm sweaty and stinky but I don't care, I don't even remove my shoes before falling on my bed face first.

Roll over. You aren't safe like this. Your back is exposed.

My entire body relaxes for a second but I can't pass out like this. My head won't let me slip into the unconscious state I so desperately want while I'm at risk.

Rolling onto my side, I push my back against the cool wall and, in the span of one breath, the world around me is gone.

When my alarm screams the next morning, no part of me is happy about it.

Fuuuuuuck.

I force myself to sit up and find the stupid thing, but it's not on my bedside table. Where the hell is it?

My gaze flitters over the room but I don't see it. It's dark since it's four AM and not even the sun is up yet, but when the alarm starts, the screen lights up.

"For the love of fuck, turn it off!" Jeremy snaps, shoving his head under his pillow.

"I can't find it." My voice is grittier than I expected but my mouth is dry and I'm thirsty as fuck.

"It fell under the bed, dumbass." His words are muffled by the cotton fluff.

I bend down and see the screen bright as shit under the bed all the way back against the wall. Great.

Sliding onto the floor, I lay flat on the shitty office carpet and stretch for the phone. Every muscle in my body objects, but I get it and shut it off.

"Thank fuck." Jeremy shoves his pillow back under his head and settles like a starfish on the tiny bed.

"You should get a workout in." The words fall from my mouth with no thought from me. "Being lazy isn't going to get us to the Frozen Four."

Not everyone is as neurotic as you.

"Fuck off. The last thing I want to do at four AM is spend it at the gym, looking at your face."

No one wants to spend time with you. You're useless. After all the time Father spent trying to fix you...

I grab my gym bag to shove clean clothes in it and find my shoes shoved under the edge of my bed.

Did I put my shoes there?

Thinking back to last night, it's kind of hazy but I'm pretty sure I fell asleep with my shoes on. As I sit to slide my shoes on, I flick my eyes to Jeremy for a second.

Did he take my shoes off after I fell asleep?

I don't know what to think about that.

The walk to the ice rink is plagued with it. Why would he care?

CHAPTER 8

jeremy

By five AM, I'm pissed. I can't fall back asleep, so I lay here and stare at the damn ceiling.

How did I get saddled with the worst roommate? I would rather have Austin, who doesn't shower regularly and doesn't pick up after himself.

You didn't hate the way he touched you.

Shut up, brain. No one asked you.

The feel of Preston holding me against the dresser with his hand on my dick, has me hardening and my skin flushing. That's what I've wanted from Brendon but never got. I wonder if he's always like that or if it was a onetime thing.

He touched you like he owned you and you loved it.

My dick stirs but I refuse to give in to the temptation. I can *not* lust after my roommate. He's a pompous, arrogant prick.

Sitting up, I slide my hand through my hair and rub my face. I stand and stretch before grabbing my discarded shirt from last night and pulling it over my head. I grab my phone and room key and leave the room, too irritated with myself to stay here anymore.

On my way out, I look back over the room and stop on Preston's bed. I've never seen him look that rough before. Normally, he's perfectly polished and put together, but when he got back from what I assume was the gym, he was rough. The look in his eyes was like he was running from ghosts. He passed out so quickly it was concerning, and if I hadn't heard the whimpering, I would have checked his pulse to make sure he was alive.

The dreams were bad, the way his big body cowered was too real. Does he have any friends he can talk to?

I close the door behind me and head to Brendon and Paul's room. Am I a dick for waking them up just because I'm irritated at my roommate for waking me up? Yes. Do I care? Nope.

I knock on the door with a smile on my face, knowing Paul is going to be pissed when he sees me and my hair isn't on fire.

I knock and knock and knock. Continuously. Until I hear someone inside.

"All right! Fuck!" Ah, Brendon is awake.

The door is ripped open and a half-asleep, angry hockey player is standing there in nothing but boxers.

"Morning, sunshine. Wakey wakey." My voice is falsely chipper, but this was more fun than I expected it to be.

"Fuck off, asshole," Paul mutters from his bed. Pushing past Brendon, who's glaring at me, I jump onto Paul and ruffle his hair.

"Come on, sugar tits, time to get up!" He struggles against me, trying to shove me off of him, but stops when my comment sinks in.

"How do you know my tits are sweet? You molesting me while I'm asleep again?"

"If I was going to molest someone in their sleep, sucking on a man titty wouldn't be my first move." I pinch his nipple.

"Ow, fuck face!" He shoves me hard this time and I fall off the bed laughing. "And I don't have moobs." He sits up, rubbing his sore nipple. "Why are you in here annoying us instead of your roommate?"

I sigh and lean back on my hands. "He was up at four and couldn't find his god damn phone to shut off the alarm."

Brendon sits on his bed, now with PJ pants on, rubbing the sleep from his eyes.

"Has he said anything to you?" Brendon's question is quiet but I hear it just fine.

"Nothing besides I need to work out more and I'm lazy."

My face heats a bit at the memory of him telling me to shut the fuck up while he was jerking me off. Brendon doesn't need to know that happened. He's not my boyfriend so I don't owe him an explanation. Right?

"Seriously, what is that dude's problem?" Paul sits up.

"He's intense, for sure," I say. All of a sudden not wanting to rag on the man I share space with. He was vulnerable last night and I don't want them to know about it. "His dad is super well known. Maybe it's a work ethic he was raised with?"

I shrug and check my phone for the time.

"Come on, time to head down to practice." I pat Brendon's knee and head back to my room to get dressed.

The blast of cold as we enter the rink puts a smile on my face, but the sound of skates on the ice has that smile falling. Fucking Carmichael. Why does he have to make the rest of us look bad?

"Show off," Paul grumbles behind me as we head for the locker room to get changed.

The locker room is full of guys changing, chugging pre-workout drinks and shoving protein bars in their faces.

"Alright, boys," Coach starts. "Today we're working on puck control and passes. Suit up."

We quickly get changed and head out to the ice for warm-ups. We circle the ice, every round faster than the last, making sure our muscles are loose and ready for the workout they're about to get.

We're lined up waiting for instructions while the coaches set up practice equipment on the ice.

"About time." Carmichael's snide voice in my ear sets my teeth on edge.

"Surprised you can move this morning. You stumbled back to the dorms like you were drunk."

"I don't drink. Too many empty calories. But I can see you enjoy it." I can hear the grin in his tone and I have never wanted to punch someone in the face so quickly. "Perhaps if you worked a little harder, you wouldn't need to drown your sorrows in alcohol."

"You don't know anything about me." I snap back.

"If you spent less time worrying about your dick and more time working out, you would be a phenomenal player. Instead, you're mediocre, *at best*." The dig hits me just as hard as he intended. Fucking prick.

"Seems you spend a decent amount of time thinking about my dick. Jealous no one wants to suck yours?"

"Hey!" Brendon whisper yells at us. "Shut up and pay attention."

"I wonder how long it will take for you to *beg* to suck my dick." Carmichael keeps right on talking as if he didn't hear Brendon. I know he did, but he just doesn't care.

Don't shove him.

Don't shove him.

Don't. Shove. Him.

My teeth ache from clenching my jaw so hard. It's going to be a long fucking day.

We break up into offense and defense then run drills until we're huffing and sweating. Muscles are definitely warmed up and we're feeling good.

"Water break!" Coach yells out and we skate over to the bench to grab a drink. I unsnap my chin strap and spit my mouth guard into my gloved hand. Squeezing the water bottle left out for us, I fill my mouth with water. Someone slams into my back, making me choke as I attempt to swallow the cold liquid. I stumble forward into the bench, going headfirst over it onto the floor, my mouth guard going flying. My helmet comes off as my face meets the floor.

"Fuck," I snap as I try to get up and face whoever hit me.

I'm stuck between the bench and the wall, my pads and gloves keeping me from getting up on my own.

"What the fuck was that?" Brendon yells as a couple of the guys lift me up. I'm wedged in such a weird position, there's no way I can get out by myself.

"Slipped." The deadpan voice of my roommate sets my anger off.

"No, you didn't! I watched you run into him!" Brendon is in Preston's face, but Preston isn't fazed or concerned. He's watching me like he can see through me. That look has me wanting to snap, to pop off and fight him, but that's what he wants. He wants to push me into making a stupid mistake and losing ice time. I have twin brothers. If he thinks a little ribbing and manhandling is going to get to me, he's wrong. I've had years of practice putting up with little shitheads.

"Albrooke, you good?" Coach asks once I'm on my feet again.

"Yeah, I'm all right."

Paul hands me my mouth guard and I shove it back in, snap my chin strap, and head back onto the ice. I can't let him see that he's bothering me.

The rest of practice is exhausting. Our new head coach is kicking our asses. Everyone is exhausted except the damn golden boy. Coach finally calls the end of practice when Paul throws up on the ice.

We all limp back to the locker room, leg muscles threatening to give out. Paul is given a water bottle and sits on a bench close to the entrance. I slap him on the shoulder pad as I hobble past him. My body is beyond exhausted. My muscles are crying for a hot shower and sleep.

I get my jersey off, pads hung up in my cubby to dry out, and my skates put up. My base layer is soaked with sweat and clings to me like a second skin.

Water bottles are passed out as we're getting ready for showers.

"Albrooke." Coach stops next to me. "Stop by my office after showers."

"Sure thing, Coach." I nod to him as dread drops into my stomach like a lead weight. Anxiety and fear send ice through my veins at the prospect of getting benched or losing my spot on the starting line.

"What did you do?" Brendon asks as I pass him to drop my base layer into the laundry on the way to the showers.

"I don't know but I have a feeling it has to do with Carmichael."

The steam of the showers is suffocating as I wash the sweat of practice off. Did Preston say something to Coach about me? Make up some lie to get me into trouble? Did I break some rule I don't know about?

Once I'm done taking the quickest shower of my life, I dry off, get dressed, and head to Coach's office, every step heavier than the last.

I raise my hand to rap my knuckles on the door when it's jerked open. Preston Carmichael is filling the doorway for a second before he raises a lip at me and shoves past me. I watch him stalking away from me, freshly showered and dressed, his black hair hanging in his eyes giving him a bad boy vibe that's normally hidden behind his perfect exterior. The jeans he's wearing cupping that amazing ass hockey players are known for is a fucked-up reminder that he's hot as well as being a pretentious dick.

"Albrooke, come in and close the door." Coach's voice has me turning away from my infuriating roommate and swallowing past the lump in my throat.

The door closes behind me with a *click* and I wait for the yelling, holding my breath and shielding my features to show nothing.

"Have a seat," he waves to the old chairs with wooden arms and upholstery that may have been new in the 90s. My ass has barely hit the seat when he starts talking.

"Have you noticed anything off with Carmichael? You're his roommate, correct?"

My mind goes blank for a second and I blink a few times as I process what he's asked.

"Uh yeah, he's my roommate." My eyebrows pull together in confusion. Anything off? Dude is crazy, seems to have some kind of superpower that tells him when I'm trying to get laid, and hates me for some unknown reason. But I doubt that's what Coach wants to know.

"You notice anything weird? Quick mood changes, stumbling or appearing out of it?" he clarifies. Should I tell him about last night? What's he getting at? We're drug tested regularly.

Now I'm really confused. "Drugs? No way. He's rarely in our room but he's always in his right mind. He won't even go out for a beer with the team. That dude lives in his routines for hockey. Up at four, to sleep no later than nine." I shake my head. "There's no way he's strung out or anything."

Coach purses his lips and nods, obviously thinking about something.

"I'm concerned about him. We received a call about him stumbling around and looking *unwell*." He holds my stare for a moment. "Just send me a message or call me if you see anything odd."

"I'll see you in the morning for workout." He dismisses me and I stand with a heavy weight on my chest.

CHAPTER 9

preston

Our exhibition game is in a few hours. I'm showered and pulling on my suit in the hotel bathroom, the newest scars on my body still bright red and angry. I had to remove the stitches myself last week since I'm not calling my father to do it.

I've already eaten my game day breakfast of eggs with grilled onions, peppers, and chicken sausage with a green smoothie, and lunch of a salad, grilled chicken, and protein shake. Like most hockey players, I'm a bit superstitious. Some are over the top and disgusting with it, but food is something I can and do control anyway. Making sure the food I put into my body fuels it to the best I can be is important. If any of my food is off today, not made just the way I need it to be, I will play like shit, which puts me on my father's radar. Not somewhere I want to be. So many little things go into making sure game day is perfect. I ironed both dress shirts I have, made sure the slacks were pressed from the dry cleaners and the jackets are wrinkle free. Being put together is important, we must look professional. Being put together makes me feel powerful, like armor.

The cufflinks glint in the light of the bathroom against my white shirt and navy-blue jacket. If I'm to believe my father, these were my grandfather's on my mother's side. I've always liked the simplicity of the gold with an anchor in the center. He loved to sail and passed down that love to my mother, who spent every summer on the yacht.

They aren't overly decorative or flashy, probably a trinket from a seaside town that they visited, but they call to me. Maybe because it makes me feel closer to my mother. I have a few memories of being a small boy on the wood deck of a big boat, my mother's blonde hair whipping around her and a big smile on her face. There was joy in her eyes as she shared the experience with me. My father was nowhere to be seen, probably at work, and she was free to enjoy the moment. I had to have been five or six so I didn't understand that she was just as much of a victim as I would become. If I remember correctly, it wasn't long after that trip that I got drugged for the first time and woke up with stitches across my chest.

Lost in my memories, I rub at the first scar I received at the hands of my father. The skin is puckered and doesn't have full sensitivity. One of the many reasons I don't like to be touched. The sensation is off. It never feels right.

I check my reflection in the mirror, dropping my shoulders and buttoning my jacket before opening the door, only to stop in my tracks at the sight in front of me.

Why did I have to room with him? Even here at the away game, I can't get away from him.

Jeremy is attempting to get a suit jacket onto his shoulders that is at least a size too small for him, looks like it was made in the 80s, and is definitely polyester.

"You're fucking with me, right?" The words are condescending and I know it. I don't care.

"What?" He turns toward me, the jacket now on his body, but he's holding his breath.

"Whose suit did you steal? That's obviously not yours." I straighten up and slide my hands into my tailored wool suit pants.

He drags his eyes over my suit, the irritation and embarrassment clear on his face. He stands stiffly, face flushed. "Not everyone can afford a custom-made suit, jackass."

His hands run down his wrinkled dress shirt.

"Your shirt isn't even ironed." I pinch the bridge of my nose, exhaling a frustrated breath, and setting my jaw. Stepping toward the closet behind the door, I grab another suit and shove it into his chest. I always bring two, just in case something happens and I need to change. Jeremy's eyes meet mine, confusion pulling his eyebrows together, crinkling the skin above his nose.

"You can wear one of mine so you aren't an embarrassment." Jeremy's gaze flicks down to the zipper bag on the hanger then back to mine. "Hurry up."

He takes a step back, insulted by the offer. There's more room in this hotel room than in our dorm but he can't escape me.

"Excuse me? I'm not wearing your shit. This is fine." He motions to the clothes on his body that are absolutely not fine.

"That costume should be tossed in a dumpster and lit on fire. I'm pretty sure it's polyester, which is notoriously flammable." I don't hide the disgust on my face as I look him over again. He looks like a waiter at a cheap Italian restaurant. "You're smaller than me but it will fit better than that travesty."

"No," he grinds out through clenched teeth.

I step into his space, tossing the suit onto his bed, then grab the lapels on his jacket, jerking him against me. It's my turn to grit my teeth against the contact, but there's enough layers of clothing that I can tolerate it. Those unmatching blue-brown eyes blazing at me from less than a foot away is intoxicating.

He smells so fucking good though. Spicy and clean. For the first time I can remember, I want to shove my face into the crook of his neck and inhale. I've never wanted to do that before. The men I've fucked in the past were just that. A quick fuck and done.

"I don't care if you hate me or not, have some self-respect and show up to the game looking like you belong there."

His eyes flick between mine. "Why do you care how I look?"

"You represent the team. Looking like shit makes us all look like shit."

My gaze drops to his mouth for just a second when he swipes his tongue over his lower lip.

I can't like him. I can't be attracted to him. I definitely can't fuck him.

Moving quickly, I grab the two sides of his shirt and rip it open, sending the buttons flying around our room.

"What the fuck is your problem?!" he yells. I pat his cheek and head to the elevator.

A few of the other guys are waiting for it as well, so I ride down with them, ignoring any attempt at conversation. I'm not here to be their friend.

We stand around the lobby until Coach appears and ushers us onto the bus that will take us to the rink for our game against University of Nevada, Las Vegas. We all file on the bus, most of them sitting with buddies, chatting or listening to something in their earbuds. I fall into the second category. Bach filters through my head, calming any pregame nerves that creep up.

"Carmichael," Coach looks at me so I pull an earbud out of my ear.

"Yes?"

"Where's Albrooke?"

Some of the guys turn to look at me.

"I don't know, Coach, he was dressed when I left our room." Close enough to the truth. He was *dressed,* I just helped him make better decisions.

"I'm here, Coach." The man in question appears over Coach's shoulder.

"Good, have a seat and we'll get going."

Coach takes a seat in the front row of the bus and I peer around the seats to see Jeremy in my dark gray suit with the light blue button up shirt. The pants are a little long but they fit his thighs perfectly.

Thighs I desperately want to feel wrapped around me.

He doesn't look at me while he finds his seat next to Johnson and sits down. The pants accentuate his ass too. I need to stop thinking about him. Oiler looks at Albrooke, takes in what he's wearing, then looks back at me. I make eye contact with him for a second, one side of my mouth lifts as I close my eyes and relax into the seat for the ride.

When we arrive at the stadium, we all file off the bus and down the tunnel to the locker rooms. I grab my workout clothes and head to the toilet stalls to get changed. It doesn't take me long to switch from the suit to the t-shirt and shorts. Rolls of tape are passed around the room and we start taping up our sticks for the night. Almost everyone does their own, every player being very particular about how it's done. Luckily, since we've all been doing it for years, it doesn't take long.

Once all the sticks are stored for the game, we grab our

skates to drop them off for sharpening while we get an off ice warm-up in.

We all know what we're doing. Most are focused on the task, but a few are laughing and joking around to lessen the tension.

Coach comes in and lets us know our skates are done and it's time to gear up.

I grab a towel to wipe my face and drink some water while I wait for my turn to grab my stuff. It doesn't take long for us to be back in the locker room changing into our gear. I grab my base layer and head back into the stall to change. Pulling on compression clothes when you're sweaty isn't the easiest thing but it gets done quick enough.

There's a high pitched "Fuck!" and running water coming from the showers. Probably Brendon if I had to guess. Taking a cold shower is probably part of his ritual for game day.

Back at my cubby, getting my gear on doesn't take long since I don't have the distraction of anyone talking to me. When you ignore people for long enough, they eventually get the message.

"Dude, did you wash those after last season?" Jeremy's question has me looking up but he's talking to Paul, who is pulling on the nastiest looking socks I've ever seen. All of his toes are sticking out of one sock, and I use the term in the loosest of senses, while the other one has a massive hole at the heel.

"Uh..." Paul stops to think about it. "Yeah, I did."

"I don't know how those things haven't disintegrated." Brendon shows up, a towel around his waist, shivering.

"Ten minutes, boys!" one of the coaches yells into the locker room.

Jeremy sits down and pulls on one sock, then his skate

and ties it, then repeats it on the other side. When his skates are on, he knocks on the toes of each one, right then left.

Why am I watching him put his damn skates on? I don't care what his pregame rituals are.

Focus.

I close my eyes and inhale a deep breath, letting the music in my ears drown out the white noise in the locker room. Ignoring everyone around me, I zero in on getting my gear on and pulling on my skates, shifting around to make sure my pads are set right.

We make it out onto the ice for warm-ups and the adrenaline of the game lights a fire in my body. I love this part. The peace before the bloodshed of battle. My muscles warm and my body loosens as I move, the skates an extension of me. I've been on the ice since I was five. It's second nature to skate, despite how much I dislike hockey because of my father. I'm good at it, it's easy, but I don't enjoy the game. Not the way someone trying to make it in the NHL should. I don't have the passion for it my father tried to cut into me. He ruined any pleasure I got from it a long time ago.

The real fucked up part is I don't know what I want to do. All I've ever done is hockey.

Coach blows his whistle and we line up on a blue line. He has us run through some drills to make sure we're good to go, passing, blocking, direction changes, then back to the locker room to wait for the game to start.

We get a drink of water and the guys break off into their cliques and a few of us listen to music as we wait. I close my eyes and lean back against my cubby, Tchaikovsky playing in my head.

After a few minutes I feel someone staring at me. Again. Opening my eyes, I find Oiler watching me like he's trying to figure me out. It's the third time today I've caught him staring at me. I lift an eyebrow at him and his gaze flicks to Albrooke. Did Albrooke tell his boyfriend that he was wearing my clothes? Or that I jacked him off?

Why do I like that he's jealous? Why do I like Jeremy wearing my stuff?

"Alright, boys," Coach starts as most of the team is pulling on jerseys, so I get my AirPods off and put them away. "This team is good but so are you. You've worked hard to get here. Keep your wits about you, don't let them in your head, and let's show them just how much Darby is a threat."

Coach calls us to go into the tunnel and Brendon, Paul, and Jeremy slap sticks right before shooting out onto the ice.

From the second we step out onto the ice, we're on the defensive. UNLV plays hard and fast and it's all we can do to keep them out of the crease. Our goalie is getting a workout and I'm two seconds from chucking one of these bastards into the boards. The refs aren't calling shit against them and they are using it to their advantage. Offsides and illegal hits left and right. My counterpart on the ice, Willis, is exhausted and it's only the second period.

We're behind on the board, two to zero and our first line is falling apart from the frustration.

By some miracle the puck lands on my stick and I fling it as hard as I can across the ice. It makes it past UNLV's defenders and lights up the lamp. I drop my head back on my neck and I let out a breath. We're on the fucking board.

My team rallies, slapping at my chest and back with "Fuck yeah!" and "Holy shit, bro!" and I try not to cringe at the touch.

The buzzer sounds and we all come off the ice for a drink and rest for the fifteen minute intermission and ice resurfacing before the third period starts. Twenty more minutes. We can come back.

After a pep talk from Coach, the team has a renewed sense of energy. The boys on the third line get the next goal on the first play, Albrooke, Oiler, and Johnson working like a well-oiled machine to get the lamp light on. The rest of the game, we struggled to get another goal in, but we managed it in the last minute of the game to break the tie and come away with the win. The most impressive part was holding UNLV to their two points.

The guys are smiling and congratulating each other as they head down the chute to the locker room. I get my gear pulled off and head toward a toilet stall to finish getting changed. I hate that I can't take a shower but I'm used to it. Like I do every time after a game, I'll rinse my head in the sink, basically sponge the rest of me off with wet paper towels, and get dressed. I'll shower in the hotel room later and have to face the awkward questions of my roommate. Normally, I can pawn it off as a post-game ritual, but I'm not sure Jeremy will take that answer.

CHAPTER 10

preston

When we get back to the hotel, I grab a change of clothes and head straight for the bathroom. I turn the shower on and strip out of my suit, doing my best not to look in the mirror. My phone rings and even though I'm standing in the bathroom in my underwear, I answer it.

"Hey, you okay?" Concern for my sister has my tone harsher than normal. Like most teenagers, she prefers text or video calls, so her calling me is strange.

"Yeah, I'm good. I watched your game, nice goal!" Her animated voice has one side of my mouth lifting in a half smile.

"Thanks. If that hadn't have worked, someone was going to get thrown into the boards." I turn and lean my ass against the counter so I don't have to look at the scars.

She laughs and I can hear noise in the background that I can't quite identify.

"Where are you?"

Knowing she's on the opposite side of the country from our father lets me breathe a little easier. If he's going to go after her, I have a few hours to get her to safety. There are a few people I have in her life that know to grab her and run if I ever give them the signal. There's a driver and bodyguard that are still around in case she needs to go somewhere away from the school. Dad pays to keep them on retainer, but he doesn't know they call me when he calls her home.

"Alison's room. She's got a show playing on her laptop," she tells me easily. My little sister is a shit liar, even if I can't see her face, so I don't question her any further. "What are you doing to celebrate your win?"

"I'm having dinner with the team then going to bed."

"Ugh!" I can see her rolling her eyes at me in my head, probably dropping her head back on her shoulders. "You are so boring! You're twenty-one! Go get drunk or something."

"Why does everyone tell me to go get drunk?" I huff. Even before college, guys I played with tried to convince me to drink with them. I've never been interested. Most of the guys kept it to one beer or one shot after a game until the season was over, then they would get hammered.

"Uh, maybe it's a sign that you need to lighten up and live a little?" The attitude coming through this phone is palpable. "You're kind of a pretentious workaholic. So, get drunk and get laid. I'm betting it'll make you a lot nicer."

"What the actual fuck, Lil? My *baby* sister does not need to think about my sex life." I bark out. It's one thing for the guys in the locker room to tell me I'm being a dick and to go get laid, it's an entirely different one for my sister to say it.

She sighs. "There's that pretentious asshat I know. Seriously, lighten up and have a drink."

"Was there a point to you calling me or are you just going to call me names?" I make sure my voice doesn't give away the amusement threatening to make me smile. I enjoy her banter and her backbone. It makes me happy that she's not afraid of me, that she's still carefree. Despite losing our mother when she was very young, the ugliness of our father hasn't tainted her. I've taken all of it on my shoulders to protect her.

"I just called to tell you to go easy on yourself for once, but I gotta go now. A few of us are having a movie night. Later!" She hangs up before I can respond. I slide my phone back onto the counter, finish getting undressed, and step into the shower.

The steam is billowing out of the stall when I pull back the curtain and step in. The hot water burns my skin, turning it pink as I let it run over me. I close my eyes again and I let myself relax and think back to the game. To Jeremy in my clothes and how well my pants fit him.

My dick perks up, wanting a piece of my damn roommate.

With images of him getting fucked in the team showers playing in my head like a movie, I stroke myself. His eyes meeting mine, helpless but too afraid to say anything, so he took it and couldn't stop himself from coming. For me.

When I walked in, he was half hard at best. Brendon doesn't know how to handle him. It's so painfully obvious he wants to be manhandled, forced, and dominated. It calls to a part of me I rarely let out. I like control. I don't mind inflicting some pain if it's wanted or pushing limits gets me off. Taking what I want and knowing that when he fights, he wants me to force him. He came so fast once he saw me watching him. He wasn't hard until he noticed me jacking off to him getting fucked. But then his cheeks flushed red and his dick perked right up. The boy was uncomfortable and that got me hot too.

My breathing increases as the images change to him staring up at me while I jerked him off. Angry, unsure, turned on. It was sexy as fuck to watch him struggle to accept it, then give in and let it happen. That moment of surrender, it's intoxicating. I want so much more of it.

I'm achingly hard, my balls full and heavy with the need to come as I stroke faster and harder, chasing the orgasm building up in my body. The whimper Jeremy made when he came for me plays in my head like I've never heard it before and my own orgasm crashes over me, spilling cum onto the wall and floor of the shower. My stomach muscles tighten as I thrust my hips against my hand.

Fuck, I needed that.

I let myself stand in the water a few more minutes before I wash off the sweat of the game and shut the water off. By the time I'm dressed in jeans and a t-shirt and step out of the bathroom, my roommate is nowhere to be found. A pang of disappointment hits me square in the chest, but I refuse to think about it. He's probably down in the restaurant getting dinner. I grab my wallet, phone, and room key then head downstairs to eat as well.

Turns out there's some convention going on this weekend so with the team all down here trying to eat, there are no open tables.

"Good evening, just you tonight?" The flirty blonde hostess in all black with a high ponytail smiles at me.

"Yes."

"We're busy tonight so there's a waitlist. Can I get a name?"

I clench my jaw and let out a breath. "Preston."

I wait to be seated by the host, standing off to one side.

"Carmichael!" I turn toward the dining room, looking for whoever called my name. Brendon is motioning me over to a table with Paul and Jeremy. My dick twitches at the mere idea of being close to him after what I just did upstairs. I hate that I want him as much as I do.

I take a deep breath and let it out slowly. Maybe I should take my sister's advice and try to relax, have some fun even.

Against my better judgment, I approach the table. It appears they haven't been here long since they only have drinks.

"Hey man, have a seat." Brendon motions to the empty chair with the glass of beer in his hand.

Paul looks at Jeremy sitting next to the empty seat and I decide to sit down based solely on the awkward expression they share.

"We haven't ordered yet, you want a drink?" Brendon looks around for the waitress and when he makes eye contact with her, he lifts his glass.

"Beer is full of empty calories." I tell him.

"Wow. Thanks for joining the party, Buzz Killer." Paul scoffs, lifting his own beer to his lips.

"Perhaps if you want to increase your performance on the ice, you should be drinking a White Claw since it's lower in calories." My eyes drill into his until he's uncomfortable and looks away.

The waitress appears by my side and smiles at me. "What can I get you to drink?"

"Water is fine."

My phone buzzes so I pull it out of my pocket to check it in case Lily needs something.

DEAREST DADDY

Decent night, were a bit sloppy in the first period. That anger in the second is going to be a problem that I will correct if you don't get it under control. Since you didn't come here to have the sutures removed, you must have done them yourself. Sounds like correction is in order, Charles. Send me a picture so I know you didn't fuck up my work.

My jaw aches and my abdomen tightens as the fear of *correction* hits me. He isn't here and he won't come fetch me, but the adrenaline doesn't know that. During the last major correction, he had to hook me up to an IV line for fluids and a caffeine drip because I was falling asleep and getting dehydrated.

"Okay, I can grab that for you. Are you guys ready to order?" The waitress's chipper voice breaks the hold my memory has on me.

They all order bacon cheeseburgers with fries while I order grilled salmon, wild rice, and steamed broccoli. I don't hold back my look of disgust at their order.

"Slow down there, party animal." Brendon laughs.

"If you were smart, you'd have a strict diet now. They expect nothing less in the NHL."

"Shots. We need shots and they're low in calories, so you'll be fine," Jeremy says, heading to the bar to order the drinks, shaking his head as he leaves the table.

Truth be told, I haven't had much experience with alcohol. My father hasn't allowed it and I didn't want it bad enough to risk him finding out. I've never really been free of him since his presence looms over me at every turn. I get a few nights away from his grasp for away games but that's it. Every home game he's there, making sure I don't fuck up and need *correction.* He even lives close to campus in case he needs to intervene during the week.

Brendon and Paul discuss something on their side of the table that I don't pay attention to. I'm scanning the room, looking for my father despite knowing he's not here. I don't like being in the middle of the room with my back to the door. It leaves me open to him sliding up behind me with no warning.

My phone vibrates in my pocket, so I pull it out and check the screen. Dearest Daddy.

"Excuse me," I stand from the table and accept the call while leaving the restaurant. My spine is straight as if going to war. I *am* fighting a battle, but it's a psychological one.

"Charles, you've been away from town for only a day and already you think you can ignore me?" My father using my first name makes me tense. I hate being called Charles. He and his high society friends are the only people to use that name.

"I'm at dinner with the team, I can't exactly strip off my clothes and send you a picture right this second." I know I fucked up the instant the words have left my mouth. I suck in a deep breath to calm my temper.

"You will watch your tone when you speak to me, you disrespectful little shit. I own you. I can pull you out of that school, and off that team, so fast your head will spin." The cold rage fills my ears and my heart starts to pound. If I was in front of him right now, at the penthouse, I would be taught a lesson in respecting my elders.

I pace the lobby for something to do with the energy coursing through me. I scan the faces of everyone who walks through my line of sight, just in case the face that looks like mine appears. It wouldn't be the first time he popped up somewhere I didn't expect him to.

The saliva in my mouth dries, a reaction to the lack of hydration he forces me to endure regularly during *correction.*

"You have nothing to say for yourself, Charles? Do you need to come home so soon? I had hoped that by now, you would have a better hold on that damn temper," he snaps. "Or perhaps, Lillian would like to come see one of your home games."

Fear races through my body, freezing the blood in my veins. A block of ice fills my stomach at the implication of him getting his hands on my sister. I've spent most of her entire life protecting her from him, I will *not* fail now.

"No!" I damn near yell the word before forcing myself to press my back against a wall, close my eyes, and take a deep breath. The sensation of being watched sends a shiver down my spine. "I'm tired and hungry. I didn't mean to take it out on you. I apologize." The words I've spoken so many times fall from my lips. I could recite them in my fucking sleep at this point.

"Do better. Stop being an embarrassment to this family."

"Yes, sir." My head hits the wall as I mumble the words. She's safe from him, that's all that matters.

"Send a picture tonight or there will be hell to pay tomorrow." The phone goes dead and the relief has my knees buckling.

A shudder zips up my spine at the memory of the music blasting in my ears and the electricity shooting through my body when he would shock me awake.

My heartbeat pounds in my ears and my body itches to flee but I'm not in danger right now. I'm okay.

Breathe.

In. Hold. Out. Release.

Over and over, I repeat the pattern of breathing until the tightness in my chest loosens and my body is no longer ready to fight for my life. When I'm calm, I head to the bathroom and luck out when there's an open stall under a light. Quickly, I pull my arm out of my shirt, take a picture of the newest incision, and send it to my father. I've got my arm shoved through the sleeve and I'm leaving the room before it's sent.

I can't handle being in public anymore. My fucking father ruined another night for me. I'm too on edge but I know going for a run right now will not help. All I need is to sleep. I don't even need food anymore.

Maybe Lily is right and I should have a few drinks.

Heading back into the restaurant, I see the waitress serving our table walking toward me and I stop her by holding up a finger.

"Is everything okay, sir?" she asks, pleasantly. Over her shoulder I can see the table and in my spot are two full shot glasses. Perfect.

"Can you have my meal boxed up and sent up with the guy I was sitting next to?"

"Of course."

I nod to her and walk to the table.

Grabbing both of the shots, I shoot one back, swallow it, then slam back the second one.

"Fuck yeah!" Brendon shouts.

I cough at the harsh burn, reaching for my water and taking a long drink then slamming it down on the table. A warmth I wasn't expecting spreads through my stomach until my entire abdomen is loose with it. I've never felt anything like it but it's comforting, like a hug but no one's touching me.

"I'm going back to my room. Night." For just a second, my eyes meet Jeremy's, surprise and confusion warring on his face. I know the closed off mask I usually wear is gone, exposing how raw and frustrated I am. There's no way I can cover it right now, I have to protect myself.

I don't stop to contemplate any of it. I don't owe him or anyone else an explanation.

CHAPTER 11

jeremy

"What the fuck was that?" Paul asks, staring at the retreating back of my roommate.

"I have no idea, but that was really weird," I mutter, chewing on a french-fry while also watching Preston leave. Who the hell was that call from? What did they say to him? He looked torn up, almost vulnerable.

Our waitress pops up with a to-go box and starts putting Preston's food into it.

"Uh, what's going on?" Brendon asks her, flicking his gaze to me like I have a fucking answer.

"The man who was sitting here, asked me to box up his meal and send it with you." She looks at me. "Is that okay?" Her hands stop moving, hovering in the air.

"Oh, sure. That's fine."

She finishes up and closes the clam shell box. "Is this being charged to your rooms?"

After we give her our room information, I grab Preston's dinner and we stand.

"I'm getting another drink," Paul announces.

"I'll join ya," Brendon steps back toward the bar.

"I'm going to take his royal highness his dinner." I motion over my shoulder with my thumb.

"Later," Paul says over his shoulder. Brendon pauses then follows me toward the elevator.

"I thought you were getting a drink?" I lift an eyebrow at him.

He shifts uncomfortably, looking around us. "You want to fool around first? We can be quick."

Shit.

Unease flitters in my stomach. I don't want to hurt his feelings, but I'm really not interested anymore. If I'm being honest with myself, I haven't been interested in a while, but he was convenient. That sucks but it's the truth.

"I'm tired, I'm just going to go to bed." I try to give him a reassuring smile but I'm pretty sure he can see right through me.

"Sure, okay. Another time." He shrugs like it doesn't matter but I can tell by how stiff his shoulders are that it stings. God damn it.

The elevator dings and I step inside with Brendon walking off toward the bar. Right now, I can't worry about Brendon's hurt feelings. I have no idea what I'm about to find. Has Preston eaten anything since the game? If not, does he know that liquor is going to hit him like a freight train?

By the time I get to my floor, I'm concerned.

Opening the door with my keycard, I'm not sure what to expect but Preston lying spread-eagle on the corner of the bed with his feet on the floor, is not it.

He lifts his head and looks at me for a second before dropping his head back down.

"Hey man, you okay?" I edge toward him, putting the food on the dresser and slowly making my way closer to the bed.

"I hate hotel rooms. The beds aren't against the wall." He sighs heavily, like this is a major inconvenience.

That was not what I asked but okay. Now that he mentions it, I don't think I've ever seen a hotel room with beds pushed into a corner.

"Who called you?"

"Doesn't matter." His eyes are closed but one side of his perfectly kissable mouth lifts in a half smile. "She's in a boarding school in New York. She's safe there."

"Who is safe from what?"

He starts humming a soft, soothing melody I've never heard before.

"Did you drink more after you left? Have you eaten anything?" He's fucking lost it. I'm concerned about a mental break here.

"Hmmm?" He lifts his eyebrows but doesn't open his eyes. He's wasted? How did he get this drunk off two shots of Jack?

I quickly scan the room looking for another drink, mini bottle, anything, but I don't see it from here.

"When did you eat last?" I step between his knees and reach for his arms to pull him up into a sitting position. He hisses and cringes away from me, pushing at my hands.

"Don't touch me."

How does someone who plays a full contact sport not like to be touched? Do the pads make that big of a difference? Or is it just me he doesn't want to touch him?

"You gotta sit up and eat," I tell him, reaching for his hand this time. He threads his fingers through mine and holds my hand. The move makes me freeze. What the hell is this?

He doesn't want to be touched but wants to hold my hand?

I stand there in my awkwardness and let him hold my hand in his while my heart thumps uncomfortably in my chest.

Less than a minute later, he's asleep and snoring lightly.

Jesus. What a mess this guy is.

I carefully lay his hand down on the bed and kneel on the floor to pull his shoes off. Why do I keep doing this for him? He's never nice to anyone, why do I keep trying to take care of him?

Because he's broken, you just don't know how much yet.

Since he's sprawled out on top of the blankets, I pull one off my bed to toss over him. He doesn't move at all. I have a feeling this was exactly what he needed tonight.

I get ready for bed and plug our phones in to charge. His screen lights up, showing a preview of a text message from Dearest Daddy. Would he have his dad saved in his phone that way or is he a lot kinkier than I thought?

DEAREST DADDY

You're a fuck up. Your mother would weep if she saw your...

The message cuts off but I don't need to see the entire thing to know it's not pleasant. Jesus. I don't know if I hope it's kinky shit or not. If that's his actual dad, what kind of parent talks to their kid like that? No wonder he pushes himself so hard. He's not good enough for his famous father.

I fall asleep pondering the life of Charles Preston Carmichael. Everyone thinks he's a spoiled, rich kid, but maybe the grass isn't greener just because your family has money.

The next morning, I'm awoken by the ringing of a Facetime call.

What the actual fuck is happening? It's too damn early for this.

Reaching for my phone, I pick up the buzzing fucker and answer it without looking.

"What the fuck do you want?"

"Um. Who are you and why do you have my brother's phone?" I don't know who that voice belongs to, but it's not my sister. "O.M.G. Did Pres really go out and get laid last night or are you a boyfriend he's hiding from me?" This girl is talking crazy at whatever the fuck o'clock it is.

I scrub my hand down my face and rub my eyes before looking at the phone screen.

"What are you babbling about?"

"Where is Preston?" She enunciates each word like I'm an idiot. A dark-haired girl with light gray eyes and a big smile fills the phone. Definitely not my sister but there's enough likeness that it's not hard to figure out she's Preston's sister. "Well, hello there, sleepy head. Aren't you adorable?"

"I don't fucking know. He was drunk and passed out last I saw him." The girl squeals as I sit up and look over at the other bed. Preston is face down on the pillow with the blanket from my bed wrapped tightly around him.

"Yo, your sister is calling." He doesn't budge.

"No, that's okay! Tell him to call me later. I'm so glad he has a boyfriend to help him relax." The video call ends, leaving me confused but too tired to give a shit. I lay back down and fall back to sleep.

At eight AM, our team wakeup call starts with a loud knock on the door of the hotel room.

"Yeah," I yell at the door to make whoever it is, probably Carpenter, stop banging on it. Opening my eyes, I roll my head toward the other bed and find Preston pulling the nightstand away from the wall.

"What are you doing?" I lift up onto one elbow, facing him.

"I can't find my phone."

A phone chimes from behind me and we both look to see where it came from.

"Do you have my phone?" Preston climbs over me to lift the pillows and pull at the blankets, finding it tangled in the sheet, irritation clear in his determined, jerky movements. "What the fuck? Why do you have it?" He sits back on his shins with it in his hand and glares at me.

Why is it in my bed?

"Oh! Your sister video called you this morning, but you were passed out. I guess I fell asleep with it in my hand." I shrug and sit up, leaning against the headboard.

Now he's furious, shaking-with-anger kind of mad.

"You talked to my sister?" The words are so quiet I almost don't hear them. My body prepares for a fight. Any minute Preston is going to swing at me, I can feel it.

"I didn't realize it was your phone when I answered it." I say carefully. I don't really want to fight this big bastard, but I will if he starts it.

Faster than I figured he could move the morning after drinking, he's flung a leg over mine and straddles my lap, leaning his forearm against my throat and dropping his head until our noses are almost touching.

My hands come up to block him but I'm too damn slow.

My heartbeat skyrockets, heat blossoming over my skin as anticipation, fear, and lust war inside of me. I lift my hands to push on his chest, trying to get some much-needed distance, my fingers gripping his t-shirt in case I need the leverage.

"Don't touch me!" Preston snarls, ripping my hands off him.

"You're the one *sitting* on me! Get the hell off me!" Anger and confusion burn my blood. I'm tired of his shit. He can't just grab me and expect me not to protect myself. That's not how this works.

His chest is heaving while he stares at me. I don't let myself look away, despite a small part of me wanting to.

It's interesting watching him reign himself back in, pull the anger back and slide that indifferent mask back over his face. His hands shake and his spine straightens. The fact that he can look completely indifferent yet superior while straddling me is fucking weird.

"What did you say to her? What did she tell you?" His voice is quiet but stern when he speaks again. He's resting his hands flat on his thighs, moving them back and forth just a little. Almost like a subconscious movement.

"She asked if you went out and got laid, called me your boyfriend, and said she was glad you had me to help you relax." One of his eye's twitches at my words but that's the only reaction he gives. "Oh, and she wants you to call her back."

There's some internal battle he's fighting while sitting on my thighs, barely rubbing his palms on his legs. He doesn't say anything and even though his eyes are on me, his gaze is unfocused, as if he's not seeing me. Is he having some kind of panic attack? What the hell is going on right now?

"Hey," I say softly, slowly moving my hand to his. The second my skin touches his, he blinks. "You, okay?"

His eyebrows pull together in confusion before he climbs off me and goes into the bathroom.

What the fuck was that?

CHAPTER 12

preston

The bathroom door closes behind me with a click. I leave the light off even though it's dark as shit in here. My head is pounding and my stomach is rolling. After my dinner consisting of two shots followed by a side of nothing else, my body isn't happy. Not to mention the two additional shots I snagged from a buzzed teammate heading up to his room with a tray of drinks.

Apparently, drinking loosens me up enough to be amicable with other people. It wasn't my best decision, but I slept better last night than I have in months, so there's that.

I tap my phone and cringe at the brightness of the screen. Once I turn it down, I call Lily.

"Hey, party boy. Enjoy yourself? Have a hangover?" Her knowing smile irritates me but I try not to show it. "Your boyfriend is cute."

"He's my roommate." I grumble.

"Then why was he answering your phone at four thirty in the morning?" She laughs like she doesn't believe me.

"I have no idea." I rub at my forehead, the damn thing not giving up the drum solo it has going on. "Why did you call me that early? Everything okay?"

I sit on the edge of the tub and close my eyes.

"Dad told me I can come out to see a game this season! I can't wait!" Her excited squeal both hurts my head and sinks a boulder in my stomach.

Fuck.

God damn it.

No.

My sluggish brain starts spinning with everything this means. The pain that will be coming my way in order to protect her. How am I going to hide everything from her? I can't have her living with the guilt of knowing what I've been doing to keep her safe.

"When?" My voice cracks a little on the word.

"I don't know yet, but I can't wait to see you! It's been *way* too long since I've seen you play!" she bounces around in her excitement, the movement giving me motion sickness. I hate that I can't fake being happier and she can see it when she looks at me.

A smile lifts the corners of my mouth a little but I can't give her a full smile.

"You know I'll fly you out anytime you want to come, you don't have to wait for him." I've told her so many times. She's busy doing a bunch of shit at school, but if she wants to come out here, I'll make it happen.

"I know, but that's a lot of extra shit for you to deal with. It's easier if I just stay with Dad." She shrugs.

"No!" I force myself to take a deep breath after snapping the word at her. "No, I'll get you a hotel room. Don't stay with him."

All the excitement from a second ago is gone in an instant. Her face falls to neutral and she falls quiet.

God damn it. I force myself to take a deep breath. Did I blow it? Am I going to lose her too? Fail to protect her?

"Okay," The excitement has left her face and it's my fault. Fuck.

I open my mouth to say something when Jeremy knocks on the bathroom door.

"Shit, I gotta go Lil. I'll talk to you later."

"Yeah, later." She hangs up the call and I feel like shit. She's the only one I'm supposed to protect and I'm fucking it up.

Getting up off the floor, I open the door to see Jeremy standing in the hallway with a water bottle and some pills.

"Ibuprofen and hydrate," he tells me, handing them over. "You also need to eat." He reaches into his pocket and pulls out an oatmeal granola bar, handing that to me too. Without waiting for a response, he turns back to the room and starts pulling his pajama pants off and digging in his duffle bag.

Turn away. Stop watching him change. You can't afford another distraction now. You're almost done with your father.

He catches me staring at his ass when he pulls his jeans up. Jeremy freezes with the waistband of the pants under his ass, lifting the muscles just enough to be enticing. I can't turn away.

Slowly, he starts to move, sliding the jeans up until they sit open on his hips. The bastard turns toward me, showing the hard planes of his body and the band of his boxer briefs riding low in the open zipper.

My dick thickens in the jeans that I didn't take off last night.

Jeremy makes a show of looking at my groin, lifts an eyebrow, then meets my eyes.

"So...do you fuck dudes too, or just stare at them like you want to?" His question snaps me out of whatever weird trance his body put me in. I don't answer the question because, both? I grab my bag from the closet and go back into the bathroom, where I don't have to look at his face and remember how good he felt under me.

Closing the door, I lock it this time, just in case, and strip out of my clothes. Where the hell are my shoes? God damn it!

I find clean clothes to wear and grab my dirty ones, shoving them in my bag. On my way out of the bathroom, I drop my duffle by the entrance door to the room and look around. Laying on my bed are my shoes and the suit Jeremy wore last night.

Jeremy zips up his bag and he watches me walk past him. I can feel his gaze on me like a physical caress. I both love it and hate it. The idea of Jeremy touching me is almost intoxicating. Part of me craves human contact, but in reality, I can't stand for anyone to touch my body. Arms and hands are okay, and sometimes a leg brush, but my torso is absolutely off limits.

I haven't felt a comforting hand since my mother died. My sister was luckier than I was, especially in those early days. I cared for her, helped her through the nightmares and her tears, but I never let her see me break. Her little five-year-old brain wasn't old enough to comfort me.

I make sure my garment bag is ready, catching a whiff of Jeremy's spicy, woody, masculine cologne as I zip up the bag, laying it across my duffle.

"Ready?" Jeremy asks, stepping too close to me. My body tenses at the nearness. The scent of his cologne makes me think of sex and it's obvious he sprayed it on while I was getting changed.

I grit my teeth and grab my things then open the door to our room. He follows me into the hallway, where other team members are crowding the space. They keep away from me, for which I'm grateful. I don't know if it's the fuck off look on my face or what, but I don't care as long as nobody bumps me.

Once we make it onto the bus, everyone settles with their normal buddies and I pop my AirPods in to ignore the noise around me. I always sit in the back row of the bus, but the others shift around a few rows every time. This time, Jeremy and Brendon end up in the row in front of me.

I take a deep breath and close my eyes, leaning back against the seat. It's not until now that I realize the throbbing in my head has lessened thanks to the ibuprofen and water. I try to relax but there's too much going on around me. I'm used to all the noise, it's always like this when we travel on away games, but something is different now. Something is telling me I'm in danger, to pay attention.

Everyone hates you.

You'll never be able to save Lily.

You're a failure and everyone knows it.

The guys shift around me, a couple guys sliding into the seats across the aisle from me. They nod at me but don't try to talk to me. By now, everyone knows I'm not interested in idle conversation. Or any conversation at all.

These bus rides are torture. The seats are not made for athletes and the buses are always packed with us, the coaches, and the team staff. No leg room, no elbow room, just packed in here like sardines. I hate it.

Paul climbs on the bus and zeroes in on Jeremy and Brendon. After a quick glance around, seeing the only empty spot is between me and the window, he grimaces on his way back here.

"Hey, can I sit here?" He looks as happy about it as I feel. My knee starts bouncing but my expression doesn't change.

No. You can't touch me.

From the corner of my eye, I notice Jeremy standing. Everyone turns to watch Brendon getting out of the way to let Jeremy out.

"Paul, take my seat. I need to study anyway."

Paul looks at Brendon, who looks pissed with his clenched jaw and stiff shoulders. He slides into the seat and Brendon stares at me like he can intimidate me. Hilarious. This kid thinks he's scary? Not a fucking chance.

I stand and move to make room for Jeremy to squeeze past me. When the front of his body brushes mine, I no longer think anything is funny. Every muscle in my body tenses and revolts, goosebumps breaking out over every inch of skin. My dick twitches as Jeremy's hip pushes against it.

I grind my teeth to keep still and not show any reaction.

He sits down, leaning into the window, and starts messing with his phone. An earbud is in his ear and he smiles at his phone.

Dropping down into the seat, I try to keep my body from pressing against his. His sensual cologne catches in my nose, and I have to force myself not to bury my face in his neck.

What would it feel like to be held by someone? To breathe them in, their hands running through my hair while we laid in bed, pressed together. I want it so bad it hurts.

But the smallest touch on my skin turns my stomach. My heart wants it but my mind can't handle it.

I want it but it hurts. Skin on my skin turns my stomach but my heart wants to be comforted.

"I swear to fuck, Stacy, if you don't let me talk to my baby, I'm pushing you down the stairs the next time I'm home." Jeremy glares into the phone, but the relaxed posture tells me he's not really upset.

"You may have carried her or whatever but she's my

baby." He rolls his eyes then starts whining like a child. "Let me talk to Ella!"

I glance at his screen and see a chubby-cheeked baby face fill the screen with a big grin. She has curly light blonde soft looking hair and big eyes, but I can't see their color from my angle.

"That's my girl!" Jeremy's entire face lights up. "Hey, baby, what are you doing today?" He pays close attention to whatever she's babbling to him. The little girl can't be two years old. Can babies that young talk?

Is that his daughter? I've never heard anyone mention him having a kid. There's no pictures in our room of one.

You'll never love anyone as much as he loves that little girl. You're fucking broken. Who will want your broken ass? Dealing with your bullshit isn't worth it.

You aren't worthy of love like that.

I close my eyes, cross my arms over my chest, and suck in a deep breath, turning up the volume in my AirPods to drown out Jeremy's voice.

I just have to make it to this summer then I can tell Dad to fuck off. He can't control me once Lily is an adult.

Jeremy's thigh presses against mine, hip to knee. I refuse to open my eyes and look at him. I don't know if he's doing it on purpose to get a reaction out of me or not, but I'm not rising to the bait.

Keep telling yourself that you hate it.

That you don't itch to touch him.

Forcing my shoulders to relax, I loosen my jaw and drop my arms, running my palms over the tops of my thighs. It's one of the few self-comforts I have.

My body itches to move, to run. I have too much energy. Since I passed out last night, I didn't set my alarm for this morning to get a workout in before getting on the bus. I hate missing that run. It calms me, clears the bullshit from my brain.

A finger touches my pinkie. My eyes pop open and my head snaps toward Jeremy. My body is tense once again, but my hands have stopped moving. What the hell is he doing?

The video call on his phone has ended, now he's scrolling through social media. Despite not looking at me and appearing completely oblivious to what is happening in my head, he hooks his finger around mine.

He mutters something I don't hear over the music in my ears but it looks like 'I've got you.'

My gaze drops to our hands, hating how much I like it. Hating how much I want to press our palms together, interlock our fingers, rub my face against the back of his hand.

For just a second, there's no one on this bus but the two of us. I'm safe.

If I look at him, will he be watching me or pretending it's not happening?

I curl my finger around his, testing the feeling of it. It's strange how my heart pounds in my throat at the little touch. I flick my gaze back up to Jeremy's face to find him watching me from the corner of his eye. No judgment, just comfort and maybe some hesitation. But why?

The spell is broken a second later when a loudmouth a few rows in front of us laughs, and I can hear it over the music in my ears. I jerk my hand back, once again crossing my arms over my chest and shifting so his thigh isn't against me anymore.

It's going to be a long ride back to school.

CHAPTER 13

jeremy

Since the second his fucking alarm went off at four this morning, Preston has been an asshole. Flicking on lights, slamming drawers and doors.

"What the hell is your problem?" I snap, sitting up in bed.

"Your lack of commitment to this team," he snaps back, pulling his shoes on and tying them.

"Your dad literally paid for you to be here, what do you know about dedication?" I work my ass off to afford to be here. Summer jobs coaching and on campus jobs during the off season to pay for books and shit like my cell phone because my family isn't made of God damn money.

"I've been waking up at four AM every day since I was twelve for workouts and practice. On top of school, after school practices, and games, I also had one-on-one training three days a week. I've put in twice as many hours as you have just since I got here. I earned my spot on this team but at least some of the guys are stepping up. You, however, are still whining like a little bitch because you *don't wanna.*" He storms out of our dorm room, slamming the door behind him.

Swinging my legs over the edge of the bed, I stand and fume. I hate that he's right and I should be putting in more time. Getting more gym time wouldn't hurt but fuck him. He's not better than me because he works out like a maniac.

As I open my dresser drawer for some workout shorts, my door opens and Brendon steps in.

Confused, I look over at him, taking in the workout clothes and water bottle in his hand.

"Hey, what are you doing up this early?" I ask, pulling up my shorts. Brendon watches me, his eyes hesitating on my ass.

"Paul and I heard the door slam and saw Carmichael storming off down the hallway. Figured we should make sure he hadn't killed you."

I grab a shirt and shove my arms through. Brendon steps behind me, splaying a hand on my stomach as I push the shirt over my head.

"It's been a while," he murmurs with his lips against my neck.

Discomfort flutters in my gut. I can't do this anymore.

"Yeah, haven't really had the time." I shrug, but Brendon doesn't get the message and presses his dick against my ass.

"We have time now," he peppers kisses across my neck.

"Paul is waiting for you, and I should get some gym time too." *Please stop pushing it. I don't want to ruin our friendship.*

"Right, sure. Okay." He steps back and I grab socks and my shoes from the foot of my bed. "We'll see you in there." He nods and leaves.

I let out a breath and finish getting ready. At some point I know I have to tell him I'm done with our arrangement, but it's not going to be a comfortable conversation. I wish he would just let it go, but much like the times we've fucked, he's not reading the situation.

By the time practice starts, I'm tired and ready to punch Carmichael right in his perfect fucking nose.

"Jesus fucking Christ, Albrooke! The puck goes *in* the net! It's no wonder you're third line!" Carmichael yells across the ice as I miss another shot.

"Hey!" Oiler yells at him, sticking up for me, but is it just me or does he sound more like a jealous boyfriend than a teammate? "You have off days too, dick head."

"When was the last one?" Carmichael gets in his face. "Have you already forgotten that *I* got us on the board on Saturday? You all went half a fucking game with nothing! Scoring is not my job!"

Coach blows his whistle and Oiler backs up, muttering something under his breath that I don't catch.

"Line it up boys. I guess we'll spend today running passing drills!" He's pissed, his barking yell echoing in the empty stands around the rink.

He gives directions and we break off into two lines against the goalie. First ones up are me and Johnson. Both of us fuck it up in spectacular fashion. This is some serious rookie shit. We are a shit show.

"Are you fucking kidding me?" Carmichael once again yells for everyone to hear. "How hard is it to pass to Johnson, Albrooke?! Get your shit together!"

"Fuck off!" I yell at him, embarrassment at my shortcomings yelled out in front of everyone, like I'm not aware of them.

"Regretting that bacon cheeseburger now?" he throws back. Half the team shakes their heads but no one says anything.

"What the fuck is your obsession with what I eat?" I skate toward him, wanting to beat him with my stick but stopping just short of him.

Carmichael straightens to his full height so he can look down on me. "Every *good* athlete knows that what you feed your body matters. All that fat and carbs you eat do nothing but slow you down." The dig hits the intended target, my insecurities.

"I get that you're everyone's God damn golden child, but not everyone wants to be you. I don't want to play in the NHL, so I really don't give a shit what *you* think I should be eating. You're a shitty teammate and when you're gone, that's all anyone on this team will remember about you." I shove him away while he smirks at me, turning my back to put some distance between us.

"Then why are you here? Are you okay being mediocre? What is it you want to do with all this hockey experience, Albrooke?" He calls after me.

"What do you care?" I snap back, spinning around to face him. Humiliation burning in my gut, making me angry.

Because he's right. Who's going to hire me to coach their kid if I suck?

"Because you're wasting everyone's fucking time. Why don't you quit so someone who actually wants to play can?" I skate toward him, shoving him into the boards and getting into his face this time. His gray eyes sear into me with anger and lust and something else. Delight? Is he getting off on pissing me off?

"You gonna hit me, Albrooke?" His words are quiet, taunting. Almost like words he would whisper in a lover's ear while he fucked them unconscious.

I want to knock him out, strangle him, push him until he snaps and attacks me.

I've got his jersey in my fist and my arms against his chest, holding him against the boards. Why isn't he telling me to get off him? To stop touching him.

"You trying to make me hit you?" I whisper back in that same threatening bedroom tone.

One of his gray eyes twitches and I smile in victory.

"That's it, isn't it? You like it rough. You get off on the fight." My gaze drops to his lips as I lick my bottom lip. "If you want to fuck, all you have to do is say something."

I watch as the mask he uses to hide slams back into place. The brightness in those haunting gray eyes dims and the grin becomes a straight line. He flips us until I'm the one being shoved against the boards. It's embarrassingly easy for him to do. "Fuck you, Albrooke. Get your shit together. I won't have you fucking up my stats." His words are meant to hurt, but he's grasping at strings to get control back.

A few of the guys hurry over to us and are pulling on Carmichael's arms to get us to break apart. Both of us are flushed with frustration and exertion. Too stubborn to back down or give in.

He's shoved away from me and for just a second, I think I can read desperation on his face. Just for millisecond, then it's gone.

Coach blows the whistle again. "That's it!" he yells, furious we're fighting instead of following orders. "Conditioning drills! Let's go!"

Everyone groans but we break off into six groups and start working our way through the exercises Coach tells us to do at each station. The first run through isn't too bad, but every time we go through them it gets harder, and by the fourth time through all the exercises everyone is exhausted. Even mister *I wake up every day at four AM to workout.*

CHAPTER 14

preston

Coach rips us a new asshole in the locker room. Yelling about in-fighting being the death of a team. We all know he's right but is that going to stop a bunch of testosterone-fueled jocks from jumping down each other's throats? Not a chance.

I get my gear off and put away in the locker room, down to just my base layer of black Under Armour long sleeve shirt and leggings. It's like a second sweaty skin that I can't wait to take off.

Once Coach is done reaming us, I grab my gym bag and head into the hallway toward the school gym. I'll change in there.

I've made it only a few steps away from the locker room before someone grabs my arm. Spinning around, I grab them and shove them against the wall, my gym bag falling to the floor before I realize who it is.

Jeremy's blue-brown eyes stare up at me in the dim light of the empty hallway.

"You really do like it rough, don't you?" He smirks up at me with a knowing look. Like he can see inside my head and roll around in my secrets. I'm not sure why that's enticing.

"What the fuck are you doing?" I growl in his face, almost close enough to kiss him. Jeremy's eyes drop to my lips, and he pulls his bottom lip into his mouth, letting his teeth drag along the plump flesh as he releases it.

I fucking hate him and his kissable fucking mouth.

"I'm testing a theory," Jeremy says as his hands land softly on my hips. My instincts kick in and I grab his hands, lifting them to the wall, and lean into him.

"Don't. Fucking. Touch. Me." My words are ground out through gritted teeth.

Before I can think to move, Jeremy lifts his mouth to mine and he kisses me. My fingers dig into his flesh as the sensation of his lips on mine explodes through me. For the first time in my life, my head is quiet. With butterflies rioting in my stomach, blood thrumming through my veins, and my dick taking notice of how close this guy is to me. He groans when I change the angle of the kiss, forcing his mouth open until I can claim it and him.

Jeremy grinds his dick against mine, the slick material of our base layers making it entirely too easy to move. I moan into his mouth as arousal hums along my skin.

I get lost in his kiss, in the nearness of him, and let my body collide with his, my chest to his and my hands releasing his arms to tangle in the long strands of his dark blonde hair. Jeremy wraps his hands around my wrists, his nails leaving half-moon imprints in my skin.

I'm so consumed by the feel of this guy against me, of the human contact, that it takes me a second to realize there are voices coming toward us.

In a moment of panic, I rip my lips from Jeremy's, pull my fist back, and punch him in the face.

"What the fuck!?" he yells, cupping his eye and turning his body away from me.

Fuck.

If my father hears about this, I'm fucked. I'll be called home for correction. God damn it.

My fear freezes me to the spot. I can't move or think.

Jeremy looks up at me and whatever he sees on my face has him jumping into action. He grabs my shirt and shoves me back a few steps until I hit the rough brick of the hallway.

"You're an asshole! Stop riding my ass!" Jeremy yells at me but it sounds far away. Running feet echo in the hallway, closer and closer to us. I shove him off me, breathing hard and lost in my head.

Father is going to make me pay for this.

I'll get more than one cut, in a painful location. I won't be able to sleep for days, no food, dehydration.

Worthless.

Useless.

Disgrace.

"Hey!" a male voice yells.

I bolt before they can touch me. Away from Jeremy, away from human touch and the desire for more.

For the first time in years, the urge to cry knots my throat, making it painful to breathe. The air in my lungs is moving too fast, my chest heaving as I find an exit and run as fast as I can outside into the fresh air. The concrete is rough and unforgiving on my bare feet but it's nothing less than I deserve.

I don't know where I'm going, I just run. Away from Jeremy, away from the rink, away from everything that's consumed my life since I was child.

Maybe if I run far enough, fast enough, I can outrun my thoughts.

You. Hit. Him.

Unprovoked.

Father is going to drag you back for this.

My muscles seize at the very thought, making me stumble and fall to my hands and knees. Like Pavlov's fucking dogs, I've been conditioned to fear what my father can and will do to me. The scrape against my palms and the pain in my knees brings me back to where I am. To now. I breathe for a second before getting up and continuing.

The concrete rips at my feet with every pounding step, jagged rocks digging into the soft part of my arches, but I don't stop. Mind over matter. Push through the pain. Show no weakness.

I find the path that leads around campus and force my feet to keep moving. It's about four miles in total and exactly what I need right now. Hills and flat sections, tree covered paved pathways, and packed dirt roads in other parts. It's not an easy run by any means, but it will do what I need it to.

CHAPTER 15

jeremy

"Hey, what the hell happened?" Doctor Butler, one of the team doctors, grabs my shoulder and turns me toward the light so he can see me better. My face hurts like a bitch. It already feels swollen. Doctor Butler presses the tender skin carefully, checking for breaks, and I hiss, pulling back out of his grasp.

"Albrooke, what happened? That was Carmichael, correct?" Doctor Butler demands an answer. The man is old enough to be my father, but by looking at him, you wouldn't know it.

"It was nothing, just a misunderstanding is all." I shift my gaze down the empty hallway, wishing I knew where he went. Preston panicked. That was clear as day. After he hit me, he looked like a little kid who broke his mom's favorite lamp and knew an ass kicking was coming his way. Was he abused as a kid? Is he afraid to get caught with a guy because of his parents?

Doctor Butler looks at me like he's considering what to say to me.

"Let's get some ice on this eye, I don't think it's broken but you're going to have a nice shiner by morning."

Grabbing Preston's dropped gym bag, I avoid the locker room and follow him into the medical room.

"Have a seat." He motions to one of the chairs along the wall and I sit.

"Are you going to tell Coach?" I ask him as I take the cold pack and turn my gaze away from him.

"That you and Carmichael got into a fist fight?"

I nod and groan when the cold hits my eye. It hurts like a bitch. That dude hits like a hammer.

"No, I won't tell him, but everyone is going to see the bruise and it may be swollen shut tomorrow." He motions to my face. "You better come up with a convincing story if you don't want him to know the truth."

"And what would be a convincing story?"

"Not running into doorknobs." He grins at me. "Perhaps someone threw a water bottle at you, and you failed to catch it."

"That's bringing another person in on the story, that's going to get dicey." The cold seeps into my skin, dulling some of the ache.

"It doesn't have to be someone you know, just make it believable." The older man in his school polo and khakis looks at me like I'm an idiot.

"Oh, that makes sense." He sighs and shakes his head at me.

"If Preston needs help, let me know. You all have my after-hours number. Use it." The older man holds my gaze, seriousness in his eyes. What does he know that I don't?

"Yeah, of course."

I sit for a few more minutes before Doctor Butler has me remove the ice pack to take a look.

"I'll give you some ibuprofen for pain and to help with the swelling, ice packs throughout the day will help too."

I nod and accept the meds he gives me, taking one at his insistence before sneaking out of the rink. It's getting cold, so I can use the hood on my sweatshirt to hide my face some. I'm not embarrassed by it, but I don't want questions before I can come up with a story.

By some miracle, I make it to my dorm with no one stopping me. The room is dark when I step inside and close the door behind me. My heart sinks when I realize Preston isn't here. I was hoping he would come here and we could talk it out, even though I know that goes against everything he believes in. Preston doesn't talk about his feelings. He belittles and pushes until you snap.

That moment of pure panic in his eyes has all my protective instincts demanding he talk to me though. I want to fight for him, but I don't know what demons he has. No one should be that afraid of a kiss. Preston is an asshole ninety percent of the time but the more I'm around him, the more I see cracks in that armor. No one deserves to be afraid like that.

I pull off the base layer I'm still wearing from practice and head into the bathroom to shower. The sweat and frustration of the day clings to me along with the lust that filled my veins when Preston was pressed against me.

Shaking off the memory, I get the water set to boiling and step in, the heat pounding into my sore muscles, forcing my body to relax even if my mind won't quiet.

Should I go look for Preston?

I have no idea where he might have gone. Or how long he'll be gone. Does he have his phone in case he needs a ride?

Did he have shoes on? We were getting changed but he was still in his hockey shit.

I scrub my body quickly and get out of the shower, drying my hair and wrapping the towel around my waist.

Digging in my hoodie for my phone, I pull up my team group messages and find Carmichael's number.

Hey, are you okay?

The symbol on the screen says the message has been sent and delivered but not opened.

I get dressed, pulling on a pair of sweatpants, and drop down onto my bed.

Am I pissed he punched me? Yes.

Am I going to have to fake that I'm not? Also, yes.

Maybe I should sleep in Paul and Brendon's room for a few days.

I should look for him.

Grabbing my shoes, a hoodie, and a ball cap, I leave the room and head down to the gym. Last time he ran after touching me, that's where he ended up. As I open the dorm door, one of my teammates sees me and starts to give me a chin up nod but stops when he sees my swollen eye. The bulky man in a t-shirt pulled tight across his chest and jeans, long chestnut hair pulled back in a small ponytail, turns to give me his full attention. Bryce is a sophomore this year and on the second line.

"Dude, what happened to you?"

For a second, my mind blanks. I stare at him but don't see him. Then Doctor Butler's story comes pouring out of my mouth.

"Dumbasses down the hall were throwing water bottles and I caught one in the face." Did that sound convincing?

"Damn, that sucks." He takes the story at face value.

Sometimes jocks are dumb and we all know it. "I'm heading to the cafeteria. You want to join me?"

I guess it is dinner time, it makes sense that he would assume I'm going there too.

"No thanks, I'm not heading to dinner yet."

He shrugs and heads toward the elevator. I go the opposite way and take the stairs down, just so I don't have to be trapped in the elevator.

The walk to the gym is quick but there's no one in there. The locker room is empty too, and same with the ice rink. Frustrated, I head back to the dorms. If he's not back in an hour or two, I'll call Coach and let him worry about it.

In my room with nothing better to do, I dig out a textbook and do some homework. I haven't finished reading the first question when my phone buzzes with an incoming call.

The screen shows my brother Keith, but it's probably both him and Jordan.

"Hey, man, what's up?" I smile at my teenage brother. Keith and Jordan are fraternal but look enough alike that people get them mixed up all the time. "Why do you have Keith's phone?"

"How can you always tell?" Jordan bitches while Keith laughs in the background.

"You always look like you're getting into something, because you normally are."

He rolls his eyes and shakes his head at me. "Whatever."

"Did you call for a reason? Girl trouble? Boy trouble? Need your big brother to beat someone up for you?" Keith laughs again and Jordan scowls.

"Just because you can't find yourself a boyfriend doesn't mean the rest of us have relationship issues." Jordan retorts.

"I don't want a boyfriend, but I get by just fine, thank you very much." Preston and Brendon flash in my head but I don't mention them.

"And how could you help with girl problems? You've never dated one." Keith scoffs.

"Just because I've never dated one doesn't mean I've never talked to one or don't have friends. Trust me, I have a much better understanding of them than your hormone-addled brain."

"Should we ask what happened to your face?" Jordan asks and Keith appears on the screen to take a look.

"Damn, that looks like it hurts." Keith adds.

My stomach tightens but I push away the memory of Preston pressing me against the wall.

"It didn't tickle." I shrug at my brothers. "Hockey injury, shit happens."

Keith returns to his video game and Jordan starts talking about a school dance that's coming up when the dorm room door opens to a sweaty, red-faced Preston.

"Hey guys, I gotta go. I'll call you later." I cut him off and end the call.

Preston closes the door and sags against it, damn near gasping for breath.

I put my stuff aside and stand up. He watches me like a scared animal.

"You, okay?" I scan his body and notice his lack of shoes. His feet are dirty and look like they may be bleeding.

"I'm fine." He pushes off the door and opens his dresser drawers, grabbing some clothes, then disappears into the bathroom. The click of the lock engaging frustrates me more than it probably should. My hand clenches into a fist then relaxes over and over while I try to calm my breathing. I'm fucking pissed.

He has the nerve to kiss me, punch me, then bounce, and now I'm not good enough to talk to? What the fuck is his problem?

"You aren't fine!" I holler at the door.

"Fuck off!" His snap feels like a slap in the face. I was worried about this asshole for nothing. He doesn't care about anyone but himself. I have a swollen fucking eye because he didn't want to get caught kissing me. Fuck him.

I grab the shit I'll need for the next few days and shove it in a bag, then head down to Paul and Brendon's room. I'm not dealing with his ass.

I knock on the door and Paul opens it then stops when he sees my bag. "Where ya going?"

"I'm sleeping here for a few days. Fuck Carmichael and all his bullshit." I throw my stuff on the ground between the twin beds. Brendon sits up and pulls his headphones off his head.

"What's going on?" he asks as I pace their room, shoving my hand through my hair.

"Carmichael is a fucking dick. I'm over his bullshit."

"He what happened to your face?" Paul crosses his arms over his chest and leans against his dresser, watching me pace.

"Oh yeah. That. This fucker pushes me all practice, right? Riding my ass for stupid shit, then he grabs me in the hallway and kisses the fuck out of me! Then. Then! He punches me in the face and takes off!" I spin around when I reach the wall and pace back, working myself up into seriously pissed off. "I was worried about him. You believe that? So, I went looking for him. Nothing."

"Wait, he kissed you?" Brendon questions. From the corner of my eye, I see Paul give Brendon a weird look and shake his head.

"He finally shows back up at the room and tells me to fuck off when I ask if he's okay!" Anger pumps through me, tightening my shoulders and clenching my fists. "You believe that?"

"What are you gonna do? You going to tell Coach?" Paul moves from the dresser to sit on his bed.

"I don't know. I should. Fuck him. But I don't want to be labeled as a problem, you know?" I stop my pacing, hands on my hips, and drop my head back on my shoulders to breathe.

"Did you want him to kiss you?" Brendon asks.

"Really? That's all you got out of what I just said?" I huff, exasperated.

"That's not really the point of this story, dude." Paul leans to one side so he can look at Brendon, who's behind me.

Despite how much I wanted that kiss, I'm not telling Brendon that. Why does this have to be so damn complicated?

Paul stands and claps me on the shoulder. "You can sleep in here. It's cool, man."

I nod and sigh. What a mess this year is turning into. Freshman year was supposed to be crazy and fun, but it's turned into a cluster fuck.

CHAPTER 16

jeremy

It's been three days since Preston punched me in the face. Coach saw it the next morning and lifted an eyebrow at me but didn't ask any questions. The swelling has gone down, but the bruising is dark purple under my eye and even bled over into the inner corner of my other eye. I look like I got my ass beat.

Practice the last few days has been brutal, Preston being even more *pleasant* than usual. Has he apologized for hitting me? Of course not. Not that I expected it. He doesn't really give off the vibes of someone who says sorry.

Practice is over and we're changing in the locker room when Coach comes in.

"Okay, guys," Coach starts. "We have a busy weekend ahead. Tonight, we are having a team dinner at Doctor Andrew Carmichael's. He has donated a lot to our team and our school, so you will be on your best behavior and dressed to impress. We've arranged vans to take us. Be outside the rink at five."

What. The. Fuck.

Preston's dad's house?

Apprehension makes my skin tingle. I'm uncomfortable with this. Can I get out of it? Will he be able to tell that Preston sucker punched me after kissing me? Is he going to pretend to be a doting father or will he be an asshole?

I run my hand through my hair with unease making me antsy. Does Preston know about this? I scan the room but don't see him, but that's not surprising. He seems to disappear a lot.

Everyone showers quickly and dresses before filing out of the locker room. A quick scan of the area tells me Preston is not in here.

We have to wear a suit? I don't fucking have one! God damn it.

I rub my forehead as I leave the rink to head to the dorms.

"Hey, man." Brendon slings an arm over my shoulders and drops into step with me. "What's your hurry? We've got a few hours still."

"You have a suit I can borrow?" I blurt out the question as Paul jogs to catch up with us.

"What happened to yours?" Paul asks.

I sigh. "It ripped." That's probably the easiest version to tell.

Neither of them says anything as we enter the dorm building.

"Well? Anyone have one I can borrow?" I look between the two of them. Paul is smaller in the waist than I am so I doubt anything he has will work, but it's better than nothing.

"We can see if we have something that will fit." Brendon shrugs as the elevator doors open and we step inside.

I lean against the back wall, frustrated and irritated. I

can't afford a suit, but I can't keep using someone else's either.

The ride to the third floor is short and we step off, walking the few doors down to their room. As Paul unlocks the door, Preston steps out of our door and immediately finds me. Our gazes lock and he lifts his head just a fraction, but I get the sense he wants me to come to our room.

"Hey, I'll be right back. Just a sec." I step around Brendon, feeling his stare on my back. Preston moves back into the room and I close the door.

"What?"

The tightness around his eyes is back, that stiffness in his shoulders, and he's vibrating with a weird energy I'm not used to feeling from him.

"Don't speak to my father."

That was not what I was expecting. Insulted, I cross my arms over my chest and lift my chin. "Why not? Afraid I'll tell him all about how you jacked me off? Or that you shoved your tongue down my throat before sucker-punching me?"

His nostrils flare and his mouth sets in a thin line. The need to kiss him and punch him war within me. I hate how confused he makes me. Why do I want to help him when he's nothing but an asshole to me? He's never nice or friendly, all he does is point out my failures, typically in public.

I hold my ground. He doesn't want me to talk to dear ol' dad? He's going to give me a fucking reason.

Preston crowds me against the door, his chest almost touching my arms as he leans his hands on the door beside my head. My body prickles with awareness that I both love and loathe. I want his hands on me so fucking badly, to use me, but he's an asshole. Who wants to fuck the guy that makes their life miserable? Apparently, this dumbass.

There's something about him that calls to me. I want to be closer.

He smells of fresh body wash and shampoo, woodsy and clean, combined to a mouthwatering scent that makes my dick ache.

"You have no idea what you're up against when it comes to my father." His body is so tense he's almost vibrating.

I drop my arms and smile smugly up at him, dragging my teeth over my bottom lip while I eye his mouth. "You seem a little tense, need to blow off some steam?"

Carefully, I grip the bottom of his shirt, so I don't touch his skin. I don't lift the fabric up, just pull on it and lean my hips forward until our bodies touch. He's watching me like he's not sure what to do, like I've thrown him off. If this is what it takes to make him stop bitching at me, I'll be using it in the future.

"Jeremy." My name is a growl, and it makes my skin break out in goosebumps.

With a knowing smile on my face, I look up at him. "I can't tell if you hate me because you want to fuck me or because you can't?"

Faster than I can blink, his hand is around my throat, pressing me into the door. My dick is at attention and throbbing.

"If I wanted you, I would have you." Preston snarls his words against my lips before taking my mouth in a brutal, harsh kiss. He holds my jaw still with a few fingers while still pushing against my throat. My body sags against him, wanting him to take whatever the hell he wants from me.

Make me.

I moan into his kiss when he grinds against me, using his free hand to grab my wrist and pin it against the door. One of my legs wraps around his ass to keep him against me.

I rut against him, needing the friction, chasing the high of orgasm.

Preston pulls back from my lips, lets go of my throat, and as my dazed eyes meet his, he slaps my cheek. Stinging heat flairs on my face and my balls draw up, readying to fucking explode.

Releasing his shirt, I reach for my dick and stroke myself quickly. I need to come so bad it hurts. I'm half-crazy from it. It's been too damn long.

"Pull my dick out." Preston's gravelly, lust-filled voice has me rushing to get him out. I'm still balancing on one leg with one arm pinned against the door. His hand flexes on my wrist and I'm sure I'll have an imprint of his fingers on my skin. I want one.

My hand wraps around both of our cocks, stroking us together while his eyes bore into mine. I can't look away.

We're breathing hard, our air mixing between us until I can taste him.

He throbs against me and knowing he's so close to the edge pushes me over. Cum shoots from me. My mouth falls open and a groan is pulled from the depths of my soul when Preston slams a hand over my lips.

His forehead drops to mine, and he thrusts into my fist, spraying more cum onto my hand and our shirts. We sag into the door and he releases his hold on me. My arm drops from the door and my leg slides off him.

I close my eyes and try not to fall on my ass while I reconnect with the world around me. I feel Preston's hand on my shirt, low on my stomach, then he slides still-warm cum across my lips. Opening my eyes, I find him staring at my mouth until I slide my tongue across it, the bitter taste of us sharp on my tongue, but not bad. Honestly, I would gladly take more if he wanted it.

His eyes meet mine for a second before he grabs his

garment bag hanging from his dresser pull and goes into the bathroom, locking the door behind him.

I put my dick back in my pants and catch sight of another garment bag on my bed. A knock on the door makes me jump. I rip my t-shirt off and turn to open the door.

"Dude, are you coming or what?" Brendon is standing there, irritation clear in the lines of his face.

I already did...

My eyes flick to the bathroom door for a second before I answer him. "Yeah, I'm coming."

CHAPTER 17

preston

There is no part of this dinner that's going to go well for me. Every breath I take, every word I say, will be used against me later. I don't know what my father is trying to achieve with this, but it will be painful for me at some point.

I close my eyes and lean against the sink.

You shouldn't have touched him.

A shudder wracks my body for a long few seconds. Being touched hurts but I want it so fucking bad.

It's better this way. My father can't use them against me if I'm alone.

I strip off my clothes, careful to wrap my shirt up so cum doesn't get on anything else and unzip my garment bag.

On autopilot, I slip into my suit, the recently ironed fabrics sliding over my skin so familiar. With the suit comes the public mask. It's second nature to shut myself off and perform. I've been in the public eye most of my life, but it got worse once my father started making a name for himself. He used me as his pawn, a marketing tool.

See what a good father I am? My son is a great hockey player. I can balance being a surgeon and a single father.

Meanwhile, my younger sister is shipped off to boarding schools so he doesn't have to deal with her while making sure his dirty secret was hidden in the shadows.

With a deep breath, I make sure my grandfather's cufflinks are aligned, my shirt is tucked in, and I am wrinkle-free.

Leaving the bathroom for socks and my dress shoes, I'm confused when Jeremy isn't in here getting dressed. Where the fuck did he go?

Striding to his bed, I grab the garment bag. The suit is still in there. What the fuck is he doing? I scan the room quickly, looking for any sign of where he would have gone. His shirt is crumpled up on the floor by the foot of his bed.

Brendon and Paul. Flinging our door open hard enough to slam it against the wall, I storm down the hallway, a few people moving out of my way without a word, until I'm in front of Brendon and Paul's room and pounding on the door.

Paul opens the door with a raised eyebrow. "You the cops now?"

"Where's Jeremy?" I'm shaking with fury. He is not wearing Brendon's fucking clothes. If I have to ruin more clothes by ripping them from his body, I fucking will. So help me, Christ.

"What's going on?" Brendon steps up behind Paul with confusion pulling his brows together.

"Where's. Jeremy." I grit the words through my teeth, ready to fucking snap. Drawing in a deep breath through my nose, I try to calm my urge to hurt Brendon.

I have no claim to Jeremy. Logically, I know that. But I

want to. It doesn't make sense and this fucking dinner with my father has set me on edge. Every muscle in my body is tight. I need Jeremy where I can fucking see him and not in Brendon's fucking clothes.

Paul and Brendon share a look before turning back to me.

"He's getting ready for dinner with your daddy. What do you want?" Brendon crosses his arms over his chest like he's won something. He's won nothing, the smug bastard.

If Jeremy's shitty mood is anything to go by, he's not getting laid anymore, which means he's not fucking Brendon.

"None of your fucking business. Get him. Now." I'm about to shove my way inside this fucking room. The eyes of people milling about in the hall are hot on me, but I don't give a shit.

Paul looks around and notices that people are watching. I'm sure there are phones out, which means Coach will probably hear about this.

"You're making a scene," Paul says quietly. "I don't know what's going on here, but this isn't the place for a dick measuring contest."

The bathroom door opens, light from inside illuminating both of them.

"Preston?" Jeremy's voice lowers the tension in my shoulders slightly. "What's going on?"

I force myself to swallow and release some of the tension in my face, allowing my public mask to come through.

"I need to speak with you."

Brendon turns and Jeremy looks at him for a second. Brendon shakes his head but he pushes past his friend. The black slacks and gray oxford look so fucking good on him, but they're Brendon's. They have to be. Paul is slimmer than Jeremy. There's no way something fitted like a suit would fit.

"Okay." He looks like he doesn't trust me but that's fine, I don't trust me either.

I lift my hand to motion for our room and realize I'm still holding the garment bag. Jesus.

The urge to rip the clothes off him and shove them at Brendon is stronger than I would like it to be, but I follow him to our room. His ass looks fucking delicious in those damn pants. I should make him come in those fucking pants before I give them back to Brendon.

In our room with the door closed, I shove the garment bag at Jeremy.

"Change." The word is a command.

Jeremy straightens, crossing his arms over his chest.

"Excuse me?"

I step closer to him, into his personal space. "Change."

"Why? What I'm wearing is fine."

I drag in a deep breath, inhaling his cologne, which goes straight to my head.

"You are going to my father's house. You have to be as perfect as humanly possible." Now he's confused. This isn't fucking fair to him, I know, but I can't stop it. I need him to just go with it and not argue.

Grabbing his shirt in both my hands, I jerk him toward me until we're face to face. He's up on his toes to make him equal in height to me. For a second, his arms flail as he tries to keep his balance. I prepare to flinch when his hands touch my chest, but they don't. He's watching me watch him.

Jeremy grabs onto my wrists. This is the second time today he's purposefully avoided touching my body. What does that mean?

"Change your fucking clothes." My body shakes with the nerves trying so hard to consume me. It would be so easy to fall headfirst into the fear and anxiety of this fucking dinner. I don't know what to expect and that's terrifying. I squeeze my eyes shut until little speckles of light dance behind my eyelids. "Please."

"Tell me why." The stubbornness from just a few minutes ago is gone.

My eyes open to find Jeremy watching me, the unevenness of his irises is impossible to look away from. So fucking different than anyone else I've ever met.

"Why does it matter so much to you?"

I rest my forehead on his, wanting so desperately to find comfort in this man while knowing I can't afford to. "I don't know."

We stand there for another moment, our exhales mixing between us. Jeremy gives my wrist a gentle squeeze before he quietly says, "Okay."

I lift my head, my eyes snapping open to peer into his. Did I hear what I think I heard?

"What?" The word sounds harsh coming from my tight throat.

"Okay. I'll change."

Something in my chest lets go, some of the pressure loosening enough to breathe. Jeremy relaxes, his shoulders dropping and his hands leaving me. I both love it and hate it. Fighting is easy, it's comfortable. Whatever this is, sucks. The urge to push him and piss him off is strong, but I don't.

Instead, I release him and step back.

"Good," I try to slide that fucking mask back on but I'm struggling. Like it's cracked or I've outgrown it. It doesn't feel right but I don't know how to survive without it.

Dropping his gaze, I look around for the garment bag, but I have no idea what happened to it. I find it on the floor by my dresser and pick it up.

"If it's wrinkled, I'll iron it, but you have to hurry or we'll be late." I hand it over, holding one side of the hanger,

Jeremy grabbing the other. I hold onto it until he looks up at me again. "I can't be late."

He nods and I let go of the bag. Turning to my dresser, I dig through my drawer for dress socks and pull out my dress shoes.

Sitting on my bed, I finish getting ready while Jeremy strips down to his boxer briefs and pulls on the suit that's slightly too big for him. The inseam is too long by an inch or more and the jacket is too wide in the shoulder and long in the arm. Fuck.

My father will definitely notice that.

"If others take their jackets off, take yours off too." I stand and adjust my pants, so they lay straight. "Do everything you can to not talk to my father."

"Why don't you want me to talk to your dad?" Jeremy asks, more curious than insulted this time. I reach for his hand and pull on the sleeves of the cream dress shirt. Digging in the bag, I find the small box with cufflinks.

"I don't want him talking to you," I say as I slip them on. These are plain white gold circles, no engraving or decoration. Simple.

My eyes meet his again when I finish with the second sleeve and drop his hand.

In my pocket, my phone vibrates with the five-minute alarm telling us to go downstairs.

"Hurry up, we need to go." I spray my cologne and check my hair in the mirror, making sure not a hair is out of place. Jeremy opens the door and we walk out into the hallway. Paul and Brendon are leaving their room too. Great.

Brendon looks at Jeremy and glowers. For some reason, it makes me want to smile. I allow a smirk to turn up one side of my lips.

"Nice suit." I hear Brendon scoff behind me as he falls into step with Jeremy.

"Uh yeah, thanks." Jeremy mumbles. I don't need to see him to know there's a red blush crawling up his neck right now. Maybe next time I give in to the temptation to touch him, I'll leave marks. I do love to see my handy work left behind.

The ride down to the main floor is quick, the space filled with Brendon's snide remarks about me being a spoiled brat.

If only.

The vans are lined up outside the rink and the weight on my chest makes itself known again. I don't know what it is about Jeremy that makes me want to stay close to him, but I do. As the vans fill, I start counting how many seats are left versus how many of us are left. Who will fit in which space, and will I be separated from him?

Paul and Brendon climb into a van with only a bench seat left, room for one more. They look at Jeremy, expecting him to get in with them, but he holds up a hand to wave them off.

"It's cool, I'll get the next one. See you guys there." Brendon's head looks like it's about to explode.

This time, I smile, following it up with a wink at Brendon before following Jeremy to the last van. He climbs in, sliding into the middle seat since someone is already against the far window. Did he know that's where I would want to sit?

I don't like having people behind me.

There's already someone sitting in the row, so I take the last seat by the door, pressed against Jeremy as we squeeze our athletic bodies into the seat made for much smaller humans. I think toddlers could fit back here comfortably.

With every mile closer to the building my father lives in, the weight on my chest grows. My hands slide across the tops of my thighs while I try to breathe through the unknowns of what I'm going to walk into. Logically, I know I will leave with no new marks. He can't get me away from the team for that long.

"If I disappear for more than five minutes, come looking for me."

The words are quiet as they tumble out of my mouth. Only Jeremy could have heard them, the rest of the guys in here are laughing and screwing around. His finger hooks around mine and my eyes close at the contact, my breathing hitching in my chest as my stomach cramps painfully.

There's no way I'm going to be able to eat. Is he going to make me sit next to him or just in his line of sight so I can't escape him?

CHAPTER 18

jeremy

This side of Preston is more terrifying than him on the ice. His leg is bouncing, hands running up and down his thighs, and I think he's counting his breaths. What the fuck kind of nightmare are we walking into?

The vans pull up in front of a high-rise in downtown Denver. This part of town is all luxury apartments, mostly made of glass and stone. It's daunting to be sure. A man that looks like a carbon copy of Preston is standing out front of the double doors with a smile on his face that I don't trust. It makes me uncomfortable. Like there's something sinister behind it.

We're led inside to a conference room set up with long tables sitting end to end covered with dark blue tablecloths. The chairs have matching blue covers over them with a white bow on the back. It reminds me of something you would see at a wedding.

"Everyone find your seats," Doctor Andrew Carmichael

announces to the room, and we all do just that. Except Preston. His father has a grip on his shoulder so he can't leave his side. There are name tags on the tables that guide us to our spots. This is so weird. I pass Paul and end up sitting across from him, Brendon on my right. We turn to the front of the room when Preston's dad clears his throat.

"I'm so glad you all could join us for dinner." A big smile stretches across his face as he looks around.

Preston has an almost vacant, lost look in his eyes, standing still as a statue.

"Two more games for preseason then off to the regular season. I have a good feeling about this team this year!" The guys clap, buying the crap he's spewing. Do they not see how tense Preston is? There's something obviously not right here.

He drones on for a few more minutes and it takes all my self-control not to roll my eyes. Some of the guys take their jackets off and hang them on the backs of the chairs so I hurry to do so as well. I'm not entirely sure *why* Preston specified this exactly, but I'm not going to argue about it.

I focus my attention back on Preston and his father. Only now, his father is staring at me. What the hell did I do? Paul looks at me with a question on his face, but I just shrug. I don't know much about him, but from that message I saw on Preston's phone, he's not a nice guy.

My eyes stray to Preston again. It's weird to watch him like this. Was this what he was like when he first got to campus? Has he really changed that much in the month we've been roommates? He's like a stranger up there. I don't know him at all. I'm learning to read him but right now, he's so shut down that I don't know where to start.

Coach stands up and thanks Doctor Andrew Carmichael, yeah we all have to call him that, for having us, and gives him tickets to tomorrow's game and the one on

Saturday. Doctor Andrew Carmichael takes them with a smile and a handshake.

Preston is eventually allowed to sit down directly across from his father and in the center of a long table. I don't think he's blinking. He's barely breathing.

Servers come out of a small door behind me and bring food to specific people. Did he get our nutrition plans from Coach? This is fucking weird. Is he poisoning us?

A plate of grilled salmon, steamed broccoli, and wild rice appears in front of me from one of the catering staff. It smells amazing, with a savory sweet glaze on the fish and herbs in the rice, but I'm decidedly not hungry. Ice water is poured into glass goblets and we're left to eat.

Who picks fish for someone else's dinner? What if I don't like fish?

Why am I so bothered by this?

Brendon's hand slides onto my thigh under the table. I tense at the touch, pushing his hand off my leg as nonchalantly as possible.

"What is going on with you?" Brendon hisses at me under his breath.

I shake my head sharply. This is not the place for that conversation. I don't want to eat this. It feels like a trap. Picking up the fork, I move the food around my plate but don't actually eat any of it.

"Is there a problem, Mr. Albrooke?" Doctor Andrew Carmichael asks and my head snaps to the left to meet his gaze. Ice shoots down my spine, settling like a snake in my gut. He's cold. Dangerous.

My eyes flick to Preston for just a second, he's watching me too. What is going through his mind? I wish I knew what was happening, why I was being singled out.

"Uh, no, sir. Just a bit of a nervous stomach the night

before a game." He zeroes in on my black eye and the skin around his eyes tightens just a little.

Fuck.

Preston pales but no one else seems to notice, everyone busying themselves with their food. The noise of the room cranks up in my head, the conversations, silverware on the porcelain plates. I reach for my glass and take a drink, just for something to do. Everyone eats and the conversations around me move to tomorrow's game, and what we need to focus on to beat Notre Dame.

I notice Preston stand and leave the room, his mask finally cracking just a little. The muscle in his jaw is jumping and his fist is clenched tight. A few minutes later, his father excuses himself from the table and disappears too.

Brendon is damn near licking his plate clean next to me. "Jesus, dude, chill out." He laughs and sits back. "That salmon was amazing."

I nod but don't comment, watching the door for Preston or his dad.

"Why aren't you eating?" I turn back to Brendon, and now Paul is paying attention along with the guys around us.

I shrug. "I'm not hungry."

"We're athletes, dude. We're always hungry," Paul says, crossing his arms over his chest. "I've never seen you turn down food. Especially free food."

Shit. I can't exactly tell them I think Preston's dad is a psycho.

I scrub a hand down my face and interlace my fingers in my lap.

"Don't know what to tell you, man." I hate lying to my friends but is it a lie if I don't really know what's going on? It's just weird and I don't trust it.

My leg bounces under the table the longer I wait for Preston to reappear.

What did he tell me? Five minutes and to come find him? How am I supposed to find him?

"Excuse me," I wipe my mouth with my napkin and place it next to my plate before standing up, pretending I need to get out of this room for a minute, get some fresh air, splash water on my face, something.

Outside the room we've been stashed in for dinner, there's a hallway with shiny granite floors, framed art on the walls, and tables with vases filled with flowers. It's like a damn hotel in here. The hallway to my right leads to the lobby and the front of the building. I doubt Preston went that way.

Look like you belong, like you know where you're going.

I shove my hands in my pockets and walk down the hallway, hoping I ooze a confidence I don't feel. I don't know where the hell I'm going but I hope I find Preston soon.

I try every door. Most are locked, which is frustrating. If he's in one of those rooms, I seriously hope I haven't just made things worse for him.

Finally, I hear voices behind a door.

"Keep your shit up and I'll transfer Lily out here so fast your head will fucking spin." Even though Preston's father isn't speaking to me, his words have dread sinking in my stomach like a stone.

"If she comes out here, she's not staying with you. I'll make sure of it." Preston snaps back.

I hesitate with my hand hovering over the knob. He said to come for him, but so far it doesn't sound that bad, just a disagreement.

"You're fucking useless. You really think you can protect her from me? I made you. Gave you everything you have. I can take it away."

What the hell kind of father speaks to his kid that way?

Jesus. I'm going to call my parents tonight and tell them I love them.

"You're a disgrace to your mother's memory. You should be ashamed of yourself. If you were a better son, I wouldn't have to correct you so often. Look at yourself."

What. The. Fuck.

With fury shooting through my veins like adrenaline, I rip open the door and barge inside. Preston spins away from me, showing me his back while his father turns that ugly, cold hatred on me.

"My bad, just looking for the bathroom."

I think Preston is buttoning his shirt. Why was his shirt open?

Like I've seen Preston do more than once, I see the second his father's public face comes out. All of a sudden, he's Mister charming, smiling and easy going. I don't believe it for a second. It's as fake as the polyester suit Preston hated so much. As he walks towards me, I keep my spine straight and my hands in my pockets. I will not cower. My stomach tightens, nerves making my skin want to crawl the closer he comes to me.

He reaches his hand out to shake mine, and begrudgingly, I take it. Over his shoulder, Preston is tucking his shirt in and adjusting his clothes.

"And you're Charles's roommate?" He looks at me expectantly, like he wasn't just berating Preston. It's really disconcerting to see Preston's face on this man. He's a little older, shorter, and not as muscular, but that face is the same. From the eye color to the set of his lips. It's eerie.

"That's correct." When is he going to let go of my hand?

"And how is that going?" His gaze is so direct, I bet it unnerves people. It would bother me if I wasn't confident he's up to something.

Preston turns around finally and his eyes lock on mine.

He's not okay but I doubt most of the other guys will notice. They haven't noticed anything fucking else all god damn night. Like hungry puppies, all they care about is food.

"It's fine. Not always easy for two athletes to share a space but we make it work." It's as close to the truth as I can get here.

"Do you share a similar work ethic?"

Are you fucking kidding me? No wonder Preston is so fucking uptight.

"Uh no, not really, but the NHL isn't my dream, so it makes sense that he works harder."

Doctor Andrew Carmichael cocks his head and purses his lips. "Then why are you on the team?"

I suck in a deep breath and let it out slowly. I've already answered this question, twice I believe, to Preston.

"I'm on a scholarship, so I play to pay for my education."

"And you don't think that's a waste of a team spot and resources that could be used for someone more talented?"

That is almost word for word what Preston said.

"Who said I didn't want to be there?" I pull my hand from his and slide it back in my pocket. I can't stand him touching me anymore. If this was all Preston had for parental support, it's no wonder he hates being touched. This dude is slimy. How anyone would pay him to do surgery on them is beyond me. I would be afraid of him slitting my throat.

"I love hockey. In fact, I plan to coach."

Preston walks toward us, places a hand in the middle of my chest and pushes me back, all without breaking stride.

"We need to get back to the team. Dinner is wrapping up and we'll be leaving soon."

I don't argue with Preston, just follow him back to the safety of the team.

"Your dad is a real piece of work." I mutter under my breath.

"Shut up."

As much as I want to ask him what the fuck that was back there, now isn't the time. We will discuss this later though. I went with what he wanted, now I deserve answers.

When we walk back into the room with our teammates, Paul lifts his chin toward us and Brendon turns around to glare. I swear to God, I do not have the energy to deal with his shit right now.

"Your boyfriend thinks I fucked you in the bathroom." For a split second, there's a small smile on Preston's face.

"Oh, now you have jokes?" He's giving me fucking whiplash.

"Are you going to tell him you jacked us off this afternoon?"

I watch my best friend stew in his jealousy. It's not fair to him that I haven't told him what we were doing is over. Shit. Can our friendship withstand this?

"No."

Preston finally looks at me instead of staring at Brendon. Why does he care what Brendon thinks?

"Why not?" His dark gray eyes are curious instead of confrontational.

I don't have an answer, so I shrug and walk to my seat.

"Everything okay?" Paul asks while Brendon continues to stew.

"Honestly, I don't know."

The dinner plates are cleared by the catering staff, and we all stand around waiting for the time to leave. Coach is shaking hands with Preston's father while Preston is, once again, standing like a statue. Or maybe a puppet. Those can speak and smile on command. It's like his dad is pulling his strings. I hate it.

While I don't want to be alone with Preston's dad, I don't want Preston to be alone with him either, so I hang back. Brendon, who I'm pretty sure is now just trying to make Preston jealous, won't leave either.

When it's just a few of us left, Doctor Andrew Carmichael speaks to me. "You know, it would be in your best interest if you stayed out of other people's business."

The muscle in Preston's cheek jumps but there's no other indication that he's even paying attention. I just want to get out of here. To put this weird damn dinner behind me and go to bed. We have two games this weekend that we have to prepare for. Sleep is crucial.

Coach pops back in, saving me from having to respond. "Let's go, boys. Vans are loading up."

Nobody else makes the first move to leave, so I do, hoping it breaks the tension and Preston will follow. Brendon is stuck to me like glue and it's driving me nuts, but maybe it will give Preston more incentive to leave as well.

I walk past Coach who is still standing there, thankfully. The vans are mostly full, one has a seat and another has two.

"Come on." Brendon tries to lead me but I don't want to leave Preston, not with him like this.

While I stand there and try to figure out what to do, Paul pops out and waves him over.

"It's cool, go ahead." I wave him off and climb into the other van. It's the middle seat, which Preston won't like, but I'm not sure what he'll notice at this point. Plus, it gets him away from his dad.

I'm buckling my seatbelt when he strides out with Coach, climbs in without a word, and Coach closes the door.

"You okay?" I ask softly.

"I'm not a child, do not treat me like one." His head barely turns while he snaps at me, but it's enough for his eyes to lock on mine. The calm mask is cracking, fury and frustration are bubbling to the surface and I'm going to be the one who's caught in its crosshairs. No one else seems to care, but for some reason, I do. So, I keep putting myself in his way, keep pushing him.

I wasn't sure which version of him I would find after this meet and greet, and honestly, I'm glad he's back to pissed off. It's a hell of a lot easier to deal with.

"Cool, glad we cleared that up." I turn back to the window and stare at the passing buildings. How did I end up here? When did I take on the job of caring about the biggest asshole on our team?

He's not an asshole for no reason and you know it.

By the time we make it back to the dorms, Brendon has texted me a handful of times, which I have not responded to or even opened. He's my best friend but he needs to read the damn room and chill out. I know I need to talk to him, tell him I'm not interested in fooling around anymore, but I'm scared it will end our friendship. I guess that's just the risk I'm going to have to take.

Preston avoids the elevator and takes the stairs up to the third floor. It's probably better that way. Feeling guilty, I wait with Paul and Brendon for the elevator.

"What's your deal with him?" Brendon demands, sounding jealous. Paul sighs, waiting for the fight we all know is coming. I don't want to fight with Brendon.

My shoulders drop and I rub at the back of my neck. "Honestly, I don't know. He's a dick most of the time but I think it's a defense mechanism."

Brendon shoves his hands in his pockets and rocks back on his heels. "He hates me."

"To be fair," Paul pipes up. "I'm pretty sure he hates everyone."

I chuckle and a smile pulls at my lips. "Paul's right. He doesn't like anyone."

"What was the deal with the suit? Why'd he freak out?"

The elevator opens and a few guys get on while we wait for the next one.

"I don't know." I shrug, not comfortable telling them how stressful this was for Preston. That feels private and they don't get that part of him. I like that it's only mine. He's so shut down about everything that those little breaks in the perfection feel like I've won a battle. Do I want the pressure of being the only one he kind of trusts? Not really, but I'll take it if that's what it takes for him to be okay.

Even I don't understand my reaction to him. Why do I care so much? I have no god damn idea.

"Dude is nuts. Half the time he's telling you how much you suck, the other half he's acting like he owns you or something. It's weird, man."

Nothing I don't already know.

"I don't think he knows how to have friends." My voice is quiet in the enclosed space.

It's finally our turn to get on the elevator. Our conversation dies in the small, crowded space and even when we get out on our floor, we don't say much.

"Night, see you in the morning." Paul pats me on the back and I nod to him.

The light is off in my room when I get back. Quietly, I strip off the button up shirt and slacks, put the cufflinks back in the box, and hang clothes back in the garment bag. I don't have the jacket.

Fuck.

Preston is going to kill me.

Anxiety swirls like a constant fucking companion in my

stomach. Is his dad going to use that against him somehow? Should I tell him or wait and see what happens? Maybe his dad won't say anything.

Pulling on my pajama pants, I jump when Preston speaks.

"Stop it."

I freeze with my pants pulled halfway up.

Uh. What?

"Excuse me?" I straighten up, still holding my pants at my thighs, and turn to look at him. My dick starts to harden at the idea of him wanting to fuck me. At how his hands feel on my skin. The rough grip he always has. I want marks. Bites, finger tips, anything.

"Stop thinking." His voice has that menacing bark to it that makes me hard. It's all I can do to stand still. That damn tone has precum sticking me to my underwear.

God. Dammit.

Is this a test? A trap? What the fuck does he want from me right now?

"Go to bed. We have a game tomorrow." His sheets rustle as he settles back into his bed.

"What if fucking is good luck and makes us play better tomorrow?" I don't really expect an answer from him as I slide into my bed, despite wanting to be in his.

"If fucking before a game worked, you wouldn't be blowing off Brendon."

Turning my head toward Preston's bed, I can barely make out the shape of his body pressed against the wall, curled on his side. He sleeps that way most nights.

I hate the fact that he's right.

"I don't have the jacket." In the dark, it's easier to confess, even if every muscle in my body tightens as I wait for his response.

I swear I can hear his eyes pop open, and his heartbeat shoot up.

"What do you mean?" His voice is so calm, it's scary.

"I left the suit jacket hanging on the back of my chair at dinner." Even to my own ears, I sound like a child, hoping I don't get in trouble. My stomach rolls and I want to fidget or pace the room.

The tension in the room skyrockets the longer he doesn't say anything. My skin prickles as the energy in my body demands some kind of release. He hasn't said anything, but I don't think he's fallen asleep either.

"I'm sorry." I blurt out the words and sit up, turning to slide my feet to the floor.

My words hang in the air with no response. I can't fucking take this. What the hell am I supposed to do? I can't go back and get the jacket now.

The tension in the air is so thick it's suffocating. I'm going to choke on it.

"Preston." I snap, getting up and pacing the short length of the space we have in here. I snap my fingers as I move, needing something to do with my hands.

"I swear to fuck, Jeremy, if you don't sit the fuck down, I'll choke the shit out of you." The growl that emanates from Preston sends a shiver up my spine and words fly out of my mouth before my brain has a chance to process them.

"Make me."

Like a shadow, Preston moves silently until he's directly in front of me, crowding my space but not touching me. Not yet. His breath fans across my lips as he stares at me.

My body stills, focusing all of my energy on the threat. A flutter of fear and arousal tickles my stomach.

"I will break you." He licks up my stubble-covered cheek. "And like it."

A moan gets caught in my throat and precum dampens my boxer briefs. Fuck. I'm painfully hard.

His fingers find my nipple and pinch it hard enough to make my body bow around it, but he doesn't ease up. I drop my head back on my shoulders, breathing through the pain.

Preston's other hand grabs my chin and turns my face away from him. He buries his face in my neck and inhales deeply for a moment. I want to touch him, but I don't want this to end.

My dick aches for attention but I don't move. I have a feeling he needs as much control as he can get after the shit show that was tonight's dinner.

And honestly, I want him to use me. No one has ever given me what I really crave, but Preston is dark enough to do it. There's a part of him that wants to cause pain, wants to take and use and hurt.

Preston's teeth sink into the flesh of my neck and I groan. My knees go weak and I reach for his arms to hold on to. I need him to ground me while I lose myself in him.

I hope there's a mark tomorrow.

"Brendon doesn't touch you again." His words are hard in my ear, a clear statement, not a question.

He finally lets go of my nipple and I hiss, flinching away from his hand as blood rushes to the abused skin.

"On your fucking knees."

There's no hesitation, only the sound of my knees hitting the floor. He runs one hand through my long hair, the other one slaps my cheek hard enough to heat and sting.

Releasing me, he reaches into his pants and pulls his beautifully thick cock out through the fly. I lift onto my knees a little to get the head into my mouth, my face upturned toward him. Preston's hand once again goes into my hair, but this time he clenches his fist around the strands and uses it to help fuck my face.

Jesus. Fucking. Christ.

I love sucking his dick. I love the way he uses my mouth, thrusting against me like he isn't concerned about hurting me. Tears trail down my cheeks from him riding my damn gag reflex but he doesn't care. My dick is hard enough to drive nails. I need to touch it but I don't dare. Before I'm ready for it to be over, he pulls away from me and lifts me under the arms, all but tossing me onto my bed.

I land on my back, staring up at the imposing man who's breathing hard. Even in the dark, I can see he's half crazed. I shouldn't taunt him when he's so close to the edge but I want him like this. He rips my pants and underwear off, crawling onto the bed. My knees fall open in invitation and he settles his hips against mine. Biting and sucking at my skin, the rough scrape of his five o'clock shadow gives me friction burns while his nails dig into my flesh to leave bright red scratches down my torso.

My back arches at the sensations overwhelming my brain. Preston cups my balls and tugs on them, teasing around the edge of my hole but not penetrating it.

"Please," I whimper, desperate to feel him inside of me. He's fucking huge and it'll hurt but I don't care. I want it. Need it. Need *him.*

My feet hook around the back of his thighs, keeping him against me and using the leverage to grind up into him.

Preston growls low in his chest and takes my mouth in a hungry, bruising kiss. I cup the sides of his head, holding him to me and ravaging him with the same intensity. His tongue tangles with mine as he plays with me, a few tugs, a stroke, his finger around my hole. It keeps me hard and on edge but not anywhere near enough to get me off.

"Lube?" he asks against my lips. "Condom?"

"Top drawer."

He sits up and reaches for the bedside table.

"They're no condoms in here." He looks at me with a questioning brow lifted.

"Your STD panel at check in was negative right?" We all have them with our physical before we can play.

"No fucking condom," he agrees and coats himself in lube. Without waiting or warning, he lines the blunt head of his cock against my hole and pushes. My body tightens around him, a hiss shooting from me at the burn, but he doesn't stop until he's all the way in.

"You're fucking leaking." Preston smirks at me, taking my weeping dick into his hand and stroking me while he sets a fast, hard pace. With his thighs on either side of my hips and one hand on my chest, pressing me into the mattress, he snaps his body for every thrust, taking me as deep and powerfully as he can. It hurts but sets my body on fire in the best fucking way.

I could drown in the sensations he's forcing on me and die happy.

The burning stretch subsides, leaving only pleasure dancing in my veins.

I'm throbbing in his grip, my hands pulling on my hair for something to hold on to.

"Oh, fuck," I growl, my impeding orgasm shooting through me like electricity.

Preston squeezes my cock to stop my orgasm and I all but cry.

"What the fuck?" I snap at him with wide, desperate eyes.

All he does is grin at me, not slowing his pace at all.

Once I've backed down, he strokes me again until I'm on the edge.

"Please, please," I beg, my body tense and ready to blow, but he squeezes me again and this time a single, frustrated sob escapes me.

"I hate you," I groan as he slows his pace, leaning hard on my chest, and slaps my cheek again. My hot skin stings at the sharp contact, yet I moan.

"Legs up," Preston orders, pumping my cock once again at the same pace he's fucking into me. I pull my legs back, changing the angle, and my eyes roll back into my head as he strokes my prostate. He finally lets me come in a mess on my stomach and chest. I'm breathing too fast, and my heart is hammering. Goosebumps erupt on my skin as he keeps hitting that pleasure spot.

I watch as he lifts his hand to his mouth and licks my cum from his skin. My spent cock twitches and he smirks at me before a shudder rocks through him. His orgasm fills me as he thrusts another few times. When he stops moving, he's leaning heavily onto my chest, panting with his eyes closed.

"Fuck." He groans, flexing his softening cock and pulling out. My entire body relaxes, spent and tired with cum cooling on my skin.

We sit there in silence for a moment, relearning how to breathe. Preston reaches for me, drawing his finger through the mess I made on my stomach, almost like he's trying to rub it in.

"Do you have a cum fetish or something?" I ask with amusement.

"It's reassuring, seeing the proof that I did well." His features change from lighthearted to introspective. Like now that he's said the words, he wishes he hadn't. He gives himself a shake and gets up, tucking his now-soft cock into his pants. "I'll let you clean up."

He's stiff and tense as he moves, lying down on his bed with his back against the wall, curled in on himself.

Grabbing my pants, I head to the bathroom with my muscles protesting and flick the light on. When I catch sight of myself in the mirror, I stop, wide-eyed. "Holy shit!" I have marks everywhere. One of my nipples is probably bruised, huge scratches down my chest look like I got into a fight with a jungle cat, and there's more bite marks and hickeys than I want to count.

I stand there and touch each one, my fingers tracing the lines his nails left on my skin, the ridges of each tooth impression, and the shape of each hickey.

This is what I've always craved but couldn't ever ask for.

He's going to break my heart.

I cannot get attached to him. I can't. It's not in anyone's best interest. All I can do is help him to the best of my ability, then walk away when it's time. I've already started thinking about him differently, but I can't lose sight of the fact that he doesn't want anything more from me than a fuck every now and then. Sometimes he lets me help calm him when he's overwhelmed, but he's already told me he isn't here to make friends. Maybe getting off and letting off some steam will make him less of a dick.

I get cleaned up and when I'm done giving myself a stern talking to, I head back to bed. Since I've been in here a while, I'm careful to shut off the light and walk quietly back to bed so I don't wake him up.

"What are you going to tell everyone tomorrow?"

"Jesus!" I jump, my heart rate spiked at the unexpected sound. "What?"

"The guys are going to see you with marks that obviously came from sex, what are you going to tell them?"

Oh. That's a damn good question. Unease makes me pause, sitting on the edge of my bed.

"That I got laid." I shrug. "Only Paul and Brendon know I'm gay, so besides them, no one will suspect it was you. A few guys may ask if you saw the chick I was with though."

"You're done with Brendon." His voice says not to argue but fuck that.

"Brendon is my best friend." I pull back my blanket and lie down.

"If he touches you, you'll fucking regret it." Oh, that's a dangerous tone. It should probably worry me that it turns me on.

"Why? You're not my boyfriend." Why? Why am I riling him up? I want him to claim me. I want him to let me in, to be his friend who he also fucks unconscious. Why am I the one fighting this now?

Self-preservation.

Preston throws off his blanket and in two steps is climbing over me. He grabs my hands and pushes them against the mattress next to my head and straddles my hips.

"Those marks on your body say otherwise." Fury is radiating off him in the heat of his skin against mine, in the tremble and strength of his fingers.

I look him dead in the eye when I respond. "Those marks mean nothing."

Looking at him is like looking at a cobra ready to strike. I know he's going to, and I know it's going to hurt when he does, but I have to push him. I have to know what he'll do, where his lines in the sand are. I need to know where I stand.

He lowers his face to mine and speaks through clenched teeth. "I. Don't. Share."

He's a possessive bastard and if I'm going to deal with his jealousy over my best friends, I have to know what this is.

"Why can't I touch you?"

As if I've struck him, he jerks away from me. His hands no longer hold mine down, his face isn't close enough to kiss. He stays sitting on my lap, rubbing his hands on his legs.

"I can't." He drops his head and gives it a little shake. "If it's that important, we're done here."

He climbs off me and lays back down on his bed. I let him go, even though I'm not at all satisfied with the conversation. Is it important? Yeah, to me it is. Not being able to touch the person I'm fucking sucks. No touching at all? Hugs? Holding hands? Cuddling?

"Go to sleep, Albrooke."

CHAPTER 19

jeremy

Our first ice breaker tournament against Notre Dame was fun. I got some ice time with Brendon and Paul, and it was like old times. We won three to one and Coach was happy. Preston has been avoiding me in our down time, but that's changing tonight. If that means I stay up all damn night waiting for him, that's what I'll do.

Brendon is also not happy with me after witnessing the bruises and scratches on my chest, but we haven't had a minute of privacy to talk about it. Partly because I avoided him last night. Carpenter, our team captain, laughed and told me to chill out on fucking 'wild cats' the night before a game.

Today's game though? Not a chance. Maine is kicking our asses like we've never played the game before. It's an embarrassment.

Carmichael has been sent to the sin bin twice and we're in the second period. I think all of our D men have been actually. It's a shit show. Our first line is beaten up and tired, our goalie is the only thing saving us. He's only let through two goals but has blocked fourteen attempts. Meanwhile, we've made seven attempts on goal.

My knee bounces while I wait for a line change, watching the game and hating not being on the ice. A fight almost breaks out after one of Maine's players runs into our goalie. Carmichael takes it as a personal attack and shoves the player, getting in his face. I can't hear what he says, obviously, but I can almost guarantee it was inventive and slightly terrifying.

Willis, the other second line D man, separates the two and the game continues. Back and forth across the ice, the puck flies from player to player. Coach yells for a line change on the fly, the first line coming off as my line shoots off the bench. As soon as my skates hit the ice, I'm racing toward the puck, trying to steal it from Maine's left winger, but I can't get to him before he shoots at the net. Our goalie blocks it and I snag it off the ice, trying to get a break away back into our attack zone.

Oiler gets to the blue line before me and I fling the puck to him. Johnson and Oiler pass it back and forth before Oiler tries for a goal. It's blocked, hits Johnson's skate and he kicks it, Oiler snagging the puck and shooting it toward goalie, this time it barely grazes the goalie's glove, and the lamp lights up.

Fuck yes!

We cheer and slap each other on the back. Finally, we're on the board. We can make a comeback again.

Coach yells for another line change, putting us back on the bench. I drop down in an empty spot next to Carmichael and grab a water bottle.

My heart is pounding and I've got a smile on my face as our fourth line faces off.

I knock my knee into Preston's. "What did you say to that player?"

"If he didn't stay off my goalie, I would make tea out of the teeth I was going to knock out of his face." His tone is so deadpan I turn to look at him. All I can do is blink for a second while my brain processes what he just said.

"What the actual fuck, man?" I don't know whether to be horrified by that mental image or impressed.

He shrugs and continues to watch the game. "I don't even drink tea."

The game keeps on the way it's been going and we don't get any more goals. It's disheartening. Our first loss as a team is always hard. We all know it's part of the game, but we never go into a game thinking we'll lose. We always think we'll win. Always.

When it's proven to us that we aren't the best, it's a hard hit. It doesn't matter how many times we've experienced it.

It takes a while to get showered and changed, deal with after-game interviews and the pep talk from the coaches.

By the time we're leaving the rink, I'm once again wearing Preston's suit pants and I stop short when I see Preston and his father talking to our head coach. Brendon walks right into the back of me at my abrupt stop.

"What the fuck, bro?" Brendon says, but I don't respond.

I can't take my eyes off Preston's back. It's steel straight, his shoulders tense, and I'm pretty sure the hand holding onto his gym bag is white at the knuckles. This isn't a good sign. Why didn't he tell me his dad was coming tonight? Was he here last night too? How long will Preston have to deal with him being here?

"Hello? Earth to Jeremy?" Paul waves a hand in my face and I turn to look at him.

"What?"

"Beers at Rocky's. Come on!" He motions toward the doors for me to follow but I'm rooted in place. I have to know if Preston is okay first.

But I'm wearing his clothes again. Should I butt in or stay away?

Before I can make a decision, Doctor Carmichael smiles at Coach, shakes his hand, and walks away with Preston following along behind him. Where the hell is he going?

I'm following too, I have to know where he's going. He's not going with his dad, is he?

My heart starts racing at the thought. He was terrified of going to dinner with his dad and there were thirty of us to run interference.

There's a town car sitting next to the curb that Doctor Carmichael is heading toward, Preston on his heels, tense and shut down.

"Preston," I say loud enough he should hear me. He doesn't even flick a glance my way. What the fuck?

I shove my bag at Brendon and break into a jog.

"Preston!" I'm about even with him, even if ten feet or so separates us. He glances at me, a second of fear breaking through the ice mask before he's hidden again.

A driver opens the door for them, both Preston and his father get into the car and the door is closed. There's nothing I can do but watch as he stares straight ahead out the front window. The car pulls away and he's gone. I'm left standing on the sidewalk outside the rink, watching the guy I care way too much about, leaving with his sketchy ass father. And there's nothing I can do about it.

I run a hand through my hair and pull on the strands in frustration.

"What's going on?" Paul asks as he and Brendon catch up to me.

"Seriously, what's your deal with Carmichael? Are you guys a thing?" Brendon demands.

"Jesus, dude. Drop it already," Paul snaps. "If he wanted to be with you, he would be. Move on."

Wait.

Shit.

I can't deal with Brendon's hurt feelings right now.

"Let's go get changed and meet the team at Rocky's," Paul says, trying to move past what he just said.

I take my bag back from Brendon and we head back to the dorms. None of us want to spend more time in these suits than we have to.

In my dorm room, I hang up the borrowed clothes and slide into a pair of jeans and a Darby University Ram's t-shirt. I'm sitting on my bed, pulling on my old Vans, when my door opens and Brendon steps in, closing it behind him.

God damn it.

He leans against the door with his arms crossed.

"I'm sorry." I clasp my hands between my knees, staring at the floor instead of my best friend. I hate that I've fucked this up.

"We had a deal." His words are full of hurt. "If we met someone, we would let the other know."

Guilt weighs heavy on my shoulders. He's right. That was the agreement we made.

"I know." My words are quiet in the tension of the space between us. "I don't know what's going on with me and Preston. We hooked up the night before last but that's the first time."

Liar.

When he doesn't say anything, I turn and look at Brendon. He hasn't moved from the door.

"I honestly don't know what will happen from here. He's..." I struggle to find a way to explain his hang ups without giving him away. I don't really know what his hang ups are, just the consequences of them. Like no touching.

Brendon scoffs, shaking his head. "He left a clear fucking message on your body. He wanted me to see it."

I rub the back of my neck. "I think that's just the way he is. I didn't have much to do with it."

He huffs a laugh before turning serious again. "But you liked it."

"I don't know what you want me to say," I admit, gripping the back of my neck with both hands.

"The truth."

I sigh and scrub my face in my hands. "I don't know what's going on between Preston and me." I grip the back of my neck with both hands and squeeze. "But one thing I do know is, what you and I were doing is done."

CHAPTER 20

preston

I am numb.

I know what happens next, since it's happened more times than I can remember. My rational thought is gone, leaving me in survival mode. I just have to make it through to the end, because there's always an end.

Jeremy calling me, trying to stop me from leaving, almost broke me. He shouldn't care about me. I've given him no reason to.

But I need it.

For once, someone cares about more than just what I can do on the ice. I don't know what to do with it. With Jeremy. How do I let him in when I've never let *anyone* in? It scares me more than anything my father threatens. Is it selfish to want it anyway?

The driver drops us off in front of the building and without a word, I climb out and follow along behind my father.

I've only been inside the penthouse once. It was enough.

The space is modern, with sleek lines and shiny surfaces. Nothing about it is inviting but it does scream money and that's all he's ever been concerned with.

"Go change," Father says over his shoulder while he pours himself a drink from the decanter on the liquor cabinet.

I don't argue or fight. That takes too much brain power. In the bathroom, I find the box with my compression shorts in it and pull them out.

The room is gleaming black stone and glass and huge. It's definitely bigger than my dorm room. One wall is a window looking out over Denver with the mountains behind it. It's beautiful but makes me feel nothing.

Compression shorts are all I'm allowed to wear during correction. He knows I hate being exposed, so he does it to make me uncomfortable and to prove he's got the upper hand. I don't think he's realized that I've given it to him and there's a countdown to when I take it back. Does that knowledge help me deal with it? No.

I strip my clothes off, take a shower, and put on the fucking shorts. Then I stand in front of the mirror and wait for him to come get me. The tension in my body grows with every passing minute, not knowing when something will happen. He's never predictable.

Sometimes I stand here for five minutes, other times it's hours. Will he start with the scalpel or cattle prod? Will I have to pick which happens first? Maybe an ice bath is what he has in store for me first.

The air conditioner turns on, the cold air prickling my bare skin.

Even I don't recognize myself in the mirror. Who is this guy?

You're a freak. Jeremy will never accept you.

What is there for him to like?

You're a constant failure.

Your mother would hate you. It's better that she's dead and you can't embarrass her now.

When the door finally opens, I don't know whether to be afraid or relieved.

I flick my gaze to him as he steps inside, holding the jacket Jeremy left at the dinner and a jar of peanut butter with a spoon sticking out of it.

Fuck.

"Tell me, Charles." He stops in front of me, lifting the jacket. "Why was that imbecile wearing this?"

I keep my stare on the mirror in front of me, trying to disassociate and lose myself in my own head, but it doesn't work. His slap across my cheek makes my body jerk and heat singes my skin. I don't make a sound or try to protect myself from him. There's no use. He'll make me regret it another way if I do.

Logically, I know I'm bigger, faster, and stronger than him. But the little boy inside me is terrified of this man. The little boy who lives in my chest trembles at the thought of my father. Shutting down, making myself numb, is the only way I've found to protect him from the pain.

"I expect an answer, Charles." He runs his finger along the newest scar on my chest. Every muscle I possess tightens, making my body shake with the effort to not shove him away from me. It turns my stomach. The skin is numb, but I can feel the pressure in the tissue underneath it, then some spots tingle like my nerves were hit with a jolt of electricity.

My teeth ache from the clench of my jaw. I can see it in my reflection, the lack of life in my eyes, the tense set of my shoulders. Why would anyone want to be around me? I'm an asshole on the best of days. Keeping everyone at arm's length to protect myself means my people skills suck.

I'm the personification of this apartment.

"Charles!"

"He doesn't own a suit right now, so I offered mine." It's as close to the truth as I can get. If my father finds out I went on a jealous rage because Jeremy was wearing Brendon's, he would find a way to use it to blackmail me or find a way to hurt Jeremy to keep him away from me. Probably both.

"Since when are you altruistic?"

"If anyone on the team looks bad, we all look bad." The motto has been beaten into me since I was a child. Father insisted on perfection for all of us. After Mom died, it was my job to keep Lily in line or pay for it later.

I usually paid for it later. Not because Lily was a difficult child, but because I refused to scare her into compliance. She was barely more than a toddler when Mom died.

"What have I told you about taking care of your things?" The cold tone sends a shiver down my spine.

"If I can't keep track of my things, I don't deserve to have anything." I don't know how many times I've said those words. How many times did he take everything from my room but a blanket on the floor and the clothes I needed for school?

A backhand snaps my head to the side again, the instant sting on my cold skin forcing a hiss from me.

He tosses the jacket on my clothes that I left on the counter, grabs the peanut butter, and shoves a spoonful into my mouth. I gag but keep it down.

I hate peanut butter. It's the only thing he allows me to eat during correction.

My stomach revolts but I have to swallow it. If I throw it up, I'll be made to eat more. Probably the entire jar.

My mouth floods with saliva, the muscles of my abdomen clench painfully, trying to get rid of the thick paste in my mouth. Father stands there with a lifted eyebrow, watching me with no emotion.

By the time the peanut butter is down my throat, sweat is breaking out across my forehead, but it's done.

Father takes my pile of clothes and turns toward the door, turning at the last second to speak to me. "If you would act right and pay attention, I wouldn't have to do this."

"Yes, sir."

The door closes and, once again, I'm left alone to stare at my reflection and wonder what he has planned. There's no way I'm leaving this place without a new cut and I won't be allowed to sleep. The only thing I have going for me now is I have to be back in my room by tomorrow night, so at least I know when this will end.

●

How long have I been standing here? The sun is down and has been for a long time. The sky above the mountains is almost black in the distance.

I keep falling asleep only to jerk awake when my body starts to relax. One of these times, I know I'm going to slam my face into the counter, probably break my nose or something.

Images of Jeremy last night filter through my exhausted brain when I'm too tired to keep them out. Even in the dark, the flush of his skin was clear. His moans when I left marks on his body haunt me now that I have zero hope of hearing them.

Why did he let me touch him?

His acceptance of whatever I wanted calmed me, soothed the fear and anxiety that is my constant companion. He seemed to need me just as much as I needed him. Why does he care about me? Doesn't he know I'm not worth the effort?

I shake my head and suck in a deep breath, rolling my shoulders to get my heart pumping a bit. The waiting might be the worst part of this. Knowing pain is coming but not *when* is a special kind of torment.

Footsteps sound in the hallway and I hold my breath. Both wanting it to open so I can get it over with and hoping it doesn't so he leaves me alone.

"Prepare the table."

Here we go.

On the top shelf of the hall closet is a black box with a lid and a label that says "CHARLES" in his handwriting. Pulling it down, I make my way to the dining room and set it on the chair at the head of the table. Inside are the sanitized tarp and the medical supplies, including his suture kit and scalpel.

On autopilot, I get the plastic sheet laid out and his supplies sealed in a bag set at the seat I suspect he'll want, the one next to my right shoulder, then climb on the table and lie down. The plastic rustling with my movements is a sound I'll remember the rest of my life.

My hands open and close in fists at my sides as I wait for my father to come in.

This room doesn't have tiles to count. The floor-to-ceiling windows on my left show the busy life of the city below and a chandelier hangs in the center of the table. The ceiling is gray and flat. Nothing to focus on.

The faucet turns on in the kitchen, probably my father washing his hands before putting on gloves and coming in here.

Goosebumps break out on my skin as the air conditioning kicks on again, blowing directly on me.

Father comes in with blue surgical gloves, a blue surgical gown, and a clear plastic face shield. This outfit haunts my fucking dreams. If I have to have surgery at a hospital, they'll have to sedate me long before I get to the table to avoid me freaking the fuck out.

The plastic sheeting under me crinkles as I breathe and he moves things around, prepping my skin with an alcohol swab. I refuse to let myself do anything more than just lay here and take it. Staring up at the ceiling while he gets started, I inhale sharply when the blade pierces my skin and the clenched muscle below.

It burns, stings, as he drags the insanely sharp blade through the flesh on my chest. Blood trickles hot against my cold skin to pool on the tarp. Sweat dampens my face, back, and the middle of my chest as my heart rate spikes, adrenaline making my hands tremble. I close my eyes to focus on my breathing, slowing my heart rate, and convincing my muscles to relax.

Behind my eyes is Jeremy dropping to his knees and swallowing my cock in an instant. His hollowed cheeks as he choked, his unmatching eyes locked on mine while he lets me use his mouth.

"Why are we here, Charles?" My father's matter of fact voice interrupts my daydream, the only coping skill I have left, the way he always does.

CHAPTER 21

jeremy

My head is aching when I wake up the next morning. I may have gotten drunk last night with the team, drowning our sorrows at losing the game that doesn't matter in the standings, and the feeling of helplessness when it comes to Preston. Honestly, I feel better than I probably should.

Really, any reason for hockey players to drink, they will accept. Well, most of them.

Cracking my eyes open, I look over at Preston's bed and see that he is not in it. That's not completely abnormal, but glancing around, I don't see any proof that he's even been here. I force myself to get up and check for his suit in the closet since that's the last thing I saw him wearing.

The hanger is empty.

Shit.

Unease starts to settle in my stomach, cold and anxious as I pick up my phone and find his number.

I click on a chat I didn't know we had and find texts I apparently sent him last night that have gone unanswered.

Hey, you cumming tonight?

See what I did there?

Where are you?

Hello? Hola? Bonjour? Guten tag?

Jesus. *Did I google how to say hello in other languages?*

I scrub my hand over my face and tap into our team group chat.

Anyone seen or heard from Carmichael?

There's a bunch of "no" but that doesn't surprise me. I think I'm the only one who talks to him. Maybe one or two of our other D men.

Shit.

I tap back into my chat with Preston and try one more time.

Hey, you okay? You coming back to the dorm tonight?

I toss my phone on the bed and grab some ibuprofen for the headache, chasing it down with a full bottle of water, then slide my feet in my shoes so I can go get breakfast.

On my way to the dining hall, I check the gym and the ice rink just in case, but don't see any sign of my missing roommate. I don't know what to do.

I don't know why Preston is so afraid of his dad, but it has to be for a good reason. You don't get that kind of fear over nothing. What am I missing?

I spend the rest of the afternoon attempting to deep

dive into Carmichael's life via Google and not coming up with much. His mom died during a home robbery gone wrong when he was ten, he has a sister that's five years younger than him and in a boarding school in New England, and his father is basically the most well-known plastic surgeon in the world. Everyone expects him to be a first-round draft pick this next season because he's terrifying on the ice. From the outside, he has almost a picture-perfect life.

But every one of these pictures I've seen of him, he's hiding behind that perfect mask. The real him isn't there. His eyes are empty and his smile is lacking warmth, if he's smiling at all.

When dinner time rolls around and I still haven't heard from him, I break down and text Coach.

Hey Coach, I haven't seen Carmichael in almost 24 hours and he's not responding to messages. Have you heard from him?

COACH

He's with his dad, he should be home tonight. If he's not home by lights out, let me know but I'm sure he's fine.

How do I tell Coach that I'm worried about Preston *because* he's with his father?

"Fuck!" I drop down on my bed, my phone dropping to my chest, and stare at the ceiling. I hate feeling helpless.

My phone rings with an incoming video call and I hurry to check it, sighing when I see it's Stacy.

"Hey dumbass, what's up?" she says when I answer.

"You called me, what do you want?"

It's quiet as she stares at me.

"What?"

"No, *you* what. What's wrong with you?" she demands.

Damn it, now she thinks there's something going on and won't let it go until I tell her. She's worse than our mom.

"I'm worried about my roommate. He didn't come home last night and I can't get ahold of him." I shrug and sit up, running a hand through my hair.

"I thought you hated your roommate?" Ella babbles in the background and I smile a little at the sound. I love that kid and miss her terribly. She was my nap buddy when I still lived at home.

"I did, but I don't know, he's not so bad. Just intense." I shrug again, trying not to think about the way he marked my skin the other night, the way he fucked me without mercy. How it was the best sex of my life.

"Anyway, how's my girl?"

Stacy picks up Ella and turns the phone so she can see the screen. Her face lights up and she starts babbling a mile a minute like she's telling me an intense story. I pretend to be intrigued by it, listening to every word and filling in any gaps with "no way" or "then what happened?"

Stacy glows as she watches her daughter animatedly telling me something. I love seeing it. I know Stacy has it hard, being a single mom, which is why I took the little rug-rat every chance I could. Our twin brothers watch her when they can, and our parents help too, but it's not the same as having a partner to share the burden with. Ella's dad bounced out of town the day he found out Stacy was pregnant. She was devastated, but honestly, she's better off. If he was able to drop her that fast, he wasn't worth keeping around.

Before I know it, we've been on the phone for an hour and it's time for Ella to go to bed.

"Night night, baby. I love you. Have a good sleep." I tell her and blow her a kiss through the screen.

"Nigh nigh. Lo u," she mimics and blows me a kiss back.

Tears threaten to choke me when the screen goes black. I miss my family and I hate that I'm missing so much of Ella's life. She's changing so fast. By the time I get back home to visit, she'll be an entirely different kid.

Checking the time on my phone, I'm more agitated that Preston isn't back and we have two hours until lights out. I should go eat dinner but I'm too stressed out to eat. I've got anxious energy that I could put to use in the gym but my gut says to stay close to the dorm, that I should be here when he gets back.

I tap my phone against my palm, sitting on the edge of the bed, zoning out when the door opens. Spinning around and jumping to my feet, my knees damn near give out in relief when it's Preston coming through the door. But my relief is short-lived.

In black gym shorts and a blue t-shirt, he looks fucked up. Deep, dark circles under his eyes, his shoulders are sagging, and his eyes are bloodshot.

I hurry toward him but don't know how to help him since he hates being touched.

"Hey, what happened to you?"

He's leaning heavily against the door, his gym bag loosely grasped in his hand, like he's too tired or weak to walk to his bed. I place my hand at his elbow to offer some support, his skin is cold, but clammy to the touch.

"Fuck off," he snaps, turning those storming gray eyes to me and pulling his arm out of my hand.

Seriously? I've been worried sick all damn day and all he has to say is 'fuck off?'

It's probably stress from seeing his dad. Don't take it personal.

"It's dinner time, have you eaten?" His stomach growls loudly in the quiet of our room. I guess that answers that.

"Go lay down and I'll grab you something from the dining hall."

Preston looks at me like he wants to say something but doesn't, just hefts himself off the door and to his bed. He drops the bag on the ground and curls up on his side with his back against the wall, not even removing his shoes first.

I sigh and pull them off, tossing a blanket over him, and force myself not to drop a kiss to his hair.

Getting dinner to-go is quick, especially this late since the rush of people has cleared out, so I can high tail it back to my room. I got him a few options, all of them healthy so I don't have to listen to him bitch about it.

When I get back to the room, he's passed out cold. I set the food on his desk in case he wants it later and settle onto my bed with my laptop. I should have been doing homework but couldn't concentrate on it. Having him back, where I can see him, calms me. He's not okay, that's very clear, but I know he's safe here.

I get about three pages into the reading when Preston starts to whimper and jerk aggressively under the blanket. Setting the laptop down, I get up and sit on the edge of his bed, unsure how to help him.

"Stop," he mumbles, his head snapping to face the opposite direction. "No."

There's something very childlike in the tone of his voice and it breaks my heart. Is it a memory he's trapped in? What kind of trauma did he live through that he had to keep hidden? Was there no one to help him?

"I'm sorry." His voice is louder this time but no less innocent. "Please."

I reach for his hand and rub circles over the back, quietly saying "Shhhh," in an attempt to comfort him.

He jerks again, his arms coming up to protect his face, but in his sleep he misses.

"Preston," I rub his arm since it's the only safe space I know I can touch besides his hair.

"Ahhhh!" he yells, sitting up straight, wide wild eyes searching the room, and his hands grab onto my arm so tight I know there will be bruises in the morning.

"Hey, you're okay," I say softly, using my free hand to run my fingers through his hair and hold the back of his neck. "You're safe."

He's breathing so hard I'm afraid he's going to hyperventilate, but he blinks a few times like he's just realizing where he is.

"Jeremy?" His voice is rough.

"Yeah?" I give his neck a gentle squeeze that I hope he takes as comforting.

"Down." He lays down and pulls me with him, turning me until my back is against his front and his arms are around me. I lay my head on his pillow and relax in his hold. One of his hands finds mine and interlaces our fingers while he buries his face in my neck. He inhales deeply and relaxes, mumbling "safe" before drifting off to sleep.

The next morning, I'm awakened by a shove and almost falling off the bed.

Luckily, my reflexes are decent and I catch myself with a hand on the bedside table and a foot on the floor, but my heart is thundering in my chest and I'm breathing too hard.

"What the fuck?" It takes me a few seconds to remember that I'm in Preston's bed. With my stomach on the mattress now, I turn my head to look into the pissed off face of my roommate.

"Get the fuck off me," he growls in a sleep-roughened voice.

"What the hell is your problem?" I snap back, frustrated at myself for continuing to put myself in this same fucking situation where Preston ends up being ungrateful.

"You in my personal space is my problem." He shoves me again and this time I fall onto the floor and glare up at him.

"If this is the thanks I get, I'm done helping you." Forcing myself to move, I get up and head into the bathroom, slamming the door closed behind me.

What the fuck?

Why?

Why does it even bother me? He fucking hates me anyway so why do I keep trying when I end up with my damn feelings hurt afterward. I spend time worrying about him only to be pushed away and yelled at. I'm done with his shit.

CHAPTER 22

preston

The four AM alarm on my phone blares, pulling me from a deep sleep. My cheek pressed against the warm skin of Jeremy's back, his ass against my dick, and my arm around his waist. As much as I want to stay wrapped up around him, I force myself to push him away.

The comfort I got from him that first night was too much. It hurt. I don't know how to accept it, accept him. For just a minute, before reality set in, I clung to him, surrounded by the warmth and the scent of his skin. My fingers itched to explore him in the slow moments of dawn, but my alarm screaming ripped the fantasy from me and I shoved him away. I want him too badly to let myself have him. He's a distraction and a weakness. I can't afford either.

There's nothing more I want than to be wrapped around him, warm and at peace, my chest against his back or my face in his neck. At night, when fear controls me, I can hold on to what he offers with both hands, but my walls rise with the sun.

It's been weeks of this. I go to bed alone and wake with Jeremy pressed against me. Weeks. Half the time I wake up rock hard and grinding on his ass, ready to come. Sometimes he's pushing back into me, moaning. Every morning it's hard to push him away and act like it doesn't bother me. Like he means nothing to me. Because he does.

Every morning I wish his skin had my marks. I wish I could fuck him out of my system but, like a parasite, he's burrowed under my skin.

With one more deep breath of his body wash, I sit up and push him. I know he's at least half awake, we do this every fucking morning.

He doesn't say a word, just gets up and leaves my bed.

Like I won't wake up in a panic tonight after we've gone to bed, fighting off the nightmares that haunt me. Like he won't wake up and climb into my bed with no resentment or judgment and let me use him to anchor myself to the here and now, my chest pressed to his back and our fingers locked together.

But I can't do it in the light of day. Once I'm awake, his touch is too much. It makes me weak to need him.

His warmth, his scent, his touch keeps the nightmares at bay. At this point, my fucking bed smells more like him than me.

I get up, grab my gym clothes, and get changed.

My workout is done, classes are dealt with, and I'm off to practice. Once again, back in the locker room to change.

Jeremy doesn't look up when I enter, he doesn't acknowledge me in any way if he runs into me during the day. Like a ghost, I don't exist. I just go on about my day without him like I'm not on the edge of a mental breakdown. He hates me and that's fine. Preferable even. He's just too nice to keep me at arm's length at night.

Out on the ice, we do a quick warm-up then get broken up into two-on-one teams. The other second line D man, Willis, and Johnson are blocking Jeremy, who is trying to get the puck in the net. Albrooke has the puck and is racing up the middle to get past Johnson. He spins in an attempt to get around him when Johnson shoves Jeremy and takes the puck, shooting toward the other end of the ice.

It has me seeing red. No one touches Jeremy but me.

I chew on my mouth guard, waiting for my turn on the ice. Coach has the teams switching around to put all of us against each other at some point. Finally, I get my shot with Johnson trying to get past me and Carpenter.

Johnson tries to get up the side of the rink against the boards. I charge for him, slamming him into the boards harder than necessary, and pass the puck to Carpenter, who makes it into the net.

Johnson shoves me off him, pissed off and red-faced. "Get the fuck off me."

"Touch him again and you'll have more than hurt pride," I seethe through clenched teeth.

"Are you fucking serious? We're running drills! The objective is to stop the guy with the puck!" He snaps back, eyeing the rest of the team waiting for their turns. "Why don't you leave him the fuck alone, huh? He's obviously not interested in whatever you're selling."

I skate up to him, chest to chest, my hands gripping his jersey. "Stay the fuck out of my business."

Coach's whistle blows and we skate back to the others. I stand off to one side because no one wants to talk to me. Which is fine. I don't want to deal with them either. I just want to get the fuck out of here.

After practice, Brendon and Jeremy get changed and

head out to meet Paul at the bar. We have a game tomorrow, so I know they won't get drunk or do anything completely stupid. Doesn't mean I don't want to clock Brendon when he turns back and looks at me as they walk away from the rink while I leave for the gym.

This is my life. It revolves around hockey, the gym, and classes. I eat the same thing every day, go to bed at the same time, shove Jeremy out of my bed at the same time every morning. And I hate it.

Once I'm exhausted in the gym, I head back to our room and find a delivery on my bed with my roommate nowhere to be found. Since my father took my suit, I had to buy another one, but that's fine, it's easier than trying to get it back from him.

Was it outside at the door and Jeremy brought it in so it wouldn't get messed with? Did he and Brendon hook up before they left? I haven't seen any evidence of that but I'm also not digging through his shit.

My phone rings with a video call and I answer it without looking at the screen. It's my sister.

"Hey, brat. What's up?" I set my phone up and go about unpacking the suit I bought. I had it sent from Boston so it cost a small fortune, but I like the guy who made my last ones.

"What the hell did you buy?" She stares at my screen like getting closer to hers will make mine clearer.

"A suit. Did you call for a reason or just to criticize my spending habits?" I get it hung up but leave it out so I can get it ready for the game tomorrow.

"Just bored. How's your boyfriend? Where is he? He's super cute." She smiles like the Cheshire cat. In that annoying way only little sisters can manage.

"He's not my boyfriend. For the last time, he's my roommate and he grabbed my phone by mistake when it rang." I huff at her, getting my school stuff set out so I can finish my homework.

"Right, sure. I believe that." She nods but is definitely messing with me.

"Are you just calling to bother me or did you actually want something?"

"Just calling to annoy you. My job is complete." She looks so proud of herself it's hard not to smile at her. She deserves a brother who's able to be there for her more, who's able to have a real relationship with her.

You're broken. Useless.

"Great, bye." She hangs up and I settle back on my bed with my textbook.

An hour later, Jeremy comes in and drops down onto his bed, face first, without a word to me. Checking the time on my computer, I save my work and close the laptop before I go about getting ready for bed. We have a game tomorrow and I know I will be fighting the monsters in my head in a few hours. Again.

CHAPTER 23

jeremy

It's a brutal game so far, we're playing a good damn team and they are kicking our asses. We're tied up two to two in the third period with ten minutes left. Preston is, once again, in the sin bin. The puck drops and I jump for it, flinging it to Paul. He passes it to me and I send it to Brendon to try for the net. It's blocked by the goalie, making everyone scramble for the puck. The other team gets ahold of it and races toward our goal with us chasing them back to our territory. Their left winger slams into our right D man, the puck is knocked around and I lose it in the shuffle as four players fight for it.

Someone's stick hooks my leg, pulling my skates out from under me. My head hits the shoulder of the left winger, flinging my helmet off. His elbow comes up and cracks me in the face hard enough to stun me. When I hit the ice, my head bounces and I have to shake it to clear it. Whistles blow around us, the coaches are yelling, someone falls on me, somehow managing to hit me in the same spot, and the ice is flooded with team members from both sides. A fist fight breaks out and someone falls on me, knocking the wind out of me.

I manage to get out from under the pile of fighting hockey players and look around at the chaos. Refs are attempting to break up the fights, Preston is straddling the chest of a guy in a red jersey, punching him in the face with his bare hands.

"What the fuck?" Blood is pouring down my face, making it hard to see, but I start for him. I'm stopped by someone grabbing my arm. Spinning around with my fist raised, I drop it when I see Paul.

"Come on, you're done. Gotta go see medical." He pulls me along like I'm going to argue. He's right, I am going to.

"It's a fucking cut, I'm fine!" I pull out of his grasp and catch movement to my right. A few players are trying to pull Preston off the player on the ice but he's fighting them off too. Fuck.

"Preston!" I holler, shaking Paul loose and skating toward him as quickly as I can. "Let him go!" I shove the big bastard as hard as I can to get his attention. "Get off him! You're going to get suspended, you dumb fucker!"

He looks up at me with fury in his face, those gray eyes a bottomless pit of pain and torment. For a second, I'm frozen. Why is he looking at me like that? It's a punch to the gut.

"Come on." I grab his arm to pull him back on his feet, wiping at the blood to get it out of my eye.

The ref yells behind me, "You're out of here! Game misconduct penalty! One game suspension!"

God damn it.

The ice is cleared of players, while someone is scraping the blood off the ice and pouring water on the scuff marks to refreeze. Coach is furious as we get to the box. I have a towel shoved at me for my face. I wipe at the blood and sit down on the bench, fully intending to continue playing. Preston is marched down the tunnel for the locker room to get changed since he's been kicked out of the game. One of the EMT's with a medical bag stands in front of me with gloves on, takes the towel from me, and looks at the cut.

"We have to get that cleaned up. You're probably going to need stitches," he tells me. "You'll also need to be checked for a concussion."

"Oh, come on!"

The EMT cleans the wound and messes with it a bit before bandaging it.

"You need stitches," he says, and I growl in frustration.

"Just butterfly it and move on. I'm fine!"

He shakes his head at me.

Coach looks over at me, his eyebrows pulling low on his eyes. "Albrooke, go. If you don't have a concussion and the doctor clears you, you can come back."

"We'll take him in," the guy says to Coach, who nods and turns his attention back to the ice where they're getting the game started again.

"Fuck!" I yell, standing up and throwing my stick in frustration. "This is bullshit. I don't have a fucking concussion!" Anger has my hands shaking and my blood hot. Now *I* want to punch someone.

One of the assistant coaches leaves with us to follow behind the ambulance so I have a ride back to the rink.

I stomp down the tunnel with the EMTs, grumbling the entire way to the ambulance.

When I pass the locker room, I try to get a glimpse of Preston, but I don't see him. Another of the assistant coaches is in there standing with his arms crossed, looking pissed off.

"How long is this going to take?" I demand as I climb

into the ambulance. I'm going back out there. This is bullshit. It's a god damn cut.

"I don't know, hopefully not long."

I missed the rest of the game and have three stitches in my forehead, but I can play tomorrow as long as I have another clear CT scan before the game. By the time I'm showered, changed, and heading back to my room, I'm tired, angry, and confused.

What the fuck was with Preston tonight? He fucking lost it out there. I know first-hand how hard of a player he is, but that was crazy.

My phone is full of text messages and missed phone calls from all of my family members. I might as well get this call out of the way.

I pull up my mom's number and call her on video since I know she won't accept anything less.

"Jeremy Rodger Albrooke!" she yells my name, fear clear in the lines of her face.

"Hey, Mom. I'm okay. Promise. Just a few stitches." I adjust the camera so she can see the stitches through the clear bandage above my eyebrow.

"I never should have let you move to that school. You should have stayed home and gone to school here!" She barely takes a breath before continuing. "Is it too late to move back?"

I can't help the smile tugging on my lips. She's the best mom and, if she'd had her way, none of her kids would've ever left the nest.

"I'm fine, I promise. I was checked for a concussion and

the CT scan was clean. As long as I have another one tomorrow and it's also clean, I can play. I'm fine."

I make my way into the dorm building and get on the elevator.

"I'm also not transferring. This is an amazing school, the team is great, and I have some friends here."

My dad appears on the video. "Hey there, bud, you all right then?"

"Yeah I'm good, Dad, just a bump on the head. I've gotten worse messing around with Jordan and Keith."

"All right. Take it easy, huh?"

"Will do, Dad. Love you."

"Love you too, bud." He hands the phone back to Mom.

I reach for my door and am relieved to find it unlocked, but when I open it to find Doctor Carmichael standing in the middle of our room, I freeze.

"Uh, Mom. I'll call you later, love you." I end the call before she can respond.

What the fuck is he doing here? A quick scan of the small space tells me Preston is not here.

"How did you get in here?" Nice one. I'm sure Mom wouldn't smack you upside the back of the head for that.

I step inside and close the door. If I'm going to pop off at this guy, I don't need an audience.

The impeccably dressed man looks at me like I'm gum stuck to the bottom of his expensive shoe. He's never done anything to me, but I don't trust him. Everything about him makes me uneasy, makes the hair on the back of my neck stand up.

"Where is Charles?" He ignores my question like he has every right to be in my personal space.

"I don't know. I've been at the ER." I point to my head like it isn't completely obvious. Was he not at the game?

Did he not see the fight break out? Isn't that why he's here?

His demeanor changes when he notices the transparent bandage on my face covering my stitches.

He walks toward me, grabs my face and turns it toward the light to get a better look.

"What the fuck? Get off me!" I shove at him, but he's stronger than I expected. His fingers dig into my face as he holds tight.

"They didn't do you any favors with this," he says, more to himself than to me. He lifts a hand and runs his finger over the wound and I hiss, jerking back from him. "Stop moving," he chastises, like I'm a petulant child who won't hold still.

The door opens behind me, making me jump and pull my head toward it to see who it is. Preston stands rooted to the floor with his eyes locked on his dad's grip on my face.

"What the hell are you doing?" Instantly, he's radiating with some mix of fear and rage. I know he's scared of his dad, but tonight, he's proven he's overly protective of me. To be honest, I'm a little afraid of what is going to happen next.

"Inspecting your friend's wound." Doctor Carmichael dismisses Preston and forces my face back into the light. "If I had my kit, I could fix this. It's a shame to scar such a pretty face."

What. The. Fuck.

His finger once again traces over the wound and I swear he gets hard. He's close enough to me that I can feel it. I'm so shocked by it, I don't know what to do. I want to knock him out.

Preston shoves his way between us, forcing his dad to let go of my jaw or bruise me. The expression when he looks at his son promises retribution.

"Stay away from him." Preston is firmly pressed against my chest. I know he doesn't like to be touched, but he put himself here. I take a step back, completely weirded out by what is happening here.

"Charles, since when do you order me around?" The tension in the room is thick enough to cut with a knife and there's nothing I can do about it. There's so much happening here that I don't understand. How can I fucking help if I don't know what's going on? What is it about Preston's life that his dad needs to control? What is he holding over Preston?

"He's not part of this. Leave him alone," Preston reiterates.

What does that mean?

Doctor Carmichael smacks Preston's face, leaving a bright red handprint on his cheek. Preston's nostrils flair, his chest expands with the force of his breathing, but he doesn't retaliate. What the fuck?

CHAPTER 24

preston

I am so fucked.

I knew this day was coming but I hoped I would get more time. More time to recover from the last correction. This one will be worse. He has days this time, not just hours. On my way out of the locker room, Coach told me he had spoken to my father, and I was excused from tomorrow's game.

"I hope your sister is okay."

The words haunt me. What did he do to Lily? What lie did he tell to my coach to get me excused from a game? I wasn't going to play anyway since I earned myself a one game suspension for attacking that player, but it was worth it. He purposefully hooked Jeremy with his stick, tripped him, and now he has stitches. Fuck that guy. Jeremy is mine. I am the only one who gets to leave marks on him.

"Go get in the car, Charles. We'll discuss this at home." My father's voice cuts through the memory of watching Jeremy hit the ice.

He walks out the door, his footsteps fading down the hallway. He knows he doesn't have to wait. I'll follow like the kicked puppy he's trained me to be. Jeremy's confusion and care almost break me. I hate this, that I have to give in to my father, that when I get back, Jeremy will have to bear the brunt force of it. This is why I never have roommates. I can't lay my shit at someone else's feet.

I'm on the verge of hyperventilating as I look at him. He looks as stricken as I feel.

"I'll be back Sunday night." The words sound far away despite coming from my own mouth.

"Sunday?" He steps closer, reaching for my hand, but I move out of the way. I can't let him touch me. I desperately want to let him hold me, wrap myself around him and lose myself in him, but I can't. Not now.

"We have a game tomorrow! You can't miss it." He gets close enough to me that if I took a deep breath, our chests would touch. "Is whatever is happening here worth getting kicked off the team?"

I close my eyes for a second and breathe, not letting the trepidation of what I know comes next take over.

"It's been cleared with Coach."

Confusion has lines forming between his eyebrows while his eyes search mine. I stare at his blue-brown eyes, memorizing them before I leave.

"But—"

I cut him off by grabbing his face and pressing a hard kiss to his lips. He opens immediately and I sweep my tongue into his mouth. Just for a second. Just to remember how he tastes. It's fucked up and selfish, but I need this memory to get through the next two days.

The spicy, woody, almost smoky scent of his deodorant fills my head. I know I'll get whispers of it for days, my mind playing tricks on me while I'm sleep deprived and in pain.

"Charles." My name is barked from down the hallway and I let him go instantly.

He grabs my wrist and I let him this time. I want his touch branded into my skin.

"Don't go. You don't have to leave with him." His eyes plead with me to stay with him.

I want to cry at how earnest he is. He means the words. He thinks it's that simple.

"I'll be back on Sunday."

"No, stay." Jeremy holds tighter to my wrist, demanding I defy my father.

I damn near break when I tell him, "I can't." My words are small and quiet in the space between us.

I turn away from him to leave. He holds onto me until the last second, finally letting my arm fall to my side as I walk away. Clearing my throat, I hide my emotions from my father and follow him down the hallway to the elevator. He doesn't say a word while we wait, just stares forward, so I do the same.

The ding announces the arrival of the elevator, and the metal doors slide open. We step in and turn to face the hallway. Jeremy is standing in the hallway outside our dorm room, fists clenched at his sides. I've never had the urge to run to someone, to know they would comfort me in a moment of weakness, but I feel the need right now and hate myself for it.

"He's a distraction, ruining the hard work you've done. Get rid of him." My father's matter of fact tone grates on my nerves.

"No."

"You aren't exactly in the position to make that call, are you?"

I take in a slow breath, forcing myself to stay calm.

"He's my roommate and teammate. I can't get away

from him." I try to backtrack but it's useless. He's going to do what he wants and I'll just have to deal with it. I won't be surprised if he calls Coach and forces his hand to get me a new roommate.

"You're allowing yourself to become distracted by him. Are you going to let a piece of ass ruin your life? Ruin your dreams?"

My dreams? I don't have dreams. Not anymore. I just hope to survive.

"What did you tell Coach to excuse me from tomorrow's game?" I'm not arguing about Jeremy with him. It's pointless and will only get me into more trouble.

"That your sister is horribly sick and we aren't sure if she'll make it," he says like he's commenting on the weather.

My head snaps to the side, staring at him. How the fuck am I supposed to keep that up? Why would he even come up with that story? It's easy to log into any social media platform and find her. Since my father doesn't talk about her much, she stays out of the public eye so she's shit with keeping her life personal.

"And I will magically be back on Sunday?" What the fuck is he thinking?

"She will have turned a corner and be getting better." He shrugs like this isn't going to blow up in my face on Monday when my teammates are asking questions I don't have answers to.

"What did you tell him was wrong with her? What is she miraculously going to heal from?" I clench my teeth so hard they ache. The elevator stops at the ground floor and we step off. His driver is standing at the curb waiting for us, holding the door open once we exit the building. My stomach rolls when I sink into the leather seat, staring out the front window like I'm just taking a trip and not about to be tortured for the next two days.

Pulling out my phone, I call Lily to make sure she's not really in the hospital.

"Hey there, caveman," she answers. Great, she saw the game.

"Hey Lily." Relief floods my system knowing she's safe.

"What the hell tripped your murder switch? I don't think I've ever seen you after someone like that."

I don't have time for this right now, and I really don't want to explain to my sister something I can't accept myself.

"Can you do me a favor and make a post on your socials like a friend is posting for you, saying you're super sick and hospitalized? Then stay off for a while, log out, and don't post anything for a few days."

"Uh, why? What the hell is going on?" I hear the sound of girls laughing in the background.

"Something came up and I need to miss the game tomorrow. Since I'm not playing anyway, I told the coach that you are basically dying." Not exactly the truth, but close enough. If she thinks she's helping me, she's more likely to do it. If I just demand she do it, she won't.

"Oh, sure. What am I dying of?"

I look at my father who is pretending like he isn't paying attention.

"Pneumonia?" I rub my forehead. "I honestly don't know. Make something up and let me know what you choose. Can't be anything crazy."

"You are the strangest brother. I doubt this is the shit normal siblings do." She scoffs.

"Do you really think siblings don't lie for each other? That's one of the perks of having siblings. It's absolutely normal." We are almost to Father's building and I know he'll take my phone as soon as I'm inside. "Thanks, Lily. I gotta go. Talk later."

"Bye, loser!"

She hangs up and I slip my phone back in my pocket.

I'm doing this to protect her. To give her as normal a life as I can.

"You talk to her regularly?" Father questions, like he's surprised.

"At least twice a week during the season, less often during the summer." I doubt he calls her even once a month. His secretary probably sends a very impersonal email.

Father puts his hand out as we get close to his building and I hand him my phone. I watch him power it off and slide it into his pocket, my lifeline gone. I knew it was coming but it's so much more crushing this time.

The driver pulls up to the building and gets out to open the door for us. We climb out and head inside to the penthouse without anyone noticing we're there. I guess it pays to live where the ultra-wealthy live.

The cold, sterile apartment is waiting for us, but this time it's even colder than before. It's probably sixty-five degrees in here. It's going to be a long weekend.

"Go change." And just like that, it's started.

Standing in the bathroom in only compression shorts, once again staring at myself, goosebumps cover my skin. It's fucking cold in here. The AC has been blowing more than it's been off. I have no idea how long I've been standing here but I'm already tired. My body sways, for comfort, for warmth, to try to stay awake. It's been a while. I can tell that by how dark the sky is outside. My body is ready to crash after the adrenaline rush of the game.

Footsteps in the hallway have my body tensing.

The door opens and Father has a bag of goodies with him. Great.

"Put these in." He hands me a pair of wireless earbuds and I hesitate for only a second to take them. I know this means I'll be subjected to painfully loud noise at random intervals to make sure I don't fall asleep.

"In the tub." He nods in the direction of the big white tub in front of the huge window.

The porcelain is cold against my skin when I sit and it seeps through the thin fabric of my shorts. Since I'm so tall, my knees are bent and the edge of the tub sits against my ribs.

Father plugs the tub and turns the cold water on before he picks up my clothes and leaves with them, coming back with a long orange cattle prod. Fuck me. The water is like needles against my flesh. It won't be long until my skin turns blue.

The thick cattle prod has a battery pack handle, a long orange rod with a U shape at the other end with two metal prongs sticking out. The fucking thing hurts like a bitch but doesn't really leave marks. If he gets me with it now, there won't even be a red mark by Sunday night.

He comes toward me, spinning it around like he has no cares in the world.

Relax.

Tensing up makes it worse.

Breathe.

I close my eyes and focus on breathing so I don't anticipate the hit.

His footsteps on the tile are quiet, but I can track him as he turns the water off with just enough in the tub to cover my feet then moves to stand behind me.

Don't tense up.

Relax.

Without a word, the metal prongs hit my shoulder, sending a snap of electricity through the muscles. My body jerks away and I hiss at the immediate pain. The shock fucking sucks. It only lasts as long as the prongs are touching me but it's sharp. If he gets the right spot, it steals my breath.

He zaps me twice more in damn near the same place. Sweat breaks out on my skin despite the temperature in the room and my knuckles are white as I grip the edges of the tub.

Moving around to the side of me, he gets me on either side of the last cut he added to my body.

"Fuck!" My pectoral muscle seizes for a second and I pant through the pain. I fucking hate getting shocked. I would rather he hit me.

In my ears, the piercing decibels of static turns on and I flinch. Father just smirks at me and leaves, closing the door behind him.

The sad fact is he doesn't have to lock me in here. I'm bigger, stronger, and faster than he is but I never fight him. I never try to escape.

My body slumps against the tub, my head hitting hard enough to echo in the room, but I can't hear it. Tired of playing this fucking game, a tear treks down my cheek as my body trembles. I'm cold, sore, exhausted, and just want to go to bed wrapped around Jeremy.

What's he doing right now?

The sound in the headphones shuts off as suddenly as it started, leaving my head ringing. My body relaxes as I'm finally able to breathe. The muscles of my shoulder and chest ache like I've gotten hit with a bat, but I can ignore it for now.

As I take in a slow, deep breath, there's a whisp of Jeremy lingering just out of reach. I know it's not possible, my head is fucking with me, but it hurts just the same that he seems so close, and I can't touch him.

CHAPTER 25

jeremy

The first night Preston is gone, I can't sleep. My body is tired but my mind won't stop spinning. Where is he? Is he okay? What is his dad doing to him? Will the nightmares be worse when he gets back? How much worse can they get? I spend the night agitated and pacing most of the time, running my hand through my hair, and obsessively checking my phone.

Assistant Coach Scott once again drives me to get my CT scan before the game. I don't tell him that my head is pounding or that I haven't slept. I hide behind my dedication to the team and a smile like all athletes are taught.

By the time I'm dressed and heading to the rink for pregame, my head is screaming, I've gotten maybe an hour of sleep, and I'm nauseated.

In the locker room, we get changed for off-the-ice warm-ups. Normally, I would be chatting with Paul and Brendon and making jokes to keep the tone light before the game.

Not today.

"Albrooke!" Coach calls me and I turn to look at him, doing my best not to squint in the bright lights.

"Yeah, Coach?"

"We're still waiting on those CT results, take it slow and easy until we have them. You feeling okay?"

"I'm good, Coach."

He watches me for a minute then walks off. When I turn back around, I sigh and stretch my neck in an attempt to loosen up the tension in my head.

"You good?" Paul finally asks after multiple attempts to get me to talk.

"Nothing." I snap, sitting to pull on my gym shoes.

"That doesn't answer the question I asked." He folds his arms over his chest and blocks the doorway when I try to leave. "We have a game soon and your head isn't in it."

The pounding behind my eyes is so intense I can barely think.

"I need to warm up, move."

Paul looks at me with pursed lips, like he's trying to read my mind.

"Johnson! Albrooke! Stop standing around, let's go!" One of the assistant coaches hollers at us. I lift an eyebrow at him, waiting for him to move.

"You have a headache? Where's Carmichael? You guys have a fight or something?"

"Fuck off, dude." I shove past him and head into the gym area. I climb onto a bike and start with an easy ride to get my muscles loose and warm.

As my heart rate increases, so does the pressure in my head. Jesus fucking Christ. I sit up and press the heels of my palms against my eyes.

"Albrooke." Coach puts his hand on my shoulder. "What's going on? Your head hurts?"

"Fuck," I groan, covering my face. I swear my head is going to explode. I rock back and forth on the bike seat.

"I need an EMT in here!" Coach yells at someone. Doesn't really matter who, it just makes the throbbing worse. It's all I can do not to cry. It hurts so fucking bad. There's nothing but the pain and pressure in my head. *Just make it fucking stop.*

"Come on, off the bike," Coach instructs, lifting an arm to help me stand. I swing my leg over and stumble my way out of the gym and into the hallway where I slide down the wall to sit on the cold floor. The cold feels good so I lay down on my back, wrapping my arm over my face.

"Did you sleep last night? When did the pain start?" Coach is trying to get information but I can barely concentrate on what he's saying.

More footsteps echo through the hallway, hurrying toward me.

"Hey, what's going on?" a new voice asks, kneeling next to me.

The pressure in my head is making my stomach turn.

"I might puke," is the only warning they get before my stomach revolts against what I've eaten today, which wasn't much.

Stomach acid burns my throat and nose, my abdomen clenching painfully, increasing the pressure in my head until I want to scream

"I want him checked again for a concussion. He hit his head last night." That's Coach, I think. "He just had a CT scan, we're waiting on the results."

I manage to roll over onto my hands and knees, hanging my head from my shoulders as I dry heave.

"He was cleared last night?" the new voice asks.

"ER cleared him to play as long as he had another clear

CT today." That's Assistant Coach Scott, he went with me last night. "Said he didn't appear to have a concussion, just the cut on his forehead and a goose egg on the back of his head."

A hand rubs my back a few times. "When did the headache start?"

"I don't know." I croak, dropping back on my knees and burying my head in my arm again. The hallway now smells like vomit, my mouth tastes like it, and I just want the lights to fuck off.

"He said he was fine an hour ago," Scott tells them.

A stretcher is pulled up next to me and I'm helped onto it. As I pass the gym a couple of guys pat my leg, but I'm not sure who it is. I don't want to open my eyes to check. Probably Paul, Brendon, and Carpenter.

I'm loaded into the ambulance and taken to the ER. They give me Tylenol to help with the pain and Zofran to put under my tongue so I don't throw it up. The EMT in the back with me calls the ER to let them know we're coming and he keeps the lights off to help with my pain. The guy sitting in the back with me gets an IV line set and hangs saline. The cold liquid going into my arm makes me shiver.

I think the guy asks me if I want a blanket but I don't answer. I can't think past the throbbing in my head.

Since I got off the bike and my heart rate has come down, the pressure isn't as bad, but it still takes most of my concentration not to scream.

The hospital isn't too busy when I get there so I'm seen pretty fast, tested for a concussion, taken for another CT scan, and discharged with Tylenol and Zofran. I'm told not to play for a minimum of two weeks, at which point I will be reassessed. Lots of rest, no gym or practice until Monday, then start slow.

By the time Coach Scott drops me off at the dorms, I'm

exhausted. Opening my door, I look at Preston's bed and hate that he's not there. Even if he wasn't with his dad, he would be at the game right now.

Needing comfort, I crawl into his bed, hold his pillow against my chest, and pull his blanket over me.

His warm, clean, masculine scent lulls me right to sleep.

I wake with a start, not understanding what woke me. My instincts are telling me to be on alert but there's nothing. I look around the room and it takes me a second to realize why I'm in Preston's bed without him. Sitting up, I check my phone, flinching at the brightness, and see it's twelve fourteen. About the time Preston normally wakes me up screaming.

With a sigh, I lay back down and adjust the pillow under my head. I hate that he's not here, that I don't know what's going on. Why does he keep going with his dad when he obviously doesn't want to? Why did he kiss me before he left after avoiding me for the last month?

Why do I want to hold him anyway?

I get comfortable and close my eyes. Sleep takes me quickly again but fills my head with Preston.

When I wake again, it's morning and the sun is bright in my room. It makes my head hurt. I check the time on my phone and since it's after eight, I get up. My head isn't happy, but I need to eat something before I can take the meds. I take care of business in the bathroom, change into sweats and a hoodie, then pull on socks and my shoes. I don't want to wear sunglasses like a dumbass, so I grab a ball cap to protect my eyes. Since it's almost Thanksgiving, it's cold. Luckily, I grew up in Michigan and am used to it.

As I open the door to leave, Brendon and Paul are standing there, Brendon with his fist lifted to knock.

"Oh, hey. You guys eat yet?" I ask them.

"We were just getting ready to head down. How are you feeling?" Brendon steps back, giving me room to enter the hallway and close my door.

"Tired. I've got a headache but I have to eat before I can take anything." I shrug. "How was the game?"

"We won last night in overtime," Paul informs me and the two of them break into telling me the highlights of the game. Who scored, who had amazing plays, who was a dumb ass.

Standing in front of the breakfast options, I decide on a mostly healthy option: eggs, toast, bacon, an apple, and some oatmeal.

"Why wasn't Carmichael at the game?" Paul asks me when he sits down with his own massive bowl of oatmeal covered in brown sugar.

I shrug, shoving more eggs in my mouth. "I'm not sure, he told me it was cleared with Coach. That's all I know."

"Has to be something serious for that to fly," Brendon says as he sits next to me.

"Coach never mentioned anything?" I verify, pulling out the pain pills and opening my bottle of water.

"Nope. He said you have a concussion and Carmichael wasn't coming so we better get our shit together." Paul shrugs. I snicker at him. Definitely sounds like something Coach would say.

A few of the other guys trickle in and stop at our table to check in with me, patting me on the back and commiserating with me.

"Game of Thrones marathon?" Brendon asks as we put our dishes away.

"The doctor told me not to watch TV or it'll make my head worse, but you guys can. I'll probably just sleep most of the day anyway." I shrug as we walk back to the dorms, the wind biting through my sweats. It's fucking cold out here. I should have grabbed a jacket to throw on over this.

The pounding in my head quiets to a dull ache, so I head to Paul and Brendon's room to hang out.

"Wanna play cards?" Paul pulls a red deck of cards from his desk.

"I think the only thing I remember how to play is Go Fish." I give him a smug look and Brendon laughs.

"Mother fucking Go Fish it is, I guess." He snorts and we sit on his bed facing each other. It's a childs game but being athletes means we're competitive. It doesn't matter what it is, if there's a winner, we each want to be it. There's no friends or allies in competition.

"Okay, but let's make this interesting." Paul shuffles the cards while Brendon and I both look at him, waiting for him to explain.

"Are we putting down pairs or four of a kind?" He looks back and forth between us.

"Four of a kind," Brendon and I say at the same time.

Paul deals the cards and I start by asking Brendon for tens—go fish. We go around and around until Brendon finally gets a set of four to put down.

"So, I obviously like girls, but I'm pretty sure I'll end up marrying a guy." Brendon shrugs and Paul studies him for a minute.

"I can see that." I nod. "I've never dated a girl, but if having a girlfriend is anything like dealing with my sister, I'll pass."

They both laugh and Paul goes next, asking me for the damn tens I've been collecting.

"You're an asshole!" I give him the cards, grumbling about payback being a bitch. He gives me a shit eating grin as he sets down his set of tens. That jackass.

"What about you? You got any specific girl in mind?" I ask him.

Paul's eyes meet mine but it's more like a deer in the headlights than anything else. What the hell is this? He's talked to us about girls before.

After a moment of awkward silence, Paul gets up and digs through his desk until he finds a bottle of rum which he opens and takes a swallow of. He looks at us then takes another drink.

I cock my head at him. "Either there's something you want to tell us or there's something you want to ask one of us. What is it?"

Paul takes his seat again and picks up his cards.

"I think I'm bisexual, maybe pansexual." He looks down at his cards.

Brendon smiles at him, cupping his shoulder. "Alright, welcome to the We Like Dicks Club!"

I snort at him and shove Brendon. "You're an idiot."

"What? You can't be pan and hate dicks." Brendon has the audacity to look at me like I'm the dumb one.

"It doesn't mean he wants to go out and start sucking dick, you moron." I shake my head at Brendon and turn to Paul. "I'm glad you felt comfortable telling us. Please don't kill him after I leave." I nod toward Brendon.

We play on and Brendon sighs heavily when he sets down another set of four. "I don't know what I want to do after college."

"What's your degree in again?" I ask.

"Boring ass business. I didn't know what to put and I panicked." He shrugs.

"Why don't you do something with sports? Coach, journalist, physical therapy? There's a lot of jobs that you can do that keep you around hockey or just sports in general," I offer. "Talk to Coach, he might have some ideas for you."

They are kicking my ass at this child's card game, and I should be a lot more upset about it, but I'm just so damn tired. But even going to bed won't help. I sleep better with Preston wrapped around me and he's not here.

"I uh...I sleep in Preston's bed most nights." The words fall from my mouth before my brain has a chance to filter them.

He's going to kill me for that.

"Yeah, we already assumed you guys were fucking and pretending to hate each other to keep it under wraps." Paul shrugs. "The way he watches you gives it away."

"What? He doesn't watch me." Now I'm confused. "And we've had sex once."

Brendon busts out with laughter. "Dude. He watches you like a hawk. Did you not realize he fucked up the guy who tripped you during the game? He's crazy protective of you. Every game, he retaliates against anyone who touches you."

I narrow my eyes at Brendon. *That can't be true.*

"You're crazy. He does *not* do that." I shake my head at him.

"I've left practices with bruises from that big bastard because I shoved you into the boards," Paul scoffs.

"What? Are you serious?" I look back and forth between the two of them. "How have I not seen that? Why haven't you guys said anything before now?"

They both look at me like I've grown a second head.

"Probably because you were avoiding him like he was a leper?" Brendon reaches for his water bottle and takes a drink.

Have I been trying so hard to ignore him that I've missed shit? Has he been trying to show me that he cares and I've not seen it?

This is making my head hurt more.

Hesitant excitement flutters in my stomach when it shouldn't. The guy is difficult, has anger issues, and is about as cuddly as a cactus, but I want him anyway. I want to be his safe space, to see a part of him that no one else sees.

"Duuuuude," Brendon whines, "Stop smiling like that. I think I'm gonna be sick."

I shove him so he falls into Paul who flushes slightly. *Oh, that's what's happening here.* I cover my smile with my hand and drop my gaze to my lap so he doesn't see me staring.

Clearing my throat, I look at my cards. "Okay, whose turn is it?"

"It's cool you think you still stand a chance of winning." Brendon sits up and looks at his cards. "Fives, P man?"

Paul shakes his head, still pink in the cheeks, but Brendon doesn't seem to notice.

The game continues and by the end of it, I'm exhausted. Brendon kicked our asses and somehow, I'm pretty sure he cheated. How would one even cheat at Go Fish? Doesn't matter, I'm sticking to my story.

"Alright, guys, I'm going to crash for a while. I'm tired." I stand and stretch, pat Paul on the shoulder, and head to my dorm room.

It's about two o'clock and if last time is anything to go by, Preston won't be home for another few hours.

Being back in my room has the darkness of the situation weighing heavy on my shoulders again. It's like being pulled down under the surface of the water. Every once in a while, you manage to break through and get a breath just to be pulled back under.

I lay down on his bed again, wanting to feel close to him, and smell him on my skin. What is his dad doing to him? Why does he keep going with him? He's twenty-one, an adult.

Settling on my side with his pillow under my head, I inhale a deep breath of him and fall asleep.

CHAPTER 26

preston

The noise in my ears makes me jerk. *Fuck.*

Now my heart is racing and I'm breathing like I just finished a run. My skin is covered in goosebumps and my teeth are chattering. I'm so tired of being cold. And hungry. And tired.

There's an IV in my arm, dripping caffeine straight into my veins to make sure I'm unable to sleep. I now have two new cuts with stitches on my stomach. Once again, I'm standing in front of the mirror, staring at my bleary-eyed face.

The door opens to the bathroom and if I wasn't so tired, I would probably flinch.

How long have I been here? Is it still Saturday?

"Time for a shower."

I'm too exhausted to hide my reaction and whimper.

"Pull yourself together. No one wants a weak man." Father comes to me, disconnects the IV and removes it from my arm. He puts a bandage on it and wraps it to keep pressure on it until it stops bleeding.

"Strip. Time to shower. Let's go." I force my body to move. My knees want to give out, but by sheer force of will I stay standing. Pulling the compression shorts off is a battle that takes longer than he wants but I can only move so fast at this point. I splay both hands on the cold black tile under the shower head and my father reaches in to turn on the cold water. It hits my skin like a thousand needles, stealing the air from my lungs. I can't stop the trembling or the flutter of my muscles desperately trying to warm me.

My feet go numb, turning blue and purple.

"Wash, let's go. The longer you stand there, the longer this will last." With shaking hands and chattering teeth, I reach for the soap pump. Thank God I don't have to pick it up, I would probably drop it.

Once I get my body soaped up, I step back under the water to rinse it off. I shout as the cold once again stings my skin, hating that this is my fucking life. That this is what I have to do to keep my sister safe.

Only a few more months.

Eventually I'm clean enough to make my father happy and I'm able to dry off and get dressed. My clothes have been cleaned and pressed, because God forbid I leave looking disheveled.

"If you would behave, I wouldn't have to do this, Charles."

The words I've always said after correction fall from my lips on reflex. "Thank you, Father."

I do my best to hide my exhaustion, the shaking of my hands, and blink to clear my vision as I ride the elevator down to the lobby. Father's driver is waiting for me, the door open and ready for me to enter.

Not yet. Don't relax yet. Just breathe.

I don't remember the drive back to the dorms, back to Jeremy, but I'm quickly losing my control. In the elevator to the dorm, I lean heavily against the wall, needing the bar to hold on to so I don't drop to the floor. I stumble down the hallway to my door and pray that it's unlocked. If it's locked, I'm fucked.

My breathing is too fast, the breakdown that always follows these corrections taking over my brain and shutting down any logic. Turning the handle, it's fucking locked and I damn near cry.

Raising my hand, I bang on the door. "Jeremy!"

I hit the door again and again.

"Jeremy!"

The door opens and I stagger into the room, slamming my shoulder into my dresser.

"Whoa," Jeremy holds his hands up like he would catch me if I fell. "What's wrong? Are you drunk? Did you take something?"

"No," I manage between breaths that are coming too fast. They're taking over and there's nothing I can do about it. I'm so tired of fighting.

A tear trickles down my cheek.

"What happened? What did your dad do?" Jeremy wraps one hand around the back of my neck, the other holds my wrist.

I can't speak, can't admit to the humiliation of my failures out loud. All I can do is shake my head and pull up my shirt. Show him how much of a fuck up I am. How broken. Useless.

Confusion creases the skin between his eyebrows as he drops his gaze to look at my exposed stomach.

"What is this?" His eyes meet mine in the dim light. "Are these cuts?"

Tears fall freely down my face now with my biggest

secret exposed. I've never shown anyone the tally marks of my failure. My eyes slam closed, not able to look at him anymore. Not able to see the disgust I know is coming on his face. He's come to mean too fucking much to me. Somehow, in the weeks we've spent in this fucking shoebox of a room, I've learned to trust him and didn't even realize it. Yet, I've done nothing but hurt him.

I drop to my knees on the thin, shitty carpet. The ache radiates through my knees but it's a dull roar in comparison to the pain in my heart.

"Jesus, Preston!" He drops down in front of me, cupping my face in his hands. His palms are so fucking warm. "Why are you so cold?"

"I don—" I shake my head, not able to speak as my throat constricts.

I'm too tired to hold it back anymore, so I don't. I let my body fall apart, hyperventilating, tears flowing down my face, shaking and weak. The walls I keep surrounding my heart have been demolished, leaving me vulnerable and defenseless.

Reaching for him, I pull him against me, burying my face in the crook of his neck, allowing myself to be comforted by him. My arms wrap around his waist until he's sitting on my thighs and his arms are wrapped around my shoulders. Once he's settled, my hands dig into his back as I find his shoulders to grip on to, needing something to ground me. Needing *him* to ground me.

For once, I allow myself to break in front of someone. I allow myself to be comforted by another person. For the first time since my mother died, I have someone who cares enough to see that I need it.

Sitting there on the floor, I shake, tears pouring from my eyes as I sob, and my hands hold him so hard there's no way he won't have bruises.

"You're okay, I've got you," he repeats, holding me just as tightly as I hold him. We rock on the floor, and I don't know if he's moving us or if I am, but it doesn't matter.

"Oh shit," someone says behind me. Some part of me recognizes the voice but I can't focus on it enough to put a name to it. I'm too far gone, too broken. Jeremy tenses against me, a hand lifting off the back of my head. I can't stand the disconnect, but I don't have the words to say that, so I sink my teeth into the side of his neck. He sucks in a breath and shudders against me.

If I wasn't so fucking tired, so fucking beaten, my dick would like his reaction, but there isn't enough energy left in my body to do anything about it. Jeremy's hand cups the back of my head again and I relax my jaw, no longer digging my teeth in but not pulling them off his skin either.

I'm so tired.

My eyes close and my body starts to relax as the realization that he has me cuts through the panic. I don't know who's behind me, but I know Jeremy won't let them touch me.

The door closes quietly, and I lean forward, putting Jeremy's back on the carpet and settling on top of him. I rub my face against his neck, soothing myself with him. With his scent, his warmth, his comfort. And I fall asleep.

Why can't I move? I have to move. Run. Hide.

All I can hear are his footsteps and my ragged breathing.

My arms are heavy, weighed down by something I can't see. Have I been drugged?

Father never drugs me, too aware of the drug testing the team does.

He's coming. I have to run.

Run.

Hide.

He's going to find you. Hurt you. Again.

Terror grips me by the throat as he gets closer.

I'm frozen in place by my fear. I know he's going to hurt me again but I can't stop it. He's bigger than me, stronger than me.

He's trying to make you better.

The bedroom door opens with a bang against the wall and I scream. Loud and long, blood curdling.

"Strong boys don't scream like scared little girls, man up." He's angry.

I messed up. Let my anger consume me and left Jeremy unprotected to get hurt during the game. *But he's mine.*

My fingers ache but I can't see them.

Father comes toward me with a cattle prod and zaps me on the back. I scream again, crying from the pain.

"I will not allow you to tarnish this family's name, you worthless little shit." Spit hits my cheek as he speaks, his fingers gripping at my arms so hard I'm sure to have bruises. Why does he hurt me? No one else on the team has parents who hurt them. Why am I such a bad kid?

"Preston."

Jeremy? Why is he here?

"Preston, wake up."

What?

There are hands on me, but they aren't hurting me. I don't understand.

With a jolt, I pop my eyes open and jerk up off the floor, expecting to find myself in my childhood bedroom, my father standing over me with a fucking cattle prod, but I'm not. I'm in my dorm room and he isn't here.

"Hey, look at me."

My eyes scan the space, watching for the shadows to move, for my father to jump out at me.

"Preston," Jeremy says my name again, reaching up to cup my face, but I grab his arm before he makes contact and stare at him.

"You're okay now."

I force myself to swallow past the constriction in my throat.

"Why are we on the floor?"

He watches me for a second before answering me. "Well, you laid on top of me and passed out. If you don't mind, I need to pee actually."

I sit up, giving him room to get up and go to the bathroom. He climbs to his feet and disappears quickly, shutting the door behind him. Sitting back against the bed, I scrub a hand over my face.

What the hell did I do? I wrack my brain for what happened after I left the penthouse but it's all blurry. *Did I show him the scars?* God damn it. He can't know about them. What does he think about me now, knowing I'm fucking useless?

CHAPTER 27

jeremy

He flinches when I open the door. I'm not sure he realizes he did it and I don't know if that's better or worse.

Does he need space? He's not very forthcoming about himself and I don't want to push him, but I have so many questions.

Starting with what the actual fuck?

Does his dad cut him up or does he do that himself and his dad stitches it when he goes too deep? There are two cuts on his stomach with four or five stitches in each one. It was hard to see in the dark last night, but he definitely has stitches. His skin is covered in scars. That's not normal.

Leaning against the doorframe, I hiss when one of my new bruises is pushed on. During his nightmare, Preston grabbed my arms and I now have fingerprints on my biceps.

Preston is sitting with his back against his bed, his suit a rumpled mess from sleeping in it. The expression on his face gives nothing away and he's put his wall back up to keep me out. I guess I don't blame him but it hurts just the same.

"Do you want to talk about it?" *It* could be so many things. The game he got kicked out of, going with his dad, the scars he showed me last night.

"No." His voice is rough from sleep and dejection at the same time.

"We missed workout this morning," I start. Maybe he just wants to talk about something normal. "Paul let Coach know that you weren't feeling well but you'll have to go see one of the team doctors."

Pulling my phone from my pocket, I check the time. "I need to go down and get checked out anyway so you can come with me, if you want."

Preston's head snaps up, gaze trained one me. "What are they checking you for? Watching your stitches?" He pulls himself up off the floor and stalks the few feet between us, grips my chin and turns my head to get a better look at my forehead.

"I have a concussion. I can start workouts today but I have to be watched by a trainer."

He pulls my face back to face him, concern and frustration in his expression. "Concussion? Are you okay?"

I shrug, butterflies flutter in my stomach from his concern. "I'm fine."

His thumb brushes along my eyebrow closest to the cut.

"It's my fault." His words are so quiet I don't think he meant for me to hear them.

"It's not. Shit happens all the time. You know that."

He shakes his head in disagreement but doesn't voice it, just holds my face. His gaze flicks between the wound and my lips, like he wants to kiss me but is afraid I won't let him.

Reaching for the back of his neck, I pull his mouth to mine. I don't care that it's morning and both of our breaths could peel paint. I want this connection to him. To show him I don't think less of him because of his father, that it changes nothing, that I want more of him.

He kisses me gently, like he's afraid I'll break. Or maybe he's afraid he will break. It's a different side of him, one that throws me off way more than the aggression. This morning, we both need to know we're okay. That I've got him and he's got me.

Preston's fingers dig into me, owning me, despite the gentle press of his lips. Like he's fighting something inside of himself. Is he fighting to let himself need me? To accept the comfort I freely offer?

He sucks on my bottom lip, brushing my skin with his teeth, with the threat of pain.

My hands hang at my sides, clenching and opening. I don't know what to do with them. Will he let me touch him or will he shove me away? Deciding to take a chance, I place my hands on his, and slowly work my way up to his shoulders, careful to read the way his body tenses and stop when he does. He doesn't stop kissing me, slow and careful, exploring and lazy.

When my hands get to his shoulders, I start back down to his hands and he relaxes, pulling me flush against him. His hard-on is notched against mine but we don't grind against each other.

Preston rests his forehead against mine, releasing my lips. His eyes are closed and he's panting slightly.

"I don't know how to touch without fucking." His confession breaks my heart. Has no one just held him because he needed it? Offered a hug?

I wrap my arms around his neck and bring him into me. "It's okay, I do."

He wraps his arms around me, splaying his hands on my back as he holds me tightly against him.

I smile when he buries his face in my neck and inhales deeply, some of the tension in his shoulders relaxing. I want to be his safe space. Everyone deserves to have that. I had my parents and I have Paul and Brendon, but who does he have?

A knock on the door has him jumping back away from me. He drops his head, rubs his forehead and takes a calming breath. I don't think he's embarrassed to be caught with me, but it's an affect of whatever happened this weekend.

"You're okay, Preston. You're safe here."

His Adam's apple bobs as he swallows. He glances quickly at me before turning to dig in his dresser, then shuts himself into the bathroom.

With a sigh, I open the door to find Paul and Brendon.

"Hey, guys." I feel weird not moving out of the way to let them in but I'm not sure if Preston wants anyone else to see him right now. It's bad enough Brendon saw him mid-meltdown last night and Paul saw him passed out on me this morning.

"Coach wants Preston to check in and I told him you were really tired this morning, so I convinced you to go back to sleep. I don't think he believed me." Paul leans against the wall next to the door.

"Thanks, I appreciate it."

The bathroom door opens and I turn to watch Preston, mask back on his face, and the muscle in his jaw jumping as he sees who is at the door.

"Still hates me then?" Brendon says more to me than Preston, but he hears the question.

Preston pulls on his socks and shoes then steps up behind me, wrapping his arm around my waist, snakes it under my shirt, and splays his hand low on my abdomen. My eyes damn near bug out of my head at the unexpected touch, especially in front of others.

Paul chuckles uncomfortably, flicking his gaze between Preston and Brendon. Preston's fingers drag slowly along the edge of my pants along the sensitive skin between my hip bones. My dick jumps to attention, making itself very well-known between the four of us in these damn sweatpants.

Brendon narrows his eyes, locked in a death glare with Preston for a tense minute, before a big smile splits his face.

"No worries, big guy, we're good. He's all yours." Brendon pats Preston's bicep. "I'm not his type anyway. I'm too nice."

My face heats as I stare at him. That did not need to be said out loud. Jesus. I close my eyes and pinch my lips together while I try not to imagine what Paul is thinking right now.

Preston snorts behind me. "Remember to keep your hands to yourself or you'll be the next one on concussion protocol."

"Is it possible for you *not* to be a pretentious dick for like ten seconds?" Brendon tosses back.

"Okay, that's enough dick measuring." Paul stands upright and pushes Brendon down the hallway. "I also didn't need to know how rough Jeremy likes it." He looks at Brendon like he's remembering something. "How have I never seen bruises on you? You never wear a shirt in our room."

Brendon smirks, looking over his shoulder at me then at Preston, who is still pressed against me.

"I rarely bottom, my guy."

Paul stops walking mid-step, spins to look at me then back at Brendon, then back at me. "Wait. Really?"

Fucking Christ. I don't think it's possible for my face to get any hotter. Why am I embarrassed? I'm a gay man. Sex feels fucking amazing. I don't have the brain power for this today. My head already hurts.

"Yeah, as much as I am loving this conversation, I have shit to do." I push Preston back into our room so I can change and head down to the rink.

"There's nothing to be ashamed about." Preston watches me pull my shirt and sweatpants off, his gaze setting off goosebumps like he's actually touched me. "I don't understand the kink-shaming people do."

"I'm not really ashamed. I like what I like, it's whatever, but I don't want it discussed in the hallway where anyone can overhear it." I shove my feet through my workout shorts and grab a sleeveless shirt.

"It won't happen again. I was making a point."

I turn on him then, frustrated that I'm embarrassed and turned on. That he's bouncing between being real with me and hiding behind this fucking mask.

"Yeah, your point was 'don't touch what's mine' but you haven't even talked to *me* about it." I stab myself in the chest with my finger. Shaking my head, I hold my hands up in front of me to stop him from speaking. "You know what, I don't want to have this conversation right now. I have to go find Coach."

"Don't." Preston barks the word and crowds me against my dresser when I turn to find socks. "You are mine and I don't share." His hands grip my hips. "No one touches you but me."

"You're going to spend a lot of time in the penalty box with that type of mentality. Hockey isn't known for being a hands-off sport." I'm only sort of kidding.

He drags in an aggravated breath. "I know."

He kisses the back of my neck and backs off so I can finish getting ready. I make myself and Preston a quick protein shake and we head down to the rink. He disappears into Coach's office and I head over to medical.

Doctor Butler waves a hand at me. "How are you feeling this morning?"

"A little better. No meds this morning, so that's something."

He has me sit on an exam table and walks behind me to check the swelling on the back of my head. Laying on the hard floor was not my favorite but luckily Brendon came in and checked on me last night and grabbed a pillow for me.

I hiss and jerk away from him when he hits a sore spot.

"Sorry about that. Still pretty tender then?" I nod at his question. "Swelling is going down but we'll keep an eye on it." He pats my shoulder. "Okay, let's do some easy exercises."

We move to the physical therapy part of the room and start with some elastic bands.

Preston comes in and joins us part way through the workout.

"Mister Carmichael, how are you feeling? I heard you weren't doing well this morning." Doctor Butler asks him.

"Sore, but I'll be fine." He's stiff and is moving like he's in pain or trying to avoid pain. It's not normal for him, I just hope no one else notices and asks him about it. I'm distracted by watching him and end up snapping myself with one of the bands.

"Albrooke, you alright?" The doctor comes over to check on me, eyeing the welt I now have on my thigh. Preston lifts an eyebrow at me, then licks his bottom lip when I pull my shorts up to look at the red welt.

"I'm fine." I flush but continue on with my workout.

I go through the steps he wants me to take and am much more tired afterward than I expected. I'm used to working out every day but Sunday and practicing twice a day during the week, except game days, during the season. These light, easy movements should not tire me out.

Even though I'm exhausted, I shower, get changed, and grab my stuff for classes when we get back to the dorm.

Swinging my backpack over my shoulder, Preston steps out of the bathroom and crosses his arms over his chest, standing in my way.

"Where do you think you're going?"

"To the ballet." I deadpan. "Where the hell does it look like I'm going?"

I try to brush past him but he doesn't let me.

"You need to rest."

"You're one to talk!"

He cocks his head at me. "I'm not the one with a concussion. I'll live. I'm used to this." The muscle in his cheek jumps as he clenches his jaw.

"And what is it you're used to?"

His face hardens, back straightening, shoulders squaring. I sigh at the response.

"Right." I nod and try to get past him again. "I need to go to class so I don't fall behind."

"You're exhausted, you need to rest. Do you actually think you'll remember anything that is said in class today?" Preston demands.

Why do I like it when he gets worked up? When he uses his full height and the broad expanse of his chest to try to intimidate me? He absolutely *can* fuck me up. Hell, I'm currently sporting bruises from him that did not happen during sex.

That thought has my dick thickening in my jeans. Damn it. Neither of us is mentally stable enough for sex right now. He's trying to hold himself together, falling back behind his walls to protect himself, and I'm pretty sure he'll re-concuss me if he fucks me right now.

Doesn't mean I don't want to though.

"Keep looking at me with 'fuck me' eyes and I'll do

exactly that. I'm not above using you to make myself feel better and wearing you out until you can't stand." He crowds my space, the air between us charged with sexual tension.

"If I have to rest, so do you." I watch his mouth as I bite on my lower lip.

"Stop. Looking. At. Me. Like. That." He grinds out. "My control is shit right now."

"Lay with me?"

He takes my backpack and sets it on the floor then nods toward his bed. Preston lays down with his back to the wall, so I kick my shoes off and lay down with my back to him. Besides last night, this is the only way we've slept. He wraps himself around me, buries his face in my hair or in my neck, and pulls me back against him.

My ass is against his hips, his dick perking up as I adjust myself to get comfortable. I know I shouldn't, but I rub my ass against him on purpose, just to mess with him.

"Jeremy." My name is a warning on his lips and it makes me smile.

"Yes?"

He grips my hip, holding me still. "Knock it off."

I chuckle but settle against him and drag in a deep breath of him. He relaxes, draping his arm over my waist. Comfortable and warm, I quickly lose my battle with sleep.

CHAPTER 28

jeremy

Every day I get a little more energy back. For ten days I wasn't allowed on the ice, mostly because putting the helmet on made me cringe, so I sat in the stands and did homework to catch up on the days I missed.

I'm finally allowed back on the ice for drills but no full contact yet. A few more days and another CT scan before I'm back at a hundred percent. Tomorrow is game day and I'm hoping to play. We'll see what the doctors say.

In the locker room after practice, everyone is getting changed back and bullshitting.

"It's Thanksgiving, where are we going to eat?" Brendon asks, rubbing his stomach.

Preston comes back from the toilet stalls changed with his workout clothes in his hand.

"You have family shit tonight?" Paul nods at Preston, who stiffens at the question. I didn't think about his dad wanting to see him or demanding to see him for the holiday.

"No." The word is full of malice, but Paul ignores it.

"You should come out with us then. We'll probably end up hitting a diner or ordering pizza." When Preston opens his mouth to talk shit about pizza, Paul holds up his hands. "I know, I know. Pizza is the worst, but most pizza places can make salads so you can eat your sad Thanksgiving Day salad while the rest of us are fat and happy with bread and melted cheese."

I laugh at the exchange and Preston turns on me.

"I'm going back to the room," he grumbles as he stalks past me.

Paul shakes his head in disapproval and I get up to follow after Preston. He's coming one way or the other because I have a surprise for him. I mean, it's not really my surprise but I know it's happening so...I'm taking credit.

Jogging to catch up, I reach for Preston's wrist to pull him to a stop. He spins on me, shoving me against the wall but cupping the back of my head in his hand so the healing bruise doesn't hit the concrete.

"Now we're talking." I wag my eyebrows at him, staring at his mouth.

"I'm not going. Don't ask."

I look down the hallway to make sure we don't have an audience then smile up at him.

"You are coming with us. You want to know why?" He lifts an eyebrow at me. "Because if you don't, Brendon will flirt with me, sit next to me at the table, maybe put his hand on my leg or around the back of my chair." With every word his posture grows increasingly tense until he looks ready to snap. His hand slides from the back of my head to my throat and he jerks me forward, growling through his teeth when he speaks.

"If he so much as looks at you longer than three seconds, I'll break his fucking nose."

"How will you know if you're not there?"

Am I riling him up on purpose? Yes. Am I risking bodily harm in doing so? Yes. Do I regret it? Not a fucking chance. I love that possessive streak he gets when it comes to me.

This time, *he* looks down the hallway, steps back to grab my hand, and pulls me along until he finds a janitor's closet. Preston shoves me inside and closes the door behind him.

He shoves me against the shelves, once again wrapping his hand around my throat. "You aren't going anywhere until your stomach is full of my cum. On your knees."

With my eyes locked on his, I unbuckle his pants and reach into his underwear to pull out his cock. It's almost at full mast so I give him a few rhythmic, squeezing strokes. Using his dick as a handle, I make him back up a step so I can drop to a crouch and suck him into my mouth.

His fingers grab onto the shelves until his knuckles are white. I use my hand and mouth in tandem, my hand rotating with every stroke while my mouth sucks and bobs on him. He hits the back of my throat and I gag, my throat contracting around him making him groan.

"Fuck." He moans when I suck his balls into my mouth, jacking him with slow, strong strokes. "I'm going to fucking come."

Pride fills my head at how quickly I was able to get him to that edge. Wrapping my lips around him again, I suck him hard, swirling my tongue around his head then taking him as deep as I can again. Over and over until he's bucking his hips into me, grunting and moaning. His cock throbs on my tongue, the first salty drops of precum making my mouth water, then cum floods my mouth. I swallow over and over again until I'm no longer drowning in cum.

I suck on his head once more to make sure I've got it all and he hisses, pulling back. Leaning forward, I kiss the tip of his cock with my eyes latched on to his then stand up with a smirk on my face.

Preston grabs the back of my neck and kisses me, tasting himself on my lips, and on my tongue. He owns me with this kiss. His tongue duels with mine, mouths crashing together with bruising force. Before I'm ready for it, he releases me and steps back, shoving his dick back into his pants and fixing his clothes.

"How am I supposed to eat dinner now?" I raise an eyebrow at him.

"Less room for pizza and lower in calories," he tosses back and opens the door. Paul and Brendon are standing there with shit eating grins on their faces. *Oh, fuck me.*

"Need to clean up a mess?" Brendon asks Preston.

"Fuck off, Oiler. Find your own closet hook up."

Brendon's smile turns to a self-satisfied grin. "Who says I've never fucked in that closet?"

I swear to God, if he insinuates that we fucked in there, I'm going to knock both of their heads together.

"We did not fuck in there. Knock it off." I shove Preston out of the way so I can leave the space that smells like floor wax, urinal cakes, and Pine-Sol.

Preston walks behind me so he can watch to make sure Brendon doesn't flirt with me or touch me. God forbid my best friend touch me.

When we step out of the rink, it's trying to snow. Tiny little flakes are falling from the sky but melting the second they touch anything. Despite it being cold as fuck outside, we walk off campus to a diner with a sign that says it's serving Thanksgiving dinner. Trudging inside, the heat of the place is a slap in the face after the biting cold that turned our skin red.

The inside looks like every diner in America. Booths along the windows, a bar across the aisle where you can see the cooks on the other side of the wall through the ticket window. It smells like fried food and coffee and feels homey. The white board by the cash register says “Specials” in big swirly letters and a breakdown of what comes in the turkey day meal. Roasted turkey, stuffing, mashed potatoes and gravy, cranberry sauce, and a roll.

“Just four of ya?” A middle-aged woman with graying brown hair and a waitress's uniform asks us as we wait.

I scan the tables looking for my surprise but don’t see who I’m looking for. Nerves flutter in my stomach but I’m not sure if it’s for what is about to happen or how Preston will react to it.

I hold up my hand behind to say five and she nods at me then looks down the row of booths before she points. “Corner booth down there, I’ll be right there!”

We make our way down the aisle, pulling our jackets off to lay them on the seat in the middle and slide in. I’m at one end with Preston next to me, then Paul, then Brendon at the other end.

“I’m getting the special, what about you guys?” I look around the table. Preston makes a disgusted face and shakes his head.

“That’s loaded in carbs, you’ll be fat and slow tomorrow.”

“Everyone is eating like that tonight, which means we’ll all be slow tomorrow. That’s the best part.” Brendon scoffs. “Lighten up, dude. Live a little.”

“I’ll be playing in peak condition.”

I sigh and roll my eyes, choosing to ignore Preston’s preaching about food.

Under the table, my knee is bouncing. I’m excited about his surprise but I want to get this part over with. Is he going to get pissed and leave? Is he going to fight me or shut me out?

The waitress comes to the table with menus and glasses of ice water.

"Here you are, I'll come back in a few minutes to take your order. Do you want something else to drink?" She looks at us expectantly.

Since I'm already annoying Preston with my food choices, I decide to stick with water. Surprisingly, so does everyone else.

The bell on the front door jingles and I tense, wanting to turn around and look but not wanting Preston to realize I'm waiting for someone. Paul and Brendon both look over, raise their eyebrows, then nod slightly at me.

She's here. Lily's here. What am I about to do?

My chest feels like there's a weight on it, crushing me into the seat back. Is Preston going to hate me? What if he doesn't see his sister unless it's for a really good fucking reason? Will he blame her being here on me?

She messaged me *yesterday* on Facebook saying she was flying in and wanted to surprise Preston. I just helped her get a hotel room set up since I know he isn't going to want her to witness his nightmares. Fuck. What have I done?

"Excuse me a second." My voice sounds weird to my own ears but I'm hoping Preston is too busy glaring at Brendon to notice. When I stand up and turn around, the girl in question spots me and a thousand-watt smile brightens her face. She waves really quickly and hurries over.

I smile, but it's tense and unsure.

The petite girl bounces over, excitement radiating off her short frame. Her hair is the same jet black as Preston's but curly and her eyes are lighter, not as haunted or closed off. She emits happiness and innocence and all things good. I wish I could bottle up her energy to share with Preston. Her features are softer, rounder, maybe. Definitely more feminine than his sharp jaw and high cheekbones. I'm betting she's a good mixture of her parents.

She slips past me and slides into the booth next to Preston. Immediately, his head swings toward her. Shock, then confusion slide over his face before that cold mask slams into place and he's looking around the place like he expects the boogey man to jump out and get him.

"Lillian, what are you doing here? Is Father with you?"

His words hold no warmth or excitement at seeing his sister. He's not cold or hurtful either, but he's definitely on guard.

Is he looking for his dad? Is he worried his dad will hurt Lily?

She cocks her head and stares at him.

"I haven't seen you in months and that's the greeting I get?"

Paul and Brendon are trying not to smile as this five-foot nothing girl chastises her six five, pain in the ass, brother.

Preston shakes himself and takes a deep breath. "I'm sorry, hello, Lily. I'm glad to see you. You caught me by surprise."

A smile lifts her pink, gloss-covered lips again and she reaches for a hug. Preston is stiff as he wraps his arm around her. I shift closer to the booth and my movement catches his attention. For just a moment there's a storm in his eyes. I don't know if he's angry or what, but something is definitely not right.

Paul and Brendon scoot over to make room for me to sit down since I'm now just standing awkwardly next to the booth. I start to sit on the cracked vinyl seat when Preston makes a noise and I freeze, flicking my gaze to him. He's staring at me, unblinking, mouth set in a thin line.

"Uh, can I get in?" I nod to the center of the booth and step back to make room for the guys to get out.

They snicker as they slide out of the way, and I sit next to Preston. His hand finds my leg and he squeezes the inside of my thigh. My dick doesn't mind the attention at all but this is not the place for it. Springing a woody in this diner is not on my list of things to do today.

Lily breaks into a story about her friends that I can barely follow. Preston seems to know all the players and looks like he understands what's happening.

"So, pretty girl, how old are you?" Brendon asks Lily and I choke on my water.

Preston's gaze snaps to Brendon, who is already on his shit list. "Young enough for me to go to jail for murdering you."

Lily rolls her eyes and waves a hand like he's exaggerating. "I'm seventeen, I'm a senior this year."

Preston grabs his phone and sends off some text messages then slides it back in his pocket.

"Does Father know you're here?" he asks as the waitress brings us food. Everyone got the special except Preston, who is eating grilled chicken and steamed vegetables.

I know Preston has serious issues with his dad, the guy is not right in the head, but what is Preston worried about? That he'll have to see his dad or that his dad will hurt Lily?

She shrugs. "I didn't tell him but I don't know if anyone else did."

"Your driver didn't and where is your guard?" he demands.

"He's in the car in the parking lot. Since I'm with you, he was fine staying put."

"Wait, you have a bodyguard?" Paul interrupts.

"Yes," Preston and Lily say at the same time, not interrupting their conversation.

"Where are you staying?"

"Embassy Suites." She points at me and my eyes widen. "Jeremy recommended it."

Oh fuck.

"Oh, did he?" His tone says he's not happy with me. "How kind of him."

Brendon chuckles. "You can sleep in our room again tonight."

Preston lifts an eyebrow at him. "Only if you want your room to reek of rotting fish."

"Hey," Paul says around a mouthful of mashed potatoes. "That's my room too, asshole!"

"And set on fire."

Lily rolls her eyes and shakes her head. "Jesus, Preston, chill out."

Preston's hand flexes on my thigh and the fork I have halfway to my mouth freezes. He's going to kill me.

"You forget how to eat there, J Bear?" Brendon smirks at me.

"J Bear?" Preston growls.

Brendon is fucking with Preston on purpose. It's both amusing and not. Lucky me.

"You know, I've known him a lot longer than you have. We have *all* kinds of history."

Lily is now looking between Brendon, Preston, and me. Great.

"Oh, snap." She sits back in her seat and drinks her water. "Did you guys used to hook up?"

"On the regular, Little Bit." He sends her a panty melting smile and Preston growls, slamming his fork on the table and rattling the dishes.

"Don't look at her like that."

Paul leans toward me, looking like he wants to tell me something, so I mimic the movement.

"Don't you fucking dare." Preston's words are quiet but

deadly. He's being pushed to his limit and is going to snap. I sit back in my seat and continue eating my dinner. I should probably be bothered by Preston bossing me around, but I find it more amusing than anything else.

And sexy as fuck.

I make it about halfway through the plate before I put my fork and napkin down.

"Are you feeling okay?" Paul asks me, eyeing my plate with food left on it.

"Yeah, I ate before we got here." I rub my stomach and put my arm across the back of the seat behind Preston, who snorts.

"Oh, so it's Preston who's the screamer? Good to know." Paul sits back and leans a little closer to Brendon.

"I told you Jay doesn't moan like that." Brendon knocks Paul's arm with the back of his hand.

Lily's face screws up like she smells something bad. "Oh, ew. Thanks for that."

"I swear to fuck, I'll make sure your next meal comes through a fucking straw." Preston snaps and Brendon laughs.

"Alright, alright. Chill out, caveman."

I pull my phone from my pocket to check the time. "We should all get back to the dorms, we have a game tomorrow."

"Lily, do you have a ticket?" Preston turns back to his sister.

"Yup, I have a ticket." She smiles at her big brother, obviously proud of him. "I'm excited to see you play in person again!"

He's worried about his dad being at the game, if I had to guess. Does he come to all the home games or just random ones?

His hand flexes on my leg again and I slide my hand on top of his.

Lily grabs Preston's arm and squeezes with a big smile on her face. "I'm so excited to be here!"

"How long are you here for? Will we have time to show you around Denver?" Brendon leans on the table closer to her.

"I wish. I fly back Sunday morning." She pretends to pout at him.

"Good. Any longer than that and I'd have to find a time and place to bury his body." Preston shoos us from the booth and reaches into his back pocket. "Let's get out of here."

We collect our jackets and slide out of the booth. Preston demands to pay for dinner and most of us are broke ass college students, so we don't argue. While his back is turned, Lily is putting her number into Brendon's and Paul's phones. No good is going to come of that, but I'm playing dumb and not saying anything about it.

CHAPTER 29

jeremy

A yell wakes me. It's dark in our room and the fingers on my arm are digging in so hard I hiss. My arms are covered in finger bruises from the nightmares that wake Preston every fucking night.

"Preston," My voice is gravelly with sleep, but sometimes I get lucky and it's enough to calm him. Tonight is not a lucky night. "Preston, wake up."

Rolling toward him, it breaks my heart to see tears on his face, his eyes clenched shut and his mouth open on a silent scream this time.

I reach for his arm to rub his skin but he swings at me, punching me in the chest.

It's not a particularly hard hit, but it surprises me. He has these nightmares every night but he's never swung at me before.

"Hey, Preston." I call his name calmly. "Wake up, babe."

I reach for him again, this time to cup his cheek, but he

jerks back and shoves my hand away, slapping at me. Jesus. This is a bad one.

His hand snakes out and grabs my arm, squeezing it like he's trying to pop it. It fucking hurts and I'm done fucking around.

Pulling his hand off of me, I quickly wrap my arms around him, pulling his face into my neck while he fights me off, yelling and crying.

"Preston, you're okay." I have to hold him as tightly as I can without hurting him. His hands slap at me, pushing and shoving to get away, but I don't let go. Just hold him and talk to him.

"Wake up, Preston. You're okay."

I wrap a leg over his hip and roll him so I'm on top of him, afraid he's going to hurt himself.

I press kisses to his forehead, hair, temple, any part of him I can reach.

Finally, he gasps awake, his movements freeze, and I relax.

"Hey." I'm panting when I pull back enough to look at him. "You're okay."

His eyes scan the room, avoiding me while he gets control of his breathing. He shoves a hand through his now-sweaty hair.

I shift to get off him but he grabs my thigh to keep me still.

"I—" he starts but cuts himself off, obviously not comfortable with whatever he needs to say.

"What do you need?"

I sit back on his hips and feel his dick rock hard under my ass. *Oh.*

I rock back on him and he clenches his jaw.

"You need to fuck?" I grind my ass over him again. "You don't have to ask, I'm always down."

His eyes finally meet mine, the hard steel of his dick letting me know I'm on a ride that I will definitely feel later.

Dragging my teeth over my bottom lip, I nod to him.

He shoves me off of him and I fall onto the floor with a loud thud. I don't have time to think about it before Preston is on me, flipping me onto my stomach and ripping at my clothes.

He straddles my thighs, shoving my pants and underwear down, and slaps my ass hard enough to sting.

A moan escapes me as fear flutters through my stomach, my skin tingling as the blunt head of his dick shoves between my cheeks. Sliding my hands up, I find nothing to hold on to while I prepare for the pain.

Don't tense. Don't tense. Don't tense.

It's been a while since he's fucked me. He's not small, and he doesn't even have lube. This is going to hurt.

Why does that idea make my dick throb?

My shirt is torn up the back, the cool air in the room setting goosebumps off across my skin. Preston leans down, bites hard at my back and shoulders, scrapes his nails down my body, and thrusts against my ass cheeks.

"Tell me you hate me," he growls in my ear.

I couldn't have heard that right. What?

Unease washes over me, cutting through the need to fuck.

"What?" I turn my head to look at him, but he leans against my shoulder to keep me facing forward.

"Say it. Tell me you hate me," he bites out the words again, trembling against me as he slaps at my ass again.

"I-I hate you." The words are awkward on my tongue. I don't hate him. Not anymore.

Preston spreads my cheeks and spits against my hole. His cock pushes against me and I force my body to relax.

"Say it again." He pushes forward, only making it part

way in before the burning pain is too much and I clench around him. He pulls back, spits on my hole again, and thrusts in.

"Oh fuck," I groan in a pain-pleasure mixture and my dick is rock hard, trapped between my body and the carpet.

Preston leans forward, shoving his hand under my chest and up to my throat.

"Say. It. Again," he seethes, setting a hard, deep pace.

"I hate you," I choke out past the grip he has on my throat. His thrusts hurt but that doesn't seem to dissuade my cock at all. Arching my hips as much as I can, the angle changes and he's dragging along my prostate.

"Lube, please," I whimper.

"Shut up," he growls, releasing my throat and shoving his fingers into my mouth. I suck on his middle fingers like my life depends on it.

He bites the muscle that runs along the top of my shoulder and groans.

"I hate you."

His free hand holds my hip as a shudder ripples through him a few seconds before heat floods my ass. His cum makes the slide of his dick so much easier, so much hotter. I love being used by him, claimed, owned.

Preston rests his forehead between my shoulders, breathing hard and trembling.

I'm panting and aching to come, afraid I'm going to have carpet burn on my dick.

Slowly, he pulls out and lifts onto his knees, still straddling me.

"Roll over."

CHAPTER 30

preston

Jeremy is naked now, stretched out on the floor under me, dick hard and leaking against his stomach, his hole wet and sloppy. I want to fuck him again.

I settle between his thighs and bite my way up his chest. The need to mark every inch of his skin is overwhelming. I suck hickies into his skin, leave bite marks and bruises from my fingers all over his body. Everyone will see them in the locker room but I don't care. I want them to. I need them to know he's taken. Owned.

"Preston," he growls when I avoid his dick.

"Shut up." I pinch one of his nipples, hard, in one hand and suck softly on the other one. He arches against me, his leaking cock throbbing against my stomach. I want to be able to feel his skin against mine but I'm not ready for it. He has questions about what he saw, I know he does, but I don't know when I'll be ready to tell him what they are.

When I release his abused nipple, he moans for me, his hips shifting restlessly. Dragging just the tips of my fingers down his body, I once again ignore his cock, cup his balls and give them a gentle squeeze, then slip two fingers in his slicked-up hole.

He groans, rolling his hips and trying to ride my fingers. Sitting back on my legs, I wrap my hand around his dick, pull the skin back from his head, and stroke him while I finger him.

"You're fucking sloppy," I growl, watching my fingers disappear into him only to slip out covered in my cum.

My dick is making a valiant effort to get hard again. It won't be much longer before I'm ready to go again. Thank fuck for quick recoveries.

Jeremy's skin heats with a flush, his muscles tightening as he gets close to the edge, but I don't let him cross the line. No, he's going to come with my dick buried deep in his ass. He'll squeeze me, ride me, while he loses it.

I crave it.

When I release his dick and pull my fingers from his body, he almost sobs.

"What the fuck?" he whines, fucking desperate to cum.

I need to feel him.

Lining myself up against his hole, I push inside in one thrust, my hips resting against his ass. He grabs his hair and pulls as his back arches off the carpet.

"Fuuuuck!"

His body sucks me in, greedy and hot and wet.

Quickly, I'm lost in him. Surrounded and consumed by this man and what he gives me.

Jeremy wraps a hand around his dick, jerking himself in fast strokes while I fuck him. His ass clenches around me in a rhythmic spasm as cum erupts from him, splattering on his stomach and chest.

Leaning a hand on his chest, I reach for his free hand and shove it under my shirt. My eyes close at the touch of his palm against my stomach, tears pouring down my face as I rut into him without mercy. Nothing matters but this, his touch on my skin. His body around mine. The pleasure and peace only he brings me. My chest tightens with the emotions threatening to choke me. I don't know what to do with them or how to deal with it. I'm overwhelmed by them and him. My anchor in the shit storm that is my life.

Jeremy wraps his legs around me to keep me deep.

"Use me," he whispers. "I've got you. Take what you need."

I break, my arms no longer holding me up, sobs wrack my body as I crash into him, trapping his hand between us. My face is buried in his neck and he holds me against him with an arm around my shoulders.

"I've got you," he says over and over again.

It takes a while for me to get my shit together and calm down again. No longer hard and not interested in sex anymore, we get cleaned up and climb back into bed. I'm emotionally raw and I don't know how to handle it.

I lay down with my back against the wall, and when Jeremy lays down in front of me with his back to me, I pull on his arm until he rolls over to face me. I need him wrapped around me tonight. To be held.

"I'm sorry," I mumble into his naked chest.

"There's nothing to be sorry for." He runs his hands through my hair, his thigh thrown over my hip and mine between his legs.

I suck in an unsteady breath and close my eyes. "My father cuts me and stitches it back up."

Jeremy's hands stop moving.

"What?"

"Every scar on my torso is from him correcting my behavior." There. I said it. My shameful secret. I'm such a fuck up that I'm covered in scars because I don't learn. Part of me knows it's wrong, knows *he's* wrong, but the little boy who only wanted to make his father proud holds onto that truth.

"How old were you when it started?" His hands run through my hair again. "How is he keeping your drug tests clean? How are you functioning so well on pain meds?"

"I was a kid, like, ten years old? I don't know. It was around the time my mom was killed." I rub my face against his chest. "I don't get pain meds. I'm stone cold sober when it happens."

"Does Coach know about this?"

My chest tightens at the question. Doesn't he get it? No one cares. No one but him.

"You're the only one who knows." My words are quiet but he hears them. He doesn't say anything for a while, just lets me hold him and draw shapes on his back with my finger as I navigate the turbulent waters in my head.

"Is that what your nightmares are about?"

"Sometimes." I press my cheek against him. "I used to fight him, hide so he would chase me. But I learned it's easier to just let it happen. The dreams are sometimes being chased by him, sometimes it's walking in to find my mom dead or finding my sister dead at his hand."

"Jesus. You found your mom?"

"No, I came home from school to the coroner parked in my driveway. I was ten when she was killed and I must have heard the cops or my father talking about it because I have this mental picture of it that I have no other way of having."

We fall quiet again while he processes my life. The shit I've kept hidden from everyone. I've never spoken about any of it before.

"It's not your fault." Jeremy cups my face and pulls it back to look me in the eye. "None of what happened to you is your fault."

Tears well up in my eyes at the seriousness in his expression. There's no arguing with him, he's made up his mind about this.

"If I was better, he wouldn't have to correct me all the time."

Fury morphs his beautiful face into hard lines. "That's bullshit. You did nothing to deserve any of that. That's not normal. Normal punishments are having your cell phone taken, not being able to go out with your friends. Your dad is a monster and deserves to die in prison."

I don't have a response for him. I want to argue but I don't want him to be angry at me, not right now. Tomorrow, I'll be happy to fight with him, but tonight, I'm too exposed. Too raw.

Jeremy lowers his mouth to mine, taking a soft kiss before settling back against the pillow. There's no more talking, just breathing. Eventually, we fall asleep, disappearing into the dark.

The next morning, we're awoken with a pounding on the door.

"Albrooke! Carmichael! Get up!" Paul is yelling through the door, banging on the wood. Jeremy groans and rolls out of bed, rubbing sleep from his eyes and stumbling to the door. It's not until he's opened the door and it's silent that I realize Jeremy is shirtless.

Shit.

I was not easy on him last night.

Popping my eyes open, I drag my gaze down his back and cringe. If his front looks anything like his back, it's very clear what he was up to last night.

"No wonder you missed breakfast," Paul comments, trying to hide his smirk.

I jerk upright in bed. "Missed breakfast? What time is it?" I demand.

"Yeah, it's lunch time, dude."

"Fuck!" I tear out of bed and dig through my dresser for clothes. I have to eat breakfast and lunch before the game. I *have* to or it fucks up everything and I'll play like shit.

I've normally been up for hours by now, gotten breakfast, showered, made sure my suit is ironed, and everything I need is packed in my gym bag.

Today is a shit show and I've barely opened my eyes.

I need my god damn routine! Fuck!

"Assistant Coach Scott is looking for you," Paul says to Jeremy.

"Oh, shit!" He races around to get dressed then disappears out the door at a sprint. I grab my phone, see about twelve missed messages and calls from Lily, and look up diners near me. Someone has to still be serving breakfast. Maybe if I eat half of breakfast and half of lunch I'll be okay?

I find a diner down the street and put in an online order that I can have delivered while I shower quickly. When I check the time, I don't have time to iron my shirt. Fuck!

I shower as fast as I can, don't shave because I don't have time, and get into my suit. My fucking shirt is wrinkled and it grates on every one of my damn nerves.

The delivery guy shows up as I'm buttoning my gray shirt. Ripping open the door, I toss some cash at him and nod, shutting the door in his face. I should probably feel sorry for that, but I don't have the brain space for it.

Opening my order, there's no fork or spoon. How the fuck am I supposed to eat this with no utensils?

Fuck today. I'm done. I can't play like this!

We're going to lose and it's going to be my god damn fault. Again.

I force myself to stop, close my eyes, and take a deep breath.

Okay. I can do this.

I dig into my food with my hands, burning my fingers in the process. It doesn't matter. Once I've eaten, I'll be better. I'll be okay. The day will be more on track.

As I shove a bite of piping hot chicken into my mouth, Jeremy bursts into the room, ripping clothes off.

"Suit?" He looks around when he doesn't see the hanger on his bed. I normally set it out for him, but in my rush to get my shit together, I didn't get a chance.

"Closet," I manage around a mouthful of food.

He doesn't hesitate, just grabs it and starts pulling it on.

I put the food down and pull on my shoes. Jeremy is sliding his on too, his shirt unbuttoned still, and grabs a piece of chicken from my container, winking at me as Paul and Brendon appear at our door and look between the two of us.

I lift my lip and growl at them but they just smile back at me.

"What the hell is wrong with you two today?"

I turn on Brendon with a snarl. "I over fucking slept, didn't eat on time, and my shirt isn't ironed. We're going to fucking lose today!"

"Fuck that. Get your shit together! We need to win today and tomorrow or we're fucked!" he says to me in no uncertain terms, pointing directly at me.

We head down to the rink, Jeremy finishing his buttons in the elevator.

"Albrooke!" Coach calls as soon as we step into the locker room. "You're cleared to play today!"

Jeremy fist pumps the air. "Fuck yeah!"

Paul and Brendon pat him on the back, with the other guys cheering as everyone gets dressed into their workout clothes.

CHAPTER 31

jeremy

These guys are fucking with us. First period, they were all over Preston, taunting him into penalties while the refs did nothing. He's been cross-checked, he's been hooked, he's been checked into the boards when he didn't have the fucking puck. And it's getting to him. He's ready to snap.

He comes off the ice for a line change and I go on, passing him by the bench. "Let it go, man." I tell him as I pass. We're in the second period and it appears the other team has changed tactics and are now gunning for me.

I'm tripped, slammed between two players, blocked for no reason, and shoved into the boards while I don't have the puck.

Paul and Brendon are passing the puck back and forth beautifully, getting down the ice. I finally manage to get away from the D men and fly down the ice, looking for an opening. The puck is passed to me and I take the shot. The puck barely slips past the goalie and the lamp lights up! Fuck yeah!

We're celebrating, with the guys patting me on the back as we make for the bench for a line change again. From somewhere behind us, someone flings a hockey stick and it cracks me and Paul in the back. Just like that, chaos ensues. Our team is jumping over the wall that separates the bench from the ice, flooding the ice with players. The team we're playing jumps onto the ice too. Players are everywhere, gloves and helmets go flying, people are yelling, the crowd is screaming.

As much as I want to join in the fray, I don't. If I get another head injury I'm going to be pissed. Instead, I search for jersey number twenty-two.

Preston is swinging at a guy but they still have gloves on, thank fuck.

The refs are blowing whistles, coaches are yelling at players to get back on the bench.

Preston grabs the other player's jersey and swings him around until he's lost his balance. This is going downhill fast and I don't want him kicked out of another game.

"Preston!" His name is out of my mouth, he'll ignore it. I jump into the mess of bodies to get to him. "Let him go!"

There's a break in the people around him and I slam into him, my body weight forcing him off the other player. I fling my gloves off and grab for the collar of Preston's jersey so he's face to face with me.

"Hey, hey, hey." I say quietly, trying to calm his fight response and bring down his heart rate. "I'm fine. You gotta chill, man. They're going to disqualify you."

"Everybody off the fucking ice!" Coach yells.

"Come on, we gotta go."

"That fucker threw a stick! That's bullshit and everyone

knows it!" he roars back, his face red in splotches. "Those fuckers are going to learn how to play the fucking game or deal with me!"

"You can't do shit from the locker room. You have got to get control of yourself. It's going to take more than a stick to the back to get me out of here."

The refs come around and hustle everyone off the ice, one of the assistant coaches is talking to Preston on the side, probably telling him the same thing I did.

I shake my head and prepare for the next face off.

"Your boyfriend ain't here to protect you now." The sneer on the face of my opponent is all I need to know. *They staged this on purpose to draw him out and get rid of him.* They think my team can't stand on their own without him. That we'll fall apart without him.

The puck drops and I fling it to Brendon, shoving my shoulder into this guy's chest as I do.

For the rest of the game, I've got players on my ass, throwing me into the boards every chance they get, tripping me, and taunting me without mercy. But I ignore all of it, they think they can break me but they're wrong.

At the end of the second period, we head to the locker room with the score sitting at two to one with us in the lead. It's a hard-fought lead that's taking every ounce of our strength to keep. They've taken more shots on goal than I can remember, but so far, our goalie is holding steady.

"Albrooke!" Coach hollers. "Those boys got a real hard-on for you. Any idea why?" Everyone turns to look at me.

"I've got a few ideas, Coach." Sweat drips down my back and my face. Reaching for a towel, I catch the drops before they burn my eyes.

"Yeah? And what's that?"

"I think they're trying to get to Carmichael, if I'm being

honest. He reacts strongly when I'm attacked so they're fucking with him. If they can get him disqualified, they think we'll fall apart."

Coach nods. "He does have a bit of a temper."

The guys chuckle at the obvious understatement. I glance at the man in question, but his face gives nothing away.

We deal with any equipment issues we have, get a drink of water, take a piss if needed, and head back to the ice.

I'm on the bench waiting for my turn, sitting next to Paul.

"I have to admit, it's nice to see him going after someone that's not me." He motions to Preston with a grin.

I chuckle and shake my head at him. "I don't know, I never seem to have that issue with him."

"I've seen you after a night of...*extracurriculars,* so I think you have it worse than everyone else."

My face flushes hot but I shrug like I'm not embarrassed and watch the game. He knocks his shoulder against mine and turns to talk to Brendon on his other side.

I struggle to take my eyes off Preston. His presence on the ice is commanding. Do I play better knowing he's there to back me up? I don't know. Maybe.

We make it through the rest of the game with no more fist fights, holding on to our two to one lead. Back in the locker room, Preston gets changed back into his suit and appears next to my cubby.

"Can you look for my sister? I don't know if my father is here and I don't want him to see her." His voice is quiet and strained. His body is tense as he asks for help when it's the last thing he wants to do.

"Yeah, of course." I pull my shirt on, buttoning the white buttons as Preston stares at my fingers. "Where do you want to meet up? We should change out of these." I motion to our outfits.

"I don't know, pick a restaurant or something? She's probably hungry." He shakes his head and shoves his hands in his pockets.

"You think she would rather go to some restaurant than come back to the dorms and just hang out with you?"

Preston steps into my space, lowers his mouth to my ear, his hot breath tickling my skin. "I don't think she wants to witness what I'm going to do to you when we get back to the dorm."

My dick is stiff and aching in the confines of these fucking pants.

"You're an asshole." I whisper back to him as he steps away from me and finishes getting dressed.

What the fuck was that? Am I going to have to wait all fucking night to find out what he has planned?

A plan starts forming in my head while I'm pulling my shoes on. I duck my head to hide the smile curving on my face.

Preston's gaze is damn near a physical touch before he walks out, probably finding some back way to sneak out of here so his father doesn't see him.

Leaning over to Paul and Brendon, I lower my voice so everyone doesn't hear me.

"Hey, I'm going to go grab Lily then head up to the dorms to get changed. You guys know of a pool house or anything we can take her to?"

Paul nods his head. "Yeah, there's a place downtown. Scratch."

"Cool, you guys want to come with us or meet us there? I know you normally go have beers with the team but this is a great opportunity for you to fuck with Preston." And for me to mess with him too.

Both smile and nod in unison. "Absolutely."

We bump knuckles and I head out of the locker room to find the girl in question. Pulling my phone out, I text her.

Where are you at?

LILY

I'm still in the stands, I figured it would be easier not to get lost in the crowd.

I coordinate where to meet her and find her standing in a now mostly deserted corridor with a few dude-bros around her. She appears okay, but when her eyes meet mine, there's relief on her face.

"Hey! Get out of here." I shove one guy back who is way too close to her. "Unless you want Carmichael to rearrange your face, you best fuck off."

He has the good sense to go pale then leaves. A couple others shrug and walk off.

"Jesus, the wild animals." I shake my head at them. "You alright?"

She smiles at me, obviously trying not to bust out laughing.

"What?"

"Using Preston as a threat. That's great." She drops into step with me as we leave the rink. "You went all big brother back there, do you have a younger sister or something?"

I smile at her and shake my head. "Nah. My sister is two years older but got herself into plenty of trouble growing up that I had to get her out of. I have twin younger brothers but they play football and handle their own shit."

We avoid the front of the stadium and head across campus. I'm not sure if their dad is still standing around or if he came at all, but I'm not risking it. If he sees Lily, Preston will murder me without a second thought.

"Are you guys close?" she asks.

A pang of homesickness hits my chest and I rub at my breastbone. I miss them. This is the first time I've been away from home for an extended amount of time. I was lucky and when I was on the juniors team, I played in my hometown.

"Kind of. It's hard to be close this far apart and hockey keeps me really busy, so with the time difference, it's hard to keep in touch regularly." I shrug and my phone goes off in my pocket. Stacy and Ella's picture is on my screen when I pull it out.

"Speak of the devil. Sorry." I answer the call and smile when Ella's adorable face fills the screen. She starts babbling immediately. "Hey, baby girl, what are you doing?"

Ella is telling me a very intense story that I, of course, don't follow since it's all gibberish, but I pay close attention anyway, giving the correct responses to any pause in her noises.

Stacy laughs in the background and speaks over her daughter. "We were watching the game and she brought me my phone and started smacking it with her hand. She was pissed when I told her we couldn't call you yet."

"You want me to come save you from your evil mommy, don't you?"

Lily giggles, covering her mouth with her hand to keep the sound in but it's loud enough for Stacy to hear.

"Who's with you? That sounded like a girl." She raises an eyebrow at me.

"It's Preston's sister, Lily." I turn the camera so Stacy can see both of us. Lily waves and smiles at my sister.

"Lily, this is my annoying sister Stacy and her adorable daughter, Ella, who is the best baby ever."

Stacy rolls her eyes and Lily laughs.

"Whatever. I'm your favorite sibling."

"That's not saying much. That's like saying you're my favorite foot fungus."

"Gross." She takes a sip from a mug. "You're coming home for Christmas, right? Mom is going nuts trying to prepare for you to come home."

Oh, shit. I hadn't thought about Christmas. Should I invite Preston? Will his dad insist on family time? Will Preston be able to sleep if I'm not here?

"Uh, maybe. I'll get back to you."

Stacy lifts an eyebrow at me. "Mom will kill all of us if you don't."

We're at the dorms and Preston is standing in the lobby with his arms crossed, wearing rich boy jeans and a t-shirt. How does he manage to look rich in jeans and a t-shirt? It's fucking weird.

"Hey Stace, I gotta go. Give Ella big hugs for me and smack the boys upside the head for me."

"Ugg! Ugg!" Ella's voice comes in the background, and it hurts my heart to hear her asking for hugs when I can't give her one.

"I love you, Ella bug."

"Lo u." A knot forms in my throat at her voice and the call ends. I shove the phone back in my pocket and force the emotions back.

Preston storms out the doors of the dorms toward us. "What the hell took you so long?"

"Relax, we took the long way around to avoid the crowds." Preston holds the door open and we step inside. "How do we feel about a pool house? We can eat shitty food, Preston's favorite." I lean into Lily's space a little like I'm telling her a secret. "And chill out."

Lily perks up. "That sounds like fun!"

Preston's lips press into a thin line and he looks at me

with a *you're going to pay for that* expression that makes my dick twitch.

"Cool, I'll go change."

Preston looks at me, his expression unreadable. He has no idea what he's in for. I wink at him as I step into the elevator and he glares at me, which makes me chuckle.

Once I'm in our room, I strip off my clothes, dig for some jeans and a hoodie, then find the bottle of lube and a butt plug that I have hidden in my sock drawer.

I hurriedly pull on my clothes but don't buckle my pants and hurry into the bathroom with the toy and lube. Leaning on the sink, I drop my boxer briefs and lube up the toy.

I press the tip against my hole and hold back a groan as I work it inside. My dick is hard and demanding attention, but I don't touch myself, not yet. It takes a minute for me to work the toy all the way in and get my pants pulled back up. My ass clenching around the silicone plug is going to make for a very long night. I catch my reflection in the mirror, surprised by the pink flush on my cheeks.

Shit.

I splash some cold water on my face and head downstairs. When I step off the elevator, Preston's jaw is clenched as he stares at Paul and Brendon with a look that promises pain. It makes my dick ache again.

"Took you long enough. What were you doing? Jacking off?" Brendon asks. Preston's head swings toward me and Lily and I both blush.

"Shut up, I had to change." I shove Brendon and Paul hides his smile behind his hand. He definitely thinks I was jacking off.

"We're leaving," Preston announces, grabbing his sister's arm and pulling her from the building. Brendon, Paul, and I follow along behind them and wait at the curb as an Uber pulls up. The front passenger window rolls down and a man leans across the seat.

"Is one of you Preston?"

Preston nods and opens a back door. The silver SUV has third row seating, but the four of us are not small so I don't know how we're all going to fit. He drops the middle seats and helps Lily in, climbing in after her and pulling the seat up.

His knees are basically in his armpits and his head is cocked to the side because the roof is too low for him to sit straight.

"Looks comfy, ya ogre," Brendon says as I climb in and buckle into the middle seats. The pressure on the plug almost makes me groan. Brendon slides in next to me, giving me a weird look, and Paul takes the front seat. Brendon drops his arm along the back of the seat like he always does in the car then smirks when Preston growls but doesn't move.

We ride along in the car, heading toward downtown in the Friday night traffic. Conversation flows around the car about the game, with Lily just as involved as we are.

Fingers play with the edges of my hair along the back of my neck as we talk. It sends shivers down my back and my ass clenches around the plug, which makes me stifle a moan. I slide my palms down my legs, pulling my jeans just a little for something to do with my hands.

The fingers in my hair disappear and Brendon yells, arching over the seat at a weird angle. Spinning around to see what is happening, Preston has Brendon's fingers bent backwards, forcing his arm at an unnatural angle.

"Touch him again and I'll break your elbow," Preston growls in Brendon's face, jaw clenched tight.

"Alright, alright! Jesus Christ!" Brendon yells.

I brush a hand down the back of my head, confused by

what started this. "Wait, that was you?" I ask Brendon. "Seriously?"

I turn back to face the front and ignore Brendon.

Paul sighs with a shake of his head. "I told you to leave him alone."

Lily snorts and the conversations end until we get to the pool house. The car pulls to a stop and Brendon opens the door and gets out. I start to slide across the seat but Preston grabs me by the throat and pulls me back over the seat, forcing my body to arch and crashes his mouth to mine. My hands find his arms, holding on as my dick jumps from a semi to hard as fuck against the unforgiving fabric of my jeans.

As Preston ravages my mouth, my hips rock, making the plug move. I moan into his kiss and he shoves his free hand inside the neck of my hoodie to scratch up my chest.

I'm so fucking close to the edge, I'm leaking precum. Jesus fucking Christ. I'm going to come in my god damn jeans with no one touching my dick.

"Hey! No sex in the car!" The driver's angry shout jolts me away from Preston. He growls at the angry man in the front seat.

I hustle to get out of the car, dick still hard and now with a hot face. Brendon and Paul are laughing hysterically at us from the sidewalk.

"Fuck off. Why am I friends with you again?" I grumble as Preston and Lily exit the car.

"I don't ever want to see my brother try to eat another human ever again," Lily says with a disgusted look on her face.

"Come on, Short Stack, let's find a table," Paul offers her his elbow and she hooks her arm though it. Preston growls and steps toward them but I pause in front of him, stopping him from following.

"What the fuck are you doing?" he rumbles in my ear, his chest against my back.

"I'm wearing a plug." Preston's body freezes, his dick twitching against my ass. I grind my ass against him once and reach for the door, grinning at the predatory look in his dark gray eyes reflected in the glass.

Stepping inside the pool house, I'm hit with the sound of pool balls crashing together, music from the overhead speakers, and conversations around the room. Since it's a Friday night, there are a lot of people in here, so we'll probably have to wait a while to get a table.

Paul waves a hand in the air to get my attention and I head in that direction, surprised when someone snags my belt loop. Before I can turn to see who it is, Preston's voice fills my ear. "Bathroom, right now."

I shudder and head toward the back, telling Paul I'll be right back on my way past him and Brendon. The bathroom is grimy and old with green stalls on one side and a wall of urinals on the other. There are a few guys taking a piss, but the stalls are open, so I go inside of one and close the door. Anticipation has my hands shaking as I wait. My dick throbs in my jeans, aching for any kind of attention. I rub the heel of my hand down the ridge and bite my lip to hold in a groan.

A few minutes later, Preston says my name and I open the stall. Striding toward me, he comes inside and locks the door, tense with sexual frustration.

"Show me." His voice is dripping with arousal and demand.

Turning to face the toilet, I open my pants, lower my underwear to my thighs, and bend over, resting my hands on the old, tiled wall. My thick cock is standing at attention, dripping precum down my shaft.

Preston puts a hand on my back to keep me still and pushes against the plug, forcing a moan from my throat.

"Are you that desperate to get used again?"

"Yes," I hiss as he pulls on the plug. My ass clenches when it's out, suddenly empty and aching to be filled again.

Preston's zipper is loud in the quiet space of the bathroom, and as badly as I want to feel his naked body against mine, I don't reach for him. He lays his hot dick against the crease of my ass and shoves his hands under my hoodie. Preston's palms splay across my body, searching for injuries. My body is beat up, there are going to be some nasty bruises and sore muscles come morning, but that's hockey. He's not exactly gentle during sex either.

He finds a particularly tender spot on my ribs and I hiss, jerking away from his fingers.

"That's gonna be a beauty in the morning," I say instinctively, trying to downplay how badly it hurts.

Preston doesn't say anything, just grips my hips and thrusts against my ass.

He's barely holding on to control. Life is spinning away from him, leaving him with nothing but me to keep him grounded. He's scared, frustrated, angry and my body takes the brunt force of it.

I crave it now.

He's ruined me for anyone else. If he walks away from me, I don't know how I'll survive.

Soft touches and sweet kisses are a foreign concept to me now. I wouldn't know how to react to them and I don't want them. I want him in his possessive, hard, demanding way.

The blunt head of Preston's cock pushes against my hole and I bite my lip to keep from groaning when he pushes in. My legs are trapped by my pants, keeping me exactly where he wants me without a damn thing I can do about it. Not that I would. I love how he controls my body, and lets me just feel what he wants me to and let go of everything else.

I love this. This part of him that only I get. I want to hate him for making me crave it, because nothing else feels as good as this. As good as him. And I am terrified he's going to get tired of me and leave me a broken shell of a human.

He slams into me, not holding back or taking it easy on me. He needs the outlet as much as I do.

Preston pulls on my hoodie to force me to stand. Arching my back, I reach back for him, needing the anchor. I cup the back of his head and hold his mouth to my skin as he digs his teeth into my flesh to leave new marks, his mouth sucking hard enough to leave dark hickies, and his nails scratch trails down my chest to mingle with the ones he's already peppered my body with.

His jean-covered hips smack against my naked ass until I'm sure there will be a friction burn.

I reach for my cock, pulling and squeezing until my balls are drawn up and my knees buckle. Preston holds his hand out in front of my dick but I don't understand why.

"What are you doing?"

"come in my hand, give it to me."

Oh fuck.

I work my dick faster, stroking and jerking myself as Preston loses his control in my ass. My head falls back on his shoulder as strings of cum shoot from me into his waiting palm. Preston's free hand slams over my mouth as I moan long and loud into the echoing room, forgetting where we are for a second as my orgasm short circuits my brain.

Preston's cum filled hand soon replaces the other one, forcing my own cum into my mouth. The bitter, salty taste catches me off guard as it slides down my throat.

Preston groans into my neck while he fills my ass with his own.

My spent dick tries to perk up but can't quite make it when he slumps against me and releases my mouth.

Preston rests his forehead against my shoulder and pants, shivering every once in a while from the power of his orgasm.

"That was fucking hot." He groans, lifting his hand that's still covered in my cum to his mouth.

My face flushes as he watches me watch him lick my cum from his skin while his dick is still buried in my ass.

When he sucks the last of my orgasm from his fingers, he takes a step back and slides out of me.

"Bend over again." He puts a hand on my back.

I lean my hands on the wall and feel him push the plug back into me. I whimper at the fullness of it and how fucking hot it is that he's forcing me to keep his cum inside me.

"Are you trying to kill me?" He pats my ass and I stand up, pulling my clothes back into place and adjusting them.

"Why would I do that? Then who would I torment?" Preston grabs my face and pulls me in for a quick, heated kiss while he still tastes like me, then steps back. "Let's get you cleaned up."

We step out of the stall and I'm glad no one is standing there. I half expected Brendon to be there, smirking at me. Bastard. I'm pretty sure he does it just to fuck with Preston.

I reach for a paper towel to get it wet and wipe my face, but Preston slaps my hand away and does it himself. This is new and I can't say I hate it.

"I can do that." I tell him, nodding to the paper towel.

"I'm aware."

I stand still as he carefully wipes away any evidence of cum from my face, rinses the towel, then gets some soap. He washes my face thoroughly then dries it before washing his hands.

I can't tell what he wants, whether he wants space or to pull me closer. Or is he trying to figure out what I need?

"Are you okay?" I finally break the silence and ask.

That damn mask slides back in place and he nods. "Yeah, you good?"

I nod and we head back into the loud pool hall where Paul, Brendon, and Lily have found a table.

CHAPTER 32

preston

I should be spending time with Lily. I should be paying attention to her before she flies back to New York tomorrow.

But I can't take my eyes off Jeremy.

Watching the way he moves, the careful way he sits when he's not taking a shot. It's us against Paul and Brendon, with Lily sometimes taking a shot for one of us since she didn't really want to play.

Spoiler alert: I suck a pool and these assholes are enjoying it.

Jeremy takes his pool cue and bends over in front of me, swaying his ass just a little as he gets set. My eyes are glued to it, to the perfectly round muscles, imagining how his sloppy, plugged hole looks right now.

I suck in a deep breath and hold it while he takes his shot. The bastard glances over his shoulder at me then hits the cue ball, sending it across the table to hit the solid orange ball and not quite making it into the corner pocket.

He stands and grunts, a frown on his face as he stands next to me against the wall with one hand on the cue stick and grabbing his Dr. Pepper with the other.

"I thought you said you were good at this?" I look at him smugly.

"Oh, I'm sorry, how many balls have you sunk?" He lifts his eyebrows high enough his hair hides them. "That's right, zero."

"Pool isn't really my thing." I shrug like it's not a big deal but it's bugging the shit out of me that I suck so bad at it. I don't do things I'm not good at, especially not in front of people. There's never been a time that I've learned how to deal with failure like this, I can't just brush it off.

Jeremy smiles at me, shaking his head and takes another drink of his soda. I turn to my sister, who is watching Paul demolish us. "Hey, do you have a ticket to tomorrow's game?"

She turns toward me with a big smile on her face. "Yeah, I've got a seat on the opposite side of the rink tomorrow."

"And you haven't talked to our father, right? He doesn't know you're here?" I watch her closely, looking for any indication she's lying to me when she answers me.

"Nope. I don't really want to see him anyway," She shrugs, picking a napkin apart. "He's never really cared about what I was doing anyway."

I hate that she's upset by his absence in her life. He's not a good man.

"It might not seem like it, but that's probably for the best. You don't need him." I say as Jeremy slides his hand into mine and gives me an encouraging squeeze. "He's not a good man, Lil."

She looks up at me like she's seeing me for the first time. "What aren't you telling me?"

The noise around us fades into the background, leaving

me with a pressure on my chest I don't know how to get rid of. All of her attention is on me and it's too much. I don't want her to know what I've dealt with, but I don't want to lie to her either. She deserves to know the truth.

I open and close my mouth, not sure what to say.

"All siblings protect each other. It comes with the territory." Jeremy buts in, giving me an out that I grip on to with all of my might.

"I was careful to make sure his attention was focused on me so he would leave you alone." I don't mean to say the words and the second they're out of my mouth, I wish I could take them back, but I can't. They're no longer mine.

"Why?" Her eyes meet mine in the dim lighting of the pool hall. "What are you protecting me from?"

Jeremy's fingers weave between mine, allowing me to use him however I need to.

His phone buzzes in his pocket, giving me the distraction I desperately want. This isn't the time or place for this conversation.

Jeremy smiles at whoever is on the screen and accepts the video call with a big, happy grin. I don't get that smile from him.

That's a smile for friends and his parents, his little girl. He's not easy going and relaxed with me.

You don't deserve him.

You're going to ruin his life.

You aren't worthy of a man like Jeremy Albrooke.

A painful, emotion-filled lump forms in my throat and I have to swallow twice to get it to loosen up.

Jeremy steps away to take his call, Paul and Brendon crowding around him and saying hi to whoever it is.

"Hey! Mrs. A! Any way you can mail that taco salad you make? It's bomb!" Brendon smiles at the phone screen.

"I can send you the recipe but I know you aren't going

to use it. Are you coming home for Christmas? I'll make it for you boys." Her voice holds a twinge of curiosity.

Jeremy looks over the top of his phone at me, raising his chin at me like he wants me to come over, but I'm not part of that group. He's friends with them and has obviously known them a long time. I don't fit.

"I think he wants you to meet his mom," Lily whispers, leaning into me.

I shake my head and lean against the wall, watching them talk to Jeremy's family. For the first time, I wish I had friends like that. People who knew me and were more like family than anything else. People I had grown up with, lived close to, went to birthday parties and had sleepovers with. That life isn't meant for me.

I'm a loner and that's fine.

You aren't meant to be loved.

"Jeremy, I bought your plane ticket today, I'll email you the confirmation." The easy smile on his face turns tense, his eyes shooting to mine.

My heart stops.

Plane ticket?

He's leaving? When? For how long?

Our nightly routine flashes through my head. How am I going to sleep without him? I can't go back to sleeping alone. I can't. I need him.

Fuck.

I try not to let my face show how panicked I am on the inside, but he can read me like a fucking book. The only person I'm fooling is myself and I fucking know it.

This is why I don't form attachments to people. I can't rely on anyone but myself.

He deserves to spend time with his parents, his daughter, and his siblings.

A healthy dose of guilt adds to the panic I'm trying not

to show. I'm a selfish asshole. He deserves time with his kid. She needs him more than I do.

Turning away from the pool table, I head to the cashier to order something to eat. There's nothing here I want but it will give me something to do. I'm sure someone will eat french fries. The grease from the fryer will just clog their arteries but I'm doing it anyway.

"Hey! Are you Preston Carmichael?" A voice calls from a pool table I'm passing. I stop and turn toward the direction of the voice, careful to school my face, create a slight smile so I don't appear aggressive unless I need to. Some people know me because of my father but typically men know me because they follow hockey.

A group of guys is staring at me from the pool table.

"Yeah, that's me." I lift a hand in greeting, hoping that's all they want.

"Dude!" One guy yells, throwing his hands in the air and hurrying toward me. Unease clenches my shoulders and tightens my stomach.

I am not alone. The guys won't make me deal with a situation on my own.

"Hi," I reach my hand out to shake his but he reaches for a hug. I immediately step back and glance around the room. People are starting to watch us. I don't want the attention.

From my position, I can glance over to see Jeremy, but I'm trying not to. I can handle this on my own even if I don't want to. There are too many people behind me, too many unknowns.

"Sorry, I'm not a hugger," I state matter of factly, offering my hand once again. "I'm happy to shake your hand though."

"It's fine, whatever," the stranger says before turning to his group of friends. "I told you that guy was weird as fuck."

From the corner of my eye, I can see Jeremy sliding his phone in his pocket and coming toward me. Relief and anxiety swirl inside of me. I don't want to deal with this, but I don't want him injured because I can't handle my shit either.

Off the ice, you don't put your hands on anyone.

My father's furious voice echoes through my head. That was cut into me on more than one occasion after fighting at school. This one fuckwad, Trent, liked to push me around, and after a while I would snap and whale on him. I broke his nose once, dislocated his shoulder another time. Every time I lost control, my father would correct my behavior.

Even if this asshole puts hands on me, I can't retaliate. I'm bigger, stronger, and better trained. It's an unfair fight.

"Hey, how's it going? Are you a Darby Ram's fan?" Jeremy's friendly voice and big smile pops up next to me, moving to stand in front of me to redirect the attention off of me.

"Yeah man, we were at the game tonight!" The man is once again excited as he chats with Jeremy.

I'm fucking useless. Why am I even here?

"Oiler and Johnson are here too. Do you want a picture with us?" Jeremy offers the guy, who cheers.

One of the guys he's with pulls out a phone and Jeremy waves the guys over. They come right over, smiling and talking hockey with the guy while I stand behind them. When they position for a photo, I step up behind Jeremy and Paul, force myself to smile, and offer to shake the guy's hand one more time. This time he takes me up on the offer and we head back to the table where Lily is waiting.

"Does that happen a lot?" she asks me.

"Not really," I shrug and grab Jeremy's soda, despite not wanting it, I need something to do with my hands. I take a sip at the sugary syrup drink and cringe. Jesus, how does anyone drink this?

Lily's laugh takes me by surprise. When I look at her, she's almost doubled over, laughing so hard. I put the cup back on the table and try not to blush.

"It wasn't that funny."

She's wiping tears from her eyes, still cackling and almost can't catch her breath.

"You-you looked at it..." She breaks off to laugh again. "Like it personally insulted you."

"So glad you find me so amusing." I deadpan.

Jeremy picks up the cup and chugs back the rest of the soda while I watch with disgust. He steps closer to me but not close enough to get attention.

"Don't worry, you can taste it on my tongue later." He winks then bends over the table again to take a shot. Bastard is toying with me.

Checking the time on my phone, I see I have multiple texts from my father and a missed call. Great.

I'm not opening anything until after the game tomorrow. I don't need him in my head.

"It's getting late, we should head back," Brendon says as Jeremy sinks the black eight ball.

"I'll call the Uber," I tell them, putting in that we have two stops and selecting an SUV that says it can hold seven people. We'll see how many hockey players we can shove in it.

We turn the table over to the next group waiting to play and head outside when my app alerts me that the driver is approaching.

It's fucking cold out here, and Jeremy offers to wrap Lily in his jacket to keep her warm, which I appreciate. If Brendon or Paul touch her, I'll break someone's nose.

She smiles and wraps her arms around his waist when he pulls open his jacket, wrapping my tiny sister in his warmth.

When the car arrives, Jeremy and I manage to squeeze into the back row, Paul and Lily in the center, with Brendon in the front. Since Lily is being dropped off at her hotel first, this was the easiest way to sit.

By the time we get to the dorms, get into our room, and get changed for bed, I'm ready to crash but my brain won't shut up.

I lay down on my bed, waiting while Jeremy deals with the plug and gets changed. Earlier, I expected to want him again before we passed out, but now I'm not entirely sure I could get it up.

The door of the bathroom opens, and the light shuts off. Rolling onto my side with my back against the wall, Jeremy climbs in, facing me.

"You know, if we were smart, we would push the damn beds together so we could sleep on a king-sized bed," he grumbles as I bury my face in his neck and inhale him, relaxing for the first time tonight.

"You're going home for Christmas?" I mumble against his skin. Jeremy wraps his arms around my shoulders, holding me against him.

"Yeah, I'm leaving after our last December game and staying for two weeks." He kisses my forehead, his fingers tracing lazy designs on my shoulder blade.

Two weeks.

Two weeks?

What the fuck am I going to do for that long? I can't sleep without him. He keeps me grounded. This guy is the light in my dark, fucked up world. How far back into the shadows will I be shoved when he's gone?

"You should come with me."

"No, you need time with your family. I'll be fine." I inhale his spicy, earthy scent and close my eyes.

We lay this way for a while, but Jeremy isn't relaxing and falling asleep. I think he's actually getting more tense.

"What are you thinking about?"

He's quiet for a minute, his chest tightening under me, then quickly blurts out the words like he's afraid to say them.

"Arewetogether?"

It takes me a minute to translate that and make sense of it.

"Together?" I pull back enough to see his face. "You're mine and I don't share."

He smiles like I've said the right thing and made him happy.

"I don't care what you call it or label it. You're mine. Only mine."

Jeremy's glowing face lifts up, pressing his lips against mine. This kiss is different from the other ones we've shared, slower, deeper, it means something. This kiss is a promise, a symbol. It's not to be rushed or hurried or angry, but explored, experienced, and enjoyed.

CHAPTER 33

jeremy

I shove the rest of my stuff in my duffle bag and zip it up. Preston is lying on his bed, pretending to ignore the fact that I'm leaving for two weeks. He's doing a shitty job of it.

Honestly, I'm scared to leave him. He still wakes up with nightmares, but they've been getting less intense since I started sleeping with him all night. What is he going to do while I'm gone? Will he sleep at all? Or work himself into exhaustion so he hopefully won't dream? None of these options are good ones.

My phone dings with a notification, telling me it's time to head to the airport.

"Alright, I'm heading out." I turn around and find him standing directly behind me. He slides his hands under my shirt to press his fingers into my skin. "You could come with me."

"I'm not ruining your family's time with you." He growls, crashing his lips to mine to stop the same argument we've had every day since Thanksgiving. Preston's tongue pushes into my mouth while he pulls my hips against him. I'm owned by this guy.

I love him.

The thought should shock me, but it doesn't. It's fucking true. I don't know when it changed from, *I could love you* to *I love you,* but I can't argue with myself.

Preston groans into my mouth when I cup his head and hold him against me. My dick hardens, notching together against his, and I roll my hips. I don't have time to do anything right now and he's already fucked my brains out this morning, but that doesn't mean my body isn't willing.

My phone goes off again, this time telling me my Uber is here. Reluctantly, I pull my lips from his and he chases my mouth, not ready to end the contact.

"I have to go," I say against his lips. Giving him quick kisses.

"I know." He sighs and steps back, pulling his fingers from inside my shirt and adjusting himself in his jeans.

He picks up my bag and heads to the door.

"I can carry that myself." I wander out after him once I've made sure my hard-on is semi hidden.

"I know."

Preston stops at Paul and Brendon's room, knowing I'll want to say goodbye to them.

The door opens and Paul is in only a pair of sweatpants.

"Hey, man, you leaving?" He eyes Preston holding my bag but steps up to give me a back patting bro hug. Preston growls at the contact and Paul chuckles.

"Take care of him for me, yeah?" I say quietly before stepping back.

Paul nods at me as Brendon comes forward, him in a t-shirt and boxer briefs.

Brendon reaches for a hug too, but Preston stops him with a hand to his chest. "Put some fucking pants on."

Brendon looks up at Preston like he's an idiot. "I'm not going to fuck him right here in the hallway, relax."

He leans into Preston's hand until Preston moves, grumbling about an ass kicking later. I hug my best friend with a grin.

"Don't drive him up the wall while I'm gone, okay? I love-" I cut myself off mid-sentence at the words. Shit. I didn't mean to say that out loud. Did he hear me?

Brendon pulls back from me with a shit-eating grin on his face. I give him a *don't you fucking dare* look and he ducks back into the room laughing like a lunatic. Fuck.

Paul lifts a brow at me but I shake it off and follow after Preston as he heads to the elevators.

He hits the call button and we stand almost shoulder to shoulder, my bag between us. Did he hear what I said? No, right? He would say something if he did. Right?

It's not long before the doors slide open and we step inside. When the doors close, Preston drops my bag and pushes me against the wall, pinning my hands above my head and sucking on my neck.

I grind against him with a moan as he bruises me, marks me for everyone to see. My torso is already covered in scratches and bite marks. I'll have to be careful around my family so I don't have to answer any awkward questions, but this one I can't hide.

When the elevator stops and dings, Preston lets go of me, his lips making a *pop* sound when the suction is broken. He grabs my bag and strides out of the elevator while I'm trying to breathe normally again and clear the lust fog from my brain.

With a huff of sexual frustration, I follow after him to

the car sitting at the curb. Preston has the door open for me with my bag already inside.

"Have a safe trip," he whispers as I slide inside. "Text me when you land."

I wink at him as he shuts the door, shoves his hands inside the front pocket of his hoodie, and steps back from the curb. I keep my eyes on him as the driver pulls away, hating to lose the connection I have with him.

Guilt eats at me with every foot of space that's put between us. I don't want to leave him.

We pull onto the freeway and my phone dings with a message. Confused at Preston sending me a message already, I open it to find a picture of his hand wrapped around his dick with a bead of precum dripping down his head.

Fuck. Me.

I almost groan out loud. Almost.

CARMICHAEL

We miss you already.

You're an asshole. I almost groaned OUT LOUD!

He replies with a bunch of crying, laughing emojis. The ass.

Better be careful or I'll set this as the background on my phone.

CARMICHAEL

Hope your mom doesn't see it.

She knows I'm gay.

CARMICHAEL

Doesn't mean she wants to see the dick you're fucking.

I snort out a laugh. He's not wrong but I'm not telling him that.

Take a selfie for me.

CARMICHAEL

Why? Need a picture to jack off to in the airplane bathroom?

HA! You wish. Just do it.

It takes a few minutes but a picture of Preston looking bored pops up and it makes me laugh. What a dick.

Another picture comes through, this time with his nose scrunched up and his tongue sticking out. That's the one.

I save the picture and set it as my phone's background then send him a screenshot.

CARMICHAEL

You trying to be my boyfriend or something? You're becoming a stage five clinger.

You are my boyfriend. You can't leave me cause I'd find you.

The scene from *Wedding Crashers* plays in my head and I chuckle.

I get a message from Paul and open it.

JOHNSON

YOU SAID THE L WORD!!!

I groan and drop my head back against the headrest. Fucking Brendon.

I'm going to kick Brendon right in the ass when I get back. He's got a big fucking mouth.

JOHNSON

Why didn't you tell me? I'm the trustworthy one of this group.

I hate you both. I'm trying to sext with my boyfriend.

JOHNSON

I fucking hope not! He's with us!

A picture comes through from Paul of Preston glaring at Brendon, who's inhaling an ice cream cone.

I flip over to my message thread with Preston.

Already over me, huh?

CARMICHAEL

They showed up mid jerk off and wouldn't leave. If Brendon doesn't stop deep throating this ice cream, I'm going to knock him out.

I chuckle at the mental image. Brendon is one hundred percent doing it on purpose to piss off Preston. It's his way of showing he cares. If Preston is annoyed by him, Preston won't have time to miss me. Brendon is a weird one, but he's a good dude and I love that he's doing his best to help Preston simply because I asked.

Careful, he might like that.

CARMICHAEL

If that were true, you would still be fucking him.

Okay, he has me there.

I arrive at the airport and grab my bag. Standing on the sidewalk outside the departure doors, I take a deep breath before heading inside to check in. This is the worst part of travel. Once I'm at the gate I'll be fine but getting checked in and through security is an anxiety attack waiting to happen.

It takes an hour and a half to get through check in and security, then I end up taking the tram to another part of the airport to get to my gate and wait there for boarding. Since I'm not a small dude, my mom sprung for business class, so I have some extra leg room. It's glorious.

For the next few hours, I watch movies on my phone and message my mom, thanks to the Wi-Fi on board.

Brendon and Paul are keeping Preston busy, which he is begrudgingly happy for. It keeps him from moping around the dorm room or working out until he passes out.

When I finally land in Michigan and make my way to baggage claim, I smile when I see the big cardboard sign my mom is holding up.

"Welcome Home Hockey Star!"

People are standing around and watching to see who this hockey star is and are disappointed when it's not someone they know.

Stacy lets go of Ella as I hit the bottom of the escalator and she runs for me with her arms up. I hunch down to catch her and twirl her around when I have her.

"Hey there, big girl!" She wraps her arms around my neck, refusing to let go. I rub her back and give her a big hug. "I missed you too, baby."

Mom rushes toward me next, wrapping her arms around my waist to hug me next to Ella, who yells at having to share me. She looks the same, though I think she's got a few more wrinkles around her eyes. At five foot nine, she's tall for a woman, but all of us boys tower over her. Her brown hair is loose down her back, and while she's never been small, she's always been able to keep up with us. She's strong as an ox and can probably work longer than the rest of us.

Stacy laughs and gives me a high five while the boys give me fist bumps. Dad wraps his arms around me and Ella, patting me on the back while Ella screams at him, pushing at him to let go. Dad went gray a few years ago. He swears it's because of the twins, and that may be true since they get into trouble chasing girls pretty often.

"Alright, baby, you're okay."

"Nice of you to steal my kid," Stacy grumbles when she tries to take the little girl who refuses to let go of me.

"Told you I'm her favorite."

Mom tucks herself under my free arm and wraps her arm around my back. "I'm so glad you're here."

While we wait for my duffle to come through the baggage claim line, the boys tell me about football, girls, and fights with friends. I don't miss the drama of high school.

I point out my bag and Dad grabs it for me. We head out to the car, stopping for everyone to put on jackets since it's cold as fuck out there. There's a good foot of snow on the ground, so the forty-minute drive home to Muskegon will probably be an hour and a half, depending on the roads.

"How long did it take to get here?" I ask Dad as I get Ella loaded in the Suburban.

"Not long, 'bout an hour." He shrugs. Jordan and Keith buckle into the back row of seats with my bag, Stacy and I take the middle on either side of Ella, and we hit the road.

"How do you like Denver?" Mom turns to face me.

"I haven't been out much. Hockey and classes keep me busy." I shrug, pulling my phone from my pocket and taking a selfie with my siblings and Ella.

Made it to Michigan, now we drive.

CARMICHAEL

How long is the drive?

"You don't get time off?" Stacy asks this time.

"Not during the season. Are you crazy?"

Could be an hour, could be four. Who knows. Depends on the roads and if the weather turns.

CARMICHAEL

How the fuck do you live like that?

I'm used to it. I was born here.

Preston's question makes me smile. Mister *has to schedule everything down to the minute*, could not handle it here.

"Who is making you smile like that?" Mom asks, a knowing smile on her face.

"That has to be the boyfriend," Stacy rats me out while I can't escape our parents.

"You're dead to me!" I turn a glare at her. "Now I'm definitely pushing you down the stairs."

"Boyfriend? When did this happen?" Mom screeches.

I slump into my seat, preparing for the interrogation.

"Thanksgiving," I sigh.

"That was *weeks* ago!" she yells and the boys snicker behind me.

Both of them muttering "Sucker," under their breaths.

"Who is it? What's his name? How did you meet?" Mom rapid fires questions at me.

"It's Preston Carmichael, he's on the team and my roommate."

Mom lifts an eyebrow at me, which I was expecting. "And what is he doing for Christmas?"

"He stayed at school with Brendon and Paul."

"I was going to ask you about that. Why didn't they come home?" She redirects the conversation, thank fuck.

"Brendon's family decided to go to Hawaii and he didn't want to spend the money on a ticket. Paul's dad is out on a big ice fishing trip, so he didn't see the point of coming back." I shrug.

"They both could have come to the house, they're always welcome," she insists.

"They know, Mom."

A picture comes through my chat with Paul.

Opening the message, I laugh at the look on Preston's face while he watches Brendon inhale what looks like a deep-fried Twinkie.

He might actually die watching Brendon eat that.

JOHNSON

He's determined to get your boy drunk. I'll keep you updated. But so far, he's holding strong and won't drink.

He's a lightweight so be careful and send me videos.

"Is Preston's family local in Denver?" Mom starts back up.

"His dad moved there the same time he did, but his sister is in New York for school."

She nods like this is what she was hoping for. "So, he's spending the holiday with his dad, good."

Ice shoots through my veins. Fuck. I hadn't thought of that. How could I be so fucking stupid? Is that why he didn't want to come out here with me? Did he know he would have to see his dad and didn't want to tell me because I already had a ticket to come home?

This time, I don't text him, I call him and hope reception holds long enough for me to talk to him.

The phone rings in my ear a few times before Preston's voice comes across the line.

"Jeremy, you okay?" His concern has a weight dropping into my stomach.

"Yeah, I'm fine. Did you not want to come out here because you have to see your dad and you didn't want me to know?" I'm fully aware that my family is listening to my conversation but oh well. I need to hear his voice when he answers me. It's too easy to lie over text.

"Hold on," I hear him excuse himself and head outside of wherever he is. "Baby," his voice is smooth like good liquor and just as enticing when he calls me that. That term of endearment does things to my insides that I wish it didn't while I'm locked in the car with my family. I suck in a breath to release some of the tension. "I'm not planning to see him. He normally leaves for Christmas, so I don't even think he's going to be in town."

"Promise? If you're lying to me, I'll kick your ass."

He chuckles, "You wish you could."

"There is so much more I could say if I wasn't locked in a car with my entire family," I grumble.

"Yeah? Like what? You won't fuck me? Won't suck my dick?" Despite the amusement in his voice, his words are turning me on, which is very uncomfortable given my current circumstances.

"Yeah, all of the above." I manage to get out through gritted teeth

"You and I both know I would take it and you would like it." The dark tone of his voice has goosebumps breaking out over my skin.

"I hate you."

He laughs again and this time, it's villainous. "You might wish that were true but we both know it's not."

I growl at him because he's right. Even when I wanted to

hate him, I didn't. Ella imitates my growl, pretending to be a bear if I had to guess, and I smile at her.

"Why did you sic your friends on me? You're going to have to make this up to me."

It's my turn to laugh this time. "I didn't expect them to drag you out of the dorms today. How did they manage to convince you to leave?"

"I was rubbing one out and they barged in, told me if I went with them now, they would go easy on me and leave me alone afterward. They lied."

I chuckle again. "So what you're saying is, you're a sucker?"

"Shut up. It'll be a miracle if I don't end up punching Brendon in the face before the end of the day."

Keith and Jordan start bickering behind me and won't quit so I tell Preston goodbye and turn to my brothers. "What the hell is your problem?"

"Nothing," they say in unison.

"Probably fighting over the girl from across the street," Stacy says, not looking up from her phone.

"Excuse me?!" Mom hollers from the front seat, turning to look at her youngest kids.

"Oh, I see how it is." I look at my older sister. "You're telling everyone's business so Mom doesn't start in on you about the neighbor you're once again sleeping with?"

Stacy flings her head at me with murder in her eyes. I smile at her, Mom yelling "Stacy!" while I chuckle. Ella babbles, pointing at the boys she can see over the back of the seat like she's telling on them too. Dad sighs and shakes his head, stifling his laugh at the ensuing chaos.

"They've been sneaking that girl into the house! I think they're pretending to be the same person to mess with her!" Stacy points behind her while facing Mom and my mouth falls open in shock.

Ella giggles and covers her mouth.

"What?!" Mom shrieks again, spinning around in her seat to yell into the back.

"You're one to talk!" they yell at Stacy.

Keith points at her, accusing, "You're screwing half the dudes on our street!"

Stacy gasps and I crack up, holding my stomach as I laugh so hard the muscles hurt.

It's good to be home.

CHAPTER 34

preston

Hanging up with Jeremy is one of the hardest things I've done, emotionally. I'm fucking lost without him. He's the light in the dark maze of my life. I want to beg him not to let me go, not to disconnect the only lifeline I have, but I don't. I can't do that to him. He's with his family and needs time to be with them, his daughter, his siblings, his parents.

"Aw don't look so sad, P Dog," Brendon knocks his shoulder into mine and I lift a lip at him.

"Do *not* call me that."

Paul smirks and shakes his head. "It's easier to just ignore the nicknames. If he knows they bother you, he'll do it more."

I let out an exasperated breath and pinch the bridge of my nose. "I'm going back to the dorms."

"We've had enough fun for today," Brendon agrees and pulls up Uber on his phone to call a ride.

Fun is definitely not how I would describe today, but I

do begrudgingly appreciate what they were trying to do. I just want to go back to the dorm and sulk. I'm not telling them that though.

The ride shows up quickly and I sit in the front with the driver so I'm not forced to talk to Brendon. He's a little shit and he knows it. I'm pretty sure he gets off on annoying the shit out of people. Specifically, me.

Back in my dorm room, I take a deep breath and let my shoulders relax for the first time in what feels like days. The last week was brutal with practices, games, and mentally preparing for Jeremy to leave. I tried to put space between us, to stand on my own like I've done since I was ten, but I couldn't. Every time I tried, I clung to him more. It was infuriating.

Classes are over for the semester so I don't even have homework to keep me busy, I'm not much of a TV or movie watcher, so what the fuck am I supposed to do for the next two weeks?

I text Lily to see what she's up to, but she's out with her friends, and I don't want to bother Jeremy again.

So, I pace my room that smells like Jeremy. Smells like comfort, safety, and home. How can a person be home?

Back and forth, back and forth. How have I not walked a hole through this floor? The anxiety tensing my body is also turning my stomach. I rub at my chest, flick my fingers, but it's not helping. Fuck. I need something to do.

Changing into workout gear, I take the stairs down to the first floor, to avoid Paul and Brendon, and head to the gym. Since it's a Sunday night, there's no one here.

You're the only one without a life. Get a grip. Paul and Brendon are only hanging out with you because Jeremy asked them to. They don't actually care about you. Who would?

I get my earbuds connected to my phone and find my running playlist to start stretching and warming up.

Once my muscles are warmed up and loose, I up the speed on the treadmill until I can't think about anything but my breathing. The pain in my side eventually goes away and the burn in my legs becomes a constant, but I focus on the air entering and exiting my lungs.

Around the four-mile mark, my phone rings with a video call from Jeremy. Shit. He's going to see right through me and know why I'm in here.

Do I answer it?

Fuck it.

I hit accept on the call and slow the treadmill down to a walk to cool down, sweaty and breathing hard when Jeremy's smiling face fills my screen.

"I had a feeling you would be at the gym." His voice fills my ears and I give him a tired smile.

"I'm not hard to figure out." Grabbing the towel I threw over the machine, I wipe my splotchy face. "What are you up to?"

"Everyone went to bed so I was hoping to get some *alone* time with you." He gives me a wink.

"You just want to get off." I shake my head in mock disappointment. "Using me for my body, such a shame, Albrooke."

It should worry me how easily I've learned how to hide from him when he's looking right at me. I know he's checking in on me because he's worried. He wants to phone sex, or whatever it's called, via video call because he knows getting off will help me sleep, but I don't tell him I'm struggling without him. I can't tell him I'm afraid to go to sleep without him. Should I? Probably. But how is that going to help? All that does is make him feel like shit for being with his family, which is where he should be.

"You going to take me in the shower with you?"

I give him a *not a chance* look and he laughs. He hasn't

seen me without clothes on. When we fuck, I stay covered. Sometimes I let him touch me, but he's only seen the damage to my body once or twice. Even that much makes it hard for me to breathe.

"You know I'm not turned off by the scars, right?" Jeremy turns serious as I shut down the machine and find a wipe to clean it.

"I am." The two words are curt, harsher than I mean for them to be, but talking about them puts me on edge.

"Boyfriend," Jeremy says, like it's my name.

"That word is so childish. Undignified." I scowl at him while he smiles at me.

"Well, manfriend sounds skeezy, guyfriend sounds like a buddy, and you're more than my fuck buddy, so deal with it."

I sigh heavily as I head into the locker room to grab my shower shit.

"Oh, baby, taking me to the showers." He wags his eyebrows at me and I roll my eyes. "Come on, don't tell me you've never thought about fucking me in the shower. I think about it all the time."

Well, that has my attention. Images of Jeremy wet and naked in the shower, moaning my name definitely has appeal.

"I don't think about anyone in the shower. I hate being in them but I hate being dirty, so I shower with the lights off." *Why the fuck did you say that? Way to ruin the mood, you fucking idiot.*

Jeremy is quiet, no longer smiling with happiness but giving me one of those sad smiles you give to someone who's grieving. Fuck.

"Get that god damn look off your face right now," I snap, clenching my jaw as I suck in a breath. "I hate it. Don't pity me."

"I'm allowed to empathize. Sometimes the shit you say is really fucking sad, dude," he snaps back. "I care about you, so sometimes when you say shit like you shower in the dark, it hurts me too. I don't want you to live like that."

"You don't get to decide how I live." How the fuck did we get here? "The way I've coped has been working for years, I'm fine. I don't need your fucking empathy!" I can't look at him. I can't see his face lined with frustration or anger or *empathy* right now.

"Since this is going nowhere, I'll talk to you tomorrow. I hope you can sleep. Call me if you need to." His voice is softer than I expected. He's obviously upset with me but trying to be the bigger person. "I lo-"

"Don't!" I bark the word at him and it echoes in the empty locker room, severe and full of fear. There's no way what he was about to say is true. None. Zero. Not a fucking chance. I can feel how wide my eyes are, the hard set of my lips as I hold my breath and beg him not to say it. The fear coursing through my veins like ice at the idea of him saying *that* word is more than I can handle.

His face falls and there's nothing I can do about it. It breaks my fucking heart.

"Good night." His murmur is as full of emotion as the lines on his face. He won't look at me now as he chews on the inside of his lip.

"Jeremy..." I try, but my voice cracks.

He shakes his head and ends the call. Now it's my turn for tears to burn my eyes and the back of my throat. God damn it! I ruin everything!

I toss my phone across the room where it hits a locker with a crunch and I yell until I'm bent over and can't breathe.

What the fuck have you done?

"Fuuuuuuuck!" Grabbing my bag, I stalk over to my

busted phone and pick it up. I'm even more furious when the screen is cracked and only parts of it light up.

He's never going to talk to you again. He hates you. He'll never love you. Ever. You've destroyed the only good thing in your life and you're going to have to watch while he picks up the pieces of his life and moves on without you.

With my chest tight and the weight of my fuck-ups heavy on my shoulders, I storm back to the dorms. I need to get out of my head. I can't live in my mind anymore.

I throw my shit in my room and head down to Paul and Brendon's room, banging on the door with shaking hands.

Paul's smile fades when he sees the emotions on my face. "Dude, what's wrong?"

"I need out of my head. How do I make it stop?" My voice breaks again, a tear escaping from my eye that I angrily wipe away.

"Uh yeah, come in." He steps back from the door to let me through. Brendon is laying on his bed with big headphones on. He takes them off and sits up when he spots me.

"Hey P Dadd—" He stops abruptly when Paul makes a cutthroat motion next to me. "What's going on?"

Paul digs a few bottles out from under his bed. "We're getting Carmichael drunk."

"Alright!" Brendon fist-bumps the air and scoots to the edge of the bed, reaching for a bottle with brown liquid. "Rum is my poison of choice."

"We've got rum, vodka, and whiskey." Paul lifts the bottles in his hands.

"I don't know and I don't care. Just get me fucked up. I don't want to think anymore." Paul looks at me like he's trying to read me, trying to figure out what's pushed me this far. Probably thinking he needs to call Jeremy.

I grab the bottle with clear liquid, unscrew the cap, and

take a chug of it. The burn down my throat makes me cough.

"Jesus," Paul mutters. "Have you ever drank before? Have you eaten recently?"

I force myself to take another big gulp of the nasty shit, coughing again at the burn. It's like drinking rubbing alcohol. It's awful but warmth is spreading from my stomach to the rest of my body.

You're so weak.

"How long until it works?" I ask Brendon, who is watching me with his mouth open.

This is why Father cuts you.

You're useless.

Another gulp and my shoulders relax.

Two more and my brain is fuzzy. I stumble against the dresser and lean heavily on it. Finally able to breathe, I close my eyes.

"You okay, man?" Brendon touches my shoulder and I jerk away from him.

"No touching." I take another swing from the bottle and drop my ass to the floor. "Touch means pain. I'm tired of the pain."

"Hey, dude. We have a situation here and I am concerned." Paul's voice sounds far away. Did he leave the room or am I losing the ability to hear? Does alcohol do that?

I hate this.

I just want Jeremy to curl up with, to smell his bodywash and deodorant, feel his heartbeat against me. I don't want to be alone anymore.

CHAPTER 35

preston

It's been three days since Jeremy went home to visit his family. I don't think I've gotten more than three hours of sleep. Even with the binge-drinking I've been doing, I wake up sweating and shaking from the nightmares.

I've sobered up enough to go for a run this morning but I feel like shit. Paul and Brendon wouldn't let me go to the gym while I was drinking, which was probably for the best, but I hate missing workouts. It stresses me out.

The shadows are moving and I'm fucking exhausted, but I'm running.

I don't know how long I run for or where I've gone. This city is still new to me and before long, I've gotten myself turned around and lost.

Air is screaming in and out of my lungs when I allow my body to stop moving. Sweat pours down my face, making my clothes stick to me. My hair falls into my face as I look around, trying to get some sense of direction.

Tall buildings everywhere, a lot of them made of sand-colored bricks and glass, and planted trees that definitely didn't grow there naturally, and manicured lawns.

Fuck.

I don't have my phone so I can't get directions back and my legs fucking ache now that I've stopped moving. The streets are crowded with people, cars on the road, and a storm is rolling in. It's cold as fuck, my breath a cloud around me.

Shuffling my way into a little hole-in-the-wall bakery, the tinkling of a bell on the door alerts someone in the back that I'm here.

"Just a second!" a feminine voice calls from the back. A knot tightens in my throat as the warmth of the small space hits my cold, damp skin. The comforting scent of sourdough bread baking tickles some long forgotten memory of my mother in the kitchen.

"Hi, how can I help—" the middle-aged woman with a name tag that says Debbi stops mid-sentence with her hands freezing in her apron. She does a quick sweep of my body before ushering me to the back.

"Come on, this way." She takes control of the situation with a calm, maternal energy that my body obeys. In the back is a small office with a desk and chairs that have seen better days, a computer that's probably older than I am, and stacks of papers. The whir of a computer fan provides a constant white noise.

"I'll get you some water and a towel." She smiles at me with empathy and it hurts. Jeremy looks at me like that sometimes. I fucking miss him. How pathetic am I that I can't survive two weeks without him? It's been three fucking days and I'm a damn mess. He probably hates me.

My entire body aches, strength draining out of my muscles, leaving me weak. How the hell am I going to get back to the dorms? My car is in the parking lot at school, I probably can't walk however many miles it'll take to get back, and I don't know where the fuck I am. I don't know anyone's number so I can't even call for a ride, not that I have anyone I can call.

Jeremy is going to call this off. The longer you put off talking to him, the longer it'll take for him to leave you.

My eyes close and I drop my head into my hands.

I can't lose him.

"Here we are." The short woman with salt and pepper hair comes back and hands me the water bottle. I twist off the top and chug the water, thirstier than I expected.

"Thank you," I say as I place the empty bottle and top into the trash can next to her desk.

"You're welcome." She puts her hands on her hips and looks me over. "Can I call someone for you?"

"I was running." *No shit, you dumbass.*

I scrub my hand over my face, pushing my hair out of my eyes, and take as deep of a breath as my exhausted body can manage.

"Do you know how to get to Darby University from here?"

Surprise raises her eyebrows. "That's like five miles from here."

I figured I had gone farther than that. Five miles is normal since running is my escape when the voices in my head are too loud, but I'm exhausted. There's no way I will be able to run back.

"Can I use your phone? I don't have mine on me." Shame for not being prepared heats my face. If my father knew how badly I've been fucking up lately, I'd wear those scars for years.

You'll be lucky to walk tomorrow. Keep being a fuck up and you'll never make it away from Father alive. He will crucify you before he allows you to be an embarrassment.

I only know two numbers by heart. Doctor Andrew Carmichael's cellphone and my little sister.

Debbi hands me a gray cordless phone from somewhere behind the desk. Trepidation makes my hands shake when I reach for it. The water in my stomach threatens to make another appearance while I dial my father's number. I can't let Lily know I'm falling the fuck apart.

"Here." She hands me a business card. "Address is on the back."

She leaves the room, probably to give me some privacy to make the call.

Sucking in a deep breath, I steel myself and dial the number.

It rings a few times in my ear until my father's polite, public voice answers.

"Hello?"

"I—" the words stick in my throat. Asking him for help is physically painful and can only lead me to more pain. "I need help."

"Charles." There's a sigh of disappointment. "What have you done now?"

"I went for a run and got turned around. I don't have my phone so I can't find my way back." I close my eyes. "I'm told I'm about five miles from the school."

"Then get directions from someone and run back."

Tears gather in my eyes so I snap them shut, refusing to let them fall. My body can't handle running back. Running on the concrete is harder on the body than the treadmill, not to mention it's not flat. God, I'm exhausted.

"I can't." The words are pathetic.

"Charles Preston Carmichael," he snaps my name and I flinch. "You got yourself into this mess, you'll deal with the consequences. Run back."

"Yes, Father." The words tumble from my lips, quiet and resigned.

The phone buzzes in my ear when he hangs up. My hand holding the phone drops to my lap and I stare at it. I hate him.

The door opens again, Debbi steps inside with another water bottle and a banana.

"Everything okay?" She hands them over to me. "Do you need a ride? The shop closes in ten minutes anyway. It won't take me long to get everything cleaned up."

I have to swallow past the lump in my throat, straighten my shoulders, and put on the face I show the public. "That's kind of you, but I'll be fine, thank you."

I stand, taking the water bottle and banana with me. My legs and feet scream in protest after the break but I grit my teeth and power through. I make it to the entrance of the shop without stumbling and find a few guys in Darby U hoodies. The one next to me has a ballcap on backwards and he turns his head.

I freeze when my eyes meet the green eyes of Paul fucking Johnson. He turns toward me, dragging his gaze down my body. Fuck. I didn't want him to see me like this. He's going to tell Jeremy.

The pang of disappointment in myself hurts more than my body does right now.

"What's going on, Carmichael?" He crosses his arms over his chest. The other guys with him turn at his voice, Brendon's red hair catching in the light, and another guy I've seen around the dorms but I haven't seen with the team.

"We've been looking for you," Brendon says sternly.

My jaw aches from clenching my teeth. It takes every ounce of self-control I have left to not snap at them, but I need their help.

Paul looks at the water bottle and banana in my hands

then at the woman still standing behind me. "Do you know her or something?"

"No, she's just a woman who was nice to me. Are you heading back to campus?"

"Yeah, just grabbing some cinnamon rolls. Debbi's are the best." The guy I don't know pipes up. Paul and Brendon are watching me like they aren't sure what to do with me. Which, I guess, is fair. I'm a dick to them most of the time and been a shit show lately. They've been babysitting me and I ditched them on purpose.

I want to tell them cinnamon rolls are the last thing they need but I don't. I'm too tired to give a shit, and who am I to judge after spending the last few days in a bottle?

They get their food and we head for the blue Corolla Paul drives. Even though I'm taller than everyone here, I climb into the back.

"I'm Nick." The kid from the dorm offers his hand. I take it and give a tight-lipped smile.

"Preston."

He laughs. "Oh, I know who you are."

Paul and Brendon have a conversation with just looks in the front seat but I don't have the energy to care. I lean my head back against the headrest and stare out the window, hoping no one talks to me.

Nick talks away but doesn't seem to need any encouragement from me to keep going so I block him out. Brendon and Paul keep looking back at me, but I don't know what they're checking for. Doesn't matter. Now they know I'm fake and a shitshow. A disappointment. No wonder my father abuses me.

When we get to the dorms, Nick climbs out, waving to the guys, and heads inside. I reach for the door but the locks engage and the guys turn around to look at me.

"This has to stop. Either go to Michigan or get your shit

together," Paul tells me in that tough love kind of way. "Jeremy is worried sick about you. So, either fucking talk to him or put him out of his misery. He's trying to find a way to tell his mom he's leaving early or he's going to end up with an ulcer from the stress."

Guilt has tears filling my eyes. He deserves so much more than me.

"He loves you, dude. He told us that and he's really worried about you," Brendon adds. "Why are you avoiding him?"

"I broke my phone." My voice cracks as tears fill my eyes. I'm so fucking tired.

"Are you kidding me? You could have used one of ours! You have a computer, send him a damn email if you have to!" Paul is almost yelling. I deserve it. I'm fucking up. "Plus, aren't you like a gazillionaire? Go buy a fucking a new one!"

"No, go to Michigan. Trust me, he wants to see you and the Albrookes are amazing. They'll be happy to have you. You can take that shit to the bank," Brendon tells me.

I nod solemnly and reach for the handle again. Paul unlocks the doors and we all go up to our floor together.

"No more taking off without letting one of us know. Pretty sure Jeremy almost came through the phone to choke us out," Brendon says before closing the door behind them.

I'm fucking exhausted but I pull out a backpack and shove some clothes in it. I need to see him and beg him to forgive me, in person. Opening my computer, I pull up an airline and buy a ticket to Grand Rapids, Michigan on the next available flight, then pass out with my arms wrapped around my laptop, my last thought being *I love you.*

CHAPTER 36

jeremy

I'm going fucking insane. I haven't spoken to Preston in days, the guys tell me he's been drinking like a damn fish and Brendon even found him smoking a cigarette once. What the fuck is happening? He won't answer my messages or calls. I can't sleep, I can't eat, and I'm definitely not doing the workouts I'm supposed to be doing for hockey.

When I was talking to Brendon at one point, he almost cried because Mom made her taco salad and I wasn't eating it. I *always* eat it.

I have to go back.

I have to.

I'm shoving clothes back into my duffle when my phone rings. Scrambling to find it, hoping it's Preston, I see it's Paul instead.

"Is he okay?"

Paul scrubs a hand down his face. "Dude is fucked up. He went for a run and didn't tell us. By sheer luck we found him at a bakery. He damn near killed himself. But we got some answers out of him. He broke his phone, I guess, so that's why he hasn't been answering you. We told him he needs to go see you."

Brendon appears on the screen. "I just checked on him and he's passed out cold, cuddling his laptop. He didn't even take his shoes off, just laid down."

Jesus. He's spiraling hard. This is exactly what I was hoping wouldn't happen. At least his dad isn't there to get a hold of him. I can't imagine what that would look like.

My heart hurts for him. He must think I'm pissed, but I'm not. Okay, I'm mad he's been avoiding me, but I love him. I want to know he's okay.

"You think he'll come?" I'm afraid to hope.

"I don't know. Dude is stubborn as fuck," Paul says.

I let out a sigh. "You're not wrong." I run my hands through my hair and pull on the ends. "Alright, keep me updated. I'm going to talk to my mom about changing my ticket and coming back early. I can't stay here if he's already this out of control after three days."

"Will do."

My bedroom door opens and Stacy comes in with Ella on her hip.

"Hey." I drop down to my bed, heavy with indecision and defeat.

"How's the boyfriend? Did you find him?" She sits next to me and Ella climbs into my lap.

I cuddle her to my chest and rub her back while she sucks her thumb. "Yeah, they found him. He went for a run and got lost, I guess. I don't know." A lump forms in my throat. "I need to go back. He's not okay."

"Is he okay for tonight?"

"Brendon says he's finally asleep but I don't know how

long that will last, he has pretty bad nightmares." I shrug, not wanting to get into the details of his life with her.

"We're going to go to Grandma and Grandpa's to do the baking tomorrow. I think the boys, Dad, and Grandpa are going ice fishing. You're probably expected to join them."

I nod and notice Ella has fallen asleep. I smile at the innocent little girl in my arms. She's such a sweet baby.

"I'll take her," Stacy says, reaching for her daughter.

"Can I just hold her for a bit?" The knot in my throat hurts to talk around but I miss the pressure of someone on my chest. The warmth of another person against me.

She looks at me for a second and nods.

"Of course." She stands and ruffles my hair, kisses my head, then turns the light off on her way out but leaves the door cracked open. I adjust myself on the bed until I'm leaning on the pillows against the headboard and cover us with a blanket.

Opening the camera on my phone, I snap a picture of her sweet face in the dimly lit room then torture myself by opening my conversation with Preston from the airport to flip through his pictures.

What happened? He seemed okay when I left, a little clingy but that was expected. Was he faking being okay?

Ella stirs on my chest, rubbing her face against my shirt. The scent of lavender from her shampoo tickles my nose. I hate that I'm missing so much of her growing up. She changes so fast these days. I'm afraid she's going to forget me and Jordan will become her favorite uncle after all.

It doesn't take long for me to fall asleep, warm and comforted by my niece on my chest.

The day is a mad rush of trying to get Mom, Stacy, and Ella ready for baking, Jordan, Keith, and Dad ready for fishing, and for me to decide what the hell I'm doing.

"I'm going to go with Mom to spend time with Ella," I tell Dad as he loads up with the boys to go get Grandpa. I sound like a fucking broken record. I'm annoyed with myself.

"Alright, bud. We'll see you later." Dad gives me a hug and leaves.

I'm getting Ella into her snow boots when my phone pings.

OILER

Little problem

Dread fills me. I can't take anymore damn problems!

What now?

OILER

He's gone and we have no idea where he went.

Again!?!

I scrub a hand down my face and growl in irritation. Looking at the time, I try to do the math to figure out the time difference. If he went to work out at four his time, he would be done by now, but if he went for a hard run last night and passed out, he probably didn't get up on time so maybe he's at the gym?

The gym?

OILER

Do you really think I wouldn't have checked there first?

Did his dad come back and grab him? He wouldn't have been in any position to fight him off. If Preston has been spiraling as badly as I think, he would have agreed to whatever his dad wanted because he felt he deserved it. Fuck.

I can't take this shit anymore! I'm telling Mom today that I'm flying back.

OILER

Might not be a bad plan. This is crazy.

We grab what we have to take with us and climb in the car. I sit next to Ella in the back and even though I know he won't answer, I call Preston anyway. I have to know I tried.

My knee is bouncing the entire drive over and my stomach is in knots. I don't know how I'm going to manage smelling baking sweets all day, but it's better than sitting in a hut on the ice with no reception.

The drive is quick enough, with not much talking since Mom is still irritated about Stacy keeping secrets for the twins, but I don't mind the quiet. It means I don't have to force myself to pay attention.

Ella babbles next to me and hands me the book she has, *Good Night Moon*.

"You want me to read it?" I ask her. She babbles happily and I open the book. "In the great green room," I start reading but she grabs the book and takes it from me. I smile at her while I zone out, consumed with worry for the man I love. Will he ever accept that I love him?

We pull up to the house my mother was raised in, and I smile at the childhood memories from this place. The bottom half of the house is brick with green wood siding and big windows on the upper half. The big tree in the front yard has an old tire swing that we used to play on in the summer.

Grandma opens the front door and I unbuckle Ella to carry her to the porch.

"Jeremy!" Grandma smiles and wraps her arms around me in a hug I didn't realize I needed. I want so badly to collapse in my worry, let her shoulder some of my troubles like she did while I was growing up, but I don't. I hold it together because I'm supposed to be an adult and handle my own problems.

"I'm so glad to see you." She kisses my cheek. "Come on, Ella, let's get in the house where it's warm." Ella races for the door and pushes on it to enter the house.

I go back to the car and help Mom and Stacy bring in the supplies.

"I knew there was a reason we brought him," Stacy says, patting me on the back.

"Yeah, yeah, shut up." I set the box on the kitchen counter and leave to get out of the way, kicking my shoes off at the door on my way to the couch.

It didn't take long for us boys to learn to stay out of the kitchen when the women are cooking, especially for holidays. It's why we all go ice fishing during prep. On Christmas, we'll watch football or Christmas movies, depending on who's controlling the TV. A few years ago, we got Grandma a little flat screen TV to mount to the wall so she could watch what she wanted while she cooked. Hopefully, she'll watch her Christmas movies there and leave the living room free for football.

Stacy gets Ella set up in her highchair in the kitchen with some ingredients to play with or eat, and I take a seat on the brown suede couch in the living room, glaring at my phone. I want the damn thing to ring and I'm pissed when it doesn't.

"What are you being so mopey about?" Grandma comes in, wiping her hands on a dish towel.

"Just worried about my boyfriend." I shrug, once again protecting his privacy and trying to avoid what's really bothering me.

"Boyfriend?" Her face brightens as she sits next to me on the couch. "Tell me about him."

I smile to myself when the screen on my phone lights up, showing me his goofy selfie.

"He's a hockey player, my dormmate, and a huge pain in my a—" I cut myself off when she gives me *the look,* "hiney."

She chuckles and swats me with the towel. "Sounds like love to me."

I want that to be true so badly it hurts, but I shrug and chew on the inside of my lip.

"If it's meant to be, it'll work out." She pats my leg and stands to head back to the kitchen. Why are adults always so quick to tell you useless crap? That's not helpful or comforting.

I'm flipping my phone around in my hands, staring off into space when it rings. My heart rate spikes as I flip it around and I'm confused when an unknown Muskegon number is calling.

"Hello?"

A shuddering breath comes across the line before, "Please come get me."

Preston. Oh, my fucking god, it's Preston. He sounds like he's damn near in tears.

"Where are you?" I'm on my feet and hurrying to pull my shoes back on.

"Trinity Health Arena." Someone says it behind him and he repeats it. Who the hell is he with?

"I'm on my way, I'll be there in like thirty minutes. Don't move." I rush for the kitchen, turning the phone away from my mouth. "Mom! I need your keys!"

"What? What's wrong? Did something happen on the

lake?" She's wiping flour off her hands onto her apron, panic in her eyes. All three women look at me as they wait for an answer.

"No, Preston is at the arena, I'm going to go get him."

"I'll drive! You're a wreck." Stacy grabs the keys Mom dug out of her purse and slides her shoes on. "Mom, can you watch El or do you want me to take her with me?"

"Uh, take her with you so we can get going on these Santa cookies." She helps Stacy get Ella ready while I impatiently pace by the front door.

"Come on! Let's go!" I'm going to vibrate out of my fucking skin if she doesn't hurry the fuck up!

"Alright! I'm coming, hold your damn horses." Stacy carries Ella to the car. I grab the diaper bag and follow behind her.

"Be careful! Drive slow!" Mom yells from the porch as we climb in the car and back out of the driveway.

My knee is bouncing a million miles an hour as I try to prepare myself for what I'm about to encounter. He sounded rough on the phone. Will he break down right there when he sees me or will he be shut down tight and emotionless? How the fuck did he even get to the arena? I lean on the door, staring out the window, lost in my head.

"You love him, don't you?" Stacy asks, glancing over at my bouncing knee.

That fucking lump is back in my throat, threatening to choke me. A tear falls from my eye and I brush it away.

"Yeah, I do." It hurts to say the words out loud when he won't accept them. Why the fuck is he here?

"Have you told him?" she asks, being nosey.

"I tried but he wasn't ready to hear it."

The drive is slower than I want it to be but we make it one piece.

"Where is he at?" Stacy asks as we pull into the arena. Shit. I didn't ask him where he was.

"I don't know. I forgot to ask!" I run my fingers through my hair and pull on the strands, frustrated with myself.

"Just pull up close and we'll drive around to see if we can see anything." It takes us a few minutes but someone in jeans and a long-sleeved t-shirt steps out from the door, hunched over against the wind.

"Stop!" I yell and throw my door open before she's had a chance to fully stop. I'm out of the car and racing for him. Preston. My boyfriend. The man I love. I run as fast as I can toward him, colliding in the middle of the driveway and wrapping my arms around him.

"Fuck!" He shoves his arms under my jacket, pressing his chest solidly against mine. He's trembling, his face pressed into my neck, as his hands slide under my shirt. They're fucking freezing.

"Your hands are fucking cold! Why don't you have a coat?" I hiss but I don't let him go, I can't. "I'm so glad you're here. Are you okay? Why haven't you talked to me in days? I've been so fucking worried!"

"I'm sorry," he says against my skin. "For everything. Please don't leave me. I need you."

His grip on me is painfully tight but I don't care, I need to feel him as badly as he needs to feel me.

"I'm not going anywhere," I say as I pull his face to mine, our foreheads resting together.

A tear slips down his cheek and I brush it away with my thumb.

"I love you," his voice cracks and the trembling increases. "I need you. Please." His eyes are squeezed together so tightly.

"I love you too." With my hands cupping the back of his head, I bring his face to mine to press our lips together. He shudders at the touch as his hands slide higher up my back. Fuck, I've missed him.

The kiss isn't rushed or heated. It's soft and slow and meaningful. A reconnecting and understanding. The anxiety that's been racing through my blood stream for days finally recedes and I'm able to take a full breath.

A car door opens behind me, a loud shriek from Ella has Preston breaking the kiss and putting some space between us.

"Shit. I'm sorry. I know I'm impeding on your time with your family. I'm a selfish fuck." He looks like he's in physical pain.

"No, it's fine. Trust me, they all want to meet you and you will probably be the new favorite." I smile at him, hoping that doesn't freak him out too much.

His eyebrows pinch together in confusion. "I'm no one's favorite anything."

"That's bullshit. You're my favorite."

"Dumbass! He doesn't have a fucking jacket! Get inside the car!" Stacy hollers from behind me.

"How did you get here? Uber?" I ask him, reaching for his hand and pulling him toward the SUV.

"No, I rented a car." He pulls keys out of his pocket and motions to a small SUV in the parking lot.

"Cool, I'll drive." I take the keys from him and turn back to Stacy. "I'll meet you at the house."

"Okay. Get him a damn jacket!"

I flip her off and we run for his car. I get it unlocked before we get to it and slide in the seats, immediately turning the key to get the engine started and heat on. Preston cups his hands in front of his mouth and blows into them.

"Here." I take my jacket off and hand it to him. He doesn't argue, just groans when he slides into the already warm coat.

"Why did you come here? To the arena?" I ask, staring up at the building I played at for years.

"I didn't know where you lived and, I don't know, something told me to come here." He shrugs and looks at the building. "A guy inside recognized me and I told him I was looking for you but couldn't remember your number. He was able to get it somehow."

I reach for his hand and thread my fingers through his. "I'm really glad you came."

He lifts one side of his mouth in a small smile but drops it quickly. "I'm sorry I'm a fucking mess."

I squeeze his hand. "I'm not. I love you the way you are."

CHAPTER 37

preston

My heart is still racing, telling me I'm in danger and have to look out, but my head is finally quiet. Mostly. I've fucked this up so badly that I'm not sure if I can really fix it. Will he trust me after this? I don't trust myself.

I'm exhausted. Physically and mentally drained from the last few days of living without him. That's pathetic and selfish but it's the truth. I caught sight of myself in a mirror at the airport and the dark circles under my eyes look like someone punched me in the face. But I'm warm again and Jeremy's hand is in mine. He's mine.

In the front pocket of my backpack is a leather cuff bracelet with hockey sticks embossed into it. I saw it while I was waiting for my flight and had to have it for Jeremy. We're going to be together on Christmas and I can't show up with nothing. I don't have anything for his parents besides a bottle of wine I already grabbed in the same little shop I got the bracelet.

Why are you here?

Wasting everyone's time, taking away the limited time he has with his family.

Selfish.

Ungrateful.

Useless.

The drive to where Jeremy is taking me doesn't take long enough. It's not enough time for me to be with just him, to get my head on semi-straight. I'm not ready to go inside and have to talk and smile and be pleasant.

"This is my grandma's house, it's baking day for the women in my family, all the guys are out on the lake fishing, but they're busy so they should leave us alone if we go upstairs." Jeremy sits back in the seat as he looks at the house we're parked in front of.

The pressure on my chest is increasing. My breaths are too fast, and my palms are sweaty. I can't do this. I shouldn't even be here.

"Preston." Jeremy pulls on my hand and reaches for me with his other hand. I flinch as he touches my cheek and pulls my face toward him. "Look at me."

I can't keep my focus on his face, my gaze swings from left to right and back.

"Why don't I go get my mom's house keys and we can just go back to the house? Would that be better?"

I nod, I think, but I can't tell. I don't have control over my body or my mind anymore. All I need is to sleep but I can't when he's not with me. Why can't he understand that?

The urge to cry is stronger than it should be. Men don't cry. They are stoic and calm and suck it up with only anger to get shit done. Suck it up and get it done. But I'm tired. I want to be weak. Why can't I be weak for just a minute?

"Hey, I'll be right back. Okay?" His face wobbles with

the tears trying to fall from my lashes. He kisses my forehead and gets out, running into the house.

I close my eyes and breathe, running my hands up and down my thighs.

Man up.

Stop being a baby.

You're a grown ass man, not some little bitch.

You're an embarrassment. Look at you, sitting in the car like a scared little girl instead of meeting his mother like a man.

He's ashamed of you.

My father's voice is sharp in my head, playing on the insecurities he put there to keep me beneath him.

The car door opens again, Jeremy's face, red with cold, turns to me as he starts up the car.

"Okay, here we go."

"Wait!" I unbuckle my seatbelt and reach for the door. "I have to introduce myself to your mom so I don't embarrass you."

I'm halfway out the door when Jeremy's hand lands on my arm and he pulls me back inside.

"What are you talking about? You are exhausted and need to rest. I told them you took a red eye and stayed up all night, and that you would meet them tonight. They understand, it's okay." He looks at me in earnest. "And you're definitely not an embarrassment. I would never be embarrassed to tell anyone you're mine."

"It's impolite to not introduce myself. I have to meet them." My argument is weak, even to me.

"You will meet them, when you are rested and in a better head space." He squeezes my hand and I buckle my seat belt again.

"Are you sure? I've already caused you a lot of problems, I don't want—"

"Stop." Jeremy squeezes my hand again. "They will love you. I promise."

I nod and relax into the seat, dropping my head to the headrest while Jeremy pulls away from the curb.

A few quiet minutes later, we're pulling into the driveway of a two-story ranch style house. It's blue with white trim and a metal roof. Homey and welcoming. It's easy to picture kids playing in the front yard, running through sprinklers and setting up a lemonade stand.

Jeremy gets out of the car and I follow him up the walkway to the door. We stop at the entrance to take off our shoes and jackets. The walls are a cream color with a natural wood chair rail and molding. The walls are lined with framed pictures and decorations I would expect to find in a cabin, bears and moose, buffalo plaid, and pine trees. It's welcoming and comfortable though, which is more than I can say for any of the places my dad has lived.

"Are you hungry?" Jeremy asks me, pulling my attention away from the pictures of him and his siblings on the wall.

"No." I shake my head. "Just tired."

He reaches for my hand and I let him pull me through the house to a staircase. We climb up and even with his sexy ass literally in my face, I'm too exhausted to appreciate it properly.

"Shower?" he asks as we stop at the landing at the top of the stairs. There's a few doors up here, probably a bathroom and three bedrooms if I had to guess.

I shake my head. I don't know how I'm still standing upright as exhaustion is taking over.

"Come on." He chuckles when I sway. He leads me to a door on the right of the stairs and opens it for me. It's definitely Jeremy's room. It smells like him. The walls are lined with hockey posters and swag from the Lumberjacks. It makes me smile, getting to see this part of him.

"Where's your bag? Do you have pajamas or are you sleeping in jeans?" Jeremy wraps his arms around my waist, his hands landing on my lower back. Our abdomens are pushed together and my hands cup his head, dropping my forehead to his.

"I missed you." I breathe the words into the space between us.

Jeremy's arms tighten around me and he lifts his mouth to mine. I don't hesitate to press my lips to his in a quick kiss. I'm too tired to do anything else.

"Do you want something to change into?" he asks me as he steps back and strips out of his jeans and t-shirt, tossing them on the foot of the bed.

I shake my head and drop my jeans to the floor, stepping out of them and looking up at him when he doesn't move to the bed. He's staring at my legs, at the scars that can be seen below my boxer briefs. I can't raise the energy it takes to be embarrassed. I'm about to pass out on my feet.

"Jeremy," I mumble, swaying toward the bed.

"Shit, sorry." He pulls back the blanket and lets me climb into the bed first so I can be by the wall. He slides in after me, laying on his back so I can collapse on his chest. I hook my leg over one of his, bury my face in his neck, and wrap my arms around him until my hands are under his back. My eyes close and it's lights out.

The next time my eyes open, the sun is streaming in the window and it makes my head ache. *Where is Jeremy?*

Sitting up, I look around the room and don't see him.

"Jeremy?" My voice is hoarse with sleep and from having a dry throat. I'm so thirsty.

I don't hear any movement, so I get out of bed and notice my lack of pants. Fuck. My shoulders droop and I scrub a hand over my face. I didn't want him to see them. Not now. Not like this.

"Jeremy?" I call again, looking for my pants. I find them at the end of the bed with my backpack. Did I put anything in there?

I pull on the jeans and open the bag to look for a change of clothes. What I find makes me freeze.

Five pairs of socks, two pairs of underwear, one shirt, and a deodorant stick. What the actual fuck?

I swipe my pits so I don't stink for now, change my shirt and underwear, then head downstairs. Sounds of sizzling bacon and brewing coffee come from the kitchen with the low hum of conversation. My stomach grumbles at the scent of food. *When was the last time I ate?*

Rolling my shoulders and straightening my spine, I school my face to neutral before I enter the kitchen. A woman with brown hair twisted into a bun wearing a blue bathrobe is standing at the stove. Eggs and bacon are cooking, with a pile of pancakes on a plate next to her and a cup of coffee in her hand.

"Good morning," she sends me a quick smile. "There's OJ in the fridge, cream and milk too. Coffee is about ready and breakfast will be ready in about five minutes."

"Thank you, ma'am." I nod to her and look around the kitchen that's open to the dining room and living room. My eyes meet Jeremy's in the living room and I shove my hands in my pockets, when he stands and comes toward us. I hate how awkward I am, how unsure of everything I am here. It's not like me. I'm confident in everything I do but here, I'm so out of my element I feel like I'm drowning.

"Mom," Jeremy says, wrapping an arm around my waist. "This is my boyfriend, Preston."

She puts down the spatula and smiles up at me. "It's so nice to meet you, Preston. We're glad to have you with us. You can call me Mom or Trish." She reaches to give me a hug but I flinch, taking a step back.

Suck it up and let the woman hug you, you worthless ass.

Her face falls and she looks to Jeremy, who pulls me into his side.

"He's not much of a hugger," Jeremy informs her while I fight with myself. "I get boyfriend privileges," he says with a smile.

She nods and offers me her hand to shake, which I take gratefully. "Thank you for having me, especially at the last minute."

"You know, you're the first guy Jeremy has brought home. I'm sure I can dig up some baby pictures." She winks at me conspiratorially and I smile at her as Jeremy groans. "Go sit, boys." Mrs. Albrooke shoos us out of the kitchen and I gratefully take the out to go sit in the living room. Jeremy offers me the seat at the end of the couch then leans against me once he's settled. Two younger boys sit on one couch, faces buried in their phones, and an older man sits at the table reading a newspaper.

I lean in to whisper to Jeremy. "I didn't know people still read the newspaper." He chuckles and reaches for a glass of water and hands it to me.

Grateful for it, I chug the glass and set it back on the table.

"Dad reads it every morning, like clockwork."

I nod and wrap an arm around Jeremy's shoulder, threading my fingers with his. The boys look up at the movement and pin me with a serious look, mouths flat, eyes staring holes into me, fists clenched. It's creepy.

Unsure of what to say, I try to give them a smile but it falls flat. I've never been in a relationship, never met anyone's family before, never had someone be important to me, so I don't know how to do this. My people skills suck on the best of days.

I'm about to ask Jeremy what to do when he looks over.

"Knock it off," he tells the boys.

Smiles burst across their faces, turning into chuckles as they relax, putting the phones down.

"I'm Keith, that's Jordan," the one on the right says.

Jeremy scoffs and shakes his head. "Liar."

"How do you tell them apart?" I ask Jeremy.

"The attitude mostly. Keith is the quieter of the two, Jordan is the troublemaker. But Jordan also has a little scar at his hairline that helps."

The one who introduced them smiles bigger.

"But don't feel bad if you get them mixed up, they do it on purpose to mess with everyone. Stacy gets it right about half the time, but I'm almost always right."

"Breakfast!" His mom calls from the table and the boys hustle over, filling their plates to overflowing. One gets orange juice while the other gets milk. I wait until everyone is done serving themselves before I grab a plate and scoop up some eggs and bacon. Jeremy smirks but doesn't say anything.

As good as those pancakes smell, I can't make myself eat them. I've done enough damage to my diet lately.

I refill my water glass and sit down at the table next to Jeremy.

There's another seat next to him and a highchair between it and Mrs. Albrooke, but I don't ask about it. I'm curious about Jeremy's daughter since he's said he's gay, but this isn't the time for it.

"Tell us about yourself, Preston," Jeremy's father says, looking up from his plate.

The blood drains from my face. What the hell am I supposed to say to that? *My father is a surgeon, likes to use me as a guinea pig. I play hockey because he tells me to, and to keep my sister safe.*

"Um, well, sir," I start, swallowing hard. "There's not

much to tell. My life revolves around hockey." God, could I sound any lamer?

Jeremy's hand rests on my leg.

"What he really wants to know is if he can talk fishing, hunting, or football with you." He looks at his dad and answers for me. "No."

Mr. Albrooke sighs and shakes his head. "Where are you from, son?"

"Boston, mostly," I answer, waiting for the comment I know is coming.

"You don't sound like you're from Boston." *And there it is.*

"My parents aren't from the area."

Footsteps sound overhead and a feminine voice can be heard, though I can't understand the words.

"Ella is up," Mrs. Albrooke says, and Jeremy pulls the highchair closer to him, putting food on it and cutting it up, then goes to the kitchen and gets a sippy cup and fills it with milk. If she's up, shouldn't Jeremy be getting her? Maybe he made arrangements with his sister for baby duty, just in case she woke up in the middle of the night so he wouldn't wake me up?

A woman not much older than me and Jeremy carrying a little blonde girl on her hip comes into the kitchen. Jeremy's face lights up when the little girl reaches for him and he takes her from the woman I assume is his sister, Stacy.

"Good morning, baby girl." He kisses her cheek and hands her the sippy cup. They come to the table and he sets her in the highchair to eat. My heart warms watching him with her. He's so happy to see her, to be with her.

You're ruining his time with her.

Jeremy sits down next to me and puts his hand back on my leg but is making faces and talking to the little girl. How is this going to work if we stay together long term? He's going to want to come back here to be with his kid, he's a good fucking dad, obviously, but I am not father material. I've never been around kids or wanted them. I don't have any clue what I want to do after college. Zero. My entire life goal is to get away from my father. After that, I have nothing.

My stomach clenches as the what ifs of the future bombard me. I don't think we can do this.

As I pick up my fork to force myself to eat, my hand shakes, making the utensil clatter against the white ceramic plate.

The woman sits down with a cup of coffee and finally sees me.

"Oh, the boyfriend is up." She grins at me.

"Don't be a bitch," Jeremy says, not looking away from Ella, who is smooshing bits of pancake with her cup.

"Jeremy! Do not call your sister names!" their mother scolds, the boys snicker and continue to shove an ungodly amount of pancakes into their mouths. Just watching them consume that much sugar and carbs makes my stomach hurt.

I force myself to eat my breakfast and watch the family interact. It's been a long time since I've been around a real, normal family. My grandparents died in a boating accident around the same time my mother was murdered, and I wasn't allowed to have friends, so I have nothing else to base normal off of.

"What time are we going to your parents'?" Mr. Albrooke asks his wife.

"Mom said one o'clock."

I look at Jeremy and he meets my gaze. "We spend Christmas Eve with my mom's parents. My dad's parents are in Northern Michigan so we go there for Thanksgiving. Tomorrow will be just us here at the house."

I swallow thickly and nod, making myself give him a small smile. The last thing I want to do is be further inundated into his life. When this falls apart, and it will because we are too different, it will be harder for me to disappear. To fade into the background of his world.

He gives me a weird look and cocks his head a little. I guess I'm not very good at hiding my expressions from him.

"Excuse me." I lift my plate and take it to the kitchen, rinsing it off and putting it in the sink before heading upstairs. I'm halfway up the stairs when footsteps sound behind me and I know it's Jeremy. I don't have anything to offer anyone here. My father would be furious if he saw how unprepared I am right now. I can't even clothe myself.

"Hey," he reaches for my hand. "Are you okay?"

"No! I'm not," I snap, pulling my hand from his and striding for his room. I can't look at him and see that rejected look I know I just put on his face. It's one more thing I've fucked up. It's why I should be alone.

The door closes behind Jeremy and I stop next to the bed with my hands on my hips. I'm furious at myself for letting myself believe I could be enough for him.

"Preston." I flinch at the hard line in his voice when he says my name. "I can't help if you won't fucking talk to me."

I spin on him to find him standing with his feet planted and his arms crossed over his chest.

"You want me to talk to you?" I stalk up to him, getting into his face, gripping his hair in my hand and forcing him to look up at me. "You want to know how I'm not good enough for you? How I have nothing to fucking offer you? How you deserve a hell of a lot better than my fucked-up ass? Someone you can show off and be proud of, someone you can touch?" His brows pull together, but I continue. "How I'm not made for kids and Christmases with grandparents? I'm unprepared for everything around me and I can't handle it. I hate myself, so how can anyone want to be around me, much less *love* me?"

When I open my mouth to vomit more words, Jeremy covers my mouth with his hand.

"Shut up." His spine straightens and shoulders square like he's ready for a fight, but I doubt it'll be physical. No, he's going to destroy me with words and it's going to hurt so much worse. "The only person who thinks you aren't good enough for me is you. I deserve whatever I say I do, and I want you. That makes you fucking worthy because I said so. You have some baggage, I'll give you that, but it's not an inconvenience or a burden to me."

I let go of his hair, my arms falling to lay limply at my sides, but Jeremy slides his hands around my head to hold me against him.

"Do you really think I won't show you off? I'll show you off to everyone and damn the consequences. The only thing holding me back is not knowing how the team will handle it because I know no one will really fuck with you, they're scared of you, but if they mess with me, you'll hurt them. I don't want that for you." He pulls my forehead down to rest on his, my chest tight with emotions I don't want to express. It hurts to be loved. So much more than I thought possible.

"And I touch you whenever I want. I know where it's okay and the limitations don't bother me. I understand why they exist. Give me a better map of where it's okay and I will touch every centimeter I'm allowed. None of that makes you unlovable or undeserving. What's happened to you is not your fault and if or when you decide to take down your dad, I will stand right next to you."

The vice grip around my ribs tightens with every word, making it hard to breathe. My heart flutters in my chest leaving me shaky and unsure of my footing. I don't know what to do with this acceptance, this love. It's the scariest thing I've ever done. Lifting my arms, I wrap them around him to pull him fully against me.

"I like that you need me, fight with me, and fuck the absolute shit out of me." He smirks at the last part and I chuckle through the knot in my throat. "Because I get to see parts of you that no one else sees. You aren't easy and I don't know how to tell you this, but I like a challenge. So, take this one day at a time with me until you're ready to plan for the future. I'll wait for you."

I take his lips in a watery, tear-filled kiss. I do need him, but I don't know *how* to need him. My throat burns and my soul screams at me to hold on to him with both hands while my head tells me to run so it doesn't hurt more later.

His tongue tangles with mine, just as invested in this moment as I am. I run my hands under his t-shirt, needing his skin. Every inch of my body craves to be against his. Not even sexually, just together.

Releasing his lips, I look him in the eye and ask him something I've never considered with another person.

"Shower with me?"

CHAPTER 38

jeremy

"Shower with me?" Preston's words choke me up. He's never let me see the scars in the light and only in bits and pieces, now he's offering to show me everything?

"You don't have to prove anything to me." I squeeze the back of his neck in my hands.

"I want to." He presses a kiss to my lips quickly. "I need to feel you against me." Preston kisses me again then takes my hand, grabs some clothes, and leads me into the bathroom.

"You want to fuck me in the most echo-prone room in the house while my entire family is downstairs?" That's ballsy, even for him.

He chuckles that dark laugh that has the hair all over my body standing up.

"I'm not going to fuck you, Albrooke." He turns the water on then backs me against the wall. "I just want to touch you."

My cock twitches and my skin heats.

"Oh, no," I cry say in a mock outrage. "Not that, the horror."

He smiles and bites his lip, eyes locked on my mouth. "Okay, fine. You don't get to come."

Preston reaches for my shirt and I lift my hands as he pulls it off and drops it on the floor.

I reach for his shirt and he tenses but doesn't stop me.

"Can I?" I ask quietly. He turns and moves away from me so I let go of him, trying not to take it personally. He takes a few steps to the door and flicks the light off, dowsing the room into dim shadow.

Preston steps back in front of me and lifts his hands, his eyes clenched tight. Careful not to touch him, I lift the shirt and drop it on the floor. My eyes are locked on his face. Now that I can see the evidence of his abuse, I don't want to. I'm scared.

It takes a minute for my head to process what I'm seeing because I can't make it make sense. There are so many scars. Everywhere. Straight lines cut into his skin in various stages of healing, some thin and white, some thick and bright red, and everything in between.

Preston lowers his hands back to his sides, hands balling in fists then relaxing, over and over. My gaze follows the movement and drags over his torso.

It hurts my heart to see the pain he's lived through.

His body is tight with tension, probably afraid of my reaction. I place my hands on his hips and lean forward to kiss one of the still bright red scars. Preston flinches at my touch and pants when my lips brush his skin.

He shudders but lets me kiss an older scar this time. Just

a gentle brush, barely a touch. No sooner than my lips have left his skin, he grips my head and pulls me up to slam his mouth over mine and presses his bare chest to mine. He gasps into the kiss when our skin meets, tears flowing down his cheeks to drip onto his chest. The light scattering of chest hair tickles my skin, the growth pattern strange because of all the scars, but that doesn't detract from how beautiful he is.

Slowly, I slide my hands inside his pants, cupping his bare ass in my hands and kneading the muscles. I groan when he flexes and thrusts his dick against mine.

Steam is filling the small room as we comfort ourselves and each other with our bodies. We remove the last of our clothes, touching and kissing until our lips are sore and swollen. There are more scars on his legs and his back, but most are on his chest and abdomen. Now I know why he doesn't change in the locker room with everyone else. My soul hurts for him.

We climb into the shower, Preston hunkering down to get his head in the water, and I snicker at him.

"What?"

"You're a giant." He glares at me but pulls me against him, shuddering when my body meets his.

"It's going to take a while to get used to that," he mutters, more to himself than to me. I kiss his throat and his dick twitches against my thigh.

"Where can I touch you?" I drag my lips along his collar bone, licking at the water on his skin.

His breathing stutters. "Everywhere."

Preston grips my biceps, his fingers digging into the muscles of my arms as I explore the expanse of his back, not staying in any one spot too long, but just enjoying his body.

"No one has touched me since my mother died, unless it

was to inflict pain," he whispers against my lips. "I crave it but it hurts."

My hands immediately leave his skin, hovering over his body. The idea of causing him more pain breaks my heart. I can't hurt him.

"No, no." He pulls my hands back against him. "I need it, please."

"I don't want to hurt you." My throat is clogged with emotion, making it hard to speak.

"You don't. You make it better."

His words fill the cracks in my heart with light, he fills in the holes I didn't know I had.

He lets me wash him and I get distracted by his thick, hard dick for a minute, stroking him until he's rocking into my fist, but he stops me to return the favor and wash me before we take it too far. We're running out of hot water so we rinse off quickly and step out. Preston dries his body off while I watch, enamored with the way his muscles flex and relax as he moves.

"You've got the best ass." I grab his ass cheek when he turns to put on his underwear. He flinches but snorts.

"Have you seen *your* ass?"

I wrap my towel around me and watch him pull his pants up. "Do you ever bottom?"

Preston catches my eyes in the mirror and lifts one eyebrow.

"No."

Feet pound up the stairs and across the hallway, the twins must be getting dressed to go.

"We better hurry up." I sigh. "My brothers will be barging in here any minute."

Preston pulls his shirt over his head and I open the door to get dressed in the bedroom.

"Thanks for using all the hot water, dick!" one of the boys yells from their bedroom.

"You're welcome!" I holler back without missing a beat.

"Sorry!" Preston says at the same time.

I smirk and shake my head. "You obviously didn't live with your sibling. We aren't sorry for shit."

"Wait," both boys say in unison.

Keith's head pops around the corner of his bedroom door. "You were *both* in the shower?"

I smile and wag my eyebrows at him. "Being an adult has perks, kid."

"There better not be jizz left in there," Jordan yells from their room.

"Twice as much as normal!" I yell back and close my bedroom door.

"What the fuck is wrong with you? You just told them we fucked in the shower!" I'm not sure if he's shocked or outraged. Both are equally amusing.

I cackle and dig in my dresser for some clothes.

"Yup."

He stares at me like I've lost my mind.

"Why would you tell them that?" The exasperation is heavy in his tone.

"Now when they come to a closed door, they'll fucking knock."

He laughs and the real smile makes my heart soar. I put that there. Me.

I walk over to him, rest my head on his chest, and wrap my arms around him. He holds me and lets me just enjoy the moment. I think he needs it too, honestly. Soft touches, anything not sexually charged, are not normal for him. I grew up with parents and grandparents who were huggers, siblings that would crowd onto a couch to watch TV, so I'm only touch starved at school. But Preston has lived a life without human contact.

It's not long after our shower that we load up in the vehicles and head to my grandparents. I help Stacy by getting Ella in their car then get into the rental car with Preston, who is wearing one of my jackets. It's at least an inch too short in the arms but it's better than nothing.

"You're really good with her," he says when I slide in and buckle up.

I can't help but smile. "I love that kid," I sigh. "I just wish I wasn't missing so much of her life right now. I don't want her to forget me."

"She can't forget you. You're too involved in her life." He's adamant, holding my hand in his lap. "You're a great dad."

Uh. What? My brain skids to a halt as I try to wrap my head around what he just said.

"She's. I'm. Wait." I shake my head and start over. "I'm her uncle."

I pull up to a stop sign and turn to look at him. He's confused now too. Great.

"Why did you think she was mine?"

"I don't know," he shrugs. "You call her baby girl, you video call with her all the time, and you've been taking care of her since I got here."

"She's Stacy's daughter but her dad isn't around. He took off right after Stacy found out she was pregnant, so we all pitched in to help. I haven't been around in months and I miss her."

"Oh." Preston's neck turns pink and it crawls up his face. It's fucking adorable.

"You know I'm gay, right? I've only been with men," I say and he plays with my fingers.

"Me too. Girls have never interested me," Preston shrugs.

While driving, I lift his hand and kiss the back of it when something he said earlier clicks into place. "Is this why you said you weren't made for babies? Because you thought I had one?"

"Yeah. I'm impatient, selfish, don't like to be touched, short-tempered, and not comforting." He's starting to spiral again, but he's wrong. All of it is wrong.

"Preston, shut up." I say it as nicely as I can. "That's all bullshit."

"No, it's not—" He starts to argue as I pull up in front of my grandparent's house and shut off the car.

"Stop." I turn to look at him. "How you are with adults is not the same as how you would be with kids. The guys on the ice with you are adult-*ish,* testosterone-driven jocks. Sometimes they need to get their asses handed to them. Kids are different."

When he says nothing, just looks defeated, I continue. "And, I would be there with you. To help you figure it all out. I have a lot of experience with different age groups because of coaching, my siblings, and now my niece. I also grew up in a neighborhood with kids at every house of varying ages." I pull his hand into my lap. "I wouldn't let you fail."

My brothers run over to the car and pound on the windows like a couple of jack-offs.

He flinches and turns to glare at them. They run off laughing and Grandma is waving us into the house.

"Come on." I lean across the center console and give him a quick kiss. "I've already told everyone you aren't a hugger so they will give you hearty handshakes instead."

"Thank you," he murmurs, a little of the tension leaving his shoulders.

"I've got you."

We head inside with his hand in mine. Grandma wraps her arms around me in a hug but I don't let go of Preston.

"We will talk later," she whispers in my ear before patting my back and letting me go. She smiles at me and pats my cheek as Preston steps up behind me, using me as a human shield.

"Grandma, this is my boyfriend, Preston." I smile at him over my shoulder.

He offers his hand to her, and she graciously takes it, shaking his hand.

"It's nice to meet you, Preston." She gives him a comforting smile. "Let's get inside, come on."

She steps inside and I mutter over my shoulder to Preston, "This will be a very carb-heavy day. We'll workout tomorrow."

He groans but doesn't say anything. We head into the living room where everyone is sitting on the couches. There's only one spot left, in the middle between Stacy and my mom. I offer it to Preston even though I'm pretty sure he doesn't want it. He shakes his head, so I sit and he takes a seat in front of me, pulling my legs over his shoulders and wrapping his arms around them like he's once again using me as a shield or an anchor.

He leans his head back on the seat, meeting my eyes, and I wink at him, running my hand through his hair. The poor guy is on edge but trying so hard. He's afraid of embarrassing me.

Mom leans down to talk to him and he flinches when she gets too close. She freezes and flicks her gaze to me for a second before turning back to him.

"Are you feeling okay?"

"Yes, ma'am. Thank you." He nods and gives her a tentative, forced smile. Mom reaches to pat his arm but stops herself. She's a touchy-feely kind of mom, so not offering physical comfort to someone in distress is difficult for her. With her, everything can be fixed with a hug and a bowl of macaroni and cheese.

Mom sits back, her hands folded in her lap. I lean my head on her shoulder and she kisses my hair.

"Preston, do you have siblings?" Stacy asks, shoving one of our traditional Santa-shaped sugar cookies in her mouth.

"Classy," I tell her. She gives me a cookie-filled smile. Ella toddles around, playing with toys Grandma has set out to keep her busy.

"Yes, a younger sister." Preston answers, sitting up straighter.

"Where's she at?" Stacy dunks another cookie in milk and breaks off a little piece for Ella, who has noticed she's got food.

"She's at school in New York." Preston watches Ella like he's afraid of her. Ella eyes Preston, and when Stacy gives her a little piece of cookie, she offers it to him. He looks too terrified to move. When he doesn't acknowledge Ella's offering, she shoves it into his mouth, and I snort. He jumps, jerking his head back at the unexpected movement.

Stacy nods as she chews. "She's in college then?"

"No, high school. She's at Calomy Academy in White Plains."

The boys pop their heads up from their phones, now interested in the conversation.

"High school?" They ask in unison. I glare at both of them.

Ella turns and sits in Preston's lap, pushing her way between my calves, and lays her head against his chest. He tenses up, completely out of his depth, but doesn't push her away. She starts babbling and lifts her little hand up to Stacy to get another bite of cookie. Preston, unsure of what to do with his hands, hovers them over Ella, puts them on his legs, then onto the floor.

Mom reaches for Ella, probably to get her to get off of Preston, but I put a hand on her arm and shake my head. He needs this. She gives me an *are you sure* look and I nod.

"Don't even think about it," Preston says to my brothers in that no nonsense way of his. Ella turns to them and babbles in a similar tone and I laugh. She's found a new love and I couldn't be happier.

"What the hell are you going to do anyway? She's in New York," I toss out, shaking my head at them. "And she would chew you up and spit you out. She's not going to deal with your crap."

"You've met her?" Stacy butts in, smiling at her daughter when she looks up at Preston and touches his cheek so he looks at her.

"Yeah, she came out for Thanksgiving and went to the games that weekend. I helped her surprise Preston." I run my fingers through his soft black hair again. Seeing Ella accept him warms my heart. Kids are such good judges of character.

"Is she spending Christmas with your parents?" Mom asks and Preston tenses.

"No, ma'am. My mother died a long time ago and my father goes to somewhere tropical every year. She's at school." The muscle in his cheek is jumping. Flexing my calves, I pull him back into the couch, putting pressure on his chest. It's as close to a hug as I can get right now without everyone getting weird.

Preston sucks in a deep breath and lets it out.

"My family isn't close," he says and I'm proud of him for it. Eyes shift around the room, Stacy looking at Dad, the boys looking at me then mom, then Stacy. Grandma looks at Dad then Mom.

"Well," Grandma speaks up. "We're happy to have you with us."

Grandpa comes down the hallway with the newspaper folded under his arm and reading glasses low on his nose.

"Who's here yet?" he asks. Preston shoves my legs off his shoulders, jumps up off the floor, putting Ella on her feet, and pulling on his clothes to release any wrinkles. I stand up behind him to make the introduction but he steps forward with his hand out.

"Hello, sir, I'm Preston," he says. Grandpa eyes him for a second, taking in how tall he is, and the serious set of his face.

He shakes Preston's hand. "Nice to meet ya, son."

My grandpa looks like a gruff country man with a few missing fingers, some gnarly scars, and some scary-as-hell hunting stories, but he's a good man. He doesn't care how much money you have or where you went to school, he'd watch a Bears game with anyone, would love to hear about that big fish you caught, or how big the buck was you took down last year. I love him. We all do.

"You're with Jeremy yet?" He motions to me and I can see the wheels spinning in Preston's head.

"Yes, Grandpa. Preston is with me." I put my hand on his hip and whisper to Preston. "He says *yet* at the end of most sentences."

"Good, good. Let's eat yet."

The twins hop up and rush for the dining room like they haven't eaten in weeks. Ella hustles to Preston and reaches for his hand. He has to hunker down to hold it, but he does and she walks him to the dining room.

Stacy stands and watches with me, the big, bad hockey player allowing this little girl to lead him around the house. It's the sweetest thing I've ever seen. Stacy smiles at the scene too.

Grandma wraps an arm around me. “I can see how much he means to you.”

“He’s definitely important,” I agree, resting my head on the top of hers.

“He seems like a good kid, kind of quiet and kind of intense, but it's clear he’s been through something though.” She gently touches my cheek. “I’m glad he has you, sweetheart.”

She pats my stomach and follows everyone into the dining room.

CHAPTER 39

preston

After lunch, we watch some Christmas movies —*Miracle on 34th Street, National Lampoon's Christmas Vacation*, and *A Charlie Brown Christmas*— while they all munch on snacks. I eat cut up vegetables while Jeremy smirks at me, shoving more chocolate-covered popcorn into his mouth.

"When you're slow and clumsy tomorrow, you only have yourself to blame." I shake my head at him and pop a cherry tomato into my mouth. It's weird being here, around a family that loves each other, but I'm starting to relax. It's hard though. I keep waiting for the other shoe to drop, and everyone to start fighting.

"It'll be worth it." He shrugs.

I lean close to his ear and whisper, "If you can't keep up, I won't suck you off afterward."

Jeremy's hand stops halfway to his mouth then drops back to his bowl. With a huff and a side-eye, he reaches for my plate and takes a carrot.

"Good boy."

"I hate you," he mumbles around the carrot, and I grin.

"Don't forget to drink water." I hand him a water bottle and he snatches it from me, untwisting the cap and chugging half of it.

Every few minutes, I glance over to the pile of presents under the tree. In the rush to get out the door this morning, I left the bracelet at the house. I'll be the only one sitting here, sticking out like a sore thumb, with nothing to contribute.

The credits roll for *A Charlie Brown Christmas* and Jordan turns to his grandma.

"Can we open presents now?" he begs, hands together like he's praying. Keith joins in and they both say, "Please?"

"Alright, start passing them out," Grandma says and the boys jump forward, reaching for the colorfully wrapped gifts.

Jeremy turns to me with guilt in his eyes. "I don't have anything for you, I'm sorry. I'll make it up to you."

I shake my head. "I don't really have anything for you either." I shrug sheepishly. He gives me a quick kiss and turns back to his family.

Ella climbs into my lap once again and Jeremy puts his hand on my leg. Ella looks at his hand, her eyebrows pull together, and she pushes his hand off of me. Jeremy looks at her with fake determination. There's something about her acceptance of me that warms my chest. Everyone else looks at me, at the fuck off expression, and gives me a wide birth, but not this little girl.

"Hey, he's *my* boyfriend." He leans down toward her, pointing to his chest.

She points to herself, babbling in a serious tone.

"Oh, I see how you are," he tells her, grabbing her off my lap and tickling her until she's shrieking. "I'm the favorite, little miss. Me." She wiggles and squirms to get free, only to climb right back into my lap.

Jeremy sighs and winks at me before looking at her again. "You're lucky you're cute, kid."

"Okay, Ella," Stacy says. "Open a present!"

Jeremy hands her one and I help her hold it. She struggles to get it started so I rip a piece to show her how to do it and end up pulling most of the paper off for her. She lifts it up and yells something, then hands it to me to open. It looks like a kid's Xbox controller with a face on it and different colored buttons. Probably makes a lot of noise.

I'm handed some scissors and get it open for her while Jordan and Keith open stuff up next, new games, then Jeremy gets a new hoodie with the Lumberjacks logo on it. He laughs and pulls it on. Around and around they go, I help Ella open all her things and show her how they work. I'm grateful for the task, honestly. By the end of it all, there's a big mess of wrapping paper and packaging. The younger boys go and grab garbage bags and everyone starts cleaning up.

Ella shows me a box she has decided is the best thing ever, puts it on the ground, and crawls inside to sit.

"Ope, hold on, there's another one." Jeremy's mom pulls something out from the other side of the tree. "Preston." She reads the name tag and hands it to me.

What the hell?

I look at Jeremy but he's watching his grandma. My palms are suddenly sweaty, so I wipe them on my pants before reaching for the box wrapped in red and white-striped paper.

The tag says *To Preston, From Grandma and Grandpa Brown.* Now I'm nervous. What the hell is it? I only got here yesterday, did they go out and buy something for me? I didn't bring them anything. Guilt eats at me as I stare at the package.

"Open it." Jeremy bumps my shoulder with his.

Glancing around, I see everyone is watching me. My face flushes at the attention.

Carefully, I open the wrapping paper to find a brown box. Jeremy hands me scissors to cut through the tape, and with shaking fingers, I lift the flaps and tissue paper. I sit in stunned silence, staring at what has to be a quilt.

Blue, snowflake, and hockey inspired fabrics laid out in a star shape. My throat burns as I stare at it, my head spinning too fast to focus on any one thought.

Jeremy clears his throat. "Grandma makes quilts in her spare time."

My eyes, glassy with tears, meet his grandmother's.

"You." I swallow past the lump threatening to choke me. "You made this?"

She smiles at me and nods. "Everyone in the family has one."

The implications of that hit me square in the chest. I don't know how to process this. Why would she give me this? She's barely met me. I don't have words for what is racing through my head.

Handing the box to Jeremy, I stand and walk up to her, wrapping my arms around her in a hug.

"Oh," she squeaks in surprise right before she hugs me back.

"I...Uh, I'm..." I sniffle tears back but don't know what to say.

She rubs my back, squeezing me tightly. "You're welcome."

"Thank you," I manage to get out, wiping tears from my face over her shoulder.

I drop down to kneeling so I'm not towering over her

and just let her hug me. I don't remember the last hug I got from my grandmother or my mother, but I know it's been at least eleven years. I don't remember what either of them sounded like or smelled like, what their laugh was like, and I was never allowed to grieve for them.

Vaguely, I'm aware of people leaving the room and I'm grateful for it. This woman that doesn't know me and has no reason to be nice to me, just holds me, giving me this moment.

"Preston," Jeremy says behind me. His hand splays on my back and, for a few minutes, we just sit here.

Wiping my eyes again, I straighten up, my head dropped toward the floor.

"I don't know your story, Preston," his grandma says, placing a hand on my shoulder. "But I can tell my grandson loves you deeply and you return that love. That's all I need to know to welcome you into this family. You will always be welcome here. Every holiday, birthday, random weekend, and family gathering."

I nod but don't look up at her. She kisses the top of my head then leaves us alone. I hate being so messed up. Who the hell cries over a blanket? God damn it.

Weak.

Embarrassment.

Useless.

Jeremy leans against my back.

"You're an asshole," I grumble at him, making him chuckle.

"What did I do?"

"You knew it was coming." I look at him over my shoulder then turn around and pull him against me. I pull his legs over mine and scoot him between my thighs to bury my face in his neck.

"I didn't know for sure, but I had a feeling."

I bite his neck and he hisses a moan.

"Tonight, your ass is mine," I growl against his skin and he shudders when I slide my hand under his shirt and drag my nails against his skin.

"Yes, mark me."

My dick hardens at his needy groan.

"Any chance we can get a few minutes in a locked room?" I slide my hand into his hair and grip it tightly. I know I don't have to explain that I need to control him right now.

"Fuck," he groans again as I bite at his scruffy jaw. He hasn't shaved since he left Colorado and I have to admit, I love it.

"You should keep this." I nuzzle the soft hair on his cheek and drag my tongue against it, the prickle of the short hairs tickling the tip of my tongue.

"If you don't stop, everyone is going to see my hard on," Jeremy moans.

"Where's the bathroom?" I demand, needing him weak and needy under me. The control he gives me calms the ragged edges of my soul. I need him to need me.

He stands and I quickly follow him up the stairs, both of us careful not to make too much noise. At the top of the stairs, directly ahead, is the bathroom. We hurry toward it and I lock the door behind me. The room is small but I don't need much room for what I have in mind. Jeremy grabs my face and fucks my mouth with his tongue. My hands drop to his pants, unbuttoning and dropping the zipper so I can pull him out. His dick springs free and I wrap my hand around it, jerking him quickly.

His groan becomes a whimper when I bite his lip hard.

Pulling away from his mouth, I drop to my knees and suck him into my mouth. Jeremy's head drops back and he bites on his hand to keep quiet.

"Is there anything in here I can use for lube?"

Jeremy fumbles for a cabinet door so I open it and find a bottle of baby oil. I'm not going to ask why that's there or how he knew it would be.

"Spread 'em." I tap his leg and coat my fingers in the oil. I'll prep him while I suck him off, kill two birds with one stone.

He shuffles his legs as far apart as the clothes will allow and I slide my slicked-up fingers against his hole while I bob on his cock. Jeremy is leaning against the bathroom counter, one hand in his mouth and the other in my hair, with my fingers pumping in and out of his greedy hole, his face flushed with arousal. It's the sexiest thing I've ever seen.

I love the way he enjoys sex. No shame in what he likes.

His cock throbs on my tongue and he gasps as he cums down my throat while his ass clenches around my fingers. The bitter taste of his release filling my mouth is fucking delicious. I suck him dry, licking my lips to make sure I get every drop before standing and opening my pants one handed.

"Turn around," I demand, and he doesn't hesitate to move. "Hands on the counter, watch how much you love being fucked."

I coat my dick in more oil and slide between his cheeks to find his puckered hole. Pushing forward, I sink in with no resistance. He groans and his eyes roll back in his head.

Gripping his hip with one hand, I cover his mouth with the other to keep him quiet and fuck into him. I use his neck to gag myself, biting and sucking on his skin and not giving a shit that everyone downstairs will see it.

He's come-drunk and loose in my hold, my favorite way for him to be, his knees and elbows not wanting to hold him up but I'm not giving him a choice. I fuck him hard, demanding, rough. I need it.

Jeremy moans into my hand, watching me in the mirror. Already, his dick is getting hard again but I ignore it.

My orgasm crashes into me like a train, damn near knocking me off my feet. I groan long and loud, the sound muffled into his neck with my teeth buried in his skin. He whimpers and clenches around me while I empty into him, making his hole sloppy with cum.

I release his mouth, my hand falling to the counter and my forehead drops to his shoulder while I pant for a minute.

"Shit, I needed that," he mumbles, come drunk like a mother fucker.

I chuckle and pull out of him. Dropping down into a squat, I pull his cheeks apart and see my cum leaking from his used hole.

Fuck, that's hot.

I kiss one cheek and stand up, pulling my clothes up and adjusting them. His neck is fucked. There's no way we can hide that. Red marks are already turning purple, teeth marks are dug into his skin. Great. Merry Christmas, I guess.

"Go downstairs while I clean up, hopefully I can sneak in and pull my hood over my neck or something." He shrugs.

I turn him around and kiss him softly. "I'm sorry, I should have been more careful."

He scoffs. "If you were careful, I wouldn't enjoy it as much. I'm not embarrassed by sex."

I smile at him and kiss him again. "Okay, I'm going."

I leave the bathroom and head downstairs to find Stacy smirking up at me from the bottom landing. I freeze mid-step and watch her watching me. The smile that was on my face falls the longer she holds my gaze and now I don't know what to do or say.

"What?" I finally ask. I don't want to be rude, but she's in my way and fucking up my escape.

"*Nothing,*" she says in *that* way that everyone knows is bullshit.

"Stacy Marie! Leave your brother alone!" her mom hollers from somewhere else in the house.

"I'm not bothering anyone!" she yells back but doesn't turn away from me.

Deciding to test my place in the family, I holler back, "Yes, she is!"

"I swear to God, Stacy! Leave that boy alone!"

Stacy rolls her eyes but moves aside and grins at me when I pass her, muttering under her breath as I go. "Tattle tale."

"You started it," I mutter back and find the empty spots at the table that were left for me and Jeremy. Pulling out a chair, I take a seat and look around the spread on the table. Roast beef, scalloped potatoes, rolls, macaroni and cheese, Watergate salad, green beans with bacon, stuffing, and sweet potatoes. It's carb overload and I have no idea what I'm going to eat.

Looks like my dinner is roast beef with all the fat cut off and green beans. Maybe a roll. Jesus. How is anyone productive after a meal like this?

"Get off me, Stacy!" Jeremy shouts from the hallway and I turn to watch when she cackles. "What the hell is wrong with you?"

She doesn't answer, just continues to laugh. An irritated Jeremy comes through the doorway with a black circle on his neck surrounding what looks suspiciously like my teeth. My eyes widen and color drains from my face.

Fuck. Me.

He stomps over and drops down into the chair next to me, everyone at the table staring between the two of us while Stacy continues to cackle like a damn evil villain.

"I swear you kids are the reason I have gray hair," their mother says, rubbing her forehead.

I drop my face toward my lap and wait for the ground to open up and swallow me whole. My face is hot with embarrassment at the obvious marks on Jeremy's neck. Everyone at this table except Ella knows what we were doing, or at least thinks they know, and while we are both twenty-one, this is his family.

Have some fucking tact!

You've embarrassed him in front of his entire family. Good going. He's not going to let you touch him ever again.

"I'm sorry," I mumble so only he can hear me.

"I'm not," he says at full volume.

"You guys exchanged gifts, in private, that's adorable," Stacy says, trying not to laugh. "We can all see what he gave you but what did you give him?" I glance up at her and almost laugh at how hard she's trying to keep a straight face and failing. "You should get that tattooed on your neck."

"You literally bring your fuck trophy with you everywhere you go," one of the twins says, sticking up for Jeremy, though I can't tell which one it was.

"Jordan Michael!" his mother scorns, his dad smacking him upside the back of his head.

The other twin snorts and covers his mouth while his entire body vibrates with laughter.

"Is your family always like this?" I whisper to Jeremy, who is also trying to hold in his laughter.

"Yes."

"I swear! We can't have one nice family get together without the four of you attacking each other and saying inappropriate things!" Mrs. Albrooke scorns her children and they all look properly chastised. It's the strangest thing. If I had said anything like that about my sister in front of my father, I would be leaving with new scars, but none of them look physically afraid of their parents.

Jeremy's grandma sighs and starts putting food on her plate. Everyone follows suit.

The dishes get passed around so everyone can get what they want onto their plates. I don't want to be rude and not eat, but I also don't want to waste food, so I put a little bit of everything on my plate and hope for the best. My stomach is already unhappy with these circumstances.

"I'm not ashamed of you or our relationship," Jeremy says, leaning into me when he hands me a bowl of rolls. "I don't care that everyone knows I have sex with you."

"I'm still sorry you look like the family whore right now."

He snorts and kisses my cheek. "I'm really glad you're here."

Our gazes meet and I smile softly at him, giving him a wink. "Me too."

After dinner, the kids all head back to the living room to fall into a food coma and Stacy puts Ella down for a nap. Somehow, even after all that food, Keith and Jordan are eating cookies. I guess I'm staring because Jordan offers me one.

"They're one of our family traditions. Every year we decorate these same cookies," he says. I take it from him since I don't want to be rude but find myself confused. It appears to be Santa on an upside-down heart, so the round humps are his beard and the point is his hat, but it's a little tilted. A white dot, and a red stripe followed by a white stripe make up the hat, a white circle with a black circle in it makes the eyes, and the beard appears to be white frosting, but because it came out of a tube or piping bag, it looks like white pubes.

I turn it around and look at it from a different angle, but

no matter what I do, it looks like a ball sack with Santa's face on it. They can't be serious. Has no one ever noticed this before?

"What?" Jeremy asks me as I continue to inspect the cookie. Seriously?

I look at his siblings and they're all looking at me with similar confusion.

"Uh, nothing." I hand the cookie to Jeremy and stand. "I need to pee."

Heading down the hallway, I find the bathroom and almost have the door closed when someone puts a hand on the door to stop it. Peering through the crack, I can see it's Jeremy.

"Seriously, what was wrong with the cookie?" he asks.

"Those are ball sack Santa cookies," I whisper so no one overhears me.

His eyes get wide and a huge smile takes over his face. "My Grandma has been making those cookies, with that same cookie cutter, for forty years!"

"Are you trying to tell me they don't look like ball sacks?" I demand.

He cracks up laughing, doubling over.

"Jeremy!" I hiss at him. I swear I will die of embarrassment if his sweet grandmother hears about this. She's a saint of a woman and I am already horrified that she knows I fucked her grandson upstairs.

"I never thought of it, but that's all I'm going to see from now on." He's laughing so hard he's crying. "Ball sack Santa!"

Another voice cackles down the hallway and I know one or both of the twins have heard. Jesus fucking Christ.

"Oh my God!" Stacy shrieks. "They *do* look like ball sacks!"

The twins and Stacy are dying laughing in the family

room, which gets the attention of the ladies in the kitchen. Jeremy stumbles his way to the living room, still holding his stomach and laughing, while I follow after him with my face on fire.

Kill me now.

"Stop saying ball sack! It's Christmas!" Mrs. Albrooke scolds her children, which just makes them laugh harder.

"What the hell is going on out here?" Jeremy's grandma stands with her hands on her hips.

"The-The..." Jeremy starts but is laughing too hard to get the words out. He wipes the tears from his face and sucks in a deep breath. "The Santa cookies look like ball sacks."

"Excuse me?" Grandma moves to stand behind one of the twins and looks at the cookies on his plate for a minute then covers her mouth with her hand. "Oh, no. They *do* look like ball sacks!

"I can tell you with absolute certainty," Jeremy announces, and everyone turns to him. "They do not *taste* like ball sacks."

The boys bust up laughing while my eyes bug out of my head and I wish the floor would open up and swallow me whole. I can't believe this is happening. Why didn't I just keep my mouth shut?

I step forward, horrified that his family now hates me and I will forever be known as the asshole that ruined Christmas. "I am so sorry! They really are delicious cookies!"

Jeremy's dad is wiping tears from his eyes, bent over and holding himself up with his hands on his knees. His grandpa is sitting in a chair and shaking with laughter.

"I hope you know, you are now a part of this family's history." Mrs. Albrooke looks at me, but she doesn't look angry. "I guess we'll be shopping for a new cookie cutter."

"Lord," Grandma says and comes to stand next to me. "Thank you, this is one of the most memorable Christmases I think we've ever had." She disappears back into the kitchen with Mrs. Albrooke, leaving me to fend for myself with this group of laughing hyenas.

The women pack up the leftovers and we pile into the cars, most of the dishes coming back to the house with us.

Everyone disappears into their bedrooms, leaving everything except the food in the living room to be dealt with tomorrow. Jeremy strips down to his boxer briefs and sits on the edge of the bed as I pull off my jeans and find my backpack. Digging in the main pocket, I find the brown leather cuff and walk over to him, sitting next to him on the bed.

"I got this for you when I was sure you hated me and were going to break up with me." I open my hand to show him what I have. It's a simple piece of leather, about half an inch wide, with a snap closure and crossed hockey sticks embossed into the top. "I saw it in the gift shop and had to have it." I shrug, uneasy. Why is it so hard to express my feelings when I'm not having a breakdown?

Jeremy puts his wrist out and looks at me. "Can you put it on me?"

I glance up at his face for a second and see an intimate smile on his lips and expectation in his eyes. I open the snap, wrap it around his wrist, and carefully close it. He pulls his arm back and inspects it with the smile still on his face.

"How does it look?" He holds his wrist out to me again and I grasp his arm in my hand, running my thumb over the design.

"It looks good."

"I think so too." He nods in agreement. "Thank you, I love it."

Some of the tension drains from my shoulders when he kisses me. Jeremy pushes me back on the bed and we adjust until we're lying on the pillows and the blankets are pulled up. This time, Jeremy lays his head on my chest, our legs intertwined, and our hearts beating together.

"Breaking up was never my plan," he says in the dark, quiet room. "I was worried, really fucking worried, about you, but you're mine and, no matter what, that's not going to change."

Quicker than I ever have before, I fall asleep knowing I'm safe and loved.

CHAPTER 40

jeremy

A week later, the vans pull up outside the hotel in Providence, Rhode Island, dropping us off from the airport for our first games of the new year.

Coach gets us checked in and hands out room assignments, Preston is with another defense player, and he does not look happy about it, while I'm with Paul.

We get our room keys and head to the elevators. Preston is wearing the quilt my grandma gave him, all folded up around his neck and refusing to answer Brendon's questions about it. He's asked about ten times since we left Denver.

The quilt lives on his bed, keeping us warm at night and bringing him a sense of peace I've never seen on him before. I often come back after classes to see him sitting on his bed with it wrapped around his shoulders like a cape. I'm also pretty sure I've heard him talking to my grandma on the phone a few times. Hopefully it's true. He needs people that care about him.

I snap a picture of him with it over his shoulders and send it to Mom.

Show this to Grandma for me.

MOM

Awww he's so sweet!

I snort at her response. Preston is a lot of things, but most people wouldn't associate him with sweetness.

We drop our shit in the hotel rooms and I text Preston.

Dinner?

CARMICHAEL

Don't be a dumbass.

I snort at his response. Paul lifts an eyebrow at me but doesn't say anything.

You're so nice to me, I can see how much you love me.

CARMICHAEL

I'm going to show you how much I love your ass the first chance I get.

Sure, sure. Just use me for my body.

CARMICHAEL

Open the fucking door.

There's a loud knock on our hotel room. With a smile on my face, I get off the bed and move to open it.

Paul bitches from his bed, "You guys are disgusting together."

Preston grabs the back of my neck to kiss me, not pulling away until I'm hard and breathless.

"Seriously, get a room," Brendon scoffs as he pushes past

us to lie on Paul's bed and puts his head on Paul's thigh like a pillow.

"Get out and we'll have one," Preston snaps back without any heat. It's just how he is. My grumpy man.

"I'm fucking hungry. Feed me." Paul runs his hand through Brendon's hair and looks at us unamused.

"I think there's a bar down the street that serves decent food," Brendon comments, scrolling through his phone. "Looks like a bunch of guys are going there."

"Decent food at a bar? I doubt it." Preston crosses his arms and shakes his head at Brendon. "I guarantee everything is deep-fried."

"And a mechanical bull! Fuck yeah!" Brendon hops off the bed and Paul follows like a lost puppy. Poor guy has it bad for Brendon but I don't think Brendon even realizes it.

Preston sighs and we follow them out of the room. In the hallway, we're careful to keep some distance between us, the team doesn't know we're together and we're not in a hurry to out ourselves. I don't think it would be much of a surprise if they found out either of us are gay but it's drama we don't need right now.

In the elevator, Carpenter and Willis join us and we all head down to the lobby. More guys from the team are there standing around when the elevator doors open and, as a group, we trudge a block to the bar, freezing our asses off. The bar is designed to look like a small-town country bar with raw wood walls, rodeo paraphernalia, and George Strait playing on the jukebox. One side of the bar is a roped off area with a mechanical bull surrounded by crash mats. All the tables are bar height with stools around them.

The team easily takes up a quarter of the tables. Preston, Paul, Brendon, and I squeezed around one table. The damn things are tiny and we all look ridiculous crammed around it.

A waitress with a high, blonde ponytail and big boobs passes out menus and takes our drink orders. We all know we have a one-drink max because we have a game tomorrow. Everyone at my table orders a beer except Preston, who orders his usual: water.

He meets all of our eyes in turn, disgruntled at being ogled.

“Beer makes you fat and slow,” we all say in unison.

“It’s true,” he grumbles while raising the menu and lifting a lip at the limited options.

I pick up mine and peruse it as well. If I eat a chicken burger, Preston will bitch less, but bacon cheeseburgers are delicious...

With a huff, he puts the laminated plastic sheet on the table with more force than necessary and I snort at him.

“So, let me guess,” I say without looking at him. “Grilled chicken burger with no bun annnnnnd...” There is really no other option that he’ll eat. “Two chicken burgers with no buns.”

He side-eyes me and I know I’ve got it right. Score one for Jeremy.

The woman comes back to take our orders and Preston orders his sad chicken breasts. The rest of us order bacon cheeseburgers.

When she walks away, we turn to look at him, waiting for his speech about nutrition.

“Nope, I’m not saying anything. You all knew what I was going to say and still made bad choices. Fat and slow it is.”

We laugh and start talking about the game tomorrow, discussing who’s who on the team we’re playing, what we need to watch out for, and who the weak links are.

"Alright, folks! Who's going to be first up to ride my bull?"

A DJ calls over the speaker system. My gaze cuts through the hazy bar lights to lock onto Preston's on the other side of the table. He's got his glass almost to his lips then freezes, his eyebrow raised, the heat in his stare almost enough to make me combust. I stand from my stool, lifting my hand in the air.

"Yeah, right here." I call to the DJ. Preston glares at me, a look that clearly says *absolutely not.*

"Our next victim!" He cheers and the room gets loud with excitement.

"You're an idiot," Preston says loud enough for the tables around us to hear. "If you get hurt, Coach will kill you."

Moving toward Preston, I lean over his shoulder so my lips are next to his ear. He barely flinches at me invading his space but doesn't move away. *Progress.*

"You gonna join me?" My tone is sultry as my breath tickles his skin.

"Why would I do that?"

"Hmm, because it's fun?" *Don't bite his earlobe. Don't bite his earlobe. Don't bite his earlobe.*

The guys at the next table are watching us so I move back a bit.

"Having my dick shoved against your ass is fun?" he says loud enough for them to hear.

I smirk. "I have a nice ass." I smack my own ass.

"You and me, cowboy!" Brendon stands up, smiling at Preston, knowing exactly how to push my man's buttons. Preston's body tenses as Brendon walks up behind me and pats me on the ass. "Giddy up!"

If looks could kill, Brendon would be on the floor bleeding out, but he shakes his head. Brendon and I head to the mechanical bull and I lift up first. I step up on the peg and swing my leg over then wrap my hand around the handle on top. Brendon uses my shoulder and the peg to hoist himself up and swing his leg over.

"You remember how to do this?" I ask over my shoulder. Brendon and I used to go to an under twenty-one club in Muskegon and ride the mechanical bull there. It was a hell of a lot of fun and we got pretty damn good at it.

"Like riding a bike." His hips are pressed against my ass and his hand is next to mine on the handle.

"Alright, you boys ready?" The DJ asks and we nod. "Oh, hold on, we've got another rider?"

We turn and see Preston has climbed over the ropes and is stalking towards us. I hide my grin by looking away but Brendon obviously feels the need to fuck with him.

"Hey there, big boy, you gonna ride my ass up here?"

"Off. Now," he demands. Brendon snorts out a laugh and slides off on the opposite side of where Preston is standing.

Preston puts his hand on my thigh, using me to pull himself up and onto the bull, dropping down behind me.

"You ever ridden before?" I ask him.

"No, but I'm a trained athlete, it can't be that hard."

A knowing smile lifts my lips. This is gonna be fun.

"It's all in the thighs." I grip the strong muscles bracketing my own. "Follow the rhythm, don't fight it."

I signal the DJ and the bull starts moving, slowly at first, then picking up a bit of speed. Preston is stiff as a board behind me, fighting the movement of the bull instead of using it. My body rolls automatically, following the rhythm, and enjoying the ride, but even with him damn near glued to me, he's not moving.

Reaching for the rope hanging above us, I use the footholds, to lift and twist my body until I'm facing him, my legs dropping on top of his.

"What the fuck are you doing?" he grits out.

"Relax. Move with the bull." I grab the waistband of his jeans and pull him against me. My body rolls sensually against him and he groans, gripping my hips with bruising force. He's starting to move but it's not enough, so I grip one of his wrists and lift his arm around my shoulders. His fingers dig into my neck, his forehead almost pressing against mine, our breath mingling between us. My heart pounds in my ears as my world zooms in on this moment. I want to kiss him. Desperately. To feel him move against me, under me. My eyes drop to his mouth and I drag my teeth over my bottom lip. He's breathing hard, glaring at me with the most aggressive, hate-filled lust I've ever seen. *God I can't wait for him to hate fuck me later.*

My body moves with the bull. I've done this too many times, muscle memory takes over. I'm in his space, he follows me into mine, over and over, suspended in this moment where nothing exists but us. There's no team members, no bar, no crowd.

Placing my palm on his chest. I push him back until he's leaning all the way back, his hands coming up to grip onto the edge of the bull for something to hold on to. His eyes don't leave mine as I lift up and grind against him to the rhythm of the fake beast below us.

He's hard.

Preston is hard, in public, for me.

I can't stop myself from rubbing my ass over the ridge in his jeans, just once. More to torture myself than him. He moans but I can't hear it, not over my pulse and the white noise buzzing in my head.

I'm hard too. Painfully fucking hard. I want to come more than I want my next fucking breath, but I can't. While the lust is clear in Preston's face, there's something else there too. Fear, maybe? What is he afraid of? Me?

I drop my ass back to the machine and grab a fist full of his shirt, pulling him up against me again.

"I hate you," he forces out while his fingers bruise my hips once again.

The bull comes to a stop, the world around us starts clicking back in place and he shoves me, hard. I fall off the bull, landing on my back on the mats while he climbs off and disappears into the crowd.

What the fuck just happened?

I'm blinking up at the ceiling when it hits me.

I just made it very obvious to half our team that Preston isn't straight.

Fuck.

The room is silent when I stand up and dust myself off, face red with guilt and embarrassment. I'm such a fucking idiot. Scanning the room, I don't see Preston.

Fuck. Me.

I race from the bar and hope to catch up with him so we can talk privately, but the streets are full of people and I didn't grab my jacket on the way out. Did he?

I run to the hotel and barely catch a glance of his face through the closing elevator doors. Damn it! If someone recorded that and uploaded it, it'll be all over the hockey blogs by morning. This is the last thing we need right now.

Hitting the elevator call button about twenty times, the doors finally open. I hit my floor number and rock back and forth on the balls of my feet as the number climbs. After the longest elevator ride of my life, it opens on my floor to a pissed off Preston standing in the hallway.

"I'm so sorry!" I reach for him but he brushes me off. Okay, he's pissed and not ready for comfort. Got it.

"Do you have any idea what you just risked?" His jaw is set but the anger is fading to something else. Fear.

He's afraid his father is going to find out and make him

come back for correction. That has to be it. His lip trembles as a different kind of tension takes over his body.

We aren't having this conversation in the damn hallway. Grabbing his hand, I pull him to my room, dig my key out of my back pocket, and get the door open.

Once we're inside, I turn on him and push him against the door, crowding into his space.

"I'm sorry, I got caught up in the moment and didn't think."

"If my father finds out about this public display, I will be taught a lesson." His voice is full of angst and pain. The sheer terror on his face breaks my heart.

"I can't let him take you again."

His dark, stormy gray eyes harden when they meet mine. "You can't stop him. I can take it, Lily can't."

I lean my forehead against his, despite wanting to rampage. It's not fair. How am I supposed to watch the man I love walk toward danger and do nothing to stop it?

"He can't keep doing this," I finally manage.

"He can until Lily turns eighteen." Preston is resigned to his fate. He doesn't fight it, just accepts it and moves on. What's the point of fighting a battle you know you'll lose?

There's noise in the hallway a few seconds before the beep of the lock on the door sounds. Preston and I move far enough away from it that Paul can enter without hitting us. He and Brendon stop in the doorway when they see us.

"Sorry, figured you'd be in the other room." Paul lifts our jackets that I had forgotten about, not realizing Preston was also in a fucking t-shirt.

"Thanks," I mutter to him, taking my coat. Preston takes his and folds it over his arm.

"We should get to bed," Preston tells the three of us.

Brendon holds up a to-go bag. "We brought dinner back."

We all shuffle further into the room and Brendon digs into the bag, handing out Styrofoam boxes.

"Thank you." Preston opens his box. His grilled chicken looks depressing and lonely.

"Seriously, just take some fries or something." I open my food and offer him some of it. "Put those poor chicken titties out of their misery."

His lip curls in disgust and shakes his head. "I ate enough carbs over Christmas to last a lifetime."

The rest of us chuckle and I shove a fry in my mouth.

Surprising all of us, Preston picks up a chicken breast and bites into it.

"Whoa, there. Chill out and find a fork like a civilized human," Paul rags on him and Preston flips him off.

"Did anyone on the team say anything?" he asks after a few minutes of us eating quietly.

"Not really," Brendon shrugs. "A couple guys were confused because you're an asshole on the ice." He looks pointedly at Preston and I snort. "A few guys thought it was a joke." Brendon shrugs again. "Most didn't seem to have a reaction."

"See anyone recording it?" I ask with a mouth full of bacon cheeseburger deliciousness.

"No, but I wasn't looking for it either." Brendon smirks at me. "I was watching the erotic show."

Preston smacks the back of Brendon's head and I laugh. He knew it was coming and braced for it.

"Idiot," Paul mutters under his breath.

We finish eating, with Paul smacking Brendon in the face with a long fry so Brendon throws a fry at Paul.

"Children. Knock it off," Preston growls and puts an arm around my shoulders, pulling me against his side. "We need to go to sleep anyway, no staying up late." He pins me and Paul with a serious look and I chuckle.

"I'm tired, anyway. Hurry up and get out so I can go to bed." I poke him in the ribs and he growls at me, pressing a quick kiss to my upturned lips before grabbing the trash and dumping it in the can.

"Oiler, out." Preston opens the door and waits for Brendon, who gives me and Paul a salute before they both leave.

Paul and I get ready for bed and lay down. He turns the TV on to some boring bullshit to fall asleep, but I struggle.

I keep tossing and turning, rolling over and huffing.

"I swear to God, I will risk being murdered by Preston and cuddle your ass just to get you to stop," Paul snaps, sitting up and staring at me with exasperation.

I flip him off and roll over again.

"It's one AM. I'm going to kill you."

Sitting up, I'm about to snap back at him when there's a pounding on our door. We both turn to look at it, then jump up and race over, ripping it open.

One of our defensive guys, Mathews, is standing in the hallway, pale, in only his boxers. "I can't get him to stop," he tells me, and that's all I need.

"Let's go," I push him back down the hallway and I can hear Preston screaming. My blood runs cold at the pain-filled wail, making me move faster. Mathews gets the door open and I race forward, sliding into bed with Preston and pulling him against me. By the angle he's laying at, he had to have put his back against the headboard to sleep.

He fights me in his sleep, pushing and slapping at me while a sob escapes him, tears staining his pillow and running into his short-cropped hair.

"Preston," I manage to wrap my legs around him and roll us so I'm on top of him with my chest pressed against his. "Wake up, come on."

I kiss his face, rubbing the soft hair of my face against his skin, and knock his hands back when he tries to pull me away. His body rocks against mine, bowing under me, but I hold on tight. These fucking nightmares are going to be the death of him. They're exhausting and traumatizing. Mathews will never forget this, and all I can hope is he won't say shit to anyone tomorrow.

Preston's shirt rides up during his struggle with the demons trapping him in his head. My body rubs against him, skin to skin, and the fight finally leaves. Both of us are panting when his eyes open, confused by my being on top of him.

His body is weak from the exertion, laying flat on the mattress while he reorients himself.

"There you are." I kiss his neck again, his forehead, his cheek. Relaxing on top of him and allowing him to accept the weight of my body against him. After these episodes, he likes the pressure of my body pushing him into the bed. He tells me it helps ground him.

"Is-is it over?" Mathews asks behind me.

Preston's body tenses, his hands coming to my waist and his eyes popping open.

"Yeah, you can go back to sleep now or go sleep in my room. I guarantee Paul won't care." I tell him, not lifting my head from my boyfriend's shoulder.

"Is he okay?"

"I'm fine." Preston's voice rumbles against my chest. Mathews lets out a breath of relief.

"I'll-um-sleep in your room," he mumbles, grabbing something and opening the door. "Oh, hey, Johnson."

"All good, Paul. Mathews is going to take my bed tonight." I tell him without looking. Paul knows Preston has nightmares and maybe he's heard a few of the bad ones, but he never asks about them. Much like me, he just makes sure everyone is okay and leaves it alone.

"Got it," my friend says and closes the door.

Preston relaxes again, his hands sliding down my body to my hips and grinding against me.

"I need you," he pants, biting at my ear lobe. My dick hardens at the lust in his voice, his cock already throbbing and rubbing against me.

"Lube?" I sit up and grind my ass on his cock, wanting to feel him stretching me, using me.

"In my bag." He palms my dick through my pajama pants, forcing a groan from my throat. "Go get it so you can ride me."

I swing my leg over and find his bag at the end of the bed. It doesn't take long for me to find the small bottle he keeps in his travel stuff and strip off my clothes. He watches me, pushing his own pants off and lifting his shirt to show part of his abdomen.

It's sexy as fuck to know that I'm the only one who gets to see him like this. Even with the scars on display, his cock is heavy and his eyes are full of lust. He's not deterred by being naked in front of me.

My dick jumps when he strokes himself while he bites his lower lip.

"Come here, baby." His voice is pure sex.

Climbing over him again, the hair on his thighs tickles my ass cheeks. I roll my hips and he takes both of our cocks in his hand, the extra skin from both of us being uncut giving us plenty of give to thrust together.

Preston sits up, reaching for the lube, and slathers his fingers in it before sliding them between my cheeks to press against my hole. I grab ahold of his head to ravage his mouth as his fingers thrust inside of me.

I whimper into his kiss, needing so much more than fingers. Pushing him back on the bed, I drip lube onto his cock and lift up to align myself over it.

"Take it, all the way down." He watches his cock disappear inside of my ass as I sink down on him. I drop my head back on a groan when my ass sits against him, fully seated on his dick. It burns a little with the stretch, but I love it. "Fuck me." Preston wraps a hand around my dick and I rotate my hips in a circle, feeling him everywhere.

I arch my back and grind his dick deep in my ass, my eyes shutting. I love the electric bursts behind my eyelids. My body is full and greedy for him.

Preston runs his hand up my body and finds my nipple, pinching it hard enough to force a gasp from me. My cock throbs at the pain, but my hips move. Leaning forward, I brace myself on his chest and lift up to slam back onto him. He groans this time and the sound spurs me on. Over and over, I take him in hard, deep, punishing movements until he can't take it anymore and he rolls us. Preston takes control, shoving my thighs wide and holding them against the mattress so he can pound into me mercilessly. My body being open and exposed to him is terrifying in the best way. I know he won't let me go or hurt me more than I want. It's freeing.

I'm moaning like a whore, back arched and needy to come with my hand around my dick.

"I love you," I grit out, craving the words from him when he's like this. Hurting and seeking comfort in me.

Preston releases my legs, one hand gripping my throat as he leans down to get his face into mine.

"I fucking love you," he snarls, slapping my cheek with the other hand. The slap is a hot sting on my face and it makes my dick leak.

Fuck.

"come for me," he demands. "Show me how much you love being fucked."

Tingles shoot up my spine and into my balls. I pant as mind-bending pleasure rolls my eyes into the back of my head and cum spurts out onto my chest while the love of my life uses my hole.

Preston's breath fans over my heated, sticky skin. He flicks his tongue out to lick at the cum on my chest and growls as his rhythm jackknifes, filling my ass with his seed then collapsing on top of me.

CHAPTER 41

preston

Sweat trickles down my back under my gear. I'm laser focused on the game and killing it out here. On the ice, nothing matters but the game. I'm able to lose myself in the muscle memory and adrenaline of it all, the real world fading to the background for an hour.

Jeremy, Oiler, and Johnson are gelling, reading each other's next move and not getting frustrated when our opponent gets the puck back.

Oiler steals the puck and flies up the ice on a breakaway, flinging the puck to Jeremy, who shoots on goal and the lamp lights up. The team is on their feet, whooping and hollering. They make their way off the ice with smiles on their faces, our first line taking over.

I slide to the end of the bench to give Jeremy room to drop down and he takes it, grabbing a water bottle and squirting some Gatorade into his mouth.

He lifts his glove covered hand to me and I fist bump him.

"Good shot." I wink at him.

"I guess that cheeseburger and fries didn't make me slow, huh?" He grins at me, his face red and sweaty.

"I wouldn't go that far," I deadpan, taking another drink of the sickly sweet liquid and he chuckles.

"Think your sister saw my breakaway?" Oiler smirks at me. *Why the fuck did I tell them she came down to the game with a few of her friends?* I lift a lip at him and he laughs, taking the Gatorade from Jeremy.

"Line change!" Coach hollers and I stand with Willis. The other guys come off the ice and we find our spots.

The puck is dropped and a big motherfucker races toward the blue line. I do my best to block him without interfering with the goalie's view of the puck. The player slams into my chest and knocks me off my feet. On instinct, I put my hand out to catch myself, but fall on another player's skate, wrenching my shoulder. Immediately there's a pop and a dull, bone-deep throb.

The puck ends up back on the other side of the ice and Willis skates over to help me up. When I try to tuck the injured arm to my body, searing pain shoots through the muscles and I shout.

"Dude, you alright?" He asks when I give him my good hand and he pulls me up.

"No, I can't move my arm." I hiss through gritted teeth.

"Coach!" Willis yells. "Carmichael's hurt!"

The refs blow whistles and the game is paused while I get off the ice and the ambulance staff come toward me.

He stays on my bad side to protect me until I'm at the bench in case anyone tries to fuck with me.

"What's wrong?" Coach is looking at me expectantly.

"My shoulder popped," I grit out. "I think it's dislocated." Jeremy stands, concern on his face, and pushes his way toward me.

"Fuck. Alright, get it checked out."

For a second, I let the fear I feel show in my eyes before I shut it back down. This isn't the most amount of pain I've been in, but it's not a vacation either. Will I be able to come back tonight? Tomorrow? Did I break something? Tear something? How long will I be out? Will this fuck up my odds of being drafted?

Do I want it to?

I walk back toward the locker rooms to get looked at by one of the assistant coaches. The EMTs meet us and I tell them what happened. They ask me the normal questions like name, date, who's president, and what happened.

"Pain, on a scale of one to ten with ten being the worst pain you can imagine." A pretty black-haired woman with big brown eyes asks.

"I don't know, like a three or four? It's constant and doesn't fucking tickle but I've had worse."

"Alright, can you move your fingers?" I try to move my fingers, but they barely budge. The ache in my shoulder joint increases when I use the muscles. "Does that make the pain worse?" I nod at her question.

Sweat drips from my forehead from the adrenaline. This fucking sucks. It's almost like a bone break, that bone-deep throb that just doesn't let up. It's not sharp enough to steal your breath but zaps your energy because it won't quit.

I'm told to sit on the gurney, so I do. My hand hangs off the edge between my legs.

"Do you feel like you're bleeding? Did you hit your head or lose consciousness?" I shake my head no at her questions.

"I need to feel around the shoulder, okay? If it hurts too bad, let me know." She tells me and I brace for the pain and for the physical contact. She slides her hand under my jersey and the shoulder pads to feel along my shoulder. I try not to flinch at the touch. She's on the outside of my base layer but it still makes my skin crawl. Jeremy is the only one who can touch me. She finds a sensitive spot and I jerk back with a hiss.

"Shoulder deformity, probably dislocated. Let's stabilize and load him up." One of the crew gets an ice pack ready. "Are you on any medications, vitamins, or supplements?" she asks.

"No," I grunt out as I swing my legs up onto the plastic mattress and wince as my arm is jostled. Once I'm settled, an ice pack is put on my shoulder and the woman is cutting the sleeves of the jersey and base layer to expose the crook of my elbow.

They take a quick heart rate and she gets an IV started in my good arm.

"We're going to give him some pain meds," she tells Assistant Coach Scott and we all head toward the ambulance. The woman is talking into her radio at her shoulder, updating the hospital on my condition, but I'm not paying attention because whatever she gave me is making my head swim a bit.

We get into the ambulance and head to the hospital.

She's saying things like "No LOC, fifty mikes, and bp," which means nothing to me.

I've never felt so light, like I'm floating for a minute.

No wonder people get addicted to this stuff. It feels like the softest, plushest fabric is wrapped around my brain. My shoulder hurts but I don't care. I don't care about anything but getting back to the ice. I don't want to go to the damn hospital. Why can't they just pop the damn shoulder back in? My father is going to be furious over this.

"Jesus, we didn't give him that much fentanyl," someone says, and it's weird to have to focus on turning my head.

"I'mma sensitive guy," I mumble, strangely aware of the movement of my lips. I feel weird but I'm still coherent.

Someone snorts and pats my knee, but I don't know who it was. It wasn't Jeremy, I know that much.

Jeremy. He's going to be worried. My boyfriend. I love him. He's going to be worried. I wish I had my phone so I could send him a message for after the game. I doubt I'll be back before the end of the game.

The IV in my arm is pushing cold liquid into my veins. I'm no longer sweating, thanks to the saline, but now I'm getting cold.

A shudder has goosebumps rising on my skin.

"Do you need a blanket?" The attendant in the back with me asks.

My eyes are closed against the bright light of the inside of the rig, but I lift my eyebrows and nod. A blanket is draped over me and for the rest of the ride, the assistant coach gives me the game play by play. Jeremy is struggling, I can tell by how he's playing. He's worried about me.

"Hey, can you call my sister?" I interrupt him.

"Sure, what's the number?"

I spout out the number and he puts the phone between my good shoulder and ear. It rings a few times before a suspicious but worried Lily answers.

"Hello?"

"Hey, it's me." She sighs. "Pretty sure I dislocated my shoulder."

"Are you okay? What hospital are you going to? I'll meet you there."

"No, no. Don't come to the hospital. Watch the game and tell Oiler and Johnson they sucked." I snort at myself. That'll teach them to flirt with my sister.

"Are you crazy? I'm not sitting in the stands and watching the game while you go to the hospital. We're already heading to the car." She says something to someone she's with. "What hospital, Preston?"

I look at Scott sitting next to me. "What hospital?"

The male EMT answers me, "Providence Memorial."

"You get that?" I ask into the phone as we pull up to the hospital. "Don't get into a car without Anthony and Mark." Her driver and bodyguard are paid for this shit and if she takes an Uber, I'm going to kill her.

"Tony is right here," she says, exasperated. I can practically see her rolling her eyes at me. "Mark is getting the car."

"Hey, message Jeremy for me. I don't have my phone."

"You got it, I'll see you in a few." The line goes dead and I nod at Scott, "Thanks."

"No problem." He goes back to checking the game highlights.

At the hospital, a tall woman with brown hair and big black cat-eye shaped glasses approaches me and quickly introduces herself, "I'm Jessica, I'll be your nurse tonight." She asks me what happened, if I'm on any medications, height and weight, and why I'm there. All the normal shit.

I nod at her. Her in-charge confidence brings me some comfort. I feel safe with her, like if my father were to show up, she wouldn't give in to his shit.

Father isn't here.

As she's talking to me, a few other staff members in scrubs come in. One short, thin man puts on gloves and has a pair of scissors. Looking at me he says, "I need to cut this off."

I eye the scissors but nod, clenching my jaw. The man makes quick work of cutting up the center and down the sleeves to pull it off then pulls the Velcro straps to take the shoulder pads off. Once the pads are removed, he pulls on the base layer shirt and cuts that off too. I don't miss the glances between the staff when they see the scars marring my chest. Luckily, my legs and most of my abdomen are covered by more pads, but my chest and arms are all on full display.

"Hello." a man in a white lab coat and scrubs comes in. "I'm Doctor Harris." He shakes my hand, pauses at my chest, asks me why I'm here and what happened, then checks for neck, head, and back issues.

He tells the nurse to order some kind of pain med that I don't hear because I'm too busy watching everyone around me. People are touching me and it's making my fucking skin crawl. Whatever they gave me in the ambulance is wearing off, which is making me even more on edge.

My good hand starts tapping on my leg, needing something to do with the energy. The ache in my shoulder is almost enough to get all of my attention but I've had too much practice shoving down pain to focus on other things.

"Alright, Mister Carmichael," The doctor says to me after pushing on my shoulder. "We're going to need to do some moderate sedation so we can set this arm. We'll have a respiratory therapist come in to monitor your breathing while we have you under, give you an amnesiac just in case, and pull that arm back into place."

That all sounds terrifying.

"Yeah, sure whatever, just fix it so I can get out of here." My eyes flitter between everyone in the room, not trusting anyone but Nurse Jessica. Why is she the exception?

Nurse Jessica comes back in with some paperwork for me to sign then injects something into my IV line. It's amazing how fast it hits my system.

My body relaxes and I slump back onto the bed, no longer giving a shit about anything around me. The world spins, someone is talking to me, but I have no idea what is happening anymore.

"Man, I wish my father would give me meds. I bet I wouldn't have nightmares." *Am I speaking? I don't know.*

My fingers feel along the ridges of scars on my chest. "Why did he have to cut me though? I was a good kid."

Sticky circles are stuck all over my chest and connected to wires that lead to whatever machines they have around me by more people I don't know. How many people are going to touch me? How many people are going to see the evidence of my torture? Of my embarrassment?

"Hey, are you related to Doctor Carmichael? The plastic surgeon?" The pretty lady sitting next to me asks.

"Doctor Andrew Carmichael is my father." I say on an exhale. "He hates me."

I close my eyes and wait for the doctor to come back with whatever other medications he said I would have. I don't know how long I wait, it could have been five minutes, could have been an hour. There's no sense of time when there's pain medication in your system. What did they even give me? I'm sure they told me, but I don't remember.

"Here we go." A doctor comes in with a syringe and injects it into my IV line. "Count back from ten."

"Ten, nine..."

CHAPTER 42

jeremy

This game has been a disaster. I've tripped over my own skates, missed passes, and been slammed into the boards more than once. We barely manage to hold on to our lead and I am definitely part of the problem.

Once the game is over, we trudge to the locker room to shower and get dressed. My body is buzzing with anxious energy, needing an update on Preston more than I need air. In the locker room, I grab my phone and check for messages.

LILY

Preston is at Providence Memorial. Dislocated Shoulder.

Uh, can you bring him a shirt? He's freaking out because he doesn't have one to put on.

Yes, I'll be there in like 45 minutes.

I shove my phone back in my cubby and strip off my

gear and base layer before hurrying toward the showers. I need to get out of here.

"Albrooke, you going to the hospital?" Carpenter asks from across the showers.

"Yes," I holler back, turning on the water and stepping in, not caring about the temperature one bit.

Is he okay? How long will he be out? How bad is his pain? Is his dad going to freak out?

I take the fastest shower of my life, aggressively scrub my skin dry with a towel, and put my borrowed suit on. Honestly, it's more mine at this point than Preston's, but semantics.

Walking over to Paul and Brendon, I stop to pull up an Uber on my phone and see I have ten minutes before they'll be here.

"Hey, either of you have an extra t-shirt or something I can take to Preston? Lily says they cut his stuff off." I look at his cubby, and while he has a suit shirt, I'm not so sure that's what he wants me to bring. I think a t-shirt would be better.

"Yeah, I've got some extra white ones, hold on." Brendon digs in his stuff and pulls a crumpled-up t-shirt from the bottom of it. "Here."

"Thanks," I take it and his suit bag just in case, and head out to tell Coach I'm leaving.

"Alright, be careful and let me know if you need anything," he says, clapping me on the shoulder.

"Will do," I tell him and fight my way to the street to meet my Uber. Luckily, it doesn't take me long to find the car or get away from the game day traffic.

The hospital isn't too far away and when I roll up to the ER, I see Lily and who I assume are a few of her friends. They all look about the same age and everything about them screams money.

Lily races up to me, pushing me back outside, her face

pale and panicked.

"What?" I demand. "Lily what is it? What's wrong? Is Preston okay?"

She doesn't speak until we're away from the doors and over to one side alone. "We have a problem and I need you to answer me honestly."

My stomach drops to my feet. What does she think she knows? I can't lie to her, but I'm not telling her all Preston's secrets either.

"Has my father been abusing Preston?" She crosses her arms over her chest and squares her shoulders.

Fuck.

"Why do you ask?" Did she see the scars? Did he say something while he was doped up on pain meds? Who else has put the pieces together?

"My friends Callie and Sara overheard two doctors talking about my father and Preston in the hallway. Something about reporting my father to the ethics board or making a report to adult protective services? I didn't even know that was a thing. One said he was forced out of Boston because of patient complaints of sexual harassment."

With every word that comes from her, dread settles heavier and heavier in my stomach. The blood drains from my face to pool at my feet as if she's sliced into my heart. This will destroy him.

Lily either doesn't notice or doesn't care because she keeps going. "They said he was talking about our father *cutting* him and how he wished he was given pain medication." She stares at me, anger coloring her cheeks. "Don't lie to me, Jeremy. What the fuck is going on?" Her arms are wrapped around herself, but I don't know if it's in defense or because she's holding herself together.

"First, they cannot tell anyone what they heard. No one. Second, I don't have many details." I say. Lily drops her gaze, looking at the concrete under our shoes, obviously uncomfortable. "What?"

She won't look at me. "They were doing a Facebook live and it's on there."

"What?!" Spinning around and racing for the ER entrance once again with Lily on my heels, I find the girls and walk right up to them. Fury and frustration and fear fighting within me. I have to protect Preston.

"Hey, delete that video. Right now. Get it off social media." I demand, one girl with curly red hair looks up at me with wide eyes and reaches for her phone. "You can't talk about this to anyone, do you understand?"

She looks down at her phone, getting into her Facebook account and finding the video.

"Deleted. It's gone." She looks up at me. "I'm sorry."

I scrub a hand down my face as the unknown future and all the possible what ifs bombard me. Do I tell him now or wait and see if something comes from it? My hands are shaking, and my stomach is twisted in knots, it hurts to breathe. Fuck. I can't protect him if this gets out. What will his dad do?

"You didn't tag him in it, right?"

She shakes her head quickly. That's something at least. I run my fingers through my still wet hair and pull on the ends.

"I'm going to see if I can go back and see him," I tell Lily and head to check in. A woman in scrubs looks up at me with a smile.

"How can I help you?" she asks.

"Can I go back and check on my friend? Preston Carmichael is his name. He was brought in by ambulance."

She chuckles, "Are you Jeremy?"

"Yes ma'am, I am." Why does she know my name?

"Come on back." She points to the door to the left.

"Through that door then at the nurses' station, he'll be right next to you."

Relief almost has my knees giving out as I head to the door. The hallway opens to a room with a nurses' station in the middle and a bunch of curtained off spaces set up around the edge of the room. I turn to the first bed on my right and step close to the curtain.

"While you were sedated, you said some things that are concerning." A feminine voice comes from behind the curtain.

"What did I say?" That's Preston's voice and he does not sound happy.

"You said that your dad cut you." My heart sinks at her answer. "Is that what all these scars are?" Her voice is full of concern and compassion, but I guarantee he hears pity. I don't know how to help him and this feeling of being helpless makes me twitchy.

I can almost imagine the blank expression on his face. He's shutting down and I don't need to see him to know it. Maybe being with him will help?

"Preston?" My tone is hesitant in case I'm not in the right place.

"Just a second," The female voice calls to me.

"Jeremy?" Preston's voice is a punch to the stomach. He's not closed off and cold right now, but scared and needy.

I reach for the curtain but a brown-haired woman in scrubs and big black glasses pulls it back a little.

"Are you Jeremy?" she asks me, taking in the suit I'm wearing and the garment bag over my arm.

"Yes, ma'am."

"Come on in." She holds the curtain open for me. "He's been asking for you."

Preston is sitting up on a bed wearing a hospital gown

and hockey pants with his skates still on. His left arm is in a sling over his chest and there's an IV in his other arm, but he looks okay. He's awake.

"Hey." His smile is tight, forced. Like he thinks I expect him to smile but he's not at all feeling it.

"Hey, how are you feeling?" I stand awkwardly next to the bed as the nurse leaves.

Preston pats the bed on his right side and I put the garment bag down then sit, relieved he wants me close. His good hand reaches for my shirt and pulls me toward him, pressing his lips against mine.

"I want out of here," he says against my mouth.

"How much longer do you have to be here?" I hope he can't see that I'm holding shit back from him. He doesn't need to worry about what could be happening on social media right now, but guilt is eating at me for not telling him already. "You should tell her."

His eyes snap to mine and his shoulders immediately tense. "What? Why?"

"Because what he's been doing isn't okay and she might be able to help you." What part of that does he not understand?

"Lily turns eighteen in a few months. Nothing is going to happen to him before that. And even if charges are pressed against him, I have zero proof. Who's to say I didn't do this myself to frame him? Not to mention, that leaves Lily vulnerable to him."

The curtain is pulled back and we both look to see Assistant Coach Scott looking between us. Preston's hand drops my shirt and I scoot back a little to put some space between us.

Scott closes the curtain again and turns to us. "Look, guys, I don't care if you're more than teammates as long as it doesn't affect you negatively on the ice. Got it?"

A breath I didn't realize I was holding comes out in a rush. Preston says nothing, his walls are back up. He puts his hand on the bed but I reach for it and run my thumb over his inner wrist, surprised when he doesn't pull away from me. Scott's phone rings and he leaves the area to take the call, once again giving us a moment of privacy.

My phone rings in my pocket so I pull it out, anxiety already spiking at the possibility that someone saw that fucking video, but I smile at my mom's picture. Answering the phone, I turn my body to get Preston in the background.

"He'll live, promise!"

"Oh, thank God! What happened? Is that a sling?" Mom asks, with Grandma behind her.

"Dislocated shoulder," Preston says. "I'll be back on the ice in a few weeks."

"Good, good. We just wanted to check in. Call me when you get home."

"Will do, thanks Mom." I smile at her.

"Thank you, Mrs. Albrooke, and Grandma," Preston says behind me, lifting his hand in a wave before I end the call.

Sliding my phone back in my pocket, I watch my finger drag along his inner wrist.

"Say it." Preston's voice makes me flinch. He's waiting for bad news and it hurts my heart. "Whatever it is, out with it."

"Lily knows your dad has been abusing you."

The air in the room has been sucked out. The tension in the air is so thick I can feel it pressing in on me like a physical weight.

"How?" The word is so quiet I almost didn't hear it over the bustle of the ER.

Closing my eyes, I inhale a deep breath and release it

before meeting his gaze. "The friends she came with overheard a couple of doctors talking about you and him. They were doing a Facebook live and got it on video." Preston's breathing increases and fear widens his eyes so I hurry with the next part. "I told them to delete it and not talk to anyone else about it, but Lily has questions." The lost little boy look on his face breaks me. This moment will forever be seared into my brain. His carefully concealed world is crumbling and there's nothing I can do to stop it. Just sit and watch it happen, then pick up the pieces of him when it's over.

The nurse comes back in with paperwork in her hand, followed by Coach Scott.

"Listen, that shoulder is going to be wonky for a while, until the muscles around it recover. Do not use that arm more than absolutely necessary." She gives Preston a pointed look. "Keep your arm against your body while you shower, get dressed and put the sling back on. I'm not kidding, you can dislocate it again very easily right now."

Preston nods at her, taking her directions seriously. Or at least pretending to.

"Excuse me," she says to me, so I get up and move to stand next to Scott. She removes the IV from Preston's arm, wraps a piece of gauze with the tan, stretchy sticky tape crap, and tells him he can get dressed. Preston doesn't flinch when she touches him. That's interesting.

He eyes Scott, not wanting to expose himself to the man, and I clear my throat.

"I'll help him get dressed and we'll meet you in the waiting room."

Thankfully, Scott takes the hint and fucks off to give Preston some privacy. Opening the garment bag, I pull out the t-shirt and help Preston get his good arm and head through it, pulling the fabric down over his slinged arm. Moving to his skates, I get them off, help him stand, and he leans on my shoulder while I pull his gear and pants off. Does he need it all off right now? No, but he'll be more comfortable in regular clothes.

"You trust her," I say as I pull his base layer down his legs. "The nurse."

"She seems like a good person, doesn't take shit from anyone, straight forward." Preston steps out of all his stuff and I get him dressed again, pulling underwear and pants up. He tucks his dick in the way he wants it situated and lifts an eyebrow at me when I smirk at him.

"I could have done that for you." I bite at my lower lip.

The unamused expression he aims at me makes me laugh.

I button and zip his suit pants and he sits back down so I can pull on his socks and shoes so we can get out of here.

In the waiting room, Lily is pissed, while Scott is leaning against the wall reading through the discharge paperwork. There's an older man standing beside Lily, talking quietly to her and her friends.

Preston walks over to talk to Lily, so I follow. The door behind us opens and the nurse pokes her head out. She nods at me and waves me over.

"I forgot something in the room, I'll be right back," I tell Preston and head over.

"Follow me," she says and walks me into what looks like an exam room with a door. "Being completely honest here, I'm worried about him. What's the deal with the scars? They aren't in the normal places where we find self-harm scars."

My chest tightens and I fight a war within myself. I want to help him, but it's not my fucking story.

"He didn't do them himself." I can't meet her eyes. My head tells me to spill it all to her, but my gut tells me it'll be worse if she knows.

"Listen, I can tell he doesn't want help right now, but if he changes his mind, call me and I will help him." She hands me a white business card with a phone number scrawled on one side, the other side is for the social worker in the hospital. "They will be happy to help too if he decides he wants it. I also highly recommend therapy if what he's been through is anything like I'm thinking."

All I can do is nod at her, the lump in my throat too big to speak around.

By the time we get back to the hotel, Preston is agitated and ready to start rampaging.

"Lily, you aren't going to that damn game!" he snaps into his phone. "I'm not even playing, what's the fucking point?"

I can hear her yell back at him but not what is said. While I realize this is a family matter, he's not doing himself any favors. He's pacing the length of our hotel room, getting more and more tense when he really should be resting.

I can't take it anymore. Standing from the bed, I step directly into his path and won't let him go around me.

Preston lifts his lip at me, his gaze promising pain if I don't back off. Luckily for me, I'm not intimidated by him.

"Let me talk to her." I put my hand out for the phone and he looks at me like I just slapped him. "She's digging in her heels because you're demanding shit from her. Let me talk to her."

"Lillian, you are not going to that damn game. Do you understand me?" he barks through clenched teeth.

With a sigh, I snatch the phone from him and run for the bathroom, locking the door behind me.

"Good evening, Lily." I say cheerfully as Preston pounds on the door.

"I swear to God, Jeremy. I don't know how you don't smother him in his sleep!" she huffs out in frustration.

I shrug even though she can't see it. "Listen, I know you and your friends came down here to watch the games. I know Preston is secretly very happy to see you, though it's probably very deeply buried at this point." I lean against the door in an attempt to counter his banging so the door doesn't break.

"He's a caveman! Just because he's my older brother, it doesn't give him the right to tell me what to do!" she yells.

"I agree. He's not handling this well. At all." The pounding on the door stops, which makes me nervous. "But can you do me a favor?"

"What?" She's suspicious, which I can't blame her for.

"Can you *not* go to the game tomorrow, please?" As soon as the words are out of my mouth she starts to argue. "I know, I know. You came all this way, I get it. *But*, I think Preston is worried about your safety. If the wrong person saw that video and spreads the word, it could go viral and you could be hounded by reporters. Which he will feel responsible for, especially since he can't do anything to help you."

She sighs but is not happy about this at all. "That makes sense, but he's still an asshole!"

"Oh, one hundred percent," I agree, and she giggles. "But he's an overly protective asshole and he's nervous right now."

"Uck. Why do you have to be so logical?" She huffs. "Fine, we'll head back to school in the morning."

"Thank you, I truly appreciate it."

"Whatever. Enjoy your night with that jackass." She hangs up and I turn back to the door, eyeing it warily. What am I going to find on the other side? Even injured, my man is freakishly strong.

Taking a deep breath and hoping for the best, I open the door. Preston shoves it open and grabs my throat, forcing me back against the wall on the other side of the bathroom. I trip over my feet but manage to stay up by sheer force of will. The last thing I want is to fall and cause him more pain.

My head hits the wall with a thud, and I stare up into the furious, almost black eyes of my boyfriend.

"You're welcome." I tell him calmly, holding up his phone before shoving it into his pants pocket. "She's heading home in the morning."

His grip on my throat tightens and he uses every centimeter of his height to try and intimidate me. I am very careful to keep my expression neutral.

"You had no right to come between me and my sister." His tone is ice cold and full of menace.

"She was digging in her heels and wasn't going to budge to your demands. All I did was ask her nicely."

One of his eyes twitches as he glares at me. He wants to fuck me up, I can see it clear as day on his face and in his body language. The need to dominate, claim, and cause destruction is strong. But he says nothing.

After a minute of staring at me and breathing heavily, I reach for his shirt and pull it up, uncovering his bad arm and sling, and bring it over his head to hang from the arm he's using to pin me against the wall. Confusion is creasing his eyebrows as they pinch together when I open his pants and shove his clothes down his legs. Since I can't help him step out of his shoes or pants, I start pulling my own suit off. Unbuttoning the shirt and dropping it on the floor, my shoes, socks, pants, and underwear quickly following, all while I keep my gaze locked on his.

When I'm bare to him and he's mostly naked, I pull him against me.

"You should shower," I say in the same calm fashion. "Let me help you."

CHAPTER 43

preston

My phone has been vibrating and lighting up since I got up yesterday morning. I have an unknown number of new emails, text messages, social media direct messages, and missed phone calls. My voice mail has been full since six AM. I had to use Jeremy's phone to call Lily's school to make sure she would be safe. They informed me that our father will not be allowed on campus, and she will not be leaving the campus until the allegations against our father were cleared or she graduated, whichever happens first. Being a rich prick has its advantages sometimes.

The video Lily's friend, Callie, uploaded Friday night was apparently seen by the right person and it's now everywhere. Despite being deleted, someone was able to download it and re-upload it. It's made the rounds in medical circles and hockey circles. It's only a matter of time before it hits mainstream media outlets. I've had more reporters call me than I can count.

I'm so overwhelmed by all of it, I'm numb. Jeremy is worried, I can see it on his face, in the way he watches me, but I can't comfort him. I can barely live in my own head right now.

"Preston." Jeremy's voice has me looking up from the ringing phone in my hand. "Turn it off."

"Is that going to stop the implosion of my life?" I hate the tone of my own voice but I can't stop it. I have no control over anything and I'm falling the fuck apart.

There's a knock on the hotel door and he sighs as he goes to check the peep hole then opens it. Coach strides in with purpose.

"Carmichael, I've spoken to the school administrators at length this morning. You are not to say anything publicly, no social media, emails, nothing. If you decide you want to make a statement, the legal team will negotiate with a reporter to get you interviewed or they will help you write up something to post if that's the way you want to go." He hands me a business card. "This is the legal office that works with the university. They have been made aware of the situation."

"Thank you, Coach." I run the card between my fingers, focusing on the texture of the expensive card stock and raised letters.

"The front desk says there are already reporters outside waiting for you, but after the media circus that was at the game last night, I'm not surprised."

I nod, accepting what he's saying but not really absorbing it. After the first period, the reporters were so bad I went to sit in the locker room by myself so they would clear out some.

"Maybe I shouldn't go to the home games this week." I flick the business card. "I'll be a distraction. The focus should be on the game, not on me."

The older man puts a hand on my shoulder. "The team stands behind you, so we will carry on like usual." He squeezes my good shoulder as a knot forms in my throat. "Get dressed, we're going to leave a bit early for the airport, just in case the reporters slow us down."

Jeremy leans against the wall next to the bathroom with a small smile on his lips, the bracelet I got him for Christmas on his wrist. I love that man.

He's already showered and half-dressed while I'm still in fucking pajamas. We had breakfast here in the room so we wouldn't have to deal with people but really, I barely picked at it. I'm not hungry. That's worrying Jeremy too.

Coach leaves and Jeremy walks over, his unbuttoned shirt fluttering open when he moves. He stands between my knees and cups my face, leaning down to kiss me softly. His beard is getting long, and I like it a lot more than I had expected to. His hair is soft against my palm when I kiss him.

"Let me help you get dressed, and if you're a good boy about it, I'll suck your dick before we leave." He's trying to distract me, but I'm not even interested in an orgasm. Not right now. Jeremy is a fixer, sitting back doesn't sit well for him. He needs a task but I can't give him one. I can barely think for myself, much less for someone else. I'm either angry or numb, there's nothing else left.

I lean my face against the bare skin of his abdomen and breathe. It's a weakness, seeking comfort from another, but somewhere along the last few months, I've learned to rely on Jeremy. Heavily. I can't handle anything without him anymore after a decade of doing everything on my own.

Sometimes I disgust myself.

He's going to get tired of your shit and leave you.

No one wants to date someone who can't take care of themselves. Who's so needy and useless.

His hands run through my hair and I relax against him.

"We're going to be okay," he tells me with conviction. "Whatever happens, we'll get through it together."

I wrap my free arm around his thighs and lean more of my weight against him.

"I love you," I say with my lips against the flesh between his belly button and his pants. Goosebumps break out on his skin and I let myself feel the bumps with my tongue.

Maybe I should suck *him* off instead. If I can keep his body satisfied, he's less likely to get tired of me and leave. Right?

Jeremy lifts my chin until I'm looking up at him, tears welling in my eyes and making him blurry. *He can't leave me. My entire world will fall the fuck apart.*

"I love you, Preston. I've got you" His hand slides across my cheek to cup my neck under my ear and brushes his thumb along my face. "Let's get you dressed."

He heads to the hanging bar behind the door and grabs my garment bag, walking it back to the bed and unzipping it. I haven't ironed any of it. Hopefully it's not too wrinkled.

"Do you want to try to take a quick shower or are you good from the one last night?"

"I'm good," I also put on deodorant right before going to bed so I should be good on that front too. I unstrap my sling and Jeremy helps me get it off without moving my arm too much. It takes both of us, but we manage to get the shirt off and my dress shirt on.

"You know, the nurse, Jessica, mentioned that you could benefit from talking to someone, like a therapist." Jeremy mentions as he helps me into my shirt.

"I barely talk to you about it. You really think I'll talk to a complete stranger? One that my father can pay off?" I shake my head and am grateful when Jeremy drops the subject.

Having him button it up is sexier than it should be. The button up shirt is easier at this point, but I feel like a tool wearing it to the airport.

"Why is it so hot to dress you? Shouldn't it be the opposite?" Jeremy grins at me.

"I'm feeling very pampered right now."

I stand and start shoving at my pants but lose my balance and stumble into the bedside table.

"Jesus, let me help you." Jeremy pins me with a hard stare and I let him pull the rest of my clothes off. I use his shoulder to steady myself as I step into the clean boxer briefs and jeans. He stands as he pulls everything up, tucking my half-hard dick into my underwear while biting his lower lip.

"Sure I can't blow you?" He tucks my shirt into the pants and buttons them, making a point to run his palm over my dick as he finds the zipper.

"One of these days..." I trail off, but Jeremy is not concerned.

"Oh yeah?" He lifts an eyebrow and grabs my jacket.

I shake my head at him. "You love being manhandled."

He chuckles as he lifts the jacket onto my shoulders and finds the sling for my arm.

"I really do."

Once my shoes are on and Jeremy finishes getting dressed, we head out to the elevators where a few of the guys are all waiting. Honestly, for a bunch of brutal hockey players, we look remarkably normal in jeans and hoodies.

Since my shirt isn't crisp with a fresh ironing job, I can't help but rub my hand down my front and button my jacket to cover as much as I can. Didn't Coach say there are reporters outside? Why didn't I iron my shirt? Now I'm going to look disheveled in any pictures they post.

We crowd into the elevator, all wanting to get going, the

guys still chatting around us. I square my shoulders and wait against the back wall.

"Hey, man, how are you feeling?" Mathews asks me.

"I'm fine." I know he's trying to form some kind of relationship, a friendship, but I don't have the mental capacity for it. Is he asking about my shoulder or the family secrets that have been splashed across the internet? I don't know, it doesn't matter, and I don't care. All I want right now is to hold Jeremy against me, but there are cameras in here. I don't know if whoever watches those tapes knows who we are, but my face is currently being plastered all over the internet. The last thing I need is for my sexuality to come out publicly and further complicate matters.

The elevator doors open and everyone falls silent and freezes. Shit. This is probably my fault.

"Everyone out, let's go." Coach waves us out of the cramped space and into the lobby. "We are going to have to push through the crowd to get to the bus. The hotel staff has agreed to help us form a barrier to get everyone in the bus, but we have to move fast." He takes a deep breath. "This is not a hockey game and these people are not athletes. Use as little physical force as you can to keep them out of the way, and do not hurt them if it can be avoided."

Guilt eats at my stomach.

"Put a hand on the shoulder of the person in front of you so you don't get separated." Assistant Coach Scott tells us. We form a line of sorts and Jeremy stands behind me. The guys look around and without anyone saying a word, they form a line on either side of me, creating a wall. Brendon and Paul on one side, Willis and Carpenter on the other and Mathews in front of me.

What are they doing?

I don't understand.

"We got your back, buddy." Brendon winks at me.

Jeremy's hand lands on my good shoulder and he gives me a squeeze. Why are they protecting me? I'm causing them more shit to deal with. They could get hurt out here just trying to get to the fucking bus.

"We're a team," Carpenter says. "Nobody fucks with you but us."

Before I can respond, the coaching staff, along with some uniformed hotel staff, move to the doors, the team following. Coach steps out, says no one will be making any statements, then the doors open and we rush the crowd.

Almost thirty big hockey players moving quickly and with determination toward anything will make people move. Most of the reporters jump out of the way before they get trampled.

"Preston, has your dad abused you?"

"Preston, do you have any proof of these abuse allegations?"

"Why have you waited so long to come out against your father?"

Questions are thrown at me left and right and it is so hard to ignore them. I want to rip into these assholes who have no idea what my life is like, pummel their faces until they understand the way my world has worked. But I don't. The crowd forces us closer, my teammates pressed against me making me feel claustrophobic and itchy.

Get to the bus. Get to the bus. Get to the bus.

I let my teammates get me safely to the bus, shoving people out of the way. We bottleneck at the doors, only one of us can fit through at a time. The people directly in front of me hurry onto the bus and into seats to get out of the way while they make room for me to get on. Someone yells "Fuck off!" and I think it was Paul, but I don't stop to look.

I'm able to get into the back row, letting Jeremy in first then sitting down and staring straight ahead.

Focus.

Don't let them see the cracks or confusion. They will exploit any weakness.

Jeremy slides his hand onto my thigh and I ignore it. I can't break right now.

"We need to be extremely careful right now." I tell Jeremy without looking at him. "If it gets out that we're together, the reporters will hound you too."

"Do you think I care?" I can feel the heat of his stare on the side of my face.

"I do." I say, looking pointedly at Jeremy. He just squeezes my thigh but doesn't respond.

Everyone gets on the bus, our bags are loaded, and the driver pulls away from the curb, even as reporters try to cling to the vehicle. Some even get into cars and chase us across town to the airport. Great.

The entire drive I stare forward, ignoring everything around me. Coach passes out flight information and tickets, reminding us about what we can and cannot have in our carry-ons. Jeremy has a backpack that he shoved some of my shit into, but it's not my problem. At the airport, the guys once again form a barricade around me to keep everyone but Jeremy back.

It's both humbling and confusing. They have no good reason for it. I've been nothing but an asshole to everyone.

It has nothing to do with you, they're protecting Jeremy.

That makes sense to me. I can't protect him right now myself, so I appreciate them caring enough about him to do something.

We grab our bags and, as a unit, move inside to check in. People turn and stare, pointing and whispering, some taking their phones out and recording us.

I'll never understand people. We're checking into our

flights. What is so damn exciting about it that you feel the need to record it?

We all get checked in, give our bags to the people at the counter, and head to security to wait in line.

We're almost to the metal detectors when a rush of reporters runs in and spots me.

"Oh, come on," I huff, turning my back to them and ignoring them.

"Preston, do you have anything to say about the sexual assault allegations that have been made against your father this morning by a former patient of his?" A man yells across the space, making sure it echoes enough for everyone in the airport to hear.

Sexual assault? That's news to me, but I guess not all that surprising. I don't have time to think about all this, I just want to get back to school and hide in my dorm room, alone with Jeremy, and decompress.

My eyebrows pinch together and I flick my gaze to Jeremy, who's looking at me just as confused. What the fuck is this guy talking about? Is he baiting me to get a response?

"Next!" The security agent yells and I step forward with my ticket and driver's license.

"Business or pleasure?" The bored tone almost makes me smile.

"Going home."

He looks at the ID with a black light and stamps the ticket before handing them back to me.

"Have a good day," he looks to Jeremy who's standing behind me. "Next!"

I move along to the metal detectors, and since my arm is in a sling, they have me step aside and wand me. Jeremy has to help me get the jacket off, which is mildly humiliating in public.

The agent waves the wand over me, front and back, rubs

some paper shit over my hands and sticks it in a machine. Jeremy finishes and waits with me, some of the guys have moved on to the gate now that there's no reporters since they can't get through security without a ticket.

I'm itching to get to the gate and look up what new allegations have been thrown at my father. The agent clears me and Jeremy. Brendon, Paul, Carpenter, Willis, and Mathews walk with me to our gate at the other end of the facility. During our walk, I pull out my phone and Google my father's name. Immediately, there's article after article of the story on mainstream outlets.

I'm so caught off guard I stop walking mid-stride, Jeremy runs into me and I reach back for him, grabbing a handful of his shirt.

"What's wrong?" Brendon asks, but I turn to look at Jeremy, my chest tight.

"I-I-" I want to tell him but I can't get the words out. I wasn't his only victim? What the fuck? He's been hurting people for years.

A woman has come forward saying she was sexually assaulted during a consult. Another one says she was forced into a surgery she didn't want. There's an article saying some of his previous coworkers reported him to hospital admin but it was swept under the rug.

Tears well up in my eyes as a realization hits me. One of the previous hospitals could have stopped this, could have saved me, but they chose money over people.

"Hey." Jeremy scans the room around us. "What is it?"

All I can do is show him my phone as the world crumbles around me. My hand is still gripping his shirt, like he's going to run and I can't let him.

"You good?" Paul asks, but I don't answer. I can't. How am I supposed to process this? I was left in the hands of my father because of *money*.

"Jesus fucking Christ," Jeremy swears under his breath and pockets my phone. He looks around again before stepping into my personal space. His chest bumps mine but he doesn't reach for me. "I know you're on the verge of breaking down, but you have to hold it together for a few more hours. What do you need right this minute?"

I wrap my arm around him and drop my forehead to his shoulder. Jeremy wraps his arms around me, careful of my bad shoulder. The guys pull the circle tighter around us, putting arms on each other's shoulders to try to block out anyone's view of us.

"I've got you," Jeremy whispers against the side of my head, kissing my hair.

I want to break. My knees almost buckle because money, power, and lies were more important than my suffering. Than the suffering of innocent human beings. I choke back the tears threatening to overtake me, shoving them behind the wall I've lived behind for years, forcing the mask back on my face that's harder to do today than it was yesterday and last week. Jeremy has cracked my walls and used the holes to scale them. My once impenetrable fortress is held together by glue and popsicle sticks. One good hit and it'll crumble around me, leaving me vulnerable.

Jeremy's hand slides under the edge of my shirt until his palm rests on my stomach. The contact anchors me to the here and now, making my mind let go of the past and the what ifs. I close my eyes and focus on the warmth of his skin on mine, our breath mingling, and that intoxicating woodsy, smoky, spicy scent he wears. With only a few lungfuls of him, my heart rate drops and the impending emotional breakdown recedes, if just for a few hours.

The sounds of roller bags, people talking, and the announcements on the intercom become clear and I'm able to stand on my own. I quickly meet Jeremy's eyes and nod, turning back around, and without a word, the guys do too. I scan the faces and see more of my teammates than when I stopped. Why are they here?

"You good, man?" one of the newcomers asks, giving me a chin lift.

With confusion still clear on my face, I give him a nod and we continue to our gate. There's a crowd of people watching and whispering but I don't pay them any attention.

The gate isn't much farther and the team has blocked out a few rows of seats so Jeremy and I are surrounded by them. I appreciate it more than I can tell them, even though I know it's not for me. I'm grateful they care enough about Jeremy to go out of their way to help him, just in case something happens to him. He's always with me, so if I'm cornered or attacked, Jeremy will be in the middle of it as well. I can't protect him right now. I can't protect myself.

CHAPTER 44

preston

Jeremy kept my phone for the duration of the flight but he shared an earbud with me so we could watch a few episodes of *The Boys* that he downloaded on his phone. I lay my head on his shoulder and he puts his hand on my inner thigh.

"This show is fucked up," I mumble.

He chuckles and squeezes my leg.

While I normally hate being confined, I find myself relaxing in the window seat with my teammates around me. No one has said anything about Jeremy and I being together, there are no questions about my father, or the abuse allegations. They're curious, they have to be, but no one has said anything to me.

"Has anyone asked you about my father?"

"No." There's no hesitation in his answer.

"Anyone given you shit for being gay?"

"Nope." Again, no hesitation. Maybe I should let some of these guys in and actually try to be friends with them. I've never had friends. That's fucking depressing, but it's the truth. Jeremy is the first person I've trusted since my mom died.

I lift my head and kiss his cheek. He smiles and glances at me before returning to the show. A notification pops up from Lily on Jeremy's phone that he flicks away. I guess he's hooked up to the onboard Wi-Fi. I've been avoiding her since my screaming match with her Friday night. Just one more thing I'm failing at. He's a better person than I am.

I'll call her when we get back.

With my head on Jeremy's shoulder, I fall asleep, finally feeling safe enough from the outside world to relax.

The captain speaking over the intercom and Jeremy rubbing my inner thigh wakes me a few hours later.

I reach for his hand to stop it as my dick perks up. Being photographed walking through the airport with a hard-on is not on the list of things I want to do today. We land and taxi for a while before pulling up to our gate, and since we're in the middle of the plane, it takes a while to get off the aircraft. My body tightens as I step out into the aisle and head toward the building. Will there be reporters waiting outside the airport? On campus? Will they start harassing my teammates and be waiting at the ice rink? Outside my classes? The dorms?

"Breathe," Jeremy says behind me, his hand sliding up the back of my shirt for a minute, while only the team is around us.

I force my shoulders down and take a deep breath as we leave the airplane and follow the rest of the passengers to baggage claim. Some people point, stare, and whisper but I ignore them, protected by my teammates. It's more than I deserve from them but I accept it because I need it. And as much as I hate it, I need them.

When we get across the airport to baggage claim, our

hockey gear is already being stacked up and guys are grabbing their personal bags to add to the pile. Jeremy grabs both of ours, a few more guys grab theirs, and we head out to the bus that's waiting for us. The guys help load up the gear while I'm told to go sit on the bus so no one gets any ideas. I hate being helpless but I do what Coach told me to and soon enough we're on our way to the dorms. It's not a long drive but I keep checking behind us to see if we're being followed. Nothing so far.

When we pull up to the school, there are news vans and security has roped off areas. My stomach drops. What the actual fuck? These goddamn soul-sucking bastards are going to be the death of me. I can't take this.

Paul turns around to face me. "One step in front of the other, ignore everything they say."

We get off the bus and the crowd goes crazy, all yelling and shouting over each other so I can't understand any of it, which is fine by me. I do my best to ignore them and grab my bag from Jeremy to carry inside. Campus security does a good job of keeping the jackasses back to allow us into the building without much hassle. Once we're inside, I let out a breath and Brendon is holding the elevator for us.

"This is some crazy shit, man." Brendon comments. "Is this what it will be like if you play in the NHL? I don't think I could handle it."

"I've been dealing with this kind of shit on and off my entire life. You learn to ignore most of it." Memories of after my mother died flash in my mind. My grandparents were famous because they were rich, which meant my mother was well known as well. Father played right into it, using the attention to boost his career and garner sympathy from the masses. *Look at how hard it is to be a single father to two children while dealing with this horrific tragedy. He's an inspiration.*

Little did they know that I was being abused, tormented by him, and my sister was sent away as soon as he was able to. She was raised in boarding schools.

We file off the elevator, Paul and Brendon unlocking their door and heading inside, giving a nod as we pass to our room. Jeremy gets our door open and I'm barely inside when my body sags. I drop my bag and stumble to my bed.

"Quilt," I say into my pillow. Jeremy chuckles but digs the quilt out of my bag and throws it at me. I pull the quilt up over my head and kick my shoes off without moving. Jeremy chuckles and slides in under the quilt with me.

"Do you want to talk about what's going on in your head?" he whispers in the dark of our space.

"No," I sigh. Ripping open the wounds sucks and I'm too tired for it. I roll over onto my back and Jeremy throws a leg over mine while sliding a hand under my shirt to rub against the skin right above my pants. My dick wakes up this time and my head is happy for the distraction.

It's awkward not being able to use one hand, but I manage to cup his face and bring his lips to mine while he opens my pants and reaches inside to stroke me lazily.

I groan into his kiss, my tongue thrusting against his at the same pace of his hand on my dick.

He rides my thigh, his own cock hard in his jeans.

"Ride me," I demand against his lips. Jeremy slides over my hips, his ass dragging against my cock in the most delicious rhythm. I reach under his shirt and dig my nails into his skin, leaving angry red scratches down his chest. He moans and leans forward to kiss me but my phone rings and we both freeze.

I instantly recognize the annoying ringing sound as my father's ringtone.

"Up, baby, let me answer that." I pat his thigh and he

sighs but gets off me. Scooting off the bed, I find my phone on the bedside table and steel myself to deal with my father.

For the first time in my entire life, I'm not as afraid of him. Lily is protected and his ugly truths are being exposed to the world.

The second I hit the accept button on the call, my father's voice fills the line.

"How dare you! You've ruined everything. Your mother would be horrified at what you've done!" The pure hatred in his voice makes me sad for him and that has to be a first. "Think of how this is going to affect your sister!"

"My sister is protected and will be fine. She's furious with you and hates you for what you've done." I snap back. Standing from the bed, I pace the floor while I work myself up into a boiling anger. For the first time in my life, I let him have it. "I hate you too. I hope you die alone and broke, your name smeared, and your medical license taken." My body is vibrating with my lost innocence, fury at the hospital for letting him continue to abuse people, and the unfairness of losing my mother so damn young. He stole my childhood and tainted it with pain and cruelty, passing it off as trying to make me better.

"You will never see either of us again."

Jeremy comes up behind me and wraps his arms around me, threading his fingers with mine and pressing his face to my back as I tremble. "You tried to break me, to make me dependent on you, but you failed.

"I've found a man that loves me despite the lies you made me believe and a family that accepts me and doesn't use pain and fear to keep anyone in line. You are just as worthless as your own father. The only difference is your addiction is to power instead of alcohol."

My father's ragged breathing fills the line.

"How could you? You hurt innocent patients. How

many women did you assault?" I demand. A door closes in the background of the call, feet slapping against concrete, then the squeaking of hinges.

"The only one I regret was your mother. I never wanted kids and she left me with two. I never wanted either of you. You've been an utter disgrace your entire life. You've never been anything other than a burden, needing constant guidance and correction. Every scar you've earned is your fault." It's windy wherever he is and it's hard to hear him. "You really are worthless, Charles. You always have been. This is your fault too." There's a clattering, like he dropped the phone, then a scream in the distance before it suddenly stops. What the fuck just happened?

"Hello?" My skin runs cold and my chest tightens like someone is sitting on my ribs. I try desperately to connect the dots, figure out what is happening, but my mind is blank. All I can do is stand here and listen, to strain my ears for any clue as to what is happening.

Did he.

Did.

Did he just jump off his building?

"Preston?" Jeremy calls my name, but I'm struggling to listen to what little I can hear through the phone. All I can hear is wind. "Preston, breathe."

I blink, spinning to look at him, barely breathing. His eyebrows are pulled together over his eyes, concern written in every angle of his face.

Finally, there's a faint siren in the background.

"I-I-" I swallow and try again. "I think he's dead."

Jeremy's face pales as I continue to stand there, holding my phone to my ear, the wailing of sirens getting louder in my ear.

"What do I do? I don't know what to do."

CHAPTER 45

preston

After calling 9-1-1 and making a statement with the police, it's been verified that my father jumped from his building's roof and is dead. They found his phone on the ledge above where he fell.

Jeremy has been stuck to my side like glue as I've called Coach, sent a text message to Lily's bodyguard, called her school, and now am staring at my phone not wanting to call my sister.

"Do you want me to call her?" Jeremy offers with his hand on my leg.

I shake my head, staring at her contact information on my phone. "No, I should do it."

The hardest part is not knowing how to feel. Part of me is relieved he's gone. He can't touch me anymore. I'm free. But my father is dead. My sister and I are now orphans. We are our only family.

Taking a deep breath, I hit call and wait for her to answer.

"Hey, what's wrong? Why are you calling me?" She's immediately on edge.

"Lily, are you in your room? Is there anyone with you?" I don't want her alone when I tell her.

"You're freaking me out, Preston. What's wrong?" Her tone goes up an octave.

"Father is dead." The words sound hollow in my head and even though I've said them a few times already, they don't feel real. It feels like a trick, like a game he's trying to play to catch me doing something wrong so he can punish me. The most recent scar he gave me tingles so I rub at it.

"Lily? Are you still there?" I pull the phone from my ear to see if the call is still connected.

"Um. Yeah." She sucks in a breath. "I'm still here." On the exhale, her breath shakes and I hate that I can't be with her. Once she graduates, I'm moving her to wherever I am. I can't take this shit anymore. We need to stay together.

"Do you know what happened?" Her voice is small, like a child, and it hurts my chest.

My throat burns with unshed tears that I don't really understand. I'm not sad he's dead but it hurts to tell her.

"He, uh, jumped off his building." She's going to see the story in the news anyway, there's no point in lying to her. "I was on the phone with him when he jumped."

She gasps, holding her breath for a minute. "What? Why would he do that?"

Hot tears stream down my cheeks but I don't bother to wipe them away.

"He was a broken man and at the end of his rope." I pushed him over the edge. That's a guilt I will carry the rest of my life. "I don't know if you've been keeping up with the news, but there's a lot of people coming forward with stories about him."

"I've seen a few but I don't know what to believe, you

know? How much is the truth and how much is the media taking a story and spinning it, you know?" She doesn't want to believe her father was a bad person. I wish I could protect her from the truth this time, but I can't. "Will you tell me the truth?"

I close my eyes and my lip trembles. My shoulders cave in and my head drops forward. The weight of what she's asking me is heavier than I anticipated. Logically, I know I shouldn't be ashamed, I am the victim and not to blame, but the words he made me believe tell me otherwise. If I would have just listened, behaved, been good, he wouldn't have had to hurt me.

"He cut me, Lil." It hurts to say the words out loud. "I was like ten when it started. He drugged me at first, it was right around when Mom died. The last one was before Thanksgiving."

Lily sobs, gut wrenching, soul shattering sobs and there's nothing I can do. Even if I was with her, I wouldn't know how to comfort her. I haven't been able to do that in years.

Jeremy reaches behind me and pulls the quilt over my shoulders like a cape, making sure I'm covered in the physical proof that his family cares about me.

"Why didn't you ever tell me?"

I scrub my hand over my face. "What was I supposed to say? I let our father scar me so he would leave you alone? That when you would leave for school every year, I was grateful I didn't have to worry about you being hurt?"

She cries into the phone and it's a knife in my heart.

"All I've ever wanted was for you to have a good life." My voice cracks and Jeremy slides a hand under my shirt, his cheek against my back. He surrounds me, grounds me, brings me peace.

"I want to be close to you. You're my big brother and you're all I have left." Her words are choked but strong.

"You got it, once you graduate, we'll move you out here. Maybe we can get an apartment or something together." Relief is a warm blanket around my heart, weaving some of the holes in my soul back together.

Jeremy's phone starts ringing.

"Shit, sorry," he mumbles and slides out from under the quilt and out to the hallway.

The door closes behind him but I can still feel him with me. For the first time in my life, I have hope. I'm looking forward to the future.

"I don't want to play hockey anymore." I blurt out, taking myself by surprise.

"What? Why not?" I've officially derailed this conversation but Lily is rolling with it.

"Father is the one who pushed me to play. I don't enjoy it. I'm good at it, but I don't want to play professionally." I shake my head to clear it. "I don't know what I'll do. Jeremy wants to coach so I guess I'll just follow him wherever he ends up." I shrug.

"Well, you're rich so you can do whatever you want, dumbass." Lily scoffs, but she's right. Mom and her parents left us a shit ton of money. Even if our father left us nothing, we would never have to work and could live more than comfortably on our inheritances. "Why don't you open a hockey thing and hire Jeremy to coach?"

"That's not a bad idea..."

We chat for a few more minutes before we hang up. There will be lots of shit we have to deal with over the next few weeks, like our father's estate, but that's not for today. I put my phone on the charger and head to the door.

"No, you are not coming out here right now." Jeremy is saying to whoever is on the phone. Probably his mother.

"There's nothing for you to do right now. No, you can come out later if you want to but not right now."

He's pacing the width of the hallway and hasn't seen me. I lean on the door jam and watch him. I love him.

"I mean, if Grandma wants to send a bigger quilt, I won't argue. Preston is a blanket hog." I snort and he swings his head up to meet my eyes, a small smile playing on his lips.

He's not wrong. I am. He mouths *I love you* then goes back to his phone call. I head back to the tiny bed we share and lay down with the quilt pulled up over me to wait for him. Maybe life doesn't always suck and I'm not destined to be alone.

CHAPTER 46

two weeks later

jeremy

I wake slowly, a muscular, warm body pressed to my back and a hard dick rubbing against my ass. Preston's prickly cheek drags against the naked skin of my shoulder as he forces his way into the crook of my neck to suck and bite at my skin. I groan, long and loud, when his teeth sink into my flesh, my dick aching for attention.

Reaching behind me, I grab a handful of his hair and hold him against me.

"Fuck." My voice is rough with sleep.

"That's the plan," Preston says against my neck. He rolls us until my stomach is flat on the bed and he pulls my pants and boxer briefs down just past my ass. His hot dick slides against my crack and I arch as much as I can with him sitting on my thighs.

He slaps one ass cheek with a sharp snap. "Hold fucking still."

Oh, he woke up and chose violence today.

My dick throbs at the prospect, a bead of precum spilling against the sheets.

Preston reaches over me to grab the lube from the bedside table and I stretch out on the bed, reaching for the headboard. I know this morning won't get too crazy since he still needs to be careful of his shoulder, but he's been working with the trainers and is making really great progress.

He shifts down my body, biting at my lower back and ass cheeks while his slick finger pushes inside me. I love when he leaves marks on my body. Physical proof of his claim on me is the hottest fucking thing. Plus, whenever a sensitive spot is bumped, I'm reminded of how it got there.

One finger quickly becomes two and he's stroking inside of me in a come here motion until he finds my prostate, sending sparks of pleasure to burst behind my eyes.

"Oh, fuck," I moan into the bed. "I'm going to come." I grind my dick into the mattress, desperate for the friction, but Preston growls with my skin still in his mouth so I stop with a whimper.

"Please," I whine. "I want to come."

"No." There's no arguing with that tone. I tighten every muscle I can to stop my incoming release. "Good boy."

Preston licks up my sack then sucks on the loose skin.

My groan of frustration when he starts with his fucking fingers again makes him chuckle. The bastard really did choose violence today. He gives me a few more pumps of his fingers then pulls out of me and pulls my clothes the rest of the way off, stripping his off too before climbing back onto the bed.

"Ass up." He slaps my ass again, hard enough to leave a fucking handprint, my skin heating.

I lift up onto my knees, keeping my chest on the bed, legs spread wide.

Preston growls, slicking his cock with lube and dragging the head of his dick over my hole to find the right angle. He leans one hand between my shoulder blades and sinks into me in one thrust. We groan in unison. It feels too fucking good to be full of him when my body is still warm and relaxed from sleep. My cock weeps and I reach back to stroke myself.

He sets a hard, fast, deep pace and I'm already sensitive from being edged, but I crave it. I crave everything he does to me. No one has ever played my body with such confidence and ease as he does. It's intoxicating.

Preston grips my hips, pulling me to get a deeper angle and snapping his body against mine to make the most vulgar sounds.

"Please," I beg, needing to come.

"Up." He slaps my other ass cheek and I lift up onto my hands. Using his good arm, Preston wraps it around my chest and pulls me to kneeling, my back arching to keep him inside of me but giving him easy access to my neck and shoulders.

He bites and sucks hickies into my skin, digging his nails into me hard enough to leave red scratches down my chest. My cock throbs and my ass clenches around him. He moans, his lips still pressed firmly against my skin, setting off goosebumps and hardening my nipples.

My hand works my dick faster, my orgasm quickly building.

"come, squeeze me. Take me with you." Preston's husky words in my ear push me over the edge and I let my orgasm overtake me, spilling cum on the sheets. Everything around me fades as I'm lost to him.

He bites me again, sinking his teeth into my neck up near my ear, growling as he spills deep inside of me. Panting and weak, he leans heavily against me, and we crash to the bed in a sweaty mess.

"I think you factory reset my brain," I pant, dropping an arm over my eyes.

He chuckles. "It's a good way to start the day." He kisses me, sucking on my bottom lip, then crawls over me to get dressed.

"What's on the agenda today?" I sit up, touching the teeth marks on my skin with my fingertips.

"I have to meet with my father's lawyer to sign some shit and pick up Lily from the airport." He pulls a clean t-shirt on and digs for some jeans. Once he's dressed, he finds one of my hoodies and pulls it on. It's a little tight on him, but I love seeing him in my clothes.

He drops a quick kiss on my lips and grabs his stuff, then heads out. It's been a rough few weeks for him and Lily but I'm starting to see happiness in him. His father left nothing to him and his sister and apparently hadn't been paying taxes, so he owes a shit ton of money to the IRS. The only thing he was allowed to take from his father's penthouse was photo albums. Thankfully, there were some in his safe so he has some pictures of his mom and grandparents. Not to mention the reporters and shit still following him around, news stations wanting to interview him, and trying to stay caught up on classes and training.

The team has been awesome about helping him get in and out of the rink and our dorm when a crowd gathers, and campus security is tired of dealing with it, so they've been slapping harassment lawsuits at people. It's finally starting to die down.

I find my underwear and pull them on to go clean up in the bathroom. In the mirror, I pause to look at the newest marks on my body. The one under my ear is pretty intense.

It's his favorite spot to bite me. I do a quick clean up and hurry down to Brendon and Paul's room.

Knocking on the door, I open it and walk in, still in my underwear because fuck it. Brendon looks up from his computer to me with a lifted eyebrow.

"Are we having a no pants day? Cause I'm down for it."

"No, I need you to trace this bite mark." He shrugs, not asking any questions, and stands. We find a ballpoint pen on Paul's desk and Brendon moves my head around to get a good angle.

"Like, the individual teeth or like, the circle it makes?"

"Each tooth." I'm smiling like an idiot but Brendon either doesn't notice or doesn't care. The bathroom door opens and Paul steps out in boxer briefs.

"Now I feel weird being the only one with pants on." Brendon complains around the pen cap in his mouth.

Paul looks confused, which is fair. "Why don't you have pants on?"

"I needed someone to trace this and didn't want to wait too long." Because this is totally normal right?

"And why is Brendon drawing on your neck?" Paul crosses his arms over his chest and cocks his head.

"I'm going to get it tattooed." I laugh at the dumbfounded expression on Paul's face.

"Fuck yes!" Brendon shouts. "That sounds like a terrible idea and I'm one hundred percent on board for this." He caps the pen and slaps my shoulder. "You should put pants on though."

"Hang on." Paul steps closer to us, holding his hands up. "Why are you going to tattoo whatever that is on your neck?"

"It's Preston's teeth." I shrug. "To show him I'm in this relationship, all the way."

"Are the two of you sharing a brain now?" Paul looks

between me and Brendon. "You could just, I don't know, tell him that?"

Brendon and I look at each other and shake our heads. "Nah, this is better."

"You guys are idiots." Paul huffs. "Do you have an appointment already or what?"

"No, I figured we could find a place and get it done." I shrug again. "It shouldn't take that long." I move to the door. "I'm going to get dressed."

"I'm obviously driving." Paul pulls open his dresser and starts digging for clothes. "I want it on record that this is a stupid idea, and I will not be taking any responsibility."

"Duly noted and ignored." Brendon claps him on the shoulder and I leave to get dressed. In a matter of minutes, we're piling into Paul's car and googling tattoo shops. There's one just a few miles from University Neighborhood, where the colleges are in Denver, so we head there.

"I want a neck tattoo," Brendon says from the front seat. "Will you bite me so I can match Jeremy?" He looks at Paul, who's starting to blush. He's got it so bad, and I can't wait to see how it all plays out. Brendon is oblivious.

"What? You want me to bite you?" Paul sputters as we pull into the parking lot.

"Well, I mean, if Jeremy did it and Preston found out he would murder both of us. So, if you do it, you'll be saving our lives."

I snort, but his logic is sound. Wait. That's terrifying. Since when does Brendon make sense?

"Okay, I'm going in," I announce and get out of the car. Paul and Brendon follow but Brendon is begging Paul to bite him and Paul is trying to hold strong. He's going to fold though. Paul wants to touch Brendon. It's clear as day.

The place has black and white checkered tile floor, light gray walls with artwork all over the place and very bright lighting. There's a table and chairs set up around the room and what looks like a red room divider in the back in case someone needs privacy.

A heavily tattooed and pierced woman with long green hair smiles at me.

"Good morning, what brings you in?"

"Hey, I want to get this tattooed," I turn my head and show her the outline Brendon drew.

She purses her lips and lifts an eyebrow. "Alright, you're wanting to get that today?"

"Yes, ma'am."

She turns to the schedule books in front of her and tells me to have a seat, fill out some paperwork, and it'll be a few minutes.

Brendon walks up to her, attempting to flirt with her while she is completely not interested, and Paul sulks. They are going to be a mess to watch and I honestly can't wait for it.

A short thin man with long brown hair pulled back in a ponytail and full sleeve tattoos calls me back and I go, still shaking my head at Brendon and Paul.

"Hey, I'm Dan." He shakes my hand and tells me to have a seat. He wheels over a stool and takes a seat, looking at my neck with a smirk. "Is that a bite mark?"

"Yeah, my boyfriend's."

He nods. "Do you have any other ink? How long have you been together?"

"This will be the first one, maybe the only one." I shrug sheepishly. "And a few months."

He looks at me, skeptical, like this is a terrible decision. "You know—"

"I know it sounds crazy, and it's probably a terrible idea, but I want to do it anyway."

"All right, man." He raises his hands in surrender and

gets his station set up. He puts on gloves, pours the ink, snaps the rubber band on the tattoo gun a few times, and cleans my neck. "You ready?"

"Yup." I lean against the back of the chair and he starts, the drag of the needle burning my skin, but the pain isn't too bad. I guess there aren't many nerves right there, but it vibrates my teeth, which feels extremely odd. It takes a total of about ten minutes and he's done. Wiping it off with some kind of cleaner on a paper towel.

Paul and Brendon show up as I'm finishing, Brendon looking triumphant while Paul looks like he's trying to hide an erection. Which I'm sure he is.

I can't hide my smile as I look at them.

"Me next!" Brendon drops into the chair I just left, and Dan raises an eyebrow at him.

"Okay then." He sanitizes everything and gets set up again. "I don't know who bit you, but they need to do it again, this has faded too fast. Unless you want me to just wing it."

"No!" Paul snaps then turns bright red when we all look at him.

I walk to the mirror to inspect the ink on my skin. Preston is either going to love this or kill me. Possibly both. The thin outline of his teeth impression on my skin brings me a weird sense of comfort. I fucking love it.

In the mirror, I watch Paul lean over Brendon and bite the fuck out of his neck. Brendon shifts uncomfortably in the seat, his face turning bright red as he tries to cover an obvious hard-on, and Dan the tattoo artist sighs. I can only imagine the weird shit he sees in here.

Paul takes a step back and discreetly adjusts himself, leaning against the wall to watch with his arms crossed over his chest.

I pay the lady at the front and as she finishes up telling

me about after care, Brendon comes walking up, looking smug. He pays her and she tells him the same spiel.

"I'm hungry, let's get some lunch."

I pull out my phone and pull up Preston's message thread.

I have a surprise for you later.

CARMICHAEL

Me too

Oh yeah? Tell me.

CARMICHAEL

If I tell you, it's not a surprise now, is it?

Spoil sport.

The three of us fuck around for a while, getting lunch and finding an arcade to waste time at before heading back to the dorms. There are some dumbasses with cameras standing around but they don't bother us as we enter the building.

"Man, I'm ready for a nap." Brendon yawns and stretches.

Paul mutters something about getting fucked and I laugh. The elevator opens on our floor and we head down the hallway, Brendon and Paul following me.

"Uh, whatcha doing?" I stop at my door and turn to stare at them.

"Movies and naps," Brendon says like the answer should be obvious.

"I'm not going to die today." Paul backs away with his hands raised.

I open the door and stop in my tracks when I see my mom and grandma sitting on my bed, Mom's phone raised like she's recording.

"What are you doing here?"

"Mrs. Albrooke!" Brendon yells behind me, pushing me out of the way to hug my mom.

"Nice hickies!" I hear my sister yell, so she must be on the phone. Great.

"How did you get in here?" I ask Grandma as I reach to give her a hug.

"Oh my God, what is on your neck?" Stacy's squeal through the phone has both Mom and Grandma looking at me, pulling my face to one side to get a good look at my neck. It's been a few hours, so the plastic wrap has been removed from the new ink.

"Fuck," I mumble as Stacy and my brothers start laughing. Good to know they're here for this too. Assholes.

"What the hell is that, Jeremy?!" Mom demands.

"It's Preston's teeth," Brendon tells her. "Look, I've got one too!" He turns his head to show her, and she glances at him.

"Why did Preston bite you? Oh no, you guys aren't doing orgies or something are you?" My mom's face falls like she's in physical pain.

Paul bursts out with a laugh, Brendon starts smiling like a loon, and I swear the blood has drained from my face.

"Orgies? What the fuck Mom?"

"Don't cuss at your mother," Dad says through the phone.

"Why would you get that tattooed on your skin?" Mom is horrified, but Stacy, Jordan, and Keith are all yelling to get a better look at it when the door opens. Preston and Lily walk in, the smile falling from his face at the chaos.

"Did you know they were coming?" I demand, staring wide-eyed at my boyfriend.

"Of course, I made plans for them to be here to meet Lily." He's confused and I'm at my wit's end.

Grandma walks over and gives him a hug, his smile softening when he looks at her and carefully wraps his arms around her.

"Mrs. Albrooke, can you make taco salad?" Brendon pleads, sticking his bottom lip out and everything.

"Are you having sex with Preston too?" she asks Brendon, who pales when he looks at Preston.

"Absolutely not!" Brendon all but yells.

"What the hell kind of a question is that?" Preston asks, clearly confused.

"They both have your teeth marks tattooed on their necks! What are we supposed to think?" Mom all but yells, frazzled.

"Excuse me?" Preston grabs my chin and jerks my face to one side then the other. "What the hell is that?" he demands.

"I got a tattoo of your teeth marks." My face is on fire. "Look, it seemed a lot more romantic in my head and didn't involve my mother being here when you found out!"

He blinks at me and starts laughing. "You're insane."

"I think you meant, an idiot," Paul chimes in.

"What the hell is on Brendon's neck then?" Preston points at my very red-faced friend. "That had better not be mine or Jeremy's teeth."

Paul steps in front of Brendon. "They're mine."

"Yeah, nobody touched your fuck boy," Brendon says with a roll of his eyes.

"What did you call him?" Grandma asks.

"Oh, for the love of Christ." I rub my eyes and pinch the bridge of my nose.

"Hello," Lily comes forward and offers her hand to Mom. "I'm Lily, Preston's sister."

"It's nice to meet you." Mom wraps her in a hug, then Grandma does too.

"I have a quilt for you too." She pats Lily's cheek.

"Oh, that's so nice of you, thank you so much." She gives Grandma another hug.

"Fuck it," Preston mumbles and takes my hands in his, forcing me to turn back to him. "Jeremy, I love you more than I ever thought possible. My life is not complete without you, *I* am not complete without you." He drops to one knee and my eyes bug out of my damn head. "Will you marry me?"

"Dude!" Brendon yells as I stare at my boyfriend, wide-eyed and speechless. He's holding a gray band that appears to be hammered so it's not perfectly smooth.

"These bands aren't perfect. Like us, they've been struck and dented, but the flaws in the metal make them unique and strong."

My throat clogs with emotion and I'm so overcome with the intensity of this moment that I can't speak. All I can do is nod and reach for him, wrapping my arms around his neck and crashing his lips against mine while I drop to my knees in front of him.

"Is that a yes?" he asks with his lips against mine as a knot clogs my throat, too overcome in this moment to do anything else. I hug him and bury my face into the crook of his neck.

"Yes," I'm able to croak. "I love you so fucking much."

Preston's arms tighten around me, holding me together like I've done for him so many times.

"I want to open a hockey camp for underprivileged kids," Preston says quickly. "Come coach for me."

"Can you stop being so fucking perfect for five seconds?" I pull back far enough to look at him.

"I'm far from perfect. Life with me will not be easy, but I swear I will love you for the rest of my life."

There's sniffling behind me but I don't turn to look, it

doesn't matter as much as this moment. Nothing will ever matter as much as this man in this moment.

"Of course, I will marry you and fight with you and love you and build a life with you. You're never getting rid of me."

Everyone behind me cheers and crowds us, wrapping us in hugs and love.

"You're a part of the Albrooke family now and we won't ever let you go," Mom says, kissing his cheek.

"I'm taking your name when we get married," Preston says with the utmost seriousness, sliding the ring onto my finger. "I don't want to be a Carmichael anymore. Make me an Albrooke."

CHAPTER 47

preston

I'm sitting in a waiting room, waiting for a therapist or psychologist or counselor, whatever they are, to call me back. I don't want to be here. How did I let Jeremy's grandma talk me into this?

My foot is bouncing like crazy and I can't stop it.

Jeremy reaches over and slides his hand into mine. "Take a deep breath."

My jaw tightens as I stare ahead at the reception desk, not really seeing it.

"I don't want to be here," I force past my teeth. "I can barely talk to *you*. Do you really think I'll be successful talking to a stranger?"

"Preston?" A woman with bright red curly hair and a comforting smile makes eye contact with me. I jerk to my feet, swallowing hard past the lump in my throat. Jeremy's hand is still in mine as I step toward her but stop when I meet resistance. My head snaps to the right where Jeremy is still sitting in the chair.

"Come on." I pull on his hand, feeling myself starting to lose my cool at the very idea of him not coming into that room with me. "I'm not going in there without you."

Jeremy's gaze flicks the woman waiting at the doorway then back to me.

"Okay." He stands and follows me as I pull him along behind me with his arm now pinned between my arm and my body. My fingers spin the ring on his left ring finger, the band bringing me some comfort. He hasn't taken off the ring since I gave it to him four days ago.

His mom and grandma are still here, staying at a short-term rental house near campus and spending most of their time feeding us, along with Paul and Brendon. I have to admit, Mrs. Albrooke's taco salad is pretty damn good. Brendon is right.

"Welcome," the woman says. "My name is Celeste Montgomery." The office has a dark teal velvet couch, a navy-blue wingback chair set across from it, a cherry wood desk in one corner, and plants. Lots of plants. Hanging from the ceiling, hanging on the walls, on her desk, in the window sill. It's like a jungle in here.

"Have a seat and take a deep breath. We don't have to talk about anything heavy today." She sits in the wingback chair and Jeremy nudges me to sit on the couch. "Today is more about getting to know each other and seeing if we'll be a good fit."

"It's nice to meet you, Doctor Montgomery." Jeremy smiles at the woman while I drag my palm over my thigh and squeeze his hand. "I'm Jeremy."

"Celeste is fine." She smiles at my fiancé because he's pleasant and friendly while I'm an asshole.

I don't want to do this. Doctors are not my friends. They aren't my saviors. Doctors have done nothing but cause me pain for the sake of money in one way or another.

My father cut me because hitting me put his hands at risk, the people above him knew he was abusing patients and did nothing to stop it, in fact they went out of their way to bury it so he could continue to be a cash cow for the hospital. I was expendable. A casualty.

Sitting up straight, I take a deep breath and close my eyes for a second.

"It's nice to meet you, Jeremy." Her pleasant voice has me opening my eyes. "It's clear you two are very close."

I say, squeezing his hand. "I don't want to be here, but the few people I have around me say I should talk to someone." The words are out of my mouth before my brain has had a chance to tell me it isn't a good idea. "I don't see how telling a stranger about how my dad cut me then stitched me back up over and over again solely for his own amusement is going to fix anything. How is it going to bring back my mom, who he admitted to killing right before he jumped off a building while on the phone with me? It's not going to take the scars off my body or change any of the facts of my life, so what's the point?"

The air is sucked from the room, but she holds my stare. Her eyes are a bright green, and for a moment, she doesn't breathe. Just blinks and adjusts in her chair to sit up straighter.

Jeremy is tense next to me, probably waiting to see what her reaction to me is. I'm already on the verge of walking out of here, so she has to walk a very careful line.

Finally, she blinks and sucks in a deep breath.

"I. Wow. That's." She takes another deep breath then tries again. "You're right, talking to me, or anyone else, isn't going to change what happened to you. I can't remove the physical scars from your body but I can help you heal the wounds that no one can see. The ones that hold you back, the ones that keep people at arm's length. I'm sure you have feelings of guilt or anxiety, probably both, which is normal, that I can help you move through so they don't control you. A lot of people forget that our brains are just as traumatized as our skin when we're hurt and if that wound isn't properly cared for, it can fester and get worse."

"I'm fine."

She purses her lips while she watches me. "Well, let's talk a bit and go from there."

I don't have a response for that, but I also don't see how telling her about any of this helps either.

"We can jump into your trauma today or we can take it easy, it's really up to you. Is there anything you want to know about me? Would you be more comfortable talking to me if you knew me better?" she offers with the lift of one shoulder.

"Whatever you tell me, really tells me nothing. Lies are easy to pass as truths."

She nods, picking up a pad of paper she had tucked into the side of her chair and writing something on it.

"Being lied to often, and by someone who is good at it, makes it hard to believe what anyone says to you." She uses the back of her pen to point to Jeremy. "What about Jeremy? Do you believe him?"

"Yes, he's not a doctor." She cocks her head as she tries to connect the dots. "Have you seen the news stories about Doctor Andrew Carmichael?"

A lightbulb practically lights up above her head. "I have seen some articles, though I don't know a lot of details about the case. Is he related to you?"

"My father, yes." I didn't have a dad. Dad's take their kids to get ice cream and pizza, throw a baseball or football round, teach you how to be a man and take care of those who are important to you. My father taught me to hide my pain and pretend to be perfect or there would be consequences. “He’s a...” I shake my head and huff a breath. “He *was* a plastic surgeon and from the time I was about ten, he used me as a guinea pig. Testing new stitch techniques turned into *correction* for unfavorable behaviors.”

Her eyes widen a little but otherwise, she says nothing.

Jeremy’s free hand wraps around my bicep and I realize I’m probably hurting him with the force of my grip on his fingers, so I release his hand and rub my palms down my thighs. I adjust on the couch and sit back against the tufted fabric, pick up the hand, and kiss the ring on his finger with my eyes on his. He gives me a soft smile and a reassuring squeeze on my arm.

“Tell me about Jeremy.” Celeste nods toward him while keeping her eyes on me.

“So you can fuck up the only good thing in my life? No.” I bite out without thinking about it. I hate this. I feel like I’m crawling out of my skin, ready to snap and hurt someone.

“Breathe.” Jeremy pinches the inside of my upper arm hard enough to hurt, but it helps me focus. “She’s not an MD. I made sure.”

“Does that make a difference?” she asks, glancing between the two of us. “That I don’t have an MD. Would that make it harder to talk to me?”

“Every medical doctor, including my own father, has been shit, so yes it matters. Every doctor I’ve ever seen has been paid off or threatened so they didn’t report shit.” I force myself to drag in a big breath. “Doctors only care about their precious licenses, making them easy to manipulate.”

“I have a license, does that make me easy to manipulate?” The question is almost a challenge, but her expression doesn’t change. She’s carefully neutral, which is something I am very familiar with.

"Possibly." I answer honestly.

"I can definitely understand why you feel that way. What would it take for you to trust me just a little bit?" She raises an eyebrow at me.

Jeremy smirks and pulls his hand off my arm. My eyebrows pull together as I turn to look at him. He lifts his shirt to show Celeste the marks I've left on his body, and there are plenty—scratches, bruises from my fingers and teeth, hickies. I should probably be embarrassed but I'm not. I love my marks on his skin.

"So, Preston and I enjoy rough sex. Now you know my secrets." He shrugs and drops his shirt. "Or, at least, one of them."

"Thank you, Jeremy." She turns her gaze to me. "Does that help? Knowing he trusts me."

"Makes me think he's naïve," I say and he slides his hand back around my bicep, pinching the tender flesh and somehow finding the same spot as last time. This time I flinch a little. I sigh but answer her earlier question. "Jeremy is my fiancé."

"Tell me about him." She makes a note on her paper.

My head blanks like I've never had a thought in my entire life. Tell her about him? What the hell kind of question is that? Like, what position does he play or what his favorite sex act is? I don't know how to answer this. I need direction.

"Like what?"

Jeremy tries to hide a snort in a cough but I hear it just fine. Jerk.

"What does he like to do? What do you love about him? Is he quick to joke in a serious moment or is he cool, calm, and collected?"

"He plays hockey and eats too much pizza, it makes him slow on the ice." He scoffs but I keep going. "I love that he knows when to call me on my shit and when I just need to... abuse him...a little." I shrug and he snorts. I take a deep breath and close my eyes, picturing him in my head. "He calms me, soothes the ragged edges my life has left on my soul." My voice is quiet now. I don't know if she can hear me or not, but that's her problem. I want to look at him, see those blue-brown eyes full of love, but this may be one of the hardest things I've ever said out loud. "He shows me that I'm lovable, even in the dark moments when everything tells me otherwise."

Why is this so hard? Why does being loved hurt so much? Accepting it as truth opens up the old scars I thought had healed. It reminds me of my mom, my grandparents, and resurfaces memories I had forgotten.

"Sounds like you've found a good man." Celeste's comment breaks through the spiral. "You said your father killed your mother?"

I nod, threading my fingers through Jeremy's as he leans his head on my shoulder.

"What was your mother like?"

My eyebrows pull together as I try to remember specific things about her. It was so long ago and so much has happened that I blocked out a lot of it because it hurt to remember. I was in enough pain.

"She was soft, gave the best hugs." I try to bring a clear image of her into my mind, but it's fuzzy. "My sister looks a little like her, short, curly hair, happy more than angry."

"Are you close to her?"

"Not until recently." I focus on spinning the ring around Jeremy's finger instead of looking at the woman across from us. "I kept her at a distance to keep her safe from our father. She's been in boarding schools most of her life."

"What made you make the effort to get closer to her?"

"Jeremy." I snort and shake my head. "He's a nosy little

shit and since he talks to his siblings all the time, he started bugging mine."

I lift an eyebrow and glance at Jeremy out of the corner of my eye to find him smiling at me.

"Now his siblings are bugging me too. I went from talking to my sister sporadically, mostly after games, to now having two sisters and two brothers blowing up my phone multiple times a week, plus his mom and grandma." I sigh. "It's weird to be accepted into a family that actually cares with no hesitation. I was just part of the group one day."

"My family loves you because I love you," Jeremy says, squeezing my arm.

"You've told me the tip of the iceberg." Celeste smiles. "But I definitely think I can help you if you want me to." She smiles as she looks between me and Jeremy. "I would love to talk to you more in-depth, and help you heal. I won't lie to you and say it'll be easy, sometimes it will feel like you're getting worse, it'll be hard and hurt, but there is light on the other side. That I can promise you."

Do I want to do this? No. But I don't want to hurt anymore, I don't want to give my father the power to continue to cause me more pain even after his death, but I think if I walk away now, I'll create more problems for myself and jeopardize my relationship with Jeremy. I can't lose him.

The suffering I will no doubt deal with will be worth it if it makes me a better man for him.

"Okay," I tell her, letting determination fill my chest. "Bring on the pain."

Our appointment time ends just a few minutes later, and Celeste shakes both of our hands and tells me to schedule another appointment for next week. By the time we leave the office, I'm wrung out.

On the street in front of the building, Jeremy pulls me

to a stop and spins me around to wrap his arms around my neck. My arms wrap around him on instinct, my hands splayed along his back.

"I'm so proud of you," Jeremy says softly in my ear.

"I'll do whatever it takes to keep you with me." I bury my head in his neck, inhaling his scent that soothes me.

"I'm not going anywhere, I love you."

"Even when I'm an asshole and push you away? When I pick a fight because I don't know how to ask for what I need?" My soul bleeds as I wait for the answer.

"Especially then." He kisses my temple. "You come after me when you need it and I'll know what's happening. I can read it on your face, in your body language, and even though I don't know exactly what triggered you or what you need in that exact moment, I know you'll take it. I'm never not willing to give you what you need."

Emotion clogs in my throat, threatening to fill my eyes with tears I don't want to let fall.

"I love you," I force out around the painful lump. "So much more than I thought I was capable of."

"I knew you were capable. There was something about you from the very beginning that called to me, that told me I needed you just as much as you would need me. That's as true today as it was then." Jeremy cups my face and lifts until our eyes meet. "You are worth so much more than you give yourself credit for and I can't wait to see what you accomplish."

"With you by my side, right?" My heart hammers in my chest. I can't do any of this without him. I don't want to try.

"I'm like an octopus to the face—hard to get rid of and really annoying." He says it with a straight face, and I burst out with a laugh. I was not expecting that.

"You've been spending too much time with Brendon." I

press my lips to his in a quick kiss, then nestle into his neck where the tattoo of my teeth is and kiss it.

"I love you, Preston," he says with a smile. "And even if we were to break up, I'm pretty sure my family would kick me out and keep you, so you would still have them."

"Ha!" I wrap my arm around his shoulders and we walk down the sidewalk to the car. I don't really like driving around new cities, but if we're going to be here for a while, I should get used to it. "Grandma would for sure. Probably the twins too, and definitely Ella."

"Fuck you!" He shoves me as we get to the car, and I hit the button to unlock the door.

I smirk at him and grab a handful of his shirt to pull him back to me. "Only if you ask nicely."

Jeremy scoffs. "Asking you nicely gets me nothing."

I back him against the car and lean my hips against his, dropping my head until our lips almost touch, but I don't give in. "Maybe you haven't asked nicely enough."

"You're a tease." Jeremy growls, gripping the back of my neck in his hand to lower my lips to his.

"But I'm all yours," I say against his mouth. "The future Mister Albrooke."

EPILOGUE

five years later

preston

Today is the day. Albrooke Hockey Camp has its first event. Kids from all over the Midwest are showing up today for training.

After we graduated, Jeremy and I started building this business, camps and training for young hockey players. We are even planning to create a few teams in the next few years. Paul and Brendon are also working with us as coaches, Lily is our receptionist, so she's the first person anyone who enters the building sees, and the Albrooke family has been pitching in too. While I never planned to live in Michigan, I now call it home.

After my father's death, I sued the hospital that brushed the complaints against him under the rug and ended up settling with a fifty million dollar payday. With that money, Jeremy and I have built this rink and made our dreams come true. We can pay for it for a few years, including salaries, before we need to stress too much about making enough money to be self-sufficient.

Jeremy and I have been married for four years and have the dumbest golden retriever, Zamboni, on the planet but he's cute so we love him. Since Jeremy taught Ella to skate, it's now a fight to get her off the ice. She's determined to keep up with the boys in this family and will make an amazing hockey player, probably a goalie.

Jordan and Keith are both playing football in Seattle with the Huskies and hoping to get drafted this year. If they go to different teams, I'm not sure how they'll handle it, but I guess that's a bridge they'll cross when we get to it.

"Babe!" Jeremy's voice pulls me from my head. I pull on my shirt and start buttoning it up. "Where are my pants?"

Sigh. That guy would lose his head if it wasn't attached.

"In here!" I yell back, tucking my shirt into my slacks. I'm not getting on the ice today and, as one of the faces of the company, I have to look the part. Plus, my husband loves the way I look in a suit.

"God damn." Jeremy stops short in the doorway of our bedroom. In boxer briefs and a polo, he drags his eyes up my body, lust filling his gaze. "Are you sure we need to leave soon?" He strides over, wraps his arms around me, and grabs my ass.

"Focus." My tone brooks no argument. He knows I'm stressing over today. We have big names coming to see us, local and national companies that may be sponsoring us in the near future. It has to go well.

"Take a deep breath. Today is going to be awesome." He smiles up at me and gives me a quick kiss. I've been up for hours, already got my morning run in, ate breakfast, showered, and ironed our clothes for the day. Some habits are hard to quit.

"Get dressed," I grumble at him, threading my belt through the loops. He smiles a shit eating grin at me and finds the pants I laid out for him on the bed. I have no idea how he missed them. Probably got distracted by the dog.

He's kept the beard, which I still love, but he keeps it on the shorter side so it's neat and tidy. Honestly, if it didn't drive me nuts when it gets scraggly, I doubt he would do anything with it.

There's a knock on the front door, so I leave Jeremy to finish getting ready and answer it.

"Good morning!" Grandma smiles up at me, patting my cheek as she hustles into the living room, the original wood floors creaking as she walks across the space to the kitchen.

"Good morning." I smile at her and shake my head. I don't have to look, I know she brought cinnamon rolls the size of my face for Jeremy. He eats like an unsupervised child. While my dietary restrictions have lessened since I stopped playing, I'm still smart with what I put in my body. Jeremy survives on white flour, sugar, butter, and cheese. He even complains when I tell him to eat something fresh like a fruit or vegetable.

A deep moan sounds from the doorway and I turn to see my husband salivating for the sugary treat.

"You are a lifesaver." He puts an arm around the woman's shoulders and kisses her head, reaching for the container, but she slaps his hand.

"You'll make a mess on your shirt if you eat it now. Go get your shoes on, we gotta go!" She claps at him like a drill sergeant, and he grumbles but does what he's told.

"I've been trying to get him dressed for half an hour. You're a miracle worker." I give her a hug too and head to put on my shoes.

"Well, sometimes he needs a good butt smack to get his ass in gear." She puts a hand on her hip and I try not to smile. I'm pretty sure there's still a handprint on his ass from last night...

"Okay, I'll see you at the rink!" She kisses my cheek and heads out. I love that woman.

Zamboni, our dumbass dog, trips following behind Jeremy down the stairs and slides on the hardwood. I can't help but sigh as Jeremy drops down to his knees to baby the dog.

"You gotta be careful, buddy. Are you okay?" The dog licks his face and wags his tail.

"Come on, we gotta go," I stand up and grab the keys for our Audi Q7 that was a graduation present when we left Denver for Michigan. Our lunches and water bottles are already packed and sitting on the table by the door, so I grab them and turn to look over the home we've created.

The overstuffed leather couches, minimalist style of décor, and a trunk hiding toys for Ella, round out our living room. It's dark wood and light, soft fabrics. Homey, comfortable, welcoming. There's love and laughter here. Above the couch is a family picture, the Albrookes, Browns, and Lily. It's not the family I was born into, but the family that chose me. I'll forever be grateful to them.

Jeremy sighs and pats Zamboni's head.

"Be a good boy." He gives the dog a chew toy and we head out.

Along the walls and on a bookcase that Jeremy argued with me about getting because "Neither of us read, what are we going to put on it?" are more framed pictures and stuff we've collected over the years. Of course, there's a stack of hockey pucks that Jeremy has from every team he's played on.

"What has you smiling like that?" Jeremy walks up to me with a smile on his face too, kissing me lightly.

"Our life."

The grin on his face widens.

"Oh, my God, you're not trying to tell me you're pregnant, right?" He gasps in mock horror.

I roll my eyes and shake my head.

"Way to ruin the moment, jackass." I sigh and walk out the door. "And if either of us was pregnant, it would be you."

He locks the door behind us and jogs to catch up as I put our stuff in the back seat.

"Oh yeah." He opens the door and gets in. "Wait, am I pregnant?"

"You're an idiot."

I back out of the driveway in the suburbs of Grand Rapids and head to our building. Our dream. I reach for his hand and lace our fingers. Jeremy lifts our hands and kisses the back of mine.

"Do you want to have kids? Be a dad?" he asks, much more seriously.

I sigh and think about his question, but I know the answer. "No. I like being the favorite uncle." He scoffs at me. "Stacy is due soon with twins so we're about to have babies coming out of our ears."

"Good thing you're pretty because I'm almost certain babies don't come out of ears."

I sigh heavily. "You've been spending too much time with Brendon."

His laughter fills our car, making me smile.

When we get to the rink, a big sign is hanging from the roof, welcoming our athletes to camp.

Butterflies riot in my stomach when I see it, excitement humming along my skin.

"We did it," Jeremy says, looking at the sign too.

"We did." I pull into our parking spot and pull his face to mine. "Come on, Coach. Time to make a difference."

Jeremy heads to the locker room to get changed into his gear while I head to my office, checking emails and making sure everyone is ready for check in at the front. Lily and Stacy are on one side to check everyone in while Jeremy's parents are handing out goodie bags with swag from our sponsors and a colored wrist band so we know where they belong. I'm the next step, directing people to locker rooms based on the color of the band.

Brendon and Paul are in the locker rooms and will be helping out on the ice along with a few other assistant coaching hires that Jeremy hand-picked.

Before I know it, an hour has gone by and Grandma knocks on my door jamb, pulling me away from the computer.

"I have something for you," she tells me, holding a wrapped box. By the shape of the box, I have to assume it's a new quilt, but I'm not sure why.

When I look at her with confusion, she smiles and hands it to me. I rip the paper off and pull the lid off the box. The quilt inside is green and white to match our facility, with hockey and golden retriever-themed squares. It's beautiful and warms me. With tears filling my eyes, I give her a tight hug.

"Thank you." My voice cracks.

"You needed an office quilt. It'll get cold in here while you're doing very important computer things." She cups my cheek with a smile. "Now, let's get out there. The lines are already crazy!"

I fold the quilt to fit on the back of my office chair and toss the trash in the garbage can before following her out. My office being clean and orderly is very important to me.

"Everyone ready?" I look at everyone and they smile at me with nods. "I want to say again how much we appreciate you all helping out and supporting us."

"Stop making us cry and open the damn doors!" Stacy wipes at her eyes while snapping at me.

"Yes ma'am." I smirk at her and unlock the doors.

jeremy

By the time the last kids are picked up, I'm exhausted. I haven't been on the ice this much in months but I loved every second of it. There were frustrating moments, some uncertain minutes, and we definitely learned that some of what we had set up was not going to work, but I wouldn't trade any of it.

In the locker room, I'm changing out of my gear when the door bangs open. There are only a few people left in the building, so I'm betting it's Preston looking for me and maybe wanting to christen the locker room.

"Yo, Jay!" Brendon's voice echoes through the room.

"Yeah?"

Brendon and Paul pop up as I'm pulling on my jeans.

"Dinner? I'm starving." Brendon rubs his stomach like the overgrown child he is. Paul shakes his head and rolls his eyes. Some things never change.

Paul has a box tucked under his arm and looks like he knows a secret. I don't trust this at all. Both of them are in track pants and t-shirts because they were smart and dressed comfortably.

"Feed yourself, I'm going home to pass out on my couch in front of the TV with my dog." I pull my shirt over my head and sit to put my shoes and socks on.

He huffs and turns to Paul with an unamused look on his face.

"I mean, if you're a good boy, I can feed you my dick," Paul offers, which Brendon is definitely considering if the lift of his eyebrows and purse of his lips is anything to go by.

"Okay, but can you feed me real food too?" Brendon asks Paul. "And beer?"

"You got it," Paul agrees and Brendon punches the air.

"This is for you." Paul hands me the box with mischief in his eyes. "And I guess Preston." He shrugs and looks at Brendon with a grin. Brendon snorts.

Okay, now I really don't trust whatever this is. I look at the box in his outstretched hand with suspicion.

"What is it?" I ask, not touching the wrapped box.

"Open it tonight," Paul says, putting it down on the bench next to where I'm standing.

"Or like, before you have sex the next time," Brendon adds.

They both laugh like that's the funniest thing they've ever heard.

"You guys are starting to freak me out." I look back and forth between them.

"Alright, we're out!" Brendon takes off for the door with Paul on his heels. I shake my head at them then grab the rest of my stuff and this terrifying box.

I find Preston in his office, a new quilt I haven't seen before wrapped around his shoulders. The image makes me smile. He's such a sap for Grandma.

"You about ready?" I lean against the door frame and check my phone for messages. "Mom and Dad let Zam out and fed him."

"Tell them thank you," he says, still typing away at his computer. "I have a few emails to finish then we can go."

Damn he's sexy as fuck sitting at that desk, handling

business. My dick twitches and I stride over to him, pulling his chair out from his desk and dropping the box onto the floor to deal with later. They said before I have sex, not before sucking dick. That's an important distinction.

"What the hell are you doing?" He jumps at the unexpected movement, but I drop under his desk and pull him toward me. I don't know who's still here, but just in case, it's better to be hidden.

I reach for him, pulling his shirt from his pants to press open mouthed kisses on his stomach while unbuckling the belt and opening his pants.

"Fuck." He runs his hands through my hair as he watches me, no longer focused on the computer.

"Finish your emails," I tell him, reaching inside his underwear to pull his cock out.

"What?" He looks at me like I'm crazy but I chuckle.

"Finish your emails while I suck your dick." I pull him farther under the desk so he can reach his computer and he slides down in his chair a little to give me better access to him.

I lick his head and hear him growl. I snicker before sucking him deep into my mouth, getting as close to his body as I can in this position. He swears, but I hear the clicking of his keyboard.

I play with him, dragging out the pleasure and not letting him come until I'm ready. Frankly, I want to drive him fucking crazy. Push him until he snaps.

I doubt he has supplies. This was not your best plan, dumbass.

Well, shit. That could be a problem…

"Last one," he groans when I suck him to the back of my throat and swallow around him. "I'm going to fuck you so god damn hard you'll see stars."

His threat sends a thrill up my spine and has my dick jumping in my pants.

I bob on his cock a few times before taking him deep again. His dick throbs on my tongue and I know he's close. Again. It's the third time tonight I've gotten him to the edge.

I start to pull off but his hand snakes under the desk, grabs a fist full of my hair and shoves me back onto him. He uses my mouth to fuck himself and comes just a few pumps later, with saliva dripping down my chin and his cock. His hand releases and I sit back, gasping for breath and wiping my face.

He backs up to let me out with a smug look on his face, but I know he isn't done with me.

"Done. Get your ass in the car," he commands and I slide out from under his desk, up between his legs to lean on his thighs, and kiss him, his spent dick still out between us.

Preston grabs my throat and kisses me back, harder than I started it. His tongue demands entrance, his teeth bite and pull on my lip. I love when he's like this. Possessive and dominating.

His dick twitches and he pulls back to tuck himself back into his pants. I grab the box I dropped on the floor and stand. Preston eyes the package and gives me a questioning brow.

"What's with the box?"

I look at it and sigh, ignoring how hard my dick is and how badly I want him to touch me.

"I have no idea. Paul gave it to me and Brendon said to open it before we have sex." Preston looks as confused as I feel.

"That could mean literally anything," he tells me, looking at the box like it might bite.

"Yeah, it could."

We grab our stuff and head out to the car. The box sits on my lap for the drive while we take guesses at what could be in it.

"Jock strap," I guess.

"An elephant g-string," Preston tosses back and I laugh. The mental picture is more than I can handle.

"A collar and leash?" I shake the box and it rattles a bit like it could have hardware. Maybe?

Preston stops and thinks about it.

"You would like that, wouldn't you?" I ask him, kind of surprised, but also not. He does like to control me, tie me up, pull me around by my tie if I happen to be wearing one.

"I wouldn't hate it." He side-eyes me.

"Kinky bastard."

"Ha! Like you don't fucking love it."

Okay he has me there. I do love it. When he takes the power, I'm free to let go and just feel. There's no pressure, just pleasure.

When we get to the house, Zamboni barks and jumps around, excited to see us after a long day. I play with him for a few minutes, love on him, and let him out again before we shut off the lights for the night.

Preston disappeared upstairs with the box a minute ago, so I head up after him, anticipation thrumming in my veins. He's naked on our bed, stroking himself, the box sitting next to him.

"Strip."

I don't argue, just rip my clothes off and climb onto the bed, straddling his thighs and rubbing our dicks together.

"On your back, open the box while I work your ass open." A shudder races through me as I do what I'm told and lay on my back with my legs open for him.

I reach for the box and tear the paper off, then lift the lid. I don't understand what I'm looking at for a minute.

What looks like black leather straps and metal rings. What is this?

"Well?" Preston asks and I lift it out of the box.

"I'm not really sure." The leather straps are all connected to metal hoops making this the most confusing thing I've ever seen. What the fuck is it?

"Oh, fuck." Preston freezes. "That's a harness."

A harness? Images from porn flash through my head, but they don't look like this. The ones I've seen in videos are thick straps across your chest and back that wrap around where your arm meets the shoulder. This is not that.

"Sit up," Preston demands and takes the contraption from me. My dick jumps at the tone of his voice. I love that bossy shit in the bedroom.

I do what he says and he starts unbuckling shit that I didn't even notice, then swings it around me. One long strap rests along my spine with two shorter ones to go around the base of my neck and another set to wrap around my waist with another long strap to sit along my chest bone and connect my neck and waist.

It's not constricting, but the leather sits flush along my skin.

"Jesus fucking Christ that's the hottest thing I've ever seen." Preston stares at me, primal lust turning his gray eyes black. He slides a hand under the chest strap and yanks me toward him with a sinister smirk. "Oh yeah, I'm going to get a lot of use out of this." My dick is aching between us, but he hasn't touched me yet. I'm about to whimper from need if he doesn't do something quick.

"They said to thank them later."

"You may be wearing this under your shirt at some point so I can torture myself with knowing it's there." Preston runs his nose along my neck, right above the leather. "And a plug in your ass so every time you move you feel it."

Oh, fuck. Now he's trying to kill me.

"Lean on your hands," he instructs, and I lean back while he adjusts to be kneeling between my thighs. He grabs the bottle of lube and slicks up his fingers.

"No, just you." My heart is racing with anticipation, but I need him. I want it to hurt, just for a minute, before it feels good and I can lose myself in him.

His eyes meet mine, but he doesn't ask. After being together this long, he takes me at my word.

"Lie back." He grabs a pillow and I lift my hips. Preston adds more lube to his hand and strokes himself before lining up the head of cock against my hole. "Hold your knees."

I pull my legs back and he pushes into me with a slow, hard thrust. He's too big to go in like this with no prep, but the burn and stretch makes the pleasure better once it stops. I have to force myself to relax, to breathe. He gives me just a few seconds before pulling back out and going again, faster this time. Every thrust is faster but just as hard as the time before. In only a few minutes, he's fucking me deep, taking his pleasure from my body and leaning into me. His hips snap against my ass with a vulgar skin-on-skin slap.

Finally, he puts me out of my misery and wraps a hand around my cock. I whimper at the pressure, at the pace that matches his thrusts.

I'm close, so fucking close already, but he lets go when my dick starts to throb and slaps my cheek. Heat blossoms on my face and I suck in my bottom lip to bite down on.

Preston spits in his hand and wraps it back around my cock.

"come for me, show me how much you like to be used." The growl in his voice is what sends me over the edge, spilling cum onto my stomach and chest, my body spasming around him, and my back arching off the mattress. Preston grunts and fills my ass with hot cum, throbbing inside of me before dropping his forehead to my shoulder.

We lay there on our bed, panting and spent for a minute, until enough brain cells have restarted to be able to move.

Preston sits up and looks down at me. “God damn it, I love this thing.” He fingers the warm leather. “Gotta get it cleaned up though.”

He pulls out of me with a hiss and goes to the bathroom. He washes up and comes back with a warm, wet washcloth and cleans me off, careful not to get the leather too wet. He drops the rag in the laundry and unbuckles the harness before we slip into bed. Tonight, he sleeps facing the door with me spooned up behind him.

“I love you.” Preston lifts the hand I have on his stomach and kisses my palm.

“I love you too.” I kiss his spine and we lay together with my bare chest against his bare back.

“I never thought I would be able to trust someone, to be happy and satisfied with my life.” Preston’s words are quiet in the dark and they make my heart soar.

“Who knew a smart ass with pain kink was all it would take?” I smile against his back.

Preston chuckles and I can feel it rumble through him.

“Thank you for not giving up on me.” Preston kisses my wedding ring.

“There’s nothing to say thank you for.” I kiss his shoulder blade. “I can’t imagine going through life with anyone else. You’re it for me. You’ve always been it for me.”

ACKNOWLEDGEMENTS

First and foremost, Denise. Thank you so much for explaining hockey to me. There were so many questions and you didn't get frustrated with me once. You are a rock star. Also, Maura, thank you for the introduction.

Nurse Jessica: the support you give me on the daily, on top of answering all of my very random medical and procedure questions have helped to make this book what it is. No ER is complete without a Jessica.

Glenna and AJ: my daily meme suppliers, the tough love givers, and my favorite bitches to bitch about bitches with. As always, this book would not have happened without you.

Braxton: fisting lengths, butt holes, and boxes of nuts. Thank you for always being happy to answer the penis questions I hit you with, along with pictures and video to answer the questions.

Whitney: orgasms, egg burgers, and sweet tart ropes. Penis.

Kayla: good lord. I swear every book I write has you doing more work than the last one. I could not do this without you.

Jordan: sorry for ruining your family's Christmas tradition by saying the cookies look like ball sacks but thanks for letting me add it to my book.\

My beta readers: Jordan, Jessica, Maura, Tal, Jessie, Braxton,

and Tara, your feedback, excitement, and encouragement keep me going and help calm the fear that comes with publishing.
To my husband: Sorry about the lack of dinners cooked and for taking over the kitchen table. For unloading my book drama all over you after working 12+ hours, and for putting up with my unwashed, sleep deprived, grumpy ass.
And of course, the readers. I can't begin to explain how much it means to me that you love the stories like I do.

ABOUT THE AUTHOR

Sarcastic and snarky, I love to laugh and read dark fucked up shit. I write about tortured pasts and hot sex, a happily ever after that has to be worked for. My stories tend to be a little dark but with some comic relief, typically in the form of sarcasm and usually include two men falling in love though I sometimes dabble in other LGBTQIA stories.

I am probably one of the most random people you will probably ever come in contact with. My favorite accessory is rainbows, big hoop earrings, and fake eyelashes (I only recently learned how to put them on). I always have coffee on hand so I can try to keep up with the three minions I've created.

http://www.andijaxon.com

Made in United States
North Haven, CT
05 June 2025